Crazy Imperfect Hearts

SAMANTHA CHRISTY

Athena
Books Publishing Group

Saint Johns, FL 32259

Copyright © 2025 by Samantha Christy

Cover designed by Maria @ Steamy Designs.

Crazy

Imperfect

Hearts

Samantha Christy

Chapter One

Lucas

"Bro." Blake's eyebrows dip low as he points to the large television hanging over the bar. "Isn't that your ex?"

I don't react. I've gotten used to the incessant teasing about my *four* exes. The women I've left at—or near—the altar over the past decade. I casually sip my drink. "Not falling for it."

"No, seriously," my other brother Dallas says, looking just as puzzled as Blake as he stares behind my head. "She's on TV."

I whip around to see the most recent bride I jilted looking as happy as a clam at high tide.

"Hey, Calloway!" a patron in the booth next to us shouts to the guy tending bar. "Turn it up."

The entire pub goes silent as Cooper sets the TV volume on max. There must be three dozen people here, a lot for this early on a Friday night, but the only sound comes from the television, and more specifically—the host of Entertainment Tonight.

"Senator Edwin McNally of New York has just announced the recent engagement of his twenty-eight-year-old son, Andrew—

currently employed at the New York Office of the Attorney General—to twenty-six-year-old Lissa Monroe from Calloway Creek, New York. Miss Monroe is a student at NYU and bartender at a popular New York City club, where the couple apparently met last fall. The wedding date and location haven't been announced, but my guess is it will be at Senator McNally's home on Martha's Vineyard."

My entire body goes numb as the host continues to talk about the upcoming wedding as if two celebrities are getting hitched. All I can do is stare at the pictures of Lissa and her new fiancé. *Did she ever look that happy with me?*

"Fuck!"

I kick the leg of the table, pick up my drink and go out on the patio. Pulling a cigarette from my pack, I notice it's equally as quiet out here. When I glance around, I see everyone staring at me.

"What?" I yell, then light up and walk over to an empty table.

People turn away and talk about me. Calloway Creek is a small town. Everyone knows my story. They all know Lissa. They know my other three exes as well. You can't fart in this town without everyone smelling it.

Dallas appears at my table with a fresh glass of whiskey. He puts it down and slides it my way before he and Blake sit.

I stare at the glass, head shaking. "She's been living thirty minutes away all this time." I flick some ashes and take a drag of the cancer stick. "And she went back to school. She always said she wanted to."

"Karma's a bitch, eh, Montana?" Dax Cruz yells from across the patio.

Standing so fast my chair falls over, I turn, ready to throw punches.

Dallas and Blake pop out of their seats and hold me back. "Not worth it," Blake says.

Dax laughs, raising his drink as if making a toast. "Public humiliation is just the cherry on top."

"Don't you have a fucking carburetor to fix?" I yell. "Maybe the car will do us all a favor and fall on your head."

A dozen pairs of eyes bounce between Dax and me as we continue to lob vocal punches.

"Luke." Dallas puts a firm hand on my shoulder. "Come on, man. Let's go back inside."

"That's probably a good idea," Cooper Calloway says, leaning in the doorway, likely making sure things don't get out of control. "Next one's on me."

I flick my cigarette across the patio, missing Dax by mere inches, before my brothers escort me inside.

On the way back to our booth, I spot Hunter McQuaid sitting with his wife and kids. I get my wallet out, fish every last dollar from it, and throw the money down in front of him.

He puts down his hamburger and stares at what is probably seven hundred dollars. "What's this?"

"Down payment."

"For what exactly?"

"The bet I lost."

Slowly, realization washes over him. It's been years since I made the idiotic wager. Seven hundred barely scratches the surface of the fifty grand I bet him that I'd actually go through with marrying Lissa.

Well, he won. Him and all the other people who bet against me. *Fuck him. Fuck all of them.*

He pushes the money toward me. "I don't want your money, Montana."

"I make good on my bets," I say, wanting to use stronger language, but refraining in front of his kids.

"I'm really sorry, Lucas," his wife Willow calls out as I walk away.

I glance at the TV as I slide into the booth, grateful it's now tuned to a Nighthawks game on ESPN.

"Senator McNally," Blake muses. "Isn't he the guy they say might run for president in the next election?"

I close my eyes and shake my head knowing I'm destined to hear about every goddamn detail of my ex's upcoming nuptials to the son of the next potential president of the United States.

"Holy shit," Dallas says. "She could be the first daughter-in-law."

I shoot him a biting glare. "Whose side are you on?"

"Always yours, brother. I'm just saying."

Cooper makes good on that drink, bringing it to the table to add to the one Dallas bought me. "This must be a real gut punch," he says, nodding to the TV. "It'll blow over."

I laugh, sounding completely unhinged. "In about ten years. You know how people in this town like to gossip."

"Nah," Blake adds. "As soon as someone's teenage kid gets knocked up or anyone is found cheating, this will be old news."

"Yeah, sure," I say and toss back one of the drinks.

"You want to get out of here?" Dallas asks. "We could pick up food and go back to my place."

I shake my head. "We came here to watch the game. Let's watch the game."

As Cooper turns to walk away, Blake swirls his hand in the air. "Another round."

"You got it," Cooper says.

Hours later, I come back inside after my umpteenth cigarette and notice the crowd has thinned out. Families have long gone. Most of the remaining patrons are young weekend bar-goers.

"The Hawks won five-to-four," Blake says.

I nod. "I was watching outside."

Dallas stares at my almost-empty pack of smokes. "I thought you were going to quit smoking."

"You're bringing that up *now? Today?*"

"Remember how hard it was to quit eight years ago?" Blake says. "We all get why you started back up, but maybe this is a sign that it's time to move on. She's obviously not coming back. To Cal Creek *or* to you."

"Gee, ya think?" I bite, so much rage simmering within, I'm ready to get into it with Blake, Dallas, Dax, or anyone else.

"Lucas Montana?"

"What the fuck is it now?"

I turn to see an attractive woman holding a microphone. A dude with a large television camera is standing behind her.

"Mr. Montana, I'm Sylvia Franco from KXTZ. I'd like to interview you about the engagement of your ex-fiancée, Lissa Monroe."

"No."

The word comes out of my mouth faster than I can even wrap my head around how quickly someone found me after the so-called breaking news.

"Mr. Montana, is it true that Miss Monroe was the fourth woman you left at the altar and you're known as the runaway groom of Calloway Creek?"

My brothers and I stare at her.

"Lady," Dallas says, coming to my defense, "I don't know who you paid to find him, but I suggest you get the hell out of here before I escort you out."

"This is a public place," Sylvia says. "We have a right to be here." She turns back to me. "Lucas, this is a chance to tell your side of the story before every media outlet finds out about you and makes you the laughingstock of New York."

"Get out," Blake says, standing and blocking me from the camera.

She pokes her head around him. "You wouldn't want any negative press to affect your family's prosperous business, would you?"

Dallas stands. "Okay, that's enough." I swear he's going to smash the video camera when Cooper comes over and interrupts.

"I own this *private* establishment," Cooper says. He points to a sign next to the door. "See that? We have the right to refuse service to anyone, especially those who are making a scene or disrupting business, which you clearly are. Now leave or I'll get the police involved. And in case you're wondering whose side they'd be on, you'd do well to remember this is a small town."

"Fine." Sylvia holds up her hands in surrender and does the cut-throat sign to her cameraman. She hands me a business card. "If you change your mind—and I think you should, to get your side of the story out before people make things up—call me." Then she eyes me up and down, as if she's just now really *seeing* me—a rich, attractive, available man. "Even if you *don't* change your mind, feel free to call."

They leave, and once again, you could hear a pin drop as all eyes are on me.

"Dude," Dallas says. "Did that reporter bitch actually just make a pass at you?"

Cooper clears some empty glasses off our table. "I wouldn't be surprised if reporters are camped out in front of your building when you go home."

My head sinks into my hands. "Shit." I pick up my smokes. "I'm going outside."

My brothers settle our tab then follow me out. "It's getting late and we have to head home," Dallas says. "You want to crash at my place?"

The wind has picked up and it takes me ten tries to light my cigarette. Finally, I get it, and I inhale deeply, the nicotine infusion calming my nerves ever so slightly. "No. I'm going to stay here and get shit faced."

"It's a long walk home when you're fall-down-drunk," Blake says.

"I think I can manage."

"Well, if you get there and find reporters, the offer stands to crash at one of our places. Call if you need a ride."

"Whatever," I say, noticing the table of ladies staring at me from across the patio. All familiar faces: Maddie, Regan, and Ava—who all own small businesses across the street—and their friends Amber, Dakota, Nikki, and Cooper's wife, Serenity.

It's a gut punch to see one empty seat at the table. It's where Lissa would have been sitting were she here. Or maybe she'd be the one serving them as one of Donovan's longest-standing employees.

But she's not at the table. And she hasn't worked here since the day I crushed her spirit. Her dreams. I spare a glance at the TV—but apparently not her future.

My brothers each clap a hand on my shoulder, seeming reluctant to leave.

"What am I, two? You don't have to babysit me. Go."

I watch them leave, envious of each of them for having someone to go home to, knowing it's my own damn fault that I don't.

I get Cooper's attention through the window, and he brings me another drink.

"Keep 'em coming until you close or I pass out," I say when it arrives.

And I mean every word.

Chapter Two

Regan

Maddie is trying her best to keep a smile on her face, but I can tell her back is killing her, especially sitting on these hard outdoor chairs. My very pregnant friend would do anything for me, including staying up late to celebrate my milestone birthday when it's obvious she needs to be in bed.

"I can't thank you guys enough," I say, looking around the table at my friends. I pack all of their thoughtful presents into one large gift bag and set it at my feet.

Ava gives me the side-eye. "You turn thirty-five and suddenly you have a bedtime?"

Laughter fills the air.

"No, but I'm well aware that almost everyone here will be woken up at the crack of dawn by at least one hungry child."

"Right," Ava says, looking sad.

I shouldn't have said anything. I know how hard she and Trevor have been trying for a baby. Seeing Maddie pregnant has been difficult enough for her, the three of us being as close as three friends can be.

Amber, Dakota, Nikki, and Serenity take my out, and get up to leave, taking turns giving me one last hug. When they're gone, I help Maddie out of her chair, trying not to laugh at the awkwardness of her huge belly.

I get it, it's hard to stand up easily with extra weight on your mid-section, especially from such a low seat. I mean, I haven't had a flat stomach since my freshman year at Houghton when Coach Minchew made us do a hundred crunches before each practice. But even my fluffy center doesn't hold a candle to Maddie's pregnant curves.

"Thanks," she says, winded from the task of simply standing.

It makes me feel guilty that I kept her out so late.

I glance around the outdoor patio at Donovan's Pub—the premier nighttime gathering place here on McQuaid Circle—and realize we're some of the few patrons left.

Sure, there are a couple of small groups scattered inside, but with most of the Calloway Creek University students on summer break, it's not as lively as it was mere weeks ago.

Lucas Montana is the only other person on the patio. He's been out here puffing on cigarettes as if the smoke could erase the past. We all know what happened. If he hadn't left Lissa literally *at* the altar, they'd be married, and she'd have never moved to the city and met the senator's son. Even though he brought it on himself, I can't help but feel sorry for him.

Everyone deserves a happily ever after.

I laugh inwardly, because unless one of the thousands of my book boyfriends comes to life, me actually getting one seems ever further out of reach.

It's not that I want to be married as much as I want companionship. And maybe someone to dust off the goods. It's been a minute. Actually, it's been two years.

"Come on," I say, taking Maddie's elbow. "We'll walk you out."

She smiles. "You guys are the best."

At Maddie's car, Ava asks, "See you Tuesday?"

The three of us have had a standing coffee date behind the ice cream shop for as long as I can remember. Ava, being the owner of The Criss Coffee Corner—an establishment that could give Starbucks a run for the money—always brings the drinks.

Others sometimes join us, but unless one of our core three is on vacation or, let's face it… *dying*… our little trio is always there. Every single week without fail.

Maddie rubs her belly. "Assuming I make it that long. I have a feeling this little guy might make an appearance by then."

"Is Tag getting excited?" I ask. "I know he's been great with Gigi, but she was five when you got together so he's never had the baby experience."

"He really stepped up as an uncle when Jaxon had his kids, so he knows how to be around babies. But, yes, he's over the moon. And Gigi can't wait to be a big sister. At eleven years old, she's going to be a huge help."

Maddie has a hard time fitting behind the steering wheel. I'm surprised she can even reach the pedals with as far back as she's got the seat.

"Drive safely," I say, closing her door. "Love you."

"Love you guys." She blows an air kiss and then she's off.

Ava and I thread our elbows and start the walk home. Both of us live in the apartments over our shops on McQuaid Circle. Maddie used to live above her flower shop, which is just a few doors down from mine, until she and Tag got together. Now she rents it out.

When we round the corner, I see a man carrying a gift bag. I stop walking. "Shoot. I forgot my gifts. I have to go back." I give Ava a squeeze. "See you tomorrow?"

"You know it." She kisses my cheek. "Happy birthday, Regan. I just know this year is going to be your best yet."

"From your lips to God's ears."

We share a laugh and then I trot off back to Donovan's.

Entering through the patio gate, I find my bag right where I left it. There are a lot of benefits to living in such a small town. Like being a single woman walking alone at night without having to look over my shoulder. And being able to leave valuables at a restaurant without anyone stealing them.

Don't get me wrong. There are drawbacks, too. Especially when it comes to men. Everyone knows everyone. Most of us grew up together. Like Ava and Trevor, and Nikki and Jaxon, many married their high school sweethearts. And there is often a shortage of good men, especially if you're a certain age.

I shake away the thought, refusing to let my age become a determining factor in how I choose to live my life. I'm happy with the life I've chosen. Running my shop. Being with good friends. And I have all the company I need with Joey. That furball is better than any man. He never talks back, always likes to cuddle, and thinks I walk on water.

Besides, men are not all they're cracked up to be. That was proven to me long ago. My friends have gotten lucky with their partners. I'm beginning to think I'm just not cut out for a long-term relationship.

"Fuck!" I hear as I collect the gift bag.

When I turn, I see Lucas yelling at the television hanging under the awning. It's another news report about his ex's engagement. In a large picture, displayed on what must be a seventy-five-inch screen, Lissa is looking dreamily at Senator McNally's son.

Oh, boy.

I try to exit unnoticed—because I'm not sure what I'd say to him if he saw me standing here—when a loud crash startles me.

I spin around. Shattered pieces of the television are scattered on the patio.

My jaw hangs loose as I stare at Lucas. "Did you just throw your glass at the TV?"

Cooper Calloway comes running out from inside and shakes his head. He's pissed. "Time for you to go, cousin."

Lucas looks up at what remains of the TV and scrubs a hand across his jaw. "Shit, Coop. I'm sorry. I'll pay for the damage."

"I know you will. Still, it's time for you to go home. Sleep it off." Lucas pulls a set of keys out of his pocket. Cooper takes them, shaking his head again. "And I know you weren't about to drive, you fucking idiot." He looks behind him into the restaurant. "I'd take you, but I still have customers."

Cooper looks over at me. He's not going to ask, but I can tell he wants to.

Why didn't I run out of here when I had the chance?

"Fine." I step forward. "I'll make sure he gets home." I hold my hand out for the keys, and Cooper drops them onto my palm.

"Thanks, Regan."

I nod. "Come on, big guy," I say to Lucas. "Let's go."

"Where we goin'?" he slurs.

"I'm taking you home."

He raises a brow.

I guffaw. "Yeah, you wish." My turn to shake my head. "I'm driving you home and then I'm driving myself home. I'll return your car tomorrow."

We approach his car. His sleek, expensive, custom-painted car. Sometimes I forget just how rich the Montana family is since they really don't act it.

When I hold up the key fob to unlock his Jag, Lucas swipes the keys and stuffs them into his pocket. "I don't wanna go home. Les go get a drink."

I stick out my hand, palm up. "Give me the keys."

"No."

"Lucas, hand them over."

He steps back and stretches his arms out to his sides. "Come get 'em if you want 'em."

"You're an idiot."

"Come on. It's your birthday. Lemme buy you a drink."

He's right. It *is* my birthday. At least for another forty-five minutes. Ava's words about me being thirty-five and having a bedtime weave through my head. I hold up a finger. "One drink. But I doubt Cooper would serve you. We'll have to go to the bar in the bowling alley."

He glances next door to Calloway Bowl, which shares the huge parking lot with Donovan's and the other establishments lining this side of McQuaid Circle. "A drink is a drink. Don't care where I get it."

Clearly inebriated, he takes the large gift bag from me and I follow him across the parking lot.

"I can't remember the last time I've been in here," I say when we enter.

The sound of pins crashing together when a bowling ball hits them thunders through the front doors.

Calloway Bowl only has ten lanes, and even at that, it's a rarity that all of them are occupied. It has a small café with mostly fried food and pizza, and a bar with exactly five stools, all empty since most people do their drinking next door.

Three lanes are being used. One by Tag Calloway's—and I suppose Lucas's—cousins (they're all related somehow), Gray, Colt, and Storm. Another by a group of girls from CCU summer school probably—all of them flirting with the handsome Calloway brothers next to them. There is a couple on the last one, the far lane at the very end. The guy is helping her bowl as if she's new to it. He's behind her, and the very large grin on her face tells me she might just know how to do it but is having too much fun to tell him.

Lucas sets my bag next to the bar. Monty Langston—owner and, at the moment, sole worker here—comes out from behind the main counter and steps behind the bar.

Monty is old. Pushing eighty I'd guess. I pretty much know everyone who works or owns businesses along McQuaid Circle as my own bookstore/boutique is one of those businesses. Like mine and Maddie's, a lot of them have been handed down from generation to generation. Monty, though, is the original owner of the bowling alley. He doesn't have kids, has never been married, and as far as I know, is always working.

I stare at him and wonder if this is who I'll be in forty-five years.

"Why, Regan Lucas," Monty says reverently. "I haven't seen you in here in a long while. You're looking sweeter than stolen honey. What can I get you?"

"Thank you, Monty. I'll have white wine please, whatever you have opened is fine."

Lucas scoffs next to me. "Swill, most likely," he mumbles.

I kick him in the shin. "Be nice," I say under my breath.

"I'm just saying, there's a winery close by, yet he doesn't stock any of our wine."

"Soon as you offer a more economical option, I'll be happy to stock it," Monty says.

"Economical," Lucas says like it's a bad word. "You mean cheap."

Samantha Christy

"Son, this is a bowling alley. My budget is as tight as a fiddle string. And you can bet on the fact that folks don't come here for expensive booze."

Lucas shakes his head and leans across the bar in a determined yet non-threatening manner. "Please don't refer to my wine as booze, old man. People drink booze to get drunk. My wine is meant to be savored."

"I tell you what," Monty says, not intimidated in the least. "I won't call your wine booze and you don't call me old man and we'll call it even."

I put a hand on Lucas's shoulder and urge him back onto the barstool. "Sounds like a good plan."

Monty pours my wine and stares Lucas down. "You drinkin' or what?"

"What's the best you got?"

Monty looks behind him. "Patrón Silver."

Lucas whistles in jest. "A forty-dollar bottle of tequila?" He pulls out his phone. "Let me check my account to see if I can swing it."

"Shush," I say. "I'm leaving if you can't be cordial."

Monty pours him a shot then says to me, "I'm guessin' we should give the lad a pass." He nods to one of the televisions on the wall. "After all, his cheese kind of fell off his cracker today."

Lucas's hand wraps around the shot glass like he's ready to launch it at yet another TV.

I put my hand over his, noting how large and warm it is. "Are you really going to let this ruin you? So she moved on. Just like all your other exes did. Instead of wallowing in it, maybe this is a sign that *you* should move on too."

He laughs bitterly. "You mean to the next woman I'm going to leave at the altar? No thank you. I'm done with that. Everyone in

16

this town knows I can't be trusted. They warned Lissa. She thought I could change. *I* thought I could change. Turns out they were right, and Lissa was wrong. I was wrong. I'm thirty years old, Regan. I'm never going to change. A tiger can't change his spots."

"Leopard," I say.

His brows knit together. "Huh?"

"Tigers have stripes. The saying is: a leopard can't change his spots."

"Whatever. So I'm a leopard."

I giggle, because with the way he's slurring, the word sounds more like leper, which is definitely what he is to all the women in this town.

With Monty back behind the main counter, cleaning shoes returned from the Calloways and the college girls they just left with, Lucas sips tequila and stares at me.

"What?" I ask.

"Regan Lucas," he says pointedly. "I almost forgot that was your last name until Monty said it. I used to joke with Ryder that if you and me got married, I could be Lucas Lucas. But that was way back in high school before your dad caught me staring out the window at you while jerking off."

There are so many things to unpack in that sentence. I start with, "You used to talk to my brother about me?"

"You're the reason I became friends with him."

I point to myself. "*I'm* the reason?"

"Well, kids," Monty interrupts. "All the lanes are clear. Time for me to put the chairs in the wagon."

Lucas opens his wallet to pay but comes up empty handed. "Shit. Forgot I gave all my money to Hunter." He slides out a credit card.

Monty waves it away. "You fall off the tater truck or somethin'? Card machine has been broken since 2016. Didn't you see the sign on the door?"

I open my purse. "I've got it. What do I owe you, Monty?"

He eyes the bottle of tequila he left on the bar to see how much is left. "Twenty-five ought to do it."

I leave him thirty. "Thank you, Monty. Have a good weekend." I tilt my glass, emptying the last bit, then vacate my barstool.

"You, too, pretty lady. And come back soon. Don't be such a stranger."

I turn. "I could say the same about you. I haven't seen you in *my* shop."

He cackles. "Next time I need a smutty novel or some of those pretty tights you like to wear, I'll pop right on over."

"I do carry other types of books, you know. Thrillers. Mysteries. You should come check it out."

"I might ought do that then," he drawls, his Texas accent coming through even though he's lived here for more than fifty years.

As soon as we're out the door, he's got it locked up and the lights off. It amazes me that a man Monty's age can still run this place alone.

Back at Lucas's car, I hold my hand out. "Keys?"

He stares blankly at my hand. "You have them."

"I don't. You took them from me before we went to the bowling alley. Remember?"

"Not hardly."

I nod to his left pocket. "You put them there and told me to get them if I wanted them so badly."

He laughs. "That does sound like something I'd say." He reaches into his pocket and comes out with his phone. He tries the other one. "I'm telling you, I don't have them."

I glance back at the darkened bowling alley. "You must have dropped them inside."

He looks at me and then his car. "Well… shit."

"I could call you an Uber."

"I have a better idea." He looks behind me at Donovan's Pub. "Cooper's probably calmed down by now."

"You destroyed his property. I doubt it. I don't think you should go back in there until you go bearing a TV twice as nice as the one you broke."

He looks at his phone. "But it's still your birthday for another seven minutes. *One* more drink, birthday girl?"

My eyes roll. Has he not had enough to forget the whole engagement debacle?

"Come on, Regan Lucas. I never got to toast your birthday. There has to be someplace we can go."

I sigh. "I have liquor at my place." I put a finger into his chest. "If you say one thing about it being cheap, I'll kick you out so quick your head will spin even faster than it will be when you wake up with a killer hangover."

His lips smash together, and he mimes locking them with a key.

Then he follows me back to my place for a drink that I know is so monumentally stupid I'll be regretting it to high heaven come morning.

But he's hot.

And it *is* my birthday.

Chapter Three

Regan

I unlock my shop and we step through the front door. It's dim, the only light coming from the display spotlight in the front window showcasing the two mannequins I've outfitted with some of the second-hand clothes donated to keep my boutique afloat.

Lucas stops walking and I almost run into him. "Didn't this used to be a bookstore?"

I gesture to the left wall, lined with bookshelves. "Still is, only now I'm a boutique as well."

He narrows his eyes. "When did that happen?"

"Years ago. You're not very observant, are you?"

"Seeing as I've never had use for a bookstore or a boutique…" His words trail off as he eyes me up and down as if he's just now really noticing me. "Why do you dress so funny?"

It's not the first time I've been asked that question. I stopped being offended by it a long time ago. Right around the time I stopped caring what other people thought of me.

I hold out a leg as if modeling my candy-stripe tights. "You don't like my choice of attire?"

His eyes sweep over my short white skirt and my pink fuzzy sweater. I can practically feel his gaze caressing every one of my curves, and it makes me all tingly inside. I almost laugh, because this is Lucas Montana, the kid who used to be my little brother's best friend. I've fantasized about a lot of guys in this town, but not him.

And now I'm wondering why. Because he's no longer that pimple-faced kid who hung around my house all hours of the day despite the fact that his own parents lived in a mansion that dwarfed our place. Now—he's a man. A tall, dark, handsome, incredibly well-built man.

I knew this had hookup written all over it when I invited him here. So I shouldn't be surprised that he's looking at me this way, like he's a starving man at an all-you-can-eat buffet.

It's laughable, though, how completely opposite we are. I stare at our reflection in the antique mirror on the wall. Lucas is wearing khakis and a light-blue dress shirt, sleeves rolled to his elbows. My guess is he was even wearing a tie earlier. It's a rare occasion that I see him in anything but business attire. Jeans sometimes, but almost always a button-down shirt. And more often than not, a suit.

My insides get all squirmy thinking of what lies under his shirt. But with the way he's looking at me, I realize how nervous I am at the idea of what I think is about to happen.

This is Lucas Montana. He's been engaged four times. He may be five years younger than me, but I'm guessing he has a lot more experience. And I'm positive he hasn't had a two-year dry spell.

"Hurry," he says, looking at the time, seeming to forget all about the question he asked me. "We only have three minutes left."

Right. My birthday. "This way," I say, leading him to the door that goes up to my apartment.

He races to the top, tripping halfway up and almost face-planting into the stairs. Sitting on the step, he braces himself with one hand as he slowly lists to the side. "Shit. I might be a little drunk."

I giggle. "You think?"

He looks up at me. "You have a nice laugh."

Joey meows loudly from the other side of the door. He hears me coming and is getting impatient.

"What the hell was that?" Lucas asks, looking around the stairwell.

I hold out a hand. "Come on. I'll introduce you to Joey."

The moment I'm through the door at the top of the stairs, Joey winds between my feet, rubbing against my calves. I reach down and pick him up, kissing him on his head.

"Hey, little... *fuck!*" Lucas withdraws his hand quickly as Joey takes a swipe at him with his claws.

"Joey," I admonish, putting him down before he scurries off to hide. I turn to Lucas. "I'm sorry about that. He's usually very friendly."

Lucas glances around. "He's not gonna like, pounce on me, is he?"

I laugh. "Joey? No. He's the sweetest thing, I assure you."

"Sweet. Yeah."

"Really, he is." I step into the kitchen and open my small liquor cabinet. "Pick your poison."

True to his word, he doesn't say anything about my collection of cheap booze. "It's your birthday. You pick."

I get two shot glasses from my small stack, and, just to egg him on, I fill them with strawberry vodka.

"Geez, woman. You drink like you dress."

Pushing his shot glass against his chest, I ask, "And how is that exactly?"

"I don't know." He shrugs. "Different."

"Different good, or different bad?"

"I'm going to plead the fifth on that one and just toast your birthday." He raises his glass and checks the time. "We just made it under the wire. To you, Regan. Happy birthday."

I clink my glass to his and we down our shots.

Wiping his lips, he does his best to hide the pucker of displeasure. I know he's accustomed to high-end liquor and fine wine, so I cut him a break. But I still tease him by refilling our glasses.

He takes both shot glasses from me, still full, and sets them on the counter. "We both know that's not why you invited me here."

All at once, chills from anxiety and warmth from desire flood through me.

I don't have to say a word. He can tell by the look in my eyes that I'm up for this. Whatever *this* happens to be.

"You're about to make a very big mistake," he warns.

"What is it they say about big mistakes? That they come with big rewards?"

"That's risks, not mistakes."

"Tomato, tomahto."

"I like the way you think." He takes a step toward me. "And you have no false impressions over what this would be? Because the only reward you'll be getting tonight will be my big cock."

I giggle. But secretly, I'm flushing with anticipation.

"I'm a grown woman, Lucas. I'm allowed to have a one-night stand. It doesn't make either of us bad people, you know."

He inches closer, leans in, and whispers in my ear, "You're so fucking sexy."

Part of me is surprised to hear him say it. He's the clean-cut businessman and I'm the eccentric shop owner. We're complete opposites in every way. I'm sure he's just saying it in the heat of the moment.

"I had a huge crush on you in high school," he adds.

Remembering what he said at the bowling alley, I tamp down the pheromones for a second. Apparently my curiosity is stronger than my libido. "So let's get back to that. What did you say about my dad catching you, um…" I shift awkwardly.

"Choking the chicken? Beatin' the meat?"

My cheeks heat. "Yeah, that."

He runs a finger up and down my arm, sending electric impulses straight to my core. "It was that time I went to the beach with your family, right before you went away to college. Jesus, you wore that red bikini. I was watching you from the bathroom window and, well, I was fourteen, I had a huge boner, and you had curves into next week. So I started going to town when the door swings open and—"

My hand flies to my mouth. "My dad walked in on you?"

He presses into me, making sure I can feel his erection. "Are we going to waste this talking about your dad, or are we going to do something about it?"

I take his hand and pull him to my bedroom, shocked by the bold move. It's quite uncharacteristic of me. "Option number two," I say, throwing him a sultry look over my shoulder.

I don't turn on the bedroom light. Through the years, since David anyway, I've become more and more secure about my plus-size body. But having that security doesn't mean I want to see myself jiggle around while a gorgeous guy rides me.

It doesn't occur to me until I'm lying down and he's peeling off my skirt that we haven't even kissed. I suppose maybe that's typical of a one-nighter. I try to think back to the only other one I've ever had. The one with Tag Calloway. Yes, he's now my best friend's husband, but this was way back when he was a player. I think he may have even slept with me on a dare. I push that thought away as I try to remember if Tag and I kissed. I can't recall, so maybe we didn't. And if we did, it wasn't memorable.

Through the dim light coming in from the living room, Lucas stares at my brightly colored tights. "Your legs look like barber-shop poles."

"Your shirt makes you look like a banker," I quip.

He chuckles and unbuttons it, tossing it to the side. "Do I look like a banker now?"

I almost want the lights to be on, because if he looks this way in the dark, I can't imagine what his sculpted abs would do to me in the light of day. I reach out and run a hand over his taut tummy. "No. Definitely not."

He skims a hand along my outer thigh. "Then do you mind if I unwrap *my* present?"

"But it's not *your* birthday."

"It's not yours anymore either."

I scoot up on the bed and poke my toes into his ribs. "Unwrap away."

He crawls up my body, hovers over me, then lowers his head until his lips are just above mine. "Happy birthday to me," he says, right before his mouth devours mine.

His lips are just like the rest of his body. Strong. Firm. Sexy. And oh, so demanding. They part slowly, allowing my tongue to slip inside, and the kiss becomes so much more than I ever expected considering this is a one-time thing.

I've done a lot of kissing in my life. Mike Gordon was the first boy I kissed. We were in seventh grade when he caught me kissing my fist behind the middle school auditorium. Instead of laughing at me and humiliating me by telling everyone he'd caught me doing it, he said I could use him for practice. What I didn't know at the time was that he was the one using me for practice. He had a crush on an eighth grader and didn't want to seem inexperienced. Mike and I made out every day for weeks. He moved away twenty years ago, and I still credit him for making me the kisser I am today. I may not be good at other things, but kissing I know.

"Mmm," he mumbles against my lips. "You taste like strawberry."

"*You* taste like strawberry."

He laughs. "I suppose I do. Now, less talking, more tongue."

"You started it."

Our prolonged make out sesh surprises me. While I'm not complaining exactly, part of me is wondering how long I have to keep this up until he pops my two-year cherry.

His lips ravage my neck. I crane my head back to give him all the space he needs. It feels sooooo good. I just know I'm already soaked down there. Lucas Montana may be even better at kissing than I am.

He licks the deep V in my neckline. "Let's get to that unwrapping."

Urging my sweater up and over my head, he then strips off my leggings and drops them both on the floor. He kneels back on his haunches, eyes raking over my body in the dim light. *Don't cover up, don't cover up*, I implore myself as the heat of his gaze consumes me.

"Holy shit." His head shakes. "I'm living out my childhood fantasy."

My eyes settle on the huge bulge tenting his khakis. Never being one to be forward, I surprise myself… *again*… by reaching out for him. As my hand skims along the outline of his impressive erection, I figure turning thirty-five has empowered me somehow.

He unbuckles his belt and loosens his pants. When I slip my hand beneath them and into his tight boxer briefs, he inhales a sharp breath through his teeth. "Fuuuuuuck." He grabs my wrist and closes his eyes tightly, almost in meditation. "If you don't want me to shoot my load like I would have in high school, you'll stop that and let me have you like I want you."

I giggle and put my hands out to my sides.

As I watch, he sheds his shoes, pants, and underwear, and gets a condom from his wallet. He's back to kneeling on the bed, his erection standing tall and proud, and, wow, I can't tear my eyes away from it. He's so… *big*.

All of a sudden, I've gone from wanting him to end my dry spell to wondering if he's going to break me.

"It'll fit," he says, as if it's not the first time a woman's eyes have nearly popped out of her head at the sight.

I guess it wouldn't be. If you're a guy with a huge penis, there are bound to be concerns.

"As long as you're ready." He grins then rips my panties clean off me and plunges a finger inside. "Jesus," he mumbles when he finds me most definitely ready. He quickly puts the condom on and hovers over me for a second. "Regan fucking Lucas." His head shakes again. "Your brother would kill me if he knew what I'm about to do to you."

I reach around and grab his ass cheeks. "Good thing he's not here then."

He sinks into me and I moan. At the stretching. The fullness. The incredible feeling of having more than a silicone-covered piece of machinery inside me.

Going slow at first and getting me used to him, he carefully glides in and out. When I don't resist, he speeds up. *Oh god, this is good.* It's exactly what I've been missing. But when some of those familiar tingles build in my lower belly, I get all up in my head like I used to.

I tell myself this is different. *He's* different. He has no expectations. No demands. And besides, I'm older now. I'm not doing this for anyone but myself.

Let go already.

I try and try and try to relax and let it happen. But the more I try, the more I know it's not going to.

I sigh in disappointment.

Lucas takes it as a sign of enjoyment. So I go with it. Just like I always have. I make the appropriate noises. I squirm and buck my hips and even give a little shout. I'm very convincing. Not my first rodeo. And he's drunk. So, how much attention is he really paying?

"Uuuuuuungh!" he calls out, spasms, then stills.

He collapses onto me, fully sated and spent.

I stare at the ceiling, ashamed.

He rolls to my side. I think he's watching me, but the light from the doorway is behind him so I can't be sure. Maybe he's just basking in post-coital bliss. I lean back into the pillow and envy him.

"You okay, Regan?"

So he *was* watching me.

I turn my head and smile. "I'm great. But tipsy and tired, so…"

He chuckles. "So, you're kicking me out." He hops up, ties off the condom, and throws it in the small trash can by my dresser.

"I open early on Saturdays."

"Right." He pulls on his boxers and the rest of his clothes then sits on the chair in the corner to put on his shoes. "Are we… good?"

I grab my robe off the bedpost. "I know what this was, Lucas. Believe me, we're fine."

"So you're not going to go all batshit crazy the next time you see me?"

"Why would I do that?"

"Isn't that what chicks do after a drunken hookup?"

I tilt my head. "Lucas, this isn't your first one-night stand, is it?"

He shrugs. "I'm more of a long-term-relationship guy."

I cover my mouth and laugh. "Oh my god, it is."

"Yeah." He stands, looking out of sorts. "So I'm not exactly sure how this works. Like, do I say thank you and leave? Obviously, I don't stay and cuddle."

Still snickering, I say, "Thank you will do just fine."

Joey jumps on the bed, rubbing himself on my thigh. He doesn't settle next to me as he usually does. He stands, tail twitching.

"Okay then." Lucas leans down and pecks my cheek with his lips. "Thank you." Joey hisses and Lucas pulls back quickly. "He really doesn't like me, does he?"

I study my cat. "That is super strange."

Lucas walks through my bedroom door and turns. "See you around, *Lucas*," he says with a wink.

"Yeah." I lift my chin. "See you around, Lucas."

He smiles. Then he's gone. A moment later, I hear the front door shut.

Joey curls up next to me. I cock my head and wonder what his problem is. Animals are usually very good at judging people. Lucas is a nice guy. Why wouldn't Joey like him? Joey likes everyone.

"Well then," I muse aloud, "it's a good thing he's not going to be a permanent fixture in my life."

I lie back and relax, not bothering to go down and lock up the shop, and think of how I'm glad it was Lucas up here and not one of the McQuaids—or at least one of the McQuaids from back in the day who would blab all over town about their conquests. I doubt Lucas would do such a thing. He *is* a nice guy, despite the fact that he's a total commitment-phobe. Which is completely fine with me. I'm the last one who needs to be committed to anyone more than the furball at my side.

Still, though, part of me wishes I could have a do-over of tonight. I'm thirty-five. Isn't that the age where women become more sexually aware? More in tune with their bodies?

Feeling defeated, I reach over and open my nightstand, determined to get the release I deserve, and shuffle through my plethora of toys until I find just the right one.

"Shoo, Joey," I say, pushing him off the bed. "I need a minute."

Chapter Four

Lucas

I'm going over Marti's latest updated designs for our rebranding. It's something she's been working on for months. As Chief Marketing Officer, I'm working closely with her. We're on the cusp of being able to debut Montana Winery's upgraded look. We've wanted to compete with the big wineries for a decade, and I think this is the first step in accomplishing that.

I glance at all of the Post-it notes lining my desk. Then I look at my calendars—all three of them—when my mind goes back to Friday night. I'd bet my left nut Regan Lucas doesn't even own a calendar. She said she opens early on Saturdays. But I have it on good authority that she opens when she damn well pleases. Sometimes eight am, sometimes ten forty-five. I guess it depends on her mood and maybe the general state of any given hangover.

It's not that I think she's a huge drinker. I mean, who in the hell gets drunk off strawberry vodka? Humorously, I shake my head at the thought.

The screen on my computer goes black with inactivity and I see my reflection. My shirt is buttoned up to the neckline. My tie matches the jacket currently hanging on a rack by the door. And every hair on my head has been meticulously combed.

What a contrast to the flamboyant brunette bombshell that is Regan.

My loins—is that even a thing?—start to burn like a fire is inside me. I wonder if she'd be up for another round. After all, I'd like to be able to remember every second of it, which is not something I'm capable of after drinking as much as I had. For a second there, I thought she might have even faked her orgasm. But I could swear her body shuddered under me. And those sounds she made have been echoing in my dreams for days.

And… did I even touch her breasts? Take off her bra? Maybe I was afraid of having a Forrest Gump moment and coming in my goddamn boxers. It's all so fuzzy. My need to have these questions answered has me wanting to risk another night with her.

And it is a risk. One night is a hookup. Two may come with expectations. Despite her lackadaisical demeanor, I suspect Regan has one hell of a head on her shoulders. She knows exactly who I am and how far away she should keep her heart from me.

Heart. Not pussy.

Unable to get my head on straight enough to work, I go down the hall to Blake's office. My youngest brother is COO—Chief Operating Officer—overseeing the day-to-day operation of the winery.

He looks up from his computer. "What's up?"

I walk in, shut the door, and sit across from him.

He reclines in his chair, perches his jean-clad legs up on his desk, ankles crossed, and eyes the door. "A closed-door meeting. We don't have many of those around here. Mind telling me what the others shouldn't be hearing?"

Settling back into the chair, I wonder how I'm going to get this out without sounding like a douchebag. But I came to Blake and not Dallas for a reason. It wasn't so long ago when Blake was a real player; a guy who's probably had more one-night stands than I have fingers and toes. Whereas Dallas has been with exactly two women in his entire life.

I fall somewhere in between, having been with my share of women, but all had been classified as a relationship. Even if some only lasted weeks or months, all of them were expected to go somewhere. I never once slept with a woman with the intention of it only being that one time, never to call or possibly even see her again. That was Blake's forte, not mine.

For as long as I can remember, I've been entranced by my parents' long, loving, carefree relationship. They make being married seem fun and easy, although I'm sure neither is true all the time. And yet, the only thing I've managed to do is disappoint my mom and dad—four times. More if you count the other breakups that never made it to engagement status. Maybe deep down, I'm afraid I could never have what they have. Or that I can't live up to the standard. So when it gets down to it, I bail rather than let myself find out it's all an illusion and the perfect marriage doesn't exist.

"Brother?"

Blake's voice pulls me from my self-analysis. I look him in the eye and do what I came here to do. "I might have done something a little stupid, and I'm embarrassed. Well, not embarrassed as in I'm ashamed of *who*. It's more like I don't want people thinking she's going to be the next jilted bride. Because it's not like that."

He holds his hand up to stop me. "Slow down. Start from the beginning."

I crack my neck. "The night we saw Lissa's engagement, I did something."

He chuckles. "You mean you did some*one*."

I nod.

"Ah, shit. Don't tell me you hooked up with Sheriff Niles's daughter."

"No. No one like that."

"Why in the hell are you dancing around this, Luke? Spit it out already."

I look at the family picture hanging behind him. The perfect portrait of the perfect family. Blake, Ellie, and Maisy look blissfully happy. Just another reminder of something I'm never destined to have. I sigh. "It's Regan."

"Lucas?" he belts out an octave higher.

On the defensive now, I blurt out, "You got a problem with that?"

"With her—no. She's one of the nicest people I know. But therein lies the problem. You got drunk, couldn't keep your dick in your pants, went after the first woman you saw, and now you're here asking me how to let her down easy."

"You've got it all wrong, Blake. She kicked me out after."

Laughter fills the air between us—all *his*.

"Come on, man," I say. "Cut me a break. I've never been kicked out before."

He cocks his head, no longer laughing. "Right. I forgot. You only sleep with the next future Mrs. Montana who never quite earns the title."

I pick up the stress ball on the corner of his desk and throw it at him.

He catches it without missing a beat and squeezes. "So you had your first official hookup." His head shakes slowly. "How you made it to thirty without one baffles me." He toasts me with his Montana Winery coffee mug. "Cheers to popping your one-night stand cherry."

When I don't smile, laugh, or get up, he stares at me strangely.

"Luke," he says, in a commanding voice reminiscent of our father. "You're not telling me you want Regan Lucas to be your fifth almost-missus, are you?"

"No. Hell no. I'm just wondering what the protocol is for… seeing if she wants to do it again."

He leans way back in his chair, thinking. The fingers on each of his hands tap together then steeple under his chin. "What you're really saying is you want a no-strings, friends-with-benefits relationship."

I shrug. "At this point, that may be the only kind of relationship I should be having. I don't intend on hurting another woman, Blake."

"Well, it's up to the girl. It's always up to the girl."

I breathe a small sigh of relief. "She said on Friday that she knew what it was, and she was okay with it."

"Be careful," he warns. "That's how a lot of problems start. She could have just been trying to…" He trails off, immersed in his own thoughts. "You know what, I doubt Regan would do that."

"Do what?"

"Try to trap you. You know, for the money. But no way, that's not her." He sits up straighter, feet now on the floor. "I say go for it, brother."

"Yeah?"

"Sure. She's single. She's got a good head on her shoulders keeping a small business going. And man… those curves. She's smoking hot." He whispers the last part as if doing so won't in any way be disrespectful to his wife. "But I'll deny ever saying it."

37

A mental picture of Regan in her underwear is suddenly front and center. "Tell me about it." I shake it away and ask, "So exactly how do I have that conversation?"

"Like a thirty-year-old adult who helps run a billion-dollar winery."

I furrow my brow. "This isn't a business transaction, Blake."

"No? Maybe it's better if you both look at it as one. No feelings. Big payout."

My head bobs up and down. I like the way he thinks. I get up to leave, then turn, one last thing niggling in the far corner of my mind. "Has a girl ever, um, faked it with you?"

He's trying to mask his amusement, but he's not doing a very good job. "I'm sure it's happened. There were a lot of girls. Honestly, though, back then I wouldn't have cared one way or the other."

He looks ashamed. He truly has changed.

"So that's what this is all about?" he asks. "You proving to yourself that you can get her off?"

"I'm not saying it didn't happen. I'm just not a hundred percent sure."

"Adulting isn't that hard, Lucas. Try being one and ask her."

"Since when does the youngest brother give the oldest one advice?"

"When he asks."

I lean against the door frame. "You've really grown. Ellie and Maisy have been good for you."

He holds both arms out in display. "Living proof that a leopard can change his spots."

And now I'm thinking of Regan again. Her mouth. Her soft, sensuous body. Her maybe-maybe-not orgasm.

I wave a hand and try to make an exit before Blake can notice my tenting trousers.

He calls me back and I stick my head around the corner. "I'm in kind of a hurry, what is it?"

"A reporter showed up earlier. Dallas urged him to leave."

I huff. "Urged?"

He shrugs. "In his own passive-aggressive way of course."

"A few have tried to intercept me outside my apartment building."

"Vultures," he says. "It'll die down."

I nod, my erection fully deflated now, and walk away.

Chapter Five

Regan

Although I'm delighted to see Maddie sitting at our usual table behind the ice cream shop—I'm not so sure she's happy to be here. My bet is she'd rather be in the hospital holding Tag's son in her arms.

She looks up as I approach, arms outstretched in frustration. "Still here, damn it."

I laugh. "Technically, you're not even due for a few more days."

She sighs and shifts uncomfortably. "I was sure he'd be here by now. Gigi is going almost as crazy as I am. We're *both* nesting. And Tag, I think he comes home with a new toy almost every day. We must have every sporting good known to man. Doesn't matter if this little guy won't be able to use them for years. My husband is dead set on his son being some kind of sports star."

"Well, he does own a sports management company."

"What's up, girlies?" Ava sings, rounding the corner with a carton of coffees. She looks at the two of us and then the empty spots on the bench. "Just us? But I brought extras." She hands Maddie and me our standing order and pushes the rest aside.

I remove the lid on mine and inhale the heavenly scent. "Actually, I'm glad it's just us three today."

Maddie seems to forget how uncomfortable she is on the unforgiving bench. Her inquisitive brows rise. "Why?"

"I don't want rumors floating around. You know how this town is. The fewer people who know, the better."

Ava sips her latte, peering at me over the rim of the cup. "Know what exactly?" she asks after swallowing.

"I'm kind of surprised nobody's said anything already. It's been almost four days."

"Regan," Maddie says impatiently. "This baby may be born before you get to the point."

I roll my eyes. "Okay, so I may have done something a little reckless the other night. On my birthday. It was stupid. Not regretful stupid, but most likely stupid in the eyes of, well… everyone."

Ava turns to Maddie and eyes her belly. "He come out yet?"

Both of my friends glare at me.

"I slept with Lucas Montana."

Maddie and Ava both gasp and then proceed to speak over each other in shrills that are hard to decipher.

I hold up a hand. "One at a time, please. Maddie, you go first since you could literally burst at any second."

Ava is practically bouncing in her seat. She opens her mouth to say something, but closes it before anything comes out. As a good friend does, she acquiesces, albeit reluctantly, and lets Maddie have her say.

Maddie sighs deeply. It's the kind of sigh you expect from your mom when she's just found out you let a boy go to second base and she's about to give you 'the talk.'

"I'm not one to give advice exactly. After all, I'm married to the ex-quintessential love 'em and leave 'em playboy of Calloway Creek. But Regan... *four times.* And he was with Lissa for a lot of years. If he couldn't go through with it with her, I fear he never will."

It's exactly what I thought she'd say. I turn to Ava. "Your turn."

"I second all that. He's almost worse than a manwhore. At least with a playboy, you know what you're getting and shame on you if you expect anything else. With Lucas though... he'll suck you in and say all the right things. He'll give you hope of that fairy tale relationship all women dream of with the nice, super-hot, rich guy... right up until he breaks your heart. So actually, shame on anyone who would touch that man with a ten-foot pole. Shame on *you,* Regan. What were you thinking?"

My eyes flit between them. "Is that it? Are you done?"

"There's really not much more to say," Maddie adds. "If you don't know exactly who Lucas is, that's on you."

"It was a one-night stand, guys."

The looks on their faces tell me they're about to explode with anger.

"Don't get your panties in a twist. It was *my* idea... more or less."

"Oh my god," Maddie cries.

"It's not that big a deal, Maddie. We're adults and have every right to—"

She grabs my arm. "Not that." She looks down. "Either my water just broke, or I just peed myself in surprise."

I fly to my feet and hold out a hand to help her up.

"Wait." She bats it away. "I want details."

I flash Maddie the eyes of a crazy woman. "Are you insane? You're in labor."

Samantha Christy

"This could take hours. You had a hookup with Lucas Montana. That's… so unlike you."

I shake my head. Her terse expression tells me she's not going to move until I talk. Behind her head, I put my thumb and pinky to my ear like a phone and mouth, "Call Tag," to Ava.

Then, knowing a tiny human needs to get out of her, I give Maddie the abridged version.

"I think it was turning thirty-five. It was freeing somehow, knowing I could have a night with zero expectations. And you know what, it was exactly that. We did it, I kicked him out after, and we haven't so much as talked, texted, or seen each other since. And I'm totally fine with it. There you have it. Can we get you to the hospital now?"

She brushes me off again. "So that's it? Wham bam? You're thirty-five and now you've gone all cougar on us?"

I belt out a maniacal laugh. "Yeah, that's me." I hadn't even thought of Lucas's age. With all he's been through, he certainly doesn't seem younger.

"You got your eyes set on anyone else?" Ava says. "I think all Jonah Calloway's boys are out of high school now."

I swat her arm. "It's not like I'm becoming the Mrs. Robinson of Cal Creek. It was a one-time thing."

"Maybe," Maddie says, still ignoring the inevitable. "Or maybe turning thirty-five set off some kind of ticking clock inside you." She rubs her bump. "Ever think of that?"

"Me? Have a kid?" I snort-chuckle. "As if. I'll leave the baby-rearing to everyone else and enjoy my life as a single cat lady, thank you very much." I touch Ava's arm gently. "It's going to happen for you, I just know it will."

She nods sadly. This must be so hard for her, especially with Maddie about to deliver.

"Woman!" Tag booms, racing up from his haphazardly parked SUV. "What the hell are you doing sitting here gabbing with your friends when my son clearly wants to come out and meet his mom, dad, and sister?"

"Girl time is important," she says.

He shakes his head, laughs, then sweeps his wife into his arms like she's a feather, and lumbers to his car.

"Call us when we can come meet the little guy!" I shout after her.

She gives me a thumbs-up over Tag's shoulder.

I go to sit back down, turning my nose up at the wet spot Maddie left behind, and shift to the other side of the table. "They are nauseatingly happy, aren't they?"

Ava nods. "Yeah."

Guilt overcomes me. "I mean, not that you and Trevor aren't. You are totally like that when he's here." I drink my now-cold coffee. "You really miss him, don't you?"

Her eyes turn sad. "I do. I thought it would get easier, but it hasn't. Still, though, sometimes when he's on leave, it's difficult to get used to a new routine. I run things the way I run things. And when he tries to help out at the coffee shop, he usually ends up just being in the way."

"How much longer does he have left?"

"Military doctors have to give seven years, not including residency. He started later than most, so he's still got about eighteen months. But after that, we'll be set. He'll never have to leave again. And we won't have to worry about money."

"But it makes it all the more difficult to get pregnant. As if you weren't having a hard enough time."

45

She looks in the direction Tag and Maddie went. "It does. Hudson McQuaid suggested he bank some sperm the next time he's on leave. At least then, I could keep trying while he's gone."

My eyebrows shoot up. "As in use a turkey baster?"

She chuckles. "Something like that, but more technical. Sperm doesn't last long. It's not like I can just put it in Tupperware and take some out when I feel like it. It has to be frozen and thawed."

"Sounds expensive."

"Not as expensive as some other methods. Don't even get me started on those. But I'm not getting any younger, so…" She looks off in the distance.

I pat her hand. "Nonsense. Women are having babies well into their forties these days."

"Fertile women," she says. "Not women with inhospitable uteruses like mine. Be that as it may, the current theory is that my uterus and his sperm just don't play well together."

I try not to giggle, because this is not a laughing matter. But every time she says inhospitable uterus, I picture little ninjas with swords in her womb, ready to attack any sperm that try to get through. "There's always adoption."

Before Ava can respond, Dakota walks up. "Sorry I'm late." She eyes the wet spot on the bench. "What'd I miss?"

Ava and I look at each other and laugh.

Chapter Six

Lucas

After parking behind Donovan's Pub, I walk out to the sidewalk along McQuaid Circle. Regan's shop, *Booktique*, is across the street, nestled between Ava Criss's coffee house and the hardware store.

I stroll down the street nonchalantly, window shopping and glancing around every so often to see if anyone is watching. Why in the fuck am I so nervous? I've never been one to get nervous around women.

It's the situation. I'm about to ask a woman to sleep with me for sport. No strings. No feelings. No attachment. She could slap me. Or laugh at me. Or blab to the town what a pathetic loser I am— as if they don't already know after the whole Lissa engagement thing.

Grow some balls, I can almost hear my brothers teasing.

I loosen my tie and jaywalk across the street. Opening the heavy glass door to her shop, the familiar tinkling of the bell over the door sounds, bringing back all kinds of flashbacks from Friday night.

There's no hush of voices as I step inside. No eyes turn to stare at me like I'm wildly out of place. In fact, the shop is empty. She's probably in the back room.

When I was here the other day, it was dim, and I didn't really get the chance to look around. This place has been here since I was a kid. When Regan's parents owned it, it was a bookstore, and they made additional income by renting out the apartment upstairs.

Surely I'd been here back in the day, when I was Ryder's friend and lusting after Regan. The two of them would have to man the store on Saturdays to learn the business and give their parents a day off. But if I've been here, I've forgotten. That, or the place is just so different now, it's hard for my brain to reconcile the two.

"Hello?" I call.

There's no answer. I pass by a small seating area that has a few chairs and a small sofa that looks to be a relic from the eighteen hundreds. I approach the counter. "Regan?" I say louder.

Still, she doesn't appear. Maybe she's in the bathroom. I walk around the counter and stick my head through the doorway to the back. Empty, and the bathroom door is open, revealing darkness beyond. She's not here. Who leaves their shop unattended?

I go back to the counter and notice the large old-timey cash register that looks like it belongs in a Five and Dime on *The Andy Griffith Show*. No way she still uses that dinosaur. Then I see a small bag, the kind you take to the bank to make cash deposits. It has several twenties sticking out of the top. I shake my head. So the register is just for show. She stuffs all her profits in there.

Receipts litter the top of the counter along with scraps of paper with scribbled notes.

One appears to be a grocery list: Cat litter. Coke. Doritos. Broccoli. Sandwich meat.

Another a to-do list: **Flower order at 5:30. Hospital. Drop off donations.**

Yet another has a list of what I think are book titles.

There's a stack of books that look like they're about to teeter off the counter. I straighten them, making a sturdy pile that won't fall.

A heap of clothes is strewn out on the floor behind the register, as if flung there by a scorned spouse.

Business cards with the name of her shop in hot pink have spilled out across the black and white tiled countertop. I pick them up, shuffle them together, and replace them in their upright holder.

My eyes rake over the mess. How can anyone work like this? It's disorganized. Chaotic. So completely random.

Then I laugh. Because all those words are words I'd use to describe Regan.

This place is her. Right down to the mismatched furniture, the contrasting wallpaper, and the distressed coffered ceiling.

The front of the store where the merchandise is—the part customers see—is also random, but at least that part is clean and inviting. Like walking into your grandmother's house for Sunday dinner.

The whole place smells like a flower. Or maybe rain. It's a scent I can't quite pin down. A thin trail of smoke in the corner catches my attention. She's burning an incense stick. I laugh inwardly. Of course she is. Don't all hippies do that? I cock my head. Is that what she is, a hippie? I honestly have no idea. All I know is that Regan Lucas is one of a kind.

I go over and look at the labels on the boxes of incense stacked under the burner. They all have strange names like Dragon's Blood, Positive Vibes, and Nirvana.

The bell over the door chimes and I turn, expecting to see Regan. But it's not her. It's Rose Gianogi—or I guess Rose McQuaid now—the former owner of the flower shop down the street, now run by her granddaughter, who I'm told is currently in the hospital after having my cousin's baby.

I grab a book from the stack so I don't look like I'm robbing the place.

Rose glances around. "Why, Lucas Montana, I've never seen you in this shop before."

"Hello, Mrs. McQuaid."

She giggles and waves me off. "Please. I might be married to a McQuaid, but I'm still just plain old Rose Gianogi. I've been signing my name that way for sixty years, ever since I married my first husband, may he rest in peace. I'm too old to go changing things up now, much to Tucker's displeasure. But he still loves me, that old grump. Even when I can't get my head to turn for someone calling that new name. I guess it's true you can't teach an old dog new tricks." She laughs hoarsely at her joke. "So tell me, what brings you here?"

"I, uh… came for a book."

She walks over with the bouncy stride of a twenty-year-old, not an elderly woman, and peers at what's in my hand, reading the title aloud. "*Managing Menopause*. Interesting choice."

I feel my cheeks heat. "I mean, not *this* book." I put it down.

Rose's head swivels in all directions. "Where's our quirky little shop owner?"

Quirky. Yeah, that's it. That's exactly it. *Quirky*.

I shrug. "The place was empty when I got here."

"Ah, well, then you'll have to do. Regan usually helps me, but with those big strong arms, I imagine you can do it in one trip."

"Do what, Mrs. Gianogi?"

50

"Come on." She waves me toward the door. "I'm double parked. Sheriff Niles won't bat an eye before he gives me a ticket, no matter who I'm married to."

I follow her out and she pops the trunk, revealing two large bags.

"Your... trash?" I ask, eyebrows knitted.

"My old clothes," she says, tugging on one bag. "You gonna help? Or is this little old lady going to pop a vein trying to get them out?"

I easily hoist one large bag out, then the other.

"Been donating clothes to Regan's shop for years. Makes me feel like I'm giving back in some way, you know?"

When I eye her like she's crazy, she adds, "You been living under a rock, Lucas Montana? How do you think she runs this shop? People donate clothes. She gives what she can't sell to Goodwill. And at the end of every month, she donates ten percent of her profits to the women's and children's shelter."

"Is that so?"

She holds open the front door of the shop for me. "Thought you would have already known that, seeing as you're a businessman and all."

"I don't really get into other people's business."

I drop the bags next to the pile of clothes behind the counter, thinking now that maybe those are the clothes she can't sell and will be taking to Goodwill.

Rose perches herself against the back of one of the chairs in the grouping. "But you'd like to get into *hers*, isn't that right?"

The door chimes again. Rose is still staring me down like she's coming up with some sinister plan. Plan for what, I have no idea— to kick me out, or finally get me married off? Most likely something in between.

I turn to find Regan bounding through the front door. "Sorry, sorry. I had to go fill an order at Gigi's for Kyla Simon's bridal shower."

I glance around, this whole time thinking she was upstairs in the bathroom or grabbing a bite to eat. "You just left your store? Unattended and unlocked? There's cash sitting on the counter."

"I'm sorry, are you new to Calloway Creek?" She rolls her eyes at me, unimpressed and like I didn't have my dick inside her just five days ago.

"Hi, Rose." She gives the elderly woman a hug. "Have you met your great-grandson yet? I can't wait to see him."

Rose's face beams. "Came from there an hour ago. The tot looks just like me." She models her face from side to side as Regan giggles.

Damn, that giggle. It does something to my insides.

"Thank you for helping with the flower order, dear," Rose says. "I'll be filling in for Maddie on a limited basis while she's indisposed. Gigi will help, too. But it's nice to know we can fall back on you and Ava in a pinch."

"You know you can. I just love how everyone on this street helps each other out. I even heard Mrs. Truman offered to take a few shifts. I'd even bet old Monty would do it if he weren't already working eighty-hour weeks."

"Be careful who you call old, dear. Monty Langston is only five years my senior. Did you know he tried to court me back in the day? He'd come in and buy me flowers right from my own shop."

"I didn't know that. Poor guy lost his chance with an amazing woman."

Rose snickers. "I suppose I was saving myself for the old fart I ended up with."

Regan raises a scolding brow.

"I have the right to use the term, dear. I've earned it with every damn wrinkle."

"That you have." Regan smiles, her deep cheek dimples making an appearance.

Rose turns and eyes me up and down. "Maybe you could get this strapping lad to man your shop while you go meet the newest Calloway."

Regan laughs and I try to ignore how my body reacts. "No worries," she says. "I'll be closing up soon and heading on over. Wednesdays are slow anyway."

As she and Rose have a conversation, I take in Regan's choice of attire. Granted I don't see much of her—I spend most of my days at the winery and only come to The Circle when socializing—but I've never seen her wear the same thing twice. And the reason I know this is that all her outfits are a bit... outrageous.

Today, she's sporting a leopard-print leotard paired with a black sweater emblazoned with the word PINK in silver glitter. I'd roll my eyes, but for some reason—same as her giggle—the carefree way she carries herself hits me somewhere in the pit of my stomach. Or maybe it's in my groin.

"Well," Rose says, looking over Regan's shoulder at me, "I'll leave you two to your business. Mr. Montana was interested in buying a book, I believe." She winks at me, then she's through the front door, making it chime, before I even say goodbye.

I quickly grab a book from the shelf behind me and pretend to read the back cover.

Regan comes near and looks over my shoulder. She reads the title. "*How to Keep the Magic Alive: Tricks to a long and happy marriage.*" She laughs, and this time I join her. Because, come on, the irony.

I put the book back in its place. "I didn't come here for a book."

Her gaze travels from my emerald-green tie down to my Ferragamo shoes. "I *know* you didn't come for the clothes. So what brings you to my neck of the woods?"

She goes over to Rose's two bags, upends one, dumps it on the floor, and starts rifling through it.

"A do-over." I stride toward her with determination. "I want one."

Her eyes snap up to mine, surprise swimming in her baby blues. "A do-over?"

I shrug. "In case you didn't notice, I may have been a little drunk. And being that it was my first and only one-night stand, I think I deserve to be able to remember it. So, yeah, I'd like a do-over."

"You're crazy, Lucas Montana."

She goes back to sorting through clothes as if I haven't just propositioned her with my cock.

"Regan, I'm serious."

She plops down in the middle of the clothes, her long sweater riding up enough so I can see the thick curve of her thigh. "You want to sleep with me again just so you can *remember* it? Lucas, that's not how one-night stands work. Look it up."

As if I weren't even here, she holds up a blouse, regarding it.

I swipe it from her. "Can we please have a conversation?"

She nods to the pile of clothes surrounding her. "Take a seat, soldier, and help a girl out."

Glancing around me and not seeing a chair, I get that she means sit on the ground. Okay then. I give myself some slack in the front of my dress pants so they don't tear at the seams, and then lower myself, grateful I'm wearing dark pants and not light ones. "What do you want me to do?"

She shoves a pile at me—the one that's not Rose's clothes. "Look for anything with holes."

I grab a pair of leisure pants and stick my hand through them from waist to cuff, wiggling my fingers out the end. "You mean like this?"

"Ha ha. Very funny." She examines them and sticks a finger through a worn hole in the knee. "I was referring to *this* kind of hole, you kook. Toss these in my donation pile." She gestures over her shoulder. "There. And anything from a discount or big box store goes there too. I only sell designer or one-of-a-kind clothes here. I have a reputation to uphold."

"Oh, *I'm* the kook," I say, letting my eyes wander her leotard.

"Dude, you're the one who came back for seconds."

"So speaking of that…"

"You know," she says matter-of-factly, "if we did it again, technically it wouldn't be a one-night stand."

I examine a shirt, thinking it's okay, so I fold it neatly and put it in her pile. "I won't tell anyone if you won't."

She looks up at me. "I already did."

I nod. "Yeah, me too. But just Blake. I mean I won't tell anyone else, and not about the repeat."

"The repeat." The words come out of her mouth like she's trying them on for size.

"So, what do you say, Lucas?"

I love the way her mouth twitches when I call her by her last name.

Her eyes widen like dinner plates. "What… like, *now*?"

"Of course not now. Saturday."

The shirt she's holding becomes a crumpled mess when her hands fall into her lap. "I'm not sure you're grasping the idea of a one-night stand. They aren't planned, Lucas. If you make plans, that's called a date. And as an intelligent woman, and one who knows your history, believe me, I know better than to date you."

"As well you should. So if they aren't planned, what do you suggest?"

She shakes her head as if she's having to explain wet to water. "Hookups are spontaneous. You run into each other accidentally or randomly. They just happen."

I think on it. "So if I were to run into you accidentally on Saturday, where might that happen?"

"Oh, I have big plans on Saturday. Movie marathon."

"At the multiplex?" I ask, already making plans on how to *randomly* bump into her.

She looks up at the ceiling. "With Joey."

For a second, a wave of something that feels an awful lot like jealousy courses through me. "Who the hell is Joey?"

"Wow, you really don't remember much. Joey—my cat."

It starts coming back to me. "Ah, right. The furball that hates me."

She giggles. "That's the one."

My ass is starting to get numb sitting on the hard floor. "How am I supposed to accidentally run into you if you're in your apartment?"

She shrugs, then sighs, like maybe I'm more of an annoyance than an opportunity. "I suppose I could do my Sunday grocery shopping on Saturday after I close up around here."

"Truman's?" I ask, thinking it's only obvious she shops at the small store down the street.

"If I told you, it wouldn't exactly be accidental, now would it?"

I cock my head, wondering if she's playing with me, or she genuinely doesn't give two shits if she watches TV with her cat or gets to knock boots with me.

I stand and hand her the pants I just folded. "Okay then, it's a
d—"

"No, Lucas. It's not."

"Right. Well, uh… I guess I'll see you when I see you."

"Yup. See you around," she says, not even glancing up.

Fully dismissed, I study the sign on the door on my way out,
making note of what time she closes on Saturday since she didn't
bother telling me. I glance back to catch her watching me do it. She
turns away, trying, but failing, to hide her dimpled smile.

.

Chapter Seven

Regan

"Knock knock," I whisper and peek around the door.

Maddie waves. "Come on in."

My hand covers my heart when I see eleven-year-old Gigi sitting on the small sofa holding her new little brother.

I deposit the flowers and teddy bear on the table with all the others. "How are you?" I ask my friend.

Maddie smiles brightly. "Perfect."

"His name is Teddy," Gigi announces proudly.

I walk over and stare down at him, only able to see his tiny face, the rest of him wrapped in a blanket and beanie. "Hey, little dude." I touch Gigi's shoulder. "Looks like you're already an amazing sister, eh, squirt?"

"Mom let me change his diaper. It was gross. But she said if I wanted to babysit someday, I had to learn how to do it. It was all yellow like mustard and—"

"Okay then," I interrupt, not wanting her to forever ruin one of my favorite condiments. "That's something I most definitely do not need a play-by-play on."

Maddie snickers on the other side of the room.

Tag comes in the room carrying a Diet Coke. He hands it to Maddie then notices me. "Hi, Regan."

I wave then point at Teddy. "Well done. Looks like he's a keeper."

Tag beams. What a far cry from the Tag Calloway I knew growing up. The cocky jock who thought he could have anything or anyone. The guy I hooked up with forever ago. That Tag is long gone. This one, the one who is Maddie's husband and now Gigi's and Teddy's dad, he's one of the most stand-up men I know.

"Come on, princess," he says to Gigi. "Let's give your mom and Regan a minute. I saw strawberry ice cream in the cafeteria."

He expertly scoops Teddy from Gigi's arms and turns to me. "Want to hold him?"

I take a step back and shake my head. I don't hold babies. Sure, some of my friends have had them over the years, but I admire them from afar. They are so small and delicate. I'm terrified I'll do something to hurt them.

Tag puts his son in the rolling bassinet next to Maddie's hospital bed. "See you girls later." He kisses his wife and then leaves with Gigi.

"You won't break him, you know," Maddie says.

I laugh quietly. "You really want to test that theory with someone who's never held one?"

"I'd never held a baby until I had Gigi. It's a natural instinct."

"For some people maybe. Not me."

"Come on. You have to do it sometime. If Gigi can do it, you can." Her stare is unrelenting.

"You're going to make me do it, aren't you?" My hands land defensively on my hips.

She shifts so she's sitting at the edge of the bed and pulls the bassinet closer. Then she picks up a sleeping Teddy and practically shoves him at me.

"If I drop your kid and he walks in circles for the rest of his life, you'll only have yourself to blame."

Her eyes roll. "Shut up. You aren't going to drop him." She settles him against me. "Keep his head in the crook of your elbow for support."

Staring down at the day-old human, I capitulate and let him mold into my arms. I don't move a muscle. I'm a friggin' statue, fearing if I even twitch, he'll cry. But he doesn't wake. After a few moments, his little mouth twists with a yawn then makes a sucking motion before he stills again.

"Damn, you guys made a cute kid."

She pulls back the beanie, showing me his dark tuft of fine hair. "He's got Tag's gorgeous hair."

"The rest of him looks just like Gigi."

"I think so too."

"Okay, you can take him back now," I say, not daring to look away from Teddy for fear of dropping him.

Maddie chuckles. "Fine. But one of these days, I'm going to get you to do a lot more."

"Yeah, we'll see."

When she takes Teddy from me, I breathe a sigh of relief. But that relief also comes with something else, a niggling in the back of my mind that I can't quite put my finger on.

I sit on the foot of her bed. "You'll never guess who came into my shop today."

When I don't immediately tell her, she asks, "Are you going to make me pull it out of you like the other—wait... it was Lucas, wasn't it? Lucas Montana came into your shop?"

I nod. "You'll never guess what he—"

"He asked you out."

"No." I shake my head vehemently. "But he did ask for a do-over."

"A *what?*" she asks incredulously.

"He spewed some bullshit about it being his only one-nighter and he was too drunk to remember it so he thought we should do it again."

Maddie's jaw almost hits the mattress. "That's ridiculous."

"It's a load of crap is what it is."

"You put him in his place, I'm sure. I would have loved to hear you go off on him, the idiot."

I shrug a shoulder innocently. "Well..."

She puts Teddy back in the bassinet and squares off with me. "Are you telling me you agreed to it?"

I shrug again.

"But you just said it was bullshit."

"It is. I think he's still pissed about Lissa and just wants to be with someone... *anyone*... to make himself feel better."

"You shouldn't do this."

"Maddie, it's *one* time. Well, one *more* time. That's it."

"As long as you're sure."

"I am. I know who he is. I know what he does. Plus, he's a smoker. You know how that disgusts me."

She laughs. "I do know. Tag used to smoke."

I cover my mouth. "I almost forgot."

As if talking about him summoned him, Tag and Gigi come back in the room. He looks at Maddie. "Did she do it?"

Maddie nods with a smile.

Tag takes out his wallet and hands her a twenty.

I look between them. "What am I missing?"

"He didn't think I could get you to hold Teddy," Maddie explains.

I roll my eyes and say to Gigi, "Your parents are toddlers."

"Toddlers aren't always making kissy faces and squeezing each other's backsides," she says, nose turned up. "Yuck."

Maddie, Tag, and I fall into fits of laughter.

"You won't think it's so yucky in a few years," I say.

Tag stops laughing. "Don't remind me."

Teddy wakes and cries. I'm amazed a teeny-tiny infant can emit such a piercing sound.

Amid the racket, the door opens and Patrick Kelsey swaggers through carrying a huge bouquet of flowers and a gift bag.

"Uncle Patty!" Gigi exclaims, rushing into his arms.

Patrick is Maddie's best guy friend. They go way back to when he was the firefighter/paramedic who rescued Gigi from her father's arms in the fire that killed him and scarred Maddie.

He holds the gift bag out to Gigi. "This is for you, squirt."

Her eyes light up and she pulls out a sweatshirt. It reads: **B·I·G S·I·S·T·E·R** in true *Friends* fashion. Underneath, it says: **I'll be there for you**.

She holds it to her chest. "I love it!"

Patrick congratulates Tag, kisses Maddie, and gives me a fist bump. He once performed the Heimlich maneuver on me, saving me from certain death by cashew.

"What's up, peanut?" he jokes and gives me a wink.

"I think it's about time for this little guy to eat," Maddie says, undoing her nursing bra.

I take a step toward the door. "My cue to leave."

"Hey, Regan?" Maddie calls.

I turn.

"Just be careful, okay?"

"Yes, Mom," I say, then I blow a kiss to Gigi and leave.

On my way out of the hospital, I pass one of Tag's brothers, Jaxon, and his wife, Nikki, carrying a stuffed bear that might be as big as Gigi.

"You see him yet?" Nikki asks.

"Just now."

"He's adorable, isn't he?" she says, patting her own slight belly. "I can't wait for this little one to arrive." She leans against her husband. "I'll have ten more if this guy will let me."

Jaxon rolls his eyes, but we all know he's up for it. The man was born to be a father.

"See you guys later," I say, starting the trek home.

I love how walkable this older part of town is. The hospital is less than ten minutes from McQuaid Circle. Everything one could need is within walking distance. There are restaurants, a bank, a hair and nail salon, a hardware store, a grocer...

A grocer.

Suddenly my thoughts are on Saturday. When I'm supposed to do my shopping and *run into* Lucas.

I'm not nervous. I don't get nervous about men. Not anymore. And I'm especially not nervous about *him*. Because this isn't a date. It doesn't matter how I look or what I wear. But I am curious. Was he being honest about the reason or is he trying to forget about Lissa as I suspect? Either way, Maddie is right, it's probably a bad idea.

I do plan on getting information out of him. Like more about this crush he had on me and how my dad caught him playing with himself.

And now, I'm thinking of him touching himself. I have firsthand knowledge of just how much there is to touch. There have been rumors. In this town, it's expected. There were nicknames. My favorite was Mountain Montana. I can't remember which of his girlfriends or fiancées would joke about climbing the mountain. Or maybe not joke… brag.

Every single rumor turned out to be true. The man is huge. Long, wide, and firm. Practically a freak of nature.

I feel myself flush. My steps quicken as I mentally go through my bedside drawer and pick out the toy that's going to make me come in about five minutes.

Chapter Eight

Lucas

I'm sweating.

Am I... *nervous?* I'm not sure why. It's not like this is a date. It's a do-over. That's all. A way to solidify the forgotten night into my memory. Only... it's not as forgotten as I thought. Bits and pieces of that night have come back to me over the past week. Her soft curves. Her inviting lips. Her delectable pussy that I long to stick more than just my dick into.

Down, boy.

It's because of the crush. The way I wore out my right hand over her. She was my fantasy for years. The forbidden sister of my best friend. The older woman who never gave a second glance to the pimple-faced friend of her annoying little brother.

I walk inside Truman's Grocery Store. It's not where I usually shop. There's a larger supermarket closer to my apartment building. This place is small. Quaint. Like most of the other establishments along The Circle.

Saturday evening is not a popular time for shopping. I only see three people in the eight aisles. Serenity Calloway, formerly Donovan, co-owner of the pub across the street, has a bag of limes and waves to me as she checks out. Althea Henry, a nurse over at the hospital, turns her nose up at me as she passes with her basket. She's my age, maybe a little younger. She—like most women in this town—has boycotted me.

Hell, most women in Cal Creek boycotted me after Simone, the second woman I left. Technically, I've only left three *at* the altar, but people in this town don't care much about technicalities.

Veronica, my third fiancée, was from the city. She's a liquor distributor I met during a wine convention in Connecticut. By the time she found out about my past, she'd already fallen for me. She's the one I left a few weeks before the wedding. Not because I didn't love her, but because I knew I'd bail and didn't want a threepeat.

Lissa—number four—knew exactly who I was and what I'd done. Our relationship started out fun and easy with a spontaneous trip to Europe to tour some wineries. From there, it grew into something neither of us expected. I should have left well enough alone and not insisted we marry. She was fine being the couple in love who just never tied the knot. Like Kurt and Goldie, she said. Soulmates who don't need a piece of paper to prove our love. If only I'd have listened. We'd still be together, and I wouldn't be the pariah of Cal Creek, destined to live and die alone.

The third shopper is Lincoln Cruz. He and his siblings own the autobody shop around the corner. It used to be a Goodyear. Maddie's ex's parents owned it until it went up for sale a few years ago and the Cruz siblings pooled their resources, took out a gigantic loan, and opened the Cruz-In Auto Repair Shop.

He, too, turns up his nose at me. For a very different reason than Althea did. The Cruzes and Montanas aren't exactly friendly.

Though Blake and Dax are friends and my sister Allie and Dax's twin, Mia, have been joined at the hip since they were teens, for the most part, our families are rivals. The Montanas always side with the Calloways and the Cruzes are closer to the McQuaid clan.

We're all related in one way or another, however, in one big clusterfuck of lineage. If I remember correctly, Lincoln Cruz is my fourth cousin.

In this town, it's not even unusual for cousins to marry. Not first cousins. I'm fairly sure that's illegal. But Addison Calloway married Hawk McQuaid—boy if that didn't stir the pot between those families—and they're third cousins. Gross, if you ask me. Inbreeding is not something I aspire to do.

"Something I can help you with?"

I turn and catch Mr. Truman himself wiping wet hands on an apron.

"I'm, uh…" *Why the fuck am I so goddamn tongue-tied?* "No, I'm just…"

"Spit it out, son."

"I just came to see what kind of wine you're stocking these days."

"Got nothin' better to do on a Saturday night, eh?" He nods because *he* knows me, too. He points to a sign in the far corner. "Wine's over there. And, just so you know, we carry a few bottles of yours."

"Glad to hear it. Thanks, Mr. Truman."

I trot off, not looking back to see if he's watching me like a man who knows he's just been fed a forkful of bullshit.

Where is she?

Maybe I gave her too much time to think about it. She said she told people. Maddie Calloway and Ava Criss, most likely. Those three are as joined together as Allie and Mia. Bet they talked her out of it. Warned her away. It's what I'd do if I were them. Hell, I'm still questioning why Regan hooked up with me in the first place.

Could it be that she really was just interested in sex? Being the kind of man who's always been in relationships, it boggles my mind.

Then again, it's not the first time a girl has wanted to get with me just to see what's *down there*.

It's always hung over my head. Just as Tom Hanesworth got teased for having a micro-penis, I got ribbed for being well-endowed. It started in high school when at fifteen, I swear I grew four inches in one year, and not in height. The guys in the locker room noticed. And once they blabbed, there was a line of girls out the front door all wanting their chance to see it.

Kaitlyn, my high school sweetheart, and the first almost Mrs. Montana, was scared when she heard the rumors. It took months to get her to touch it. Years before she'd let me put it inside her. And she was so tight we always had to use lube or she would chafe badly.

By the time junior year rolled around, I had several nicknames. While poor Hanesworth was dubbed Tom Thumb, I was graced with versions of Long Dong Lucas. Meat Stick Montana. Or the one that finally stuck with me for life after Simone: Giganta Montana.

Having a huge cock comes with pros and cons, much like I imagine is the same with large-breasted women. We both have trouble running. No way could I ever go commando or my meat would be swinging like a pendulum, thwacking my thighs with every step. And then there's the wondering, as I am now, if a woman likes me for my dick or my personality. And of course the biggest downside: blowjobs. I rarely get a good one. I'm just too large. Women choke on me. Their jaws get tired from opening wide. It's just something I've become accustomed to living without.

Condoms are a problem, too. I always have to carry my own. Women rarely have a size that fits me. Too-small condoms make me feel like I'm wearing a tight turtleneck. Not to mention they're likely to slip off or break.

And not all men's underwear takes endowment into consideration. Pants, too. I have to choose carefully. Tight jeans can be an issue. And then there's the issue of actually fitting inside a woman.

Is that why I asked for a do-over? Because no matter how you slice it, of all the girls I've been with, Regan Lucas is the one who seems to be the best 'fit.'

The way she took me in was like finding the perfect pair of gloves.

"Excuse me," a feminine voice sings as a hand reaches for a bottle of wine in front of me.

I know that voice. And that hand. I have to play Jedi mind tricks to keep myself from getting hard. Because when you're hung like I am, even a half-chub is going to be conspicuous. And I do not need anyone thinking what I've come to accept over the past week—that even after all these years, I still have a massive fucking crush on Regan Lucas.

Chapter Nine

Lucas

Without smiling, and like she's totally playing the part, she picks up a bottle of Montana Winery chardonnay, reads the label and muses aloud, "I wonder if this one has a good body."

My lips turn upward. "It does." I take it from her. "This is one of our full-bodied wines."

"Mmm. And is that how you prefer them? Full-bodied?"

Facing the wine display, we're not looking at each other, both pretending this is some random meeting. I like this game. I like it a lot.

Finally, I turn and let my eyes rake over her from head to toe. Her curves are electric beneath the well-fitting top, that looks straight out of a seventies psychedelic hippie movie, tucked into frayed bell-bottom jeans with carefully placed rips on the outer thigh and knee and more frayed ruffles encircling the calves. My mouth actually waters. "That's *exactly* how I prefer them."

When the words come out, I realize just how true they are. In a flash, all my previous girlfriends cycle through my head like I'm looking through a lens of one of those retro-style view master toys. All of them were slender. You might even say they were petite. Beautiful, sure. Hot even. And most of them sufficiently endowed. But, my god, I thought some of them might actually snap in half in bed.

With Regan, a whole different kind of reel cycles through my mind. Pictures of what I want to do to her and all the ways I want to do it. Fantasies far more daring than what I used to whack off to.

She doesn't even flinch under my heated perusal and obvious objectification.

"Some men are put off by the weight and viscosity of full-bodied wine, which is why they prefer the lighter ones."

"Au contraire. I would argue exactly the opposite. That light-bodied selections are deemed inferior. They are less complex, lacking fullness and deep flavor." I hold out my free hand. "Why, Regan Lucas, what a pleasure it is to run into you."

Now is when she smiles so big, it practically splits her soft round face in two. She extends her arm and places her hand in mine. "Imagine that." She pulls back her hand when Mr. Truman walks by. Then she narrows her eyes. "In fact, I'm having a hard time remembering our last meeting."

"Hey, now," I whisper, drawing closer. "Don't go stealing my line. Besides, things have started coming back to me."

"Oh, so all this is quite unnecessary."

She spins as if she's going to walk away.

"Wait," I say to her backside. "There are still some blanks that need to be filled in."

She stills, as if contemplating, then turns slightly, her playful expression cluing me in to the fact that she's still playing the game. "I've got a few more things to pick up." She glances at the basket on the floor next to her. I hadn't even noticed it. She really is doing her shopping. "It's been nice seeing you, Lucas." She turns away, studies her list and mumbles, "I wonder where the condoms are."

"I'll take care of those," I whisper into her ear as I pass.

With the wine still in my hand, I head to the store's one register, manned by Mr. Truman's wife. She looks oddly at the bottle as she scans it, then up at me. "You're Lucas Montana."

"Yes, ma'am, I am."

"Don't you have an endless supply of these at your winery? Why would you want to pay retail?"

"Wine emergency," I say.

"Ahh." She nods, still looking confused. "Well, enjoy."

"Oh, I plan on it."

Outside, I light up a cigarette and lean against the building, watching the world go by as I wait. I am supposed to wait, aren't I? We didn't talk about it. Maybe she doesn't even want to be seen with me. Last time, it was late. Nobody was out and about. But now, people are walking along The Circle. Kids are racing down the sidewalk. A few couples walk hand-in-hand going to or coming from dinner.

Across the street, Hawk McQuaid emerges from the ice-cream shop, his daughter perched on one hip, her hand dripping with the sticky remnants of the cone she's licking. Hawk lifts his chin when he sees me. To be neighborly, I do the same.

I watch him walk away. That could have been me if I hadn't ruined every single one of my relationships. Hell, I could very well have a gaggle of kids by now if Kaitlyn and I had married after high school like we'd planned.

Just as all the bad thoughts of my failed engagements come creeping back in, Regan comes out of the grocery store, two bags in hand. She eyes the wine bottle I'm holding. "You bought it? You could have just brought one from work, no?"

I shrug. "Why would I have had one with me? This *is* accidental after all." I nod in the direction of her shop down the street. "If it bothers you to be seen walking with me, I'll go on ahead." I take a drag of my smoke.

"I couldn't care less what people think, Lucas." She eyes my cigarette. "It's *that* thing that bothers me. Must you?"

I throw it down and stomp it out. "Don't worry, the flavor of the wine will mask the taste of it."

"So we're actually *drinking* the wine? It's not just for show?"

I laugh. "Regan, I may not be an expert at one-night stands, but I'm fairly sure most of them happen because of alcohol."

She giggles. "You wouldn't be wrong."

I offer to carry her bags, but she doesn't let me. I'm not sure if I should be offended or not. But it's just one more indication that she has no intention of taking this beyond what it is. And as a smart woman, she's wise to think that.

We don't pass anyone on this side of the street, but there are a few families strolling the other side. I look at Regan to see if she has any reaction, like putting distance between us to prevent the rumors that will most definitely spread if anyone sees us together. But she doesn't. It makes me think she was telling the truth when she said she doesn't care what people think. Then again, looking at her clothes, I'm not surprised. Someone who dresses as outrageously as she does wouldn't give a rat's ass about the opinions of others.

Just outside her door, I hold out my hand for the keys.

"It's open," she says, skirting around me and pushing into it with her behind.

Once through, I ask, "You left your door unlocked?"

"Where have you been living all your life? I've been here in Calloway Creek where people respect one another."

"But you don't leave it unlocked at night, do you?"

She shrugs. "I lock it when I remember to."

"Regan." I admonish her with a stern look. "We're not that far from the city. There are still a lot of bad people out there. And you're a beautiful single woman."

"Who knows self-defense."

I raise a brow. "Really?"

"Learned it several years back. Anyway, here"—she finally hands the bags over—"my arms are killing me."

"I would have carried them all the way, Regan."

"I know." She turns, hands on hips. "I may not care what people think, but sometimes it's best not to pour fuel on the fire, you know?"

"Right."

She opens the door to the stairway and I follow her up.

Halfway up, I have a memory. "Did I fall down the stairs the other night?"

She laughs. "Almost rearranged that handsome face of yours."

I perk up. "You think I'm hot, eh?"

"I said handsome. There's a difference."

We walk into her apartment and immediately her rabid cat comes into view. He greets her with a rub on her calf, then looks up at me and runs in the other direction.

She giggles. "He still likes you, I see."

Heading straight for the kitchen and depositing the bags on the counter, I find some wine glasses, uncork the wine, and let it breathe as she puts her groceries away.

She holds a package of pasta in her hand and glances back at me. "I just realized I didn't buy enough for two, because this—"

"Isn't a date," I finish, stepping over and brushing her hair behind her shoulder.

Taking the box from her hand and putting it in the pantry, I snoop around, find some crackers, and then open her fridge and pull out a brick of cheese. I hold both items up. "This will do. It'll go with the wine."

I find a knife, slice the cheese, and then search for a small platter to put it on. I arrange the crackers and cheese on a rainbow-colored plastic serving tray that's the shape of a fish, trying not to laugh because the serving tray is so *her*. Then I look under her sink for cleaning supplies and sanitize the entire counter.

"Shall we sit?" I ask, tray in hand, motioning to her couch.

She grabs the glasses and the bottle and we go to the living room, which is really just an extension of her kitchen, making it one large room. Her cat peeks out from behind the couch. He looks at me like I'm a cat butcher in search of fresh meat.

"How was your day?" I pour the wine and hand her a glass before shoving a piece of cheese in my mouth.

"I'm not one for small talk, Lucas. Besides, that's not really why we're here. But there is one thing I've been curious about."

"What's that?"

"I really want to know what the hell happened when my dad walked in on you."

I laugh heartily. "Is that why you agreed to this? Curiosity?"

She shrugs and I wonder if it truly is the reason.

I lean back with my wine and put my feet on her coffee table, crossing them at the ankles. A story like this one definitely calls for settling in.

She palms a few cubes of cheese then curls herself into the corner of the sofa, watching me expectantly.

"In order for me to properly tell the story, I have to start from the beginning. Back in middle school, probably when I sprouted my first pubic hair, I was at the town fair and saw this amazing dark-haired girl playing volleyball in the sandpit."

A smile overtakes her face. "I remember those town fairs. What ever happened to them?"

"I think they still happen. We just outgrew them."

She looks at me oddly, like she's disappointed that we did.

"Anyway, you were this voluptuous older girl, in high school by that time, but I'm fairly sure seeing you in those tight shorts resulted in my very first boner. Or maybe it was the top you wore. It said *I like big balls*. It was a volleyball shirt, but even at my young age, I got the double entendre."

"You remember what I was wearing?" she asks in surprise.

"Hell yeah, I do. Regan, that image of you was the very thought I jerked off to for years."

Her jaw slackens. "Years?"

"It was the reason I became friends with Ryder. I figured if I was his friend, I'd be closer to you. And it worked. By the time I was a freshman and you were a senior, you were driving us around in your parents' Nissan."

"Oh my god. I remember that. I hated having to drive you to football practice. I'd sit in the stands and do my calculus homework."

"I know you did. Why do you think I didn't make the team that year? I was too busy staring at the rockin' captain of the girls' volleyball team. You never looked back at me, though, and that pissed me off."

She giggles. "Sorry. I did end up with a B+ in calc, so it was worth it."

"That summer, your parents invited me on your beach vacation."

"Right. Ava was there too."

"Was she? I can't remember," I joke. "All I could see was you. And one afternoon, I was in the bathroom and looked out the window and there you were, sunning on the back deck in your tiny red bikini. I couldn't help myself, and I knew *that* was the visual I'd be jerking off to from then on."

"But then my dad walked in on you?"

My head shakes as I remember the horror. "It's still the single most terrifying moment of my life."

She giggles and takes a sip.

"He looked me up and down, my pants lowered, hand on my stiffy, then he looked out the window and saw you." I run a hand across my jaw. "Jesus, Regan, I thought he was going to pummel me into the ground."

"He didn't?"

"Worse. He told me I'd never touch myself again at the thought of his daughter, because if I did, the only thing I'd see was *his* face. Then he took two steps closer, not even caring that my drawers were still dropped, pointed to his stern expression—one I can still see to this very day, right down to the small scar on his forehead—and he said, 'This is what you'll see, Lucas Montana. Every motherfucking time.'"

Regan's hand flies to her mouth. "My dad said *motherfucking*?"

"He did."

"I've never heard the man curse. Not one time. Both of my parents have always been so strait-laced and traditional."

"Well, he did that day. And fuck me if it wasn't effective. I was never able to do it again. Every goddamn time I'd start thinking of you and got hard, his face was front and center in my mind. It was a genius move on his part, effectively ending my years-long Regan Lucas masturbation streak, and a tactic I'll remember if I ever have kids. I gotta respect the guy for that, even if he did ruin you for me."

She leans forward, intently interested. "What did you do after that? I mean when you…"

"Polished the banister?"

Her cheeks redden.

"I moved on, I guess. You went away to college, and I took up with Kaitlyn Carmichael."

She nods. "Your first fiancée."

"That's the one."

"So you never thought about me that way again?"

"Not until this week. Believe me, though, after Friday night, *your* face is the one I'm seeing again."

"Again? You mean…" Her gaze goes to my lap. I'm confident she can see how I'm already getting hard.

"Are you asking if I fantasized about you this week, Regan?"

"Maybe I am."

I put down my glass, hop off the couch and hover over her. "How about I just *show* you what I thought about."

Her breath hitches. She pushes me back, gets up, takes my hand, and pulls me toward the bedroom.

Fuck yeah.

Chapter Ten

Regan

He laughs as I eagerly drag him back to the bedroom. Of course I do. He has, after all, been the inspiration for all six orgasms I've had since we last did this. Getting this under my belt will surely give me more to draw upon.

Crossing the threshold of my bedroom, he points across the hall. "What's behind that door?"

"Bedroom. Or it would be, but I've made it into a closet."

He laughs. "Of course you have. I'll bet your collection of crazy-ass leggings is even more impressive than my collection of ties."

I giggle, flip off the light and pull him toward the end of the bed. He drops my hand, looks me right in the eye and tugs the hem of my shirt out of my jeans. I might be taller than the average woman, but he still towers over me and easily lifts it over my head.

He tosses the shirt to the floor and stares at my breasts. Large-breasted women have more limited sexy lingerie options. But having advanced knowledge that this was going to happen, I broke out one of the few very pricey pieces in my collection. It's not quite as supportive as my day-to-day bras, and the straps do cut into my shoulders, but sometimes it's worth it.

The way he's staring at my chest—this is definitely one of those times.

"I have to apologize," he says, practically salivating. "I don't think I gave these proper attention last time." He reaches around and unhooks my bra, freeing my size Fs from their satin captivity. "I won't be making that mistake again."

Instantly, his large hands cover my breasts—massaging, kneading, caressing—sending bolts of pleasure shooting through me, especially when he touches my nipples.

"They're fucking spectacular." His head dips and he flicks a nipple with his tongue. Then he takes my entire areola into his mouth and sucks like a baby getting his first meal.

I take the opportunity to run my fingers through his ever-immaculate hair. Unlike his brothers, Lucas never has a hair out of place, and now I can feel the reason—styling gel. I rake my fingers through the stiff strands, hell-bent on making his hair as messy as possible. Am I doing so to please myself or irritate him?

Doesn't matter. Because he doesn't seem to notice. He's a bit... preoccupied.

When he bites down lightly, I yelp and push back, trying to decide if I liked the sting or didn't. "Did you just *nip* me?"

"Sorry. I heard some girls like that."

"You *heard?*"

He shrugs. "Never tried it."

This shocks me to my core. He's been with at least a half dozen women that I know about, most of them long term. Don't couples in long relationships try things?

"Oh. Well, the jury is still out."

He chuckles. "Noted. Mind if we get naked now?"

"Considering I'm halfway there..." I hold out my arms in invitation.

He unbuttons my jeans and lowers the zipper. I sit, toe off my wedges, and assist him in getting my pants off. They're pretty darn snug and I don't want him flying across the room and falling on his ass. Although now that I think of it, it might be quite entertaining.

"Now you." I'm at eye level with his crotch and can't keep my eyes off the massive bulge.

When he untucks his shirt and lifts it over his head without undoing all the buttons, I can't help but stare at the tip of his erection. Because it's jutting out of the top of his pants. *Holy, wow!* He either doesn't notice my gawking or is so used to it that it means nothing to him.

His shoes and socks come off in a flash. Then his pants and boxer briefs are discarded in one fell swoop. When he stands up straight again, his cock thwaps his lower abs then rebounds, bouncing back and forth like an inverted pendulum.

Oh my god, that thing was inside me?

I swallow and scoot myself fully onto the bed, amazed at the capability of the vagina to accommodate penises this size. Then again, women push babies out of them, so I shouldn't be surprised. I guess I'm more perplexed that it didn't hurt, and that I actually enjoyed it. I did enjoy it, didn't I?

Since David, it's been hard to enjoy much of anything unless it's at my own hand under my own control.

Regan, now is not the time to think of that snake.

Lucas sits on the bed beside me and stares at my naked form. "I promise I'll last longer this time."

I rise up on my elbows. "How can you possibly know that? Did you take those pills or something?"

"Nah, I pre-gamed." When I narrow my eyes in confusion, he explains, "You know, rubbed one out earlier so I won't shoot off like a pubescent hornball."

I can't help it; I belt out incredulous laughter. "Are you serious?"

He laughs along with me. "It's kind of nice to be able to talk about shit without wondering if you'll judge me. Benefits of a one-night stand I guess."

I hold up two fingers. "Two, but who's counting? And I agree. But, Lucas, there's a fine line between honesty and TMI."

His abs shake with silent laughter. "I guess you know way more than you ever wanted about my masturbation habits, huh?"

My hand goes for his cock. "So I can do this now?"

His eyes close briefly and his head seems to float above his shoulders. "Oh, hell yes."

I can't completely wrap my hand around him, but he doesn't seem to mind. I pump him the best I can, wondering for a moment how any woman could fit that thing in her mouth. *Could I? Would I want to?*

"Fuck, that's good," he moans after I've worked him for a good minute or two. "Your turn again."

I lie back flat and he pushes my legs apart, running a finger along my wet folds before sliding it inside me.

"Admit you think I'm hot and not just handsome."

I look at him like he's crazy.

"Come on, Ray, tell me you think I'm hot. I know you do. Your pussy doesn't lie."

My thighs squeeze together. The combination of his words and the low, growly timbre of his voice has me experiencing a quivering in my belly unlike anything I've felt before.

It registers that he called me *Ray*. Nobody ever calls me that. Not after I insisted on it way back in middle school when I thought it sounded too manly. But, oh my, when he says it, it's like sex on a stick. A big wet juicy lollipop on his lips. So I don't bother correcting him.

"Say it," he demands.

"You're hot, okay? Jeez."

He smiles, then dips his head and feasts on me.

There's something about getting eaten out that is better than anything else a man could ever do to a woman. In comparing notes with friends, I've found that men don't tend to frequent the area on me, a plus-size woman, as much as my slender friends get treated to it. Now I'm wondering if maybe it's not my size. Maybe it's just me. Is it possible I give off a vibe that tells them I'm not up for it?

Vibe or not, Lucas seems intent on being there and I've no plans to push him away. In fact it feels so good that...

Holy hell, is it going to happen?

... no, I don't think so.

... well, maybe.

... ah, shit.

Like I've done more times than I can even count, I go through the motions, make the noises, squeeze my vag muscles, and gyrate my hips. Then, I still.

"Damn, woman." He rises, lips glistening in the muted light.

I try to keep the guilt off my face. "Condom?"

"Coming right up."

He hops off the bed and moments later I hear the tearing of the package. He rolls it on as I remember the conversation from earlier when I offered to get condoms. *Do they make special sizes for guys like him?*

"I lied," he says, back on the bed and hovering over me. "I'm not going to last long."

I giggle and reach around to grab his ass cheeks, encouraging him inside.

He slides in easily. Much more so than last time. I wonder if he notices too. He glides in and out, his groans of pleasure getting more frequent and louder with every thrust.

I groan a bit too. It does feel good, but I don't kid myself into thinking I'll get more out of it than I am.

His elbows lock as he comes, grunting loudly as he rides the wave. His head slumps and he rolls to the side, breathing heavily.

How long do I let him lie there before kicking him out and giving myself the release I need? Because I'm wound as tight as a spring in a mattress factory.

He breathes out deeply. "Thanks for that."

"Sure thing."

He lifts his head. "Regan?"

"Mmm?"

"You faked it, didn't you?"

Chapter Eleven

Lucas

"What? No…"

She turns away slightly. She's lying.

"And you faked it last time." I give her a nudge. "No judgment, remember. We can be ourselves here."

An arm flies over her face, covering her embarrassment. "Okay, yeah."

"Can I ask why?"

She laughs maniacally. "How much time do you have?"

I get rid of the condom and lie back on one of her pillows. "As it so happens, a lot."

Her arm falls to the side of her head as she pulls a sheet over herself. "I thought you were too drunk to remember. Or was that just a ruse to get me back into bed?"

"I didn't remember much at first. It was fuzzy. It came back to me slowly, but I just had this… feeling. About you faking it."

She blows out a huge sigh. "I thought I'd perfected it."

"Okay, wow." I turn and prop up on an elbow. "I'm not sure if it makes me feel better or worse that I'm not the only one you faked it with."

"There's nothing to feel bad about. Some women just have a hard time."

"I get it. But why make us think you got there when you didn't? If you don't give us a chance, it'll never happen."

"Men don't get it." She shakes her head. "There's the point you get to where you're all in your head. You're thinking too much. Am I going to come? Why's it taking so long? Is he getting bored? And once you reach that point, it's pretty much over."

"So you don't even try? Not even with new guys?"

"Been there, done that." She snorts. "I gave up hope a long time ago. It's just easier this way, believe me."

"So you've never?" I try to wrap my head around it. She's thirty-five. What a fucking shame if it's never happened for her.

"I have. I used to sometimes. Sparingly. Never during actual sex, but it happened. Not for well over a decade though."

"Ten years?" I bolt up, staring down at her in the dim light. "You haven't had an orgasm in over ten years?"

"Oh, I've had plenty. Just not with men."

I scrub my hands across my jaw. "Shit." I brush an errant hair off her forehead. "What happened ten years ago that changed things?"

"It was thirteen, actually. And his name was David."

Hairs on the back of my neck prickle. "David? Who the fuck is David?" I think. "Wheeler?"

She shakes her head. "You don't know him. I met him in college."

"Who was he?"

Her eyes close briefly. It's so telling. "Nobody."

"I don't believe that for a goddamn second. Did he hurt you?"

When she doesn't respond. I touch her arm firmly but gently. "Regan, did he hurt you?"

"Not in the way you're thinking."

"There are other kinds of hurt, Regan. Not just the throwing punches kind."

She nods, eyes closed once again. "Then, yeah, I suppose he did." She rolls over, away from me. "Be a sport and cork the wine before you leave. It'd be a shame if it went to waste."

And there it is. She's kicking me out again. "Sure thing."

I get out of bed, dress quickly, and go into the other room, the whole time my mind on this David and what he could have done to put her in the position she's in.

The wine corked and the cheese tray covered and put away, I turn to the sound of hissing.

It's her damned cat. The creature fucking hates me.

"Joey, is it?" I say. I crouch down thinking it's my size he doesn't like. "We can be friends, can't we?"

He scampers out from behind the couch, never taking his eyes off me, then darts into Regan's bedroom.

What's the point? I'm fairly sure I'll never see the feline again after tonight.

On my way out, I glance at a few pairs of those crazy tights she wears tossed over the backs of chairs.

My hand on the front door handle, I look behind me, realizing how it saddens me to think this is the last time I'll be here.

The entire way home, I can't stop thinking about her. She's faked it for thirteen years. Almost all of her adult life. Does she not like sex? No—not possible. She was wet. Really wet. So wet in fact, she's one of the few women I've not needed lube with. She wanted it. She wasn't faking *all* of the sounds she made. The ones when I sucked her tits. Drew her clit into my mouth. Crooked my fingers inside her.

She *can* come. She admitted it. So it's not physiological. It's psychological—in her head like she said. It's a damn shame, though, because I've heard women tend to enjoy sex more the older they get. She should be entering her prime years. She should be able to enjoy them.

I wish there was something I could do.

I laugh out loud in my car, thinking how stupid that sounded in my head. It's not like I can teach her how to have an orgasm.

I stop at the one and only traffic light in town and look up at the darkening sky.

Or can I?

When the light turns green, I stomp on the gas, go back to my place, and devise a plan.

Chapter Twelve

Regan

I turn over in bed, stretching. Joey complains when I almost squish him. I laugh. "You've got to be quicker than that."

He trots off to use his litter box, but I stay put, lazily staring at the indentation on the empty pillow next to me. What was I thinking telling him the things I did? What if he blabs all over town and I become the laughingstock woman who can't come? The middle-aged masturbating cat lady.

Oh my god, what have I done?

Can't blame it on the alcohol—I only had one glass.

I wish I could take it all back. I should have lied through my teeth and convinced him of what I'm so good at—making them think they're all good lovers.

This is something I can't undo. There's no way to take it back or talk my way out of it.

"Stupid, stupid, stupid," I chide myself loudly.

"What's stupid?"

My heart pounds and I dart up in bed when I hear the deep male voice. I'm reaching for the baseball bat under my bed when Lucas comes around the corner.

The bat thumps to the carpet as I exhale my relief.

He stares at the bat. "You keep a bat under your bed?" His head cocks. "Weren't you the one just telling me this town is so safe, you didn't need to lock your door?" He laughs. "In this case, it worked in my favor." He raises his arms. In one hand is a beverage carrier with two tall coffee cups from The Criss Coffee Corner.

The other hand holds a bag emblazoned with the name of the pastry shop down the street. Ava carries a small selection of breakfast items and snacks, but this place... my mouth waters despite the presence of my uninvited guest.

Joey hisses, skitters around Lucas, and jumps to my side.

"What's with him, anyway," Lucas asks. "Why does he hate me?"

I pet Joey. "He's a very good judge of character. He's warning me away."

"He's protecting you?" he muses. "Maybe you should tell him we're just friends and he has nothing to worry about. That I can't break your heart because no woman in her right mind would let herself fall for a guy like me."

I chuckle at how right he is, even though he has yet to tell me why he's here. I cross my arms. "Friends don't break into each other's apartments."

"If you never lock up, that's what happens."

I think of his words. "*Are* we friends, Lucas?"

"Yeah, of course we are. And sometimes friends bring each other breakfast. So get up before the coffee turns cold." He spins and leaves the doorway.

Joey stares at me as if he understood the conversation, wondering what I'm going to do next. I shrug. "He brought pastries."

I get out of bed, pull on a robe, hit the bathroom, and join Lucas in the kitchen.

When I get there, he's arranged a dozen pastries on my Scooby Doo mystery machine platter. I'm busy deciding if I'm upset that he was rummaging through my cabinets when he sees me. "Pick your poison."

I peruse the donuts, bear claws, gooey cinnamon rolls, and chocolate-drizzled croissants. Settling on a croissant, I pull it apart and take a bite of the heavenly confection, moaning when it explodes across my taste buds.

"That right there"—Lucas points at me—"that's the sound you make when you fake it."

Still mortified over the embarrassingly private details I divulged, I take a seat and beg, "About that. Can we never speak of it again? And please, please don't tell anyone. I never should have said anything."

"Sorry. No can do."

I drop the croissant in anger. "No can do what? Speak of it, or tell anyone?" My heart sinks. "You already did, didn't you? Who did you tell?"

"Calm down and eat your breakfast," he says, pushing my small paper plate toward me. "I meant the speaking of it part. I was up half the night thinking what a shame it is that you can't enjoy fucking enough to get there."

I almost choke at his bluntness. "I enjoy sex, Lucas. For the most part."

"Tell me what that means exactly."

"I enjoyed it with you. With the last few guys I've been with. Just not with—"

"That asshole, David."

I nod.

"So you enjoy it. Good. We can work with that."

I cock my head, unsure of where this is going and why he's here. "We can *work with that?*"

He shoves an entire cinnamon donut into his mouth, chews, swallows, then takes a drink of his coffee. He leans forward, elbows on the table, fingers steepled underneath his chin. He looks all businesslike. In fact, it's now that I realize it's Sunday morning, yet he's dressed in gray linen pants. At least he's traded his usual button-down dress shirt for a short-sleeved Polo. "I have a proposition for you."

My appetite now lost—something most unusual for me—I stand and pull my robe tightly around my body. "A proposition?"

"One that will benefit us both."

I narrow my eyes. "Why don't I believe that?"

Joey darts across the kitchen floor, eyeing Lucas carefully as he sniffs his empty food bowl.

I walk over, open a cabinet, and peel back the film of his favorite salmon cat food. As I spoon it onto a dish, Joey glares at Lucas as if he might steal it from him, then turns and digs in.

"I'm gonna get that cat to like me if it's the last thing I do," Lucas says.

Hands on my hips, I stare at Lucas, wondering exactly what kind of proposition he has that would be mutually beneficial. His words echo in my head. *So you enjoy it. We can work with that.* My jaw hits the floor.

"You have some gall," I snap.

He holds up his hands and looks from wall to wall. "What? I haven't even said anything yet."

I stride over and tower over him where he sits at my table. "You want to *fix* me, don't you? Make me your pet project. And all the while you'll be getting your rocks off instead of spilling into your hand considering nobody in this town is crazy enough to sleep with you."

The surprise on his face tells me I'm spot on. A hand rakes through his perfect hair, rendering it not so perfect. His mouth opens, closes, then opens again. "Um... how in the hell did you know?" He stands, getting leverage over me. "Regan, you don't need fixing, and you wouldn't be my pet project. It would be a journey into exploring your sexuality."

"Ha!" I bend over and snort laughter. "Are you serious? Do you think I was born yesterday?"

"You're not wrong in that I'd be getting something out of it too. Before you, I had a long dry spell. Lissa was the last woman I was with. And with her engagement and all the reporters spreading my business on the news, I'll be hard pressed to find any woman in the tri-state area to take a chance on me. So I like sex. I'm a red-blooded guy, of course I do. We can make this work, Regan. I'm nobody to you. Who cares what happens in the bedroom? Lots of fucking, no strings. No complications. But maybe, just maybe, we can get you to the point of letting go. Think of how that could help you in the future. Do you really want to spend the rest of your life sticking pieces of plastic in your pussy?"

His proposition is so outrageously idiotic, I contemplate slapping him across the face. If not for myself, for all womankind. But then why, in the back of my head, is there something telling me to consider it?

"Listen," he says, taking a seat again and sifting through the pastries for his next selection. "I'm going to be out of town for two weeks. I'm headed to Napa for a wine convention and then I'll be touring and meeting with some CMOs at wineries along the west coast. Think about it. That's all I'm asking."

I'm honestly stunned into silence as I watch him nonchalantly eat a bear claw after everything he just said. Does he have no shame?

Joey, now finished with his own meal, watches Lucas from around the corner, only his head sticking out as he appraises our uninvited guest. I should take my cues from him. Animals are smart. They sense things. Things humans can't.

Lucas wipes his mouth with a napkin, throws his trash away, and approaches me. He leans close, his hot breath flowing over my neck causing goosebumps to erupt over my entire body, and whispers into my ear, "I'm not him. And I swear, I'm going to make you come. I'm going to make you come with my fingers. My tongue. My cock. I'm going to make you come so hard and in so many different ways, you'll forget all about that motherfucker. I'm going to make you come so spectacularly, your toys will be jealous. I'm going to make you come so often, you won't be able to think about anything else. Work. Food. Friends. They'll all be secondary. Your every thought will be of what's going to happen next. You'll be an addict to orgasms, Ray. And your life will change forever."

He picks up his coffee, walks to the front door, and leaves.

Wetness pools between my legs. *Ho-lee shit.*

I race off to my bedroom and consider his proposition.

I consider it three times.

Chapter Thirteen

Regan

"Are you fucking crazy?"

Ava snickers at Maddie's reaction. "Does this really surprise you?" she asks. "Regan doesn't exactly follow social or cultural norms." She turns to me. "But I totally agree with our sensible friend—you've gone off the deep end."

This is precisely why I've kept my mouth shut for almost two weeks. I knew they would try to talk me out of it.

Maddie's head shakes disapprovingly. "He's trying to lure you in like the rest of them."

"You think he wants to make me his next ex-fiancée?" I laugh, because they haven't heard the entire story. "Quite the opposite, ladies. I believe he's making me his pet project."

Both of them look confused.

"You guys know I have trouble... you know... getting there. Well, he called me out on faking it and he swears he can get me to the finish line."

"I knew it," Ava barks. "I knew he had some ulterior motive. I mean, you aren't exactly his type."

I try not to take offense, because it's absolutely true, but still... it hurts a little to be called out on it.

Seeing my expression, she puts a hand on mine. "I think you misunderstood." She scoots closer and hugs me. "Friend, you are one of the most beautiful women I know, inside and out, and any man would be lucky to have you. But we all know he goes for the types who are—"

"Less eccentric and far more malleable," Maddie finishes.

My head bobs sideways. "Malleable?"

"You know, someone he can get to do the stuff he likes, act like he acts, do what he says. Pretty much the opposite of you."

"You think they were all doormats?"

"No, of course not," Maddie says, then thinks on it. "I don't know... maybe. But, Regan, by agreeing to this, isn't that exactly what you're becoming?"

"You think I'm his doormat?" I toss her a punishing stare. "Who says *I'm* the one being used in this scenario?"

Suddenly Ava perks up. She claps her hands. "It's brilliant. Work out all the bugs with the unattainable, uncatchable, unweddable guy of Cal Creek, then you'll be ready when *the guy* comes along."

"Exactly," I say, smiling.

"You know what this is, then," Ava practically sings. "It's a situationship."

Maddie and I both gaze at her with tilted heads.

"All the Gen Z-ers are saying it," Ava says proudly, like she's ten years younger than she is.

"Situationship," I say, trying out the word. "I think I like it. It's better than the tired old friends-with-benefits."

"Or fuck buddies." Ava giggles.

Maddie isn't as jubilant as Ava. In fact, I'm not sure she's convinced at all. Of the three of us, she's always been the most cautious. She blinks a few times, studying me. "Regan Lucas, if you get tied up with him and catch feelings and think he's somehow going to change and—"

"Stop." I put fingers to her lips. "You and I both know something's been missing in my life. Maybe it's this. A little spice. A fun, no-strings relationship. There isn't a rule that says only guys can want one of those, is there?"

"Well, no, but—"

"Do you think I'm stupid?"

"Of course not. I think you've got a great head on your shoulders. One of the best."

"Then don't worry about me. I'm not going to fall for him."

"Tag aside, you've fallen for all the guys you've slept with. Why would this be any different?"

I grasp her hand. "Maddie, it's not going to happen. There's something about him. Maybe it's that I know this can't go anywhere and that makes me able to just be myself around him."

She laughs. "Since when have you ever been anyone but yourself?" Then her eyes turn serious. "Oh, sweetie, I totally forgot about David."

"That asshole," Ava adds.

"Mom says we can't say asshole," Gigi says, having snuck up behind us. "Right, Mom?"

Maddie's amused eyes flash to us and then back to her daughter, who had been eating ice cream with friends. "Right."

"My friends wanted to see Teddy. Can I bring him over?"

Maddie glances at her sleeping son in the stroller. "Push him carefully. Try not to wake him. And nobody picks him up, okay?"

"Okay."

Gigi pushes the stroller like it's carrying a bomb, and when she gets to her friends, she stands in front of it, lecturing them on the rules.

I laugh. "That kid is going to make one heck of a babysitter."

Maddie looks on, beaming with pride.

"How are you feeling?" Ava asks Maddie. "Is it nice to get out again?"

"Great." Maddie grabs her larger-than-normal breasts. "But these things are leaking all over the place. Teddy doesn't even have to cry to start the flow. I have to wear pads so I don't look like a freak…"

They continue the conversation, but my mind is stuck on *pads*. Oh, Jesus. With everything going on, the Lucas thing, helping to cover Maddie's flower orders, and Teddy's arrival, I totally forgot— my period should have come on Friday.

It's Tuesday.

I've never been late.

I stand, conjuring up a lie so as to not alert my friends to my predicament. "I totally forgot what day it is. I should have filed my quarterly sales tax. I'll see you guys later."

As I hurry in the other direction, Maddie calls out, "But it's not even due yet."

It was a stupid excuse. One I shouldn't have used with other small business owners. Obviously they'd both know the current quarterly sales tax period ended May 31st and with today being June 4th, isn't even due for another sixteen days. But it was the first excuse I could think of.

I don't turn and try to explain. My mind is on a one-track reel at the moment.

I pass by Truman's and the pharmacy. I don't dare go to either of those. People talk. I rip open the front door of my shop and march right through to the back door, grabbing my car keys from behind the counter along the way.

My old VW Beetle sits there, rarely used. If it weren't for the donations at Goodwill all the way across town and the occasional trip to Target, I'd never have to drive anywhere at all.

Dropping down behind the wheel, I turn the key, but nothing happens. I try again and again, getting the same nothing. I bang my forehead on the steering wheel, wondering why the world seems to be so against me right now.

I look down the back alley. Could I sneak into the grocery store and make Mr. or Mrs. Truman swear on their life they won't blab?

I could say it's for a friend. I laugh out loud, because that's the stupidest thought I've ever had.

I could steal it.

No. Even in this critical situation, as a small business owner myself, I refuse to go to such lengths.

I close my eyes and let my head fall back against the headrest. Then it hits me. The train. It's perfect. I'll take the train into the city where nobody knows me and cashiers won't even bat an eyelash at someone buying a pregnancy test.

Slamming the door of my car, I race off in the direction of the train station at the far corner of McQuaid Circle, on the other side of Truman's. I can be there and back in ninety minutes. Then I'll know. Then I'll know for sure.

I spend the entire train ride feeling sick to my stomach.

Chapter Fourteen

Regan

Two days and four pregnancy tests later...

I sit and stare at the test, not believing it. I take another one. And then another.

Still negative.

It doesn't make sense.

I google early signs of pregnancy. Technically, based on my last period, I'd only be five weeks pregnant. Most sites claim a woman may or may not experience any pregnancy symptoms at that time. I palm my breasts to see if they're more sensitive. They aren't. I *have* felt a little queasy over the past few days. My shoulders slump. Despite the six tests claiming I'm not knocked up by the runaway groom, I know deep down I am.

On my way out of the shop, I turn my sign to *CLOSED*. I don't bother setting a return time. I can't even think about work right now.

As inconspicuously as possible, I walk down McQuaid Circle on this mild afternoon and make my way to the medical complex where my gynecologist's office is adjacent to the hospital.

Inside, I step up to the front desk. "I'd like to see Dr. Russo please."

Carrie, the receptionist, looks up. "Oh, hey, Regan. I didn't know you had an appointment today. You're not on her schedule."

"I'm not. But I really need to see her."

"What's the problem?"

I know everyone here is bound by that law that says you can't talk about stuff, but I know how things go. Carrie will go home and tell her boyfriend, Stu. Stu will tell his best friend, Cameron. Cam will tell his poker buddies. Each of those will spill to their wives or significant others. Before you know it, the whole freaking town will be abuzz with the latest hot newsflash: Regan Lucas, single and pregnant, who's the father?

"Carrie… I just really need to see her."

She nods. "I'll try to fit you in." She smiles cordially. For all she knows, I could be harboring an STI. Or have some other gynecological emergency. I'm sure pregnancy is the last thing on her mind when it comes to me—the ever-single eccentric boutique owner who hasn't been seen with a man in who knows how long.

I sit in the waiting area, hoping nobody will see me. Then again, I could just be here for my annual. The realization of that has me not so quick to wish I was hiding under a rock.

Time stands still. I glance at the many magazines, infants and babies adorning the covers, and shake my head. How is this happening?

An hour and twenty minutes later, I'm called back. The nurse— a new face in town I'm not familiar with yet—takes my weight and vitals, escorts me to a room, and asks why I'm here.

"I'd rather just talk to the doctor."

She sighs, and I could swear she rolls her eyes on the way out the door. "It's not like I won't find out later," she mumbles loudly enough for me to hear.

My head slumps into my hands knowing *everyone* will find out later. There are no secrets in Calloway Creek.

The door opens and Dr. Russo comes in carrying my file. It's a paper file, not an iPad. She's been my gynecologist since I started going to one. She was my mom's before that. In fact, she was the doctor who delivered Ryder and me. My guess is that she's approaching retirement age. Mid-sixties perhaps.

She sets my file on the counter and pulls over the rolling stool. "Nice to see you, Regan. I've been told you have a private matter to discuss?"

I nod, embarrassed to have even thought for a second this wouldn't spread like wildfire no matter who I tried to keep out of the loop. "I think I'm pregnant."

She smiles. "Oh, well that's not such a terrible thing, dear."

"It is if you weren't trying to be and the father is… well, I just need to know for sure."

She picks up my chart. "When was your last period?"

I tell her. "Hmm," she mumbles. "Five weeks ago. And you've had a positive pregnancy test?"

"No. That's the problem. They've all been negative. But my periods come like clockwork. And I've been nauseous."

"First thing's first." She reaches into a cabinet and pulls out a cup. "Let's get a urine sample, shall we? The bathroom is across the hall."

I hesitate, looking at the cup.

"You can bring it right back in here and I'll do it myself."

I let out my breath and nod.

"I have another quick exam to do." She spreads a paper towel on the counter. "Leave it here. I'll be back in a bit."

"Thank you, Dr. Russo."

I palm the cup and follow her out, going into the bathroom. I know I'll be able to pee, I've been drinking more than usual in order to take all the tests.

After peeing in the cup and washing my hands, I make sure the coast is clear and go back across the hall, shutting the exam room door behind me. I set the cup with the pale-yellow liquid on the paper towel and stare at it for a full twenty minutes before the doctor returns.

Dr. Russo puts a test strip into my pee and turns to smile. "This is basically the same kind of test you took at home. We'll have the results in a few minutes." Her body blocks the cup as she faces me. "In the meantime, how are your mom and dad doing down in Florida? It's been ages since I've seen them. Do they ever make it back here?"

Small talk. She wants to make small talk at a time when my life is turning upside down.

"They don't like to make the long drive," I say. "And ever since the pandemic, my mom swears she gets sick whenever she flies, so she avoids it whenever possible. I mostly see them when I go to Sarasota for a visit. Ryder, his wife, and I went down for Christmas last year."

"That sounds heavenly. Christmas at the beach. Was it warm?"

I know she's just trying to kill time. I see her glancing at her watch every so often. But the wait is killing me.

Finally, she claps a hand on her knee and says, "Let's find out if you're going to be a mother."

A *mother*. The word stabs me right in the heart. But for a second, I feel it's not a wound that would kill me. In fact—for one fraction of a second—it feels like something totally different. And the feeling takes my breath away.

"Well, there you go," she says. "No need to worry yourself further. It's negative, dear."

"But… I'm late. And nauseous."

"When did the nausea start?"

"Tuesday night when I realized I missed my period."

"Nerves probably, at the thought of being pregnant."

"Well, yeah, but—"

"Didn't your friend, Maddie Calloway, recently have a baby?"

I nod.

"Sometimes our minds and bodies can play tricks on us, Regan."

I scoff. "You think I *wanted* to be pregnant?"

As soon as the words come out, however, that strange feeling hits me once again.

She looks at my chart. "I see you had a birthday recently. Thirty-five. For some women, that's an age at which they believe they are running out of time to have a child. It's not true, of course, women can be fertile well into their forties. But fertility does diminish. In fact, it starts to decline around age thirty."

"But my period."

Her head shakes. "As we age, we tend to become more irregular."

I sigh. But for the first time, I'm just not sure it's in relief. "I was so sure." I look up. "Isn't there a more definitive test?"

"We could do a blood test. But it'll have to be sent to the lab. Odds are you'll get your period by then." She nods to the test strip. "Those are very reliable. Over ninety-nine percent."

"But what if I'm the one percent?"

"Do you know how many times I hear that, Regan?"

"Please, Dr. Russo. I have to know for sure." I glance at the machine in the corner. "Can you do an ultrasound?"

"A five-week fetus is smaller than a grain of rice."

"But there would be other signs, wouldn't there?"

She sighs. I know I'm being pushy. But I *have* to know.

"At five weeks, the only thing we're likely to see is the gestational sac and yolk sac, but even those aren't guaranteed."

"Please?"

"Okay. But like I said, no guarantees."

"Thank you."

"Remove your lower clothing. It's a vaginal ultrasound."

I quickly do as she asks as she powers up the machine, types things on the keyboard, and rolls it over.

She lowers the head of the exam table. "Just lie back and relax."

Right. I couldn't relax now if my life depended on it.

I feel her insert the long steel rod covered by what looks like a condom and lube. *He used a condom*, I think, not for the first time.

She studies the screen for quite a long time before she speaks. Then she says, "Regan, what I'm seeing here is the normal uterus of a woman who is about to have her period. Your uterine lining is thicker, and I can't see any indication of a gestational or yolk sack. Dear, you're not pregnant."

"I'm... *not?*" I say in a morose tone that surprises even me.

"If you really need further verification, I'll do a blood test. But, honestly Regan, all you'll be doing is adding to your bill." She pulls out the wand, removes her gloves, and places a hand on my arm. "When you came in, I was sure this was something you didn't want. But now... I'm getting the feeling that perhaps you did."

I look up at the ceiling and blink away traitorous tears. What the hell is happening to me?

She lets me lie here and puts her things away.

"I'll send a nurse in for the blood if you really want it."

I shake my head.

"Okay then." She pauses before she reaches the door. "Regan, if it's in your plans to become a mother, you may want to start solidifying those plans. I know you're not married, but there are plenty of single women having babies. I can even refer you to a sperm bank. You have options. And you still have time. I'm just saying, you might want to figure out sooner rather than later how you really feel."

She offers one last smile, then she leaves.

Me—I break down in tears, sobbing for the baby that never was. The one I never knew I wanted.

Chapter Fifteen

Lucas

She texted me two words on Monday: **I'm in.**

When I read them, I was instantly hard. I've been thinking about it all week, how I'm going to make her come. It's definitely like I'm right back in high school.

My flight landed two hours ago. I'm showered, groomed, and ready for the mission. And let's face it, I'm downright giddy.

I show up right before seven o'clock, when she usually locks up for the day, and the bells over the door alert her to my arrival. She glances my way without a single reaction as she deals with a customer. I try not to let her blatant indifference bother me and pretend I'm browsing the book section.

When I don't hear voices, I turn. I'm surprised to see Regan and a customer talking in ASL.

With Blake's wife and daughter both being deaf, I've learned some American Sign Language myself over the past year, but I had no idea Regan knew it. I know enough, and pick up from contextual clues, to figure out the two women are talking about a book.

I watch Regan stealthily from behind a rack of clothing. The fluid motion of her hands. The way her colorful skirt swishes back and forth with every movement. How her lips move, forming words with no sound.

Fuck.

I turn away and pick up a book about Europe to tamp down my growing problem.

A few minutes later, the front doorbells chime again. The customer has left. We're alone. Regan sits on her stool behind the counter, pulls a pen from over her ear, and writes in a ledger, not even bothering to acknowledge my presence.

Finally, it clicks—it's all part of the game. Like our *accidental* meeting in the grocery store.

I smile to myself, go over and turn her sign from *OPEN* to *CLOSED*, and lock her door. My pulse quickens with each step as I stride the length of the store to the register, knowing I'm that much closer to doing what I've been dreaming up these past weeks.

Without even making eye contact, she puts down her ledger, walks around the counter, follows the same path I just blazed from the front door, and unlocks it again. She holds it open and looks at me. "Sorry, we're closed."

She's really getting into character. I backtrack, join her where she stands, and tug on the open door. She doesn't allow it to budge. I study her face. There's no mystery. No amusement like before. Is she... kicking me out?

"Regan?" I take a step closer, putting a hand on her curvy waist.

She shrugs me off. "Not gonna happen."

"But you said—"

"I changed my mind. Women do that."

Women do that. She sounds just like Allie does when it's her time of the month.

I hold up my hands in surrender, disappointed, but with complete acceptance. "I get it. So I'll come back, say, next Wednesday?"

Five days. That's enough time, isn't it?

"No, Lucas. I've changed my mind as in forever. This isn't happening."

"Aw, come on. Maybe you'll feel differently in a few days."

"I'm not going to stand here and tell you my reasons. I just don't want to do it. Not now, not ever." She side-steps me, letting the door shut with me still inside. She turns off most of the lights, does a few things behind the register, and heads for the door to the stairs to her apartment. "You can let yourself out. Bye, Lucas."

That's it? *Bye, Lucas?*

I stand here stunned. Without thinking about what a monumentally bad idea it is, especially after being lectured by my mother, Allie, and multiple fiancées on what not to do when a woman is hormonal, I step over to the door she just went through and take the stairs two at a time.

As suspected, her apartment is unlocked. I really need to get her to change her habits.

I open the door like I own the place and march across the floor to the kitchen where *she* now stands stunned.

"You can't just storm into my apartment and demand sex, Lucas."

I step back so as to not seem threatening. "I'm not demanding sex, Regan. I'd never do that. I just thought we could talk about it."

She laughs. "You mean you wanted to find out why I shut off the gravy train you thought you'd hopped onto. Can you just leave it at I changed my mind? There are all kinds of reasons your proposition had bad idea written all over it. The least of which is that it would have made me look like a doormat. Maybe it just took me a while to realize it."

"Since when have you cared what people think of you?"

She turns away. Another uncharacteristic movement.

"Does this have something to do with that David guy?"

Spinning around to face me, her lips turn into a sneer. "Of course not. Why would you even ask that?"

I shrug. "Because you look sad. Even when you were signing with that woman, I didn't see you smile. Not once. I'm not sure I've ever gone more than a few minutes without seeing you smile. Something's changed, and I doubt very much that it has anything to do with it being your time of the month."

She frowns. "It's not him. I just don't want to. Will you leave now? Please, Lucas?"

There's only so much begging a man can do, even for something as epic as I anticipated this being. But I'm not about to pressure her or do anything more stalkery than following her up to her apartment uninvited.

"Fine. If you ever change your mind, you know how to find me. I hope everything is okay with you."

Starting for the door, hopes dashed, I see brochures scattered on her kitchen table. I focus on two particular words on the front of one of them: *Sperm Bank.*

When I go to pick it up, Regan tries to stop me. I swipe it away from her and open it, reading aloud some of the text inside. "Go to our online catalog and select the donor of your choice based upon physical attributes, ethnicity, childhood photos, and other characteristics." The next page reads, "Donor sperm may be purchased as single vials for IUI or IVF, or in multiple vials."

When I look at Regan, she's sitting down, a mask of defeat across her face.

"Wow. I'm sorry. I had no idea you were interested in kids. I always got the opposite impression."

She laughs sadly. "Tell me about it. I'm more surprised than you are. Believe me."

"What happened?"

She tells me about her pregnancy scare. Her trip to the gynecologist. Her out-of-the-blue reaction to finding out she wasn't pregnant.

She's quiet for a minute when she finishes, then raises her shoulders. "I guess turning thirty-five really messed with my head. Pretty pathetic, huh?"

"It's not pathetic." I hand her the brochure. "I think you'll be a great mom, Regan."

"You might be the only one."

"What? No. Come on, you're super fun. And your kid will be one lucky sonofabitch. I bet he or she will never have a curfew or be told what to wear or how to act. Every kid's dream mom."

"Yeah. I guess we'll see. I'm sorry to have to disappoint you. I know you had a mission." She touches the front cover of the brochure, the one with the baby on it. "I guess I have my own mission now. I've finally figured out what's missing in my life." She laughs softly. "The whole time I thought it might have been a man. Now though…"

I pat her hand, resigned to accept my fate. "Well, good for you. I wish you the best of luck."

"Thanks," she says, finally smiling.

I thumb to the door. "I'll let myself out."

"Lucas?" she calls after me.

I turn.

"You're a really good guy. Someday, you'll find the one that sticks. I'm sure of it."

I nod, even though I don't agree, and shut the door.

Walking down the stairs and out of the shop, a spike of envy hits me. She's going after what she wants despite any unintended consequences. I mean, I know business. She's probably barely breaking even here. Having a baby will put a lot of strain on her finances. She must know that, yet she's going for it anyway. Because that's who she is, a woman who knows what she wants and doesn't give a fuck if what she wants doesn't conform to social norms.

Back in my car, I wonder what it would take for me to actually get what I want. A wife. A family. What I've *always* wanted despite circumstances to the contrary.

I could move. Go someplace where nobody knows me. But that would mean leaving the family business, something I'm not sure I could ever bring myself to do.

At home, I spend the entire night tossing and turning. I'm thirty goddamn years old. I should be able to figure this shit out. And by *this shit*, I mean figure out what's so fucking wrong with me that I can't commit to anything beyond my nine-to-five job.

By dawn, I've convinced myself I'm a lost cause. But then a revelation breaks through the dejection and I bolt up in bed with a renewed sense of excitement I haven't felt in a long time.

Maybe having a wife was just a means of getting what I really want: a child. A son to play baseball with or a daughter who will have piano recitals. Maybe I can take a page out of Regan's book and skip the partner, going straight to the one thing that really matters.

And then reality hits and my excitement wanes. It's not as easy for a man. I can't just go to a sperm bank, get some jizz, inject it inside me and—poof—nine months later I have a kid.

Surrogate.

The word rolls around in my head.

"It could work," I say out loud.

I have money. A lot of it. That's all it really takes.

I hop out of bed, do a little research on the internet, and write down a plan. I jot things down on Post-it notes and arrange them in order of priority. I make a list, then another, of all the things I'd have to do to make this happen. I laugh, wondering if Regan did the same, but I know she didn't. That woman's lists consist of chicken scratches on napkins.

Once again, I'm amused at how completely opposite we are.

I glance at the pieces of paper in my hand. The meticulously planned mission I've devised. And I rip it to shreds.

Then I dress quickly, get my keys, and race out the door.

Chapter Sixteen

Regan

The sound of pounding has me pulling a pillow over my head. Mr. Kastapulous at the hardware store I share a wall with must be doing some remodeling again.

The knocking noise doesn't stop. It's soon followed by someone shouting my name.

I push the pillow off my head and look at Joey, who seems annoyed as well. "He's kidding, right?" Well, at least he had the decency to knock this time.

Rolling out of bed, I pull on a robe as I make my way to my front door and swing it open. "I'd give you points for persistence, but the answer is still no."

When I shut the door, he jams his foot into it. Then he shoves a bag from my favorite bakery up to the crack. "Come on. I brought treats. And I promise I'll keep all my clothes on."

I put my eye to the door crack. "Bribing me with bear claws?"

"It's not what you think. I have another proposition for you. A different one."

Curious, I release my pressure on the door and swipe the bag. "This better come with coffee."

I know it does, I could smell the magical elixir before I even saw the cups, but he holds them up proudly. "Straight from Ava's."

"She's going to start questioning why you're suddenly getting coffee at her place rather than the Starbucks closer to your apartment."

"She already did. With a huge smile, I might add. You told her about my first proposition, didn't you?"

"She's one of my best friends." I walk through to the kitchen and drop the bag of pastries on the table next to the brochures. "She doesn't know everything, though."

His eyebrow shoots up. "You haven't told her about these?" He picks one up.

I shake my head. "I'm still trying to wrap my own mind around it. Besides, I don't want anyone trying to talk me out of it like they tried to talk me out of... you."

He laughs. "Good friends want you to make good decisions."

"Are you saying you aren't a good decision?"

He picks up the bag. "Donut?"

I get two plates from the cabinet and sit, perusing the choices. "Mind telling me why you're breaking into my apartment again?"

"You're the one who leaves the store unlocked. On some level that means you want me here."

I *have* been leaving it open more than normal. Is he right? Or is it just a coincidence?

"You didn't answer the question," I say, then take a bite of an apple fritter.

He gathers up the sperm bank brochures and tears them up. "You don't need these. I'll do it."

I cough and sputter and practically choke on my breakfast. "Wh-what?"

"I'll be the sperm donor. Well, not the donor really. I'll be the father. I'll impregnate you."

Finally… and quite obviously… it occurs to me. "You're saying that just so you can stick to your original mission. Oh, my god, you'll stop at nothing to get what you want."

"This isn't about winning. It's about me having an epiphany. The same one you had." He looks at my clock. "It's after nine and you just got out of bed, didn't you? I'll bet you stayed up at least half the night looking at sperm donor profiles online."

I shrug. He's not wrong, but I don't admit it.

"Did you find the perfect one?"

I shrug again.

"You didn't. Want to know why? The perfect one doesn't exist. Why do you think I've bailed so many times? I'm beginning to think perfection is an illusion. But it's too little too late. I'm fucked around here. But last night, when I couldn't sleep either, I came to realize that maybe all this time what I've really wanted was a kid. So you see, it's the perfect solution."

"Let me get this straight. You want me to have your baby? But I want to have *my* baby."

"It can be yours and it can be mine."

"You actually came over here thinking you'd talk me into this and that we'd *share* this child?"

"Well… yes."

I get up so fast, the chair falls over. "You're off the deep end crazy, Lucas. The plan was to find an anonymous donor and be a single mom. *Single*—as in by myself." I throw up my hands. "Perfect solution? Perfect would have been you having a kid with Lissa and me with Bentley Fitzgerald."

"Who the hell is Bentley Fitzgerald?"

"A character in the book I'm reading." I shake my head. "It's not important. What I'm saying is that this"—I motion a hand between us— "is most definitely not perfect. In fact, it's the most imperfect situation I can think of."

"Maybe that's why it makes sense." He follows me across the room. "Maybe both of us have been waiting for something that's never going to happen. Maybe imperfect is all we get in this life. That doesn't mean it's wrong. Or bad. Think about it, Regan. I have money. The kid will want for nothing. I know you're barely in the black. Childcare is expensive. Diapers. Clothes. Sports. College. They say it takes hundreds of thousands of dollars to raise a child—do you have that kind of money? I can provide. All I'm asking is that I get time with him or her. That the kid will know me. That I can teach him how to throw a ball and warn her away from guys like me. That I can show them the business and that maybe, one day, he or she can even work at the winery."

"But it's ludicrous."

"Regan, do you have any savings?"

"Enough for a rainy day."

"So, what, a few thousand? That won't even cover the hospital bill to deliver the baby. You'll have to take time off at first and that means even less money coming in. Have you thought this through? Do you have a plan? Because I do. And I can help you do this."

I hate to admit that he's right. Hell, the cost for the sperm alone will drain my savings. I didn't even think about childcare. Or college. Or… anything in between. But women like me—regular women with regular jobs and not a lot of extra income—do this all the time. Don't they?

"You could find worse candidates, you know." He holds his arms up and turns, showing me the merchandise. "You have to admit, I've got what most women going to a sperm bank would kill for: looks, pedigree, intelligence, no family history of terrible diseases."

Am I going crazy here, or is his proposition starting to sound appealing?

"Come on, Ray." He smiles. "What do you say? I promise it'll be amazing."

And this is where I turn on a dime. "You're hardly the poster boy for keeping promises. No, this is a terrible idea. I'll just work hard to save up more money and then in a few years—"

"When you're thirty-seven? Forty? When it might be too late to even get pregnant?"

God, I hate him a little bit right now. Everything he's saying is true. But what he's offering is just… insane.

"You're worried about my commitment here? Afraid I'm going to bail? What's to worry about? You said yourself you wanted to be a single mom. If I change my mind, you're no worse off than you are now. Actually, you'll be far better off because you could demand child support." His eyes light up. "In fact, if you want, we can even do this through a lawyer. You know, have contingencies and rules in place in case you think I'm going to fuck this up like I fuck up everything else."

I narrow my eyes. "You really want a kid?"

He squares his shoulders and looks me right in the eyes. "I really do."

I go over and take the lid off my coffee, sipping as I think. Then thinking as I sip. "I don't know. It's all so confusing in my head right now. I mean, this could be the stupidest mistake of all time."

"Or it could be the best thing that ever happened to either of us."

I put down the cup, walk behind him, and push him toward the door. "Right now, you need to go. Any decision I make at this moment would be totally hormonal. I need time to think."

"I'll go," he says. "But promise me you won't go to any of those sperm banks without really considering what I'm offering. I'm talking Ivy League education, Regan. No anonymous donors can offer that much. Or *anything*."

"Stop. I heard what you said, and I know exactly how rich you are, Lucas. Everything isn't always about money."

"But—"

I stomp my foot. "Quit it."

"Reg—"

My hand flies up to his mouth. He talks through it anyway, his words coming out muffled.

"I really wanted a bear claw."

I roll my eyes, go fetch the bag, shove it into his ribs, and push him out the door.

Then I lean against it, sliding to the floor, feeling like I've just been offered Sophie's Choice.

Chapter Seventeen

Regan

The past several days have been spent deep in self-reflection. I've thought about a lot of things. My job. My life. My future. While most things are about as clear as mud, the one thing I've determined is that I most definitely want a child. Even enough to pare down my coveted wardrobe and turn my closet into a nursery.

I'm just not sure having one with Lucas is the right call.

But he is a Montana. It would mean lifelong financial security for the baby. It would mean local grandparents who are about the nicest people I can think of. It would mean aunts and uncles and cousins, something my child would never have if I did this alone.

The one thing I keep coming back to, however, is it also means having to be accountable to someone else. Lucas and I are wired differently. Would he want to control how I raise the baby? Dictate when and where and how and why, just because he's providing financial support?

I lower my head into my hands, knowing there isn't one right answer.

My grumbling stomach reminds me it's time for lunch. I set my sign to *CLOSED* and turn the dial to 2PM. Forty minutes will be plenty of time to get back.

I cross the street and eat a bowl of Goodwin's macaroni and cheese. It's the dish the diner is famous for, and one I get at least once a week. Then I head out down The Circle and go to the auto shop where my car was towed earlier today.

They have a bell over the door just like I do. It rings as I step through. A few heads go up, customers on their phones waiting for oil changes or whatever. I stroll to the counter. The Cruz-In Auto Repair Shop is both a retail auto parts store and a repair garage. All four Cruz siblings run it, including Mia, who towed my car.

Nobody is at the counter, so I stand and wait.

After a few moments, I hear the familiar sound of forearm crutches. I smile when Christian Cruz comes slowly around the corner, looking at me through thick Coke-bottle glasses.

"Hey, Christian. What are you doing here? Shouldn't you be in school?"

"Hi, Ms. Lucas," the polite twelve-year-old says. "It's summer break now and Dad said I could start working here a few hours every afternoon."

"Learning the family business?"

He nods. "I'm going to be a mechanic."

"That's amazing. I'm sure you'll make them all proud."

"Are you here to check on your Beetle?"

"Yes, I am."

"I'll go ask my dad. He's the one who's been looking at it."

"Thanks, Christian."

I watch him walk away, his torso twisting a bit unsteadily as he uses his crutches. There's also a walker over by the door in case he needs it. Christian—the result of a scandalous teen pregnancy—has never let his cerebral palsy be a deterrent. When Christian's mom Denise bailed shortly after Christian was diagnosed, the whole town rallied behind Christian and his dad, Carter. Eventually, the shame became too much for Denise and she left town.

It's her loss, though. Because despite the struggles Carter had with Christian as a child, all his persistence paid off, and Christian is a well-adjusted, happy kid who brings joy to everyone he meets.

He's smart too. And I have every confidence that he *will* become a mechanic in spite of his physical limitations.

I study him through the glass separating reception from the garages as he talks with his father.

What if I have a special needs child? What if I go with a sperm donor and end up with a baby who has medical expenses I just can't cover? Would I lose the shop? Would the town set up a fund like they did for Carter? No—they wouldn't. Because I'm not a naïve hormonal teenager who got himself into a situation and didn't have the foresight to plan for such things. I'm a grown woman who has to live with the choices she makes.

Carter comes through from the garage. "Hi, Regan." His smile immediately disappears, alerting me that what he says next isn't going to be anything I want to hear. "I'm afraid the news isn't good."

My heart sinks. "Give it to me."

"It's the engine. It needs replacing."

My eyes go wide. "The entire engine?"

"Sorry, but yes. And the air-cooled, flat-four engine design in these older Beetles can be intricate, adding to the cost of replacement."

"How much?"

He rubs his chin in thought. "That depends if you're going new or used. I might be able to scrounge up a used engine for a little over a grand. Add in the other parts and labor required for installation and we're talking somewhere around twenty-five hundred out the door. I have to warn you, though, that while any used parts come with a six-month warranty, the same thing could happen a year or two down the road."

"What about a new one then?" I ask, already seeing the numbers in my savings account dwindle down to nothing.

"Ten thousand." He shakes his head. "But honestly, Regan, I'm not sure it would be worth it. The transmission is old. I don't know how much time you have left on it. You may have reached the point with this old car where things just keep going out one after the other."

I sigh and sit on the stool next to the counter.

"I'm really sorry. I wish I could help. But even if I gave you the good neighbor discount, you're still looking at a significant bill."

The good neighbor discount. As a small business owner on The Circle, I know exactly what that means. It means basically zero profit for the business because they either really like you, or feel really sorry for you. I'm wondering which would be the case in this instance.

For a second, I look at Carter in a way I haven't before—as a single, good-looking father. Younger than me, but available. Does he even date? I try to remember ever hearing anything about it. I think his whole life revolves around this shop and his son. Sure, he has a few tattoos, which I don't normally go for, but then again, who am I to talk? He's probably thinking the exact same thing about me and the clothes I wear.

"Regan?"

I bring my thoughts back to the here and now. "I'm not sure I can afford either, even with your discount. Maybe I can go without a car altogether."

"It's not unheard of. You've got the train if you need to go to the city or over to White Plains. And everything you need is pretty much along McQuaid Circle. I can see how much the scrapyard I use would give you for the car. And if you want, I could keep my eye out for another affordable option."

"That's okay. If I can't afford to fix this one, no way can I afford another one." I nod in resignation. "See what you can get for it." I get out my purse. "How much do I owe you for the tow?"

"It's not that much. I'll just take it out of the price Stan gives you for the car."

I smile, knowing it's not what he's going to do at all. He's being neighborly. It's why half the businesses around here don't make very good profits. But I do the same, so I understand. "Thanks, Carter." I turn to leave, but then stop to ask, "Hey, Carter, how's Christian doing? He says he's going to be working here."

His face beams. "He is. The boy's been telling me for years he wants to follow in his old man's footsteps."

I tilt my head. "Has it been hard for you? With Christian."

He looks at his son across the room, sorting spare parts into bins. He nods, but smiles. "It has. But I tell you what, it's been worth it. He's a hell of a kid. I'm a lucky man."

"Yeah," I say, my mind reeling. "I can see that."

"I'll call you when I hear from Stan."

I thank him then trot over to strike up a conversation with Mrs. Henderson over in the corner. She's one of my best customers.

~ ~ ~

"Your head is anywhere but here," Ava says during our usual weekly meet-up behind the ice cream shop.

I look away from Teddy, who is sleeping peacefully in his stroller beside our table. "It's my car," I lie. Well, it's not exactly a lie, I do worry about what I'll do if I really need transportation. In this moment, however, my car is the furthest thing from my mind.

"You know you can borrow mine whenever you need to."

"Mine, too," Maddie says.

"Thanks, guys. I think I have it all figured out, though. I can order a ton of stuff online. The only time I absolutely need a car is when I take my donations across town. But with the money I'll be saving on car insurance and repairs, I can easily pay for an Uber."

"Or"—Maddie puts her hand on my arm—"you can borrow one of our cars and save even more money."

"I tell you what," Ava says. "You know I rarely use mine. I'll leave the keys under the floor mat. That way if I'm busy at work or sleeping or whatever, it's there and available."

"Okay. Thanks."

Teddy begins to fuss, gratefully cutting off any further attention to my transportation problems.

"I've got him," Ava says, scooping him up and smelling his head. "God, I can't wait to have one of these. My ovaries explode every time I'm near this little nugget."

I reach over and touch his little cheek, wanting to hold him, but not wanting to draw attention to the fact that I've completely changed my stance on children over the course of the last week.

"It must be a lot different this time than when you had Gigi," I say. "I mean, I know you had Gigi's dad at first, but then you were a single mom for quite a while before you got together with Tag. How'd you do it?"

I'm hoping I asked nonchalantly enough so as to not raise suspicion.

"It was incredibly hard. But I had Gran."

"What would you say was the hardest thing about it?"

Maddie thinks on it. "I guess knowing that I was solely responsible for a small human. And knowing I'd be the only one to blame if something happened to her or if she'd turned out bad."

I laugh. "Nothing to worry about there. Gigi is fabulous."

"She is, isn't she," she says like the proud mother she is. ˉ

"So you wouldn't change anything?" I ask. "Like if you could go back and do anything differently?"

Her hard stare alerts me to my ridiculous question. "You mean other than leaving my hair straightener on and burning down my house, and my baby's father going back in to rescue her and then dying?"

I swallow my guilt. "I'm sorry, I didn't mean that."

"I know what you mean," she says with a sad smile. "I just had to state the obvious. To answer your question honestly, I'd have to say I wish I'd stopped the self-pity and self-loathing a lot earlier. Maybe I'd have gotten with Tag sooner. He's been so great with Gigi. I don't know what I'd do without him." She sighs, looking at Teddy in Ava's arms. "And now he's given me a son. I don't think my life could be any better than it is at this very moment."

I've been sitting on Lucas's offer. Waiting for a sign. Maybe it's come. Yesterday in my conversation with Carter. And now. It's like the universe is trying to tell me something. Maybe I should listen.

I stand up. "Excuse me for a second. I need to respond to a text."

I walk over, lean against a tree, take a very large breath, and type into my phone.

Me: Okay.

I slip my phone back into my pocket, surprised to hear a ping a moment later. I pull it back out and read the reply.

Lucas: Okay? As in you agree to my proposition?

Me: I want a lawyer to draw it up.

Lucas: I'll have it done tomorrow. She'll want to meet with both of us.

I roll my eyes. Must be nice to be so rich that you have a lawyer at your beck and call.

Me: Fine. Just tell me when and where. But I no longer have a car.

Lucas: I'll send one for you.

I try not to roll my eyes again, knowing I may have just agreed to a lifetime of such statements. Or eighteen years of them anyway.

Me: See you then. Over and out.

He gets my drift and doesn't reply. This isn't like before. It's not a sex thing. This isn't a courtship. It's not even a relationship really. It's more like a business deal. Or a *situationship* as Ava called it.

I look over at my friends and wonder just what they're going to think about *this* situation. Which is exactly why I decide not to tell them.

Chapter Eighteen

Lucas

"Thanks for coming in the middle of the afternoon," I say as Regan gets out of the car I sent. "I know it's eating into your business hours."

"Not a problem." She glances back at the black SUV. "But if anyone saw me get into that thing, they'll be asking about it for sure. It's like the FBI picked me up for questioning."

Regan looks up at the nice, new, modern three-story building that houses my lawyer's office. It's all the way across town from McQuaid Circle in what has become the recent town expansion. We pass a fountain out front. In the center, there's a marble elephant leaning over to take a drink with its trunk.

"That's weird," she says, stopping to examine it.

"Oh, *that's* weird?"

I let my gaze wander up and down her body. Her long floral print tunic hits her mid-thigh, and the yellow and black striped tights peeking out below it make her look like a bumblebee. The chunky black platform shoes make her inches taller than she is, but still not as tall as me.

"You don't like my choice of attire?" she asks, not looking the least bit ashamed that she looks totally out of place. "Embarrassed to be seen with me?"

"It's not that." I chuckle. "I was just imagining the outrageous clothes you're going to dress our kid in."

Her face turns serious. Has my mention of *our kid* made this all too real for her?

"Lucas, are you sure you want to do this? I mean, it's crazy, right? You and me having a kid. People will talk. They'll say things. They—"

I put a hand on her shoulder. "Since when do you care what people think? Is this you having second thoughts? I get it, believe me. I've backed out of more things than the average bear." I thumb to the building. "Just come inside. See what Candace has to say. Nothing is set in stone yet."

She nods hesitantly, looking nothing like her carefree, casual self. "Your lawyer is a woman?"

I chuckle. "I'll bet you expected some stuffy old white guy, huh? Candace is quite the opposite."

Holding the outer door for her, we enter the building and ride the elevator to the third floor. While inside, I imagine us taking the elevator to my penthouse. I imagine doing things to her while *in* the elevator. Things like stripping those ridiculous tights off her.

My thoughts are halted by another. Would she even want to go there? To my place? Ever since she texted me yesterday, I've been imagining all the places I could try to impregnate her. My penthouse. The dressing room in her shop. A beach house on Martha's Vineyard.

But then I remember how many times she's kicked me out of her apartment. How she ended the text conversation. How she told me she changed her mind about my first proposition.

While I'm looking at this as a fun way to get what we want, she may be looking at it as strictly business. *Ah, damn.* Is she going to want me to jizz in a cup so she can use a turkey baster? I hadn't even thought of that.

When the elevator dings and the doors open, pulling me back to our present reality, I gesture for her to go first. "Second door on the left."

"Oh, hey, Regan," the receptionist says, when we walk in.

Stacey, I believe, looks between the two of us, seemingly confused.

"We're uh…" Regan looks to me to save her.

"We're here on winery business," I say.

"Right. Of course." Stacey still seems confused as to why the CMO of Montana Winery would be taking the quirky boutique owner to a business meeting with his lawyer. I wonder what the gossip line will do with this information.

As if reading my thoughts, Regan leans close as we wait for Candace. "If we end up doing this, we're going to have to figure out what to say to nosey people."

I laugh. "You mean everyone in this town?"

She sighs heavily as if she hadn't yet thought of the repercussions or the criticism she'll face. I suppose I haven't either. Will people assume she's trying to trap me by getting pregnant? Will they call her stupid for thinking I'll finally settle down and commit?

Suddenly it dawns on me that she has a lot more at stake here than I do.

And what about our age difference? Will people have a problem with it? In the overall scheme of things, five years isn't that much.

But people do tend to have a bias when the woman is older than the man—idiotic ideals if you ask me. Older women are fucking hot.

Faces flash in my mind. Faces of all the women I've dated. All of whom were my age or younger.

Huh… interesting.

"Lucas," Candace says, emerging from her office. "So nice to see you."

"Good afternoon, Candace. Thanks for working this in on short notice."

"That's what your daddy pays me to do. Come in, come in."

Regan catches my eye and grins. As I thought, she's amused that Candace is not, in fact, an old fart of an attorney, but an attractive plus-size black woman in her forties.

"Regan Lucas," Candace says. "I thought I recognized your name when Lucas asked for this meeting. I've been in your shop once or twice. I just love McQuaid Circle." She extends a hand. "Candace McMillan."

Regan nods. "Yes. I remember you, Ms. McMillan."

"Splendid." She motions to a large table in the corner of her massive office. "Have a seat."

As Candace sits at the head of the table in front of an open laptop, Stacey opens the door and pops in with a tray of coffee and various sugars and creamers.

"Thank you," I say, watching Stacey eye Regan suspiciously. We're definitely going to have an issue on our hands if that look means what I think it does.

"Candace." I motion to Stacey. "This meeting is going to remain confidential, correct?"

She gets my meaning and smiles. "The two of you were never here." Sending a firm look Stacey's way, she confirms, "Were they?"

"No, ma'am."

"Okay, then, shall we get started?"

Stacey leaves, never giving Regan another glance. One look from her boss was warning enough apparently. Good, I hope that settles the issue. We don't need rumors floating around before anything even happens. Regan and I will have to sit down and discuss when and what to tell people when the time comes. I look at her, sitting across the table like we're a divorced couple meeting to divide our property, and I wonder if she already has told people. People like Ava and Maddie.

I'm pretty sure she hasn't. They'd never let her do it. Then again, when has anyone ever told Regan what to do? Perhaps having a lawyer run this show isn't the worst thing in the world. I do have rights, too.

"Okay then," Candace begins. "While this agreement we're about to draw up may be a bit unconventional, it's not that different from say a prenuptial agreement. In the end, though, they're all the same thing, business transactions." She turns to Regan. "I don't mean for that to sound cold, but things like this are necessary to protect both of you. And I'll have my friend in family law go over the contract before you sign it."

"You don't already have one?" Regan asks. "I thought that's why we're here."

"You're here to set the terms of the contract. It's up to you and Mr. Montana, not me. I'm just here to guide you and bring up matters you might not have thought about. That's also why I'll have Richard Livingston take a look at it—to make sure we covered things *I* might not have thought of. I'll redact the names of course. Lucas came to me because he knows I'll be discreet." She waves a hand at the door. "Everyone in my office will be discreet."

Regan nervously pours herself a cup of coffee from the carafe. She rips open two packets of sugar and pats them until they're empty.

"It's okay, Regan," I tell her. "This is just an informal meeting. We're not teaming up on you. This is for your benefit. You need to just tell us what you want."

Candace holds up a hand. "Before we begin, I want to make it clear that this contract will only cover what happens *after* the baby comes. It presumes you will successfully conceive and deliver a baby. I told Mr. Montana I did not wish to take part in any preconception agreement or contract. How, if, and when you try to conceive this child is entirely up to you."

Regan visibly relaxes, as if she thought I could somehow have legally coerced her into having sex if she doesn't want to. I can see she's warming up to Candace.

"Let's start with any questions you have, Regan," Candace says.

"I guess I want to know why Lucas needs to be protected. He's the one with all the money."

"Well, he will be the father. The other biological parent. It's my understanding he wishes to be much more than just a sperm donor, and in return, he plans on providing financial support. There's a lot that goes along with it. Why don't we start out by listing what Mr. Montana intends to pay for."

Both women look at me, waiting for an answer.

I hold up my hands. "Everything, I guess."

"Define everything," Candace says.

I pull out the itemization of expenses I'd drawn up and start going down the list. "Education. Childcare. Medical."

Candace makes notes on her laptop. "And what about monthly child support?"

"I'll pay whatever she wants."

We turn to Regan. "Don't look at me," she says. "I have no idea what a kid costs." She shrugs. "Like a thousand dollars a month?" Regan catches Candace's surprised reaction. "Is that too much?"

"Here's how this works, Regan," Candace explains. "If both parents are in agreement, child support payments can be reduced, raised, or waived altogether. It's important to note, however, that a judge has the right to supersede this if they feel it's unfair. But as you're not going through a divorce, it's unlikely this would ever appear before a judge unless one of you so requested. So it's basically up to the two of you to decide. But knowing this issue would come up, I did some digging. And Regan, with Mr. Montana's current yearly salary at the winery, he'd be required by law to pay at least six times that."

Regan's jaw hits the table. She's speechless. I'm fairly sure she's calculating in her head what that adds up to. And I'm confident it's far more than she nets owning her boutique.

I try not to smile. I don't want Regan to think I hold all the cards here. Because it's quite the opposite. She's the one who can call all the shots. She's driving this train and she doesn't even know it.

"I... but..." She covers her mouth. "That's ridiculous. I couldn't possibly take that kind of money. I don't even know what I'd spend it on. Gold encrusted onesies?"

Candace laughs, types something into the laptop, and then turns serious again. "What you need to understand, Ms. Lucas, is that Mr. Montana's family is quite wealthy. They give him a generous salary as Chief Marketing Officer, and he's one of four heirs of the business. Were you married and having a child together, the child *and* you would benefit from that wealth. The standards for child support are set with that in mind, so the child will grow up with the same standard of living as the primary bread-winning parent. Sadly, this doesn't happen a lot of the time." She tilts her head toward Regan. "You're one of the lucky ones, Regan. Lucas has indicated to me he's eager to be generous where this child is concerned. Has he told you about his plans for a trust fund?"

"Trust fund?" Regan asks, her eyes snapping to mine.

I shrug. "I want to make sure any kids of mine are set up should anything happen to me."

"Lucas asked me to establish a sizable fund for the child," Candace tells her. "Should he pass before the child is twenty-five, you'll be named trustee."

"Me?" Regan points to herself. Then her eyes narrow and she targets me with her glare. "There's a catch. There's always a catch. What are you asking for in return?"

"I told you before, I just want to be involved in his or her life."

"Let's get into the weeds of that," Candace says. "Living arrangements. Custody. Will it be divided equally?"

"No," Regan says. "This whole thing started because I wanted a baby. *I* wanted one. For *me*. Not a kid I had to share."

"Well, there's always the sperm bank," I say, maybe a little too sarcastically. "I looked it up, Regan. It could be in the thousands of dollars. More if you have to keep doing it over and over until it sticks. I also researched out of pocket expenses for having a baby. Unless you have bougie insurance, it could cost you five to ten grand, and that's assuming no C-section or complications. Childcare, education, sports. I can't even tell you how much sports cost, it's way more than you—"

"I get it," Regan says, slapping the table. "But I'm not going to let you hold me over a barrel here just because you have money. You want a kid so badly, go buy one."

"Let's calm down," Candace says. "You each have something to offer here. We just need to work something out that is mutually agreeable." She turns to me. "What are your thoughts on custody?"

"She can have custody for the most part. Like on a day-to-day basis. But I'll want time with him or her. Weekends. Vacations. Some holidays."

"How many weekends? How often?"

Candace's fingers are busy typing as she fires off the questions.

"I haven't really thought about it. Every other?" I look at Regan to see her reaction. She's pretty stoic now, on the defensive for sure, but I think I detect a hint of relief. "I mean, I'm not sure I want anything set in stone. What if I want to see the baby more often? Like come over after work? Or when he or she gets older, maybe have him for a longer visit. I don't want to be cornered into anything here."

"I wouldn't keep you from seeing the baby, Lucas," Regan says. "I'd never do that. You'd have free access. Not a key to my apartment or anything, but I'd be happy to let you come over often. And I'm not opposed to two weekends a month, maybe even a little more. This is all new to me, and based on what I see with friends, a lot of hard work. It might be nice to have a break every once in a while."

"Okay then," Candace says. "We're in agreement on two weekends minimum, with Lucas free to ask for more time as needed. And shall we say split holidays equally?"

"*All* of them?" Regan asks sadly.

I can almost picture her in those candy cane tights she wore, sitting on her couch on Christmas morning, gutted because the kid is with me and not her. It's a painful thought. I could never do that to her.

"My family loves holidays. The more the merrier. You'd always be welcome to spend them with us."

"Why don't we go with splitting the holidays as the official stance." Candace types out notes. "You can alter that on the fly. Agreed?"

Regan nods.

"Fine," I say.

"What about residency?" Candace asks. "What if one of you decides to move out of Calloway Creek, or out of the state?"

"No," I say. "No way. That's a hard stop for me." I turn to Regan. "I know you aren't the type of person who would do it, but with the kind of child support I'm offering, you could potentially sell your business and go anywhere. If we're doing this, we're going all in. Until the kid is eighteen, neither of us can move out of town."

"I've lived here all my life, Lucas. My friends are here. I'm not going anywhere."

"Your parents live in Florida."

"You think I'd run off with your kid to Sarasota to parents who will most likely disown me when they find out I'm having a baby out of wedlock?"

"So you're in agreement on this point?" Candace asks, moving things along.

We both nod.

"I'd like to buy you a car," I say to Regan. "A safe one. If you're driving my kid around, I want him or her surrounded by airbags."

"I really don't drive much."

I raise a brow. "You're turning down a free vehicle?"

She thinks on it. "Do I get to choose?"

"As long as it's got a high safety rating, yes."

"Agreed."

Candace smiles and types away, her fingers sailing across the keyboard like she's transcribing every word. She looks up. "Let's talk about decision making. Usually the primary custodial parent is given authority over decisions regarding education, health care, and other major issues."

"I'd like to have input," I say. "Regan and I have vastly different lifestyles. And while that may be one of the many things I like about her, I don't really want my kid going to clown school."

Regan laughs out loud. "I'm not going to indoctrinate him or her into some secret society, Lucas."

"What I would suggest," Candace interjects, "is that you make decisions together as co-parents. If you really come to a stalemate, you can always bring in a neutral third party to arbitrate based upon the child's best interest."

"So we fight about it until one of us gives in, or we hire someone to make the decision for us?" Regan shakes her head, clearly irritated.

"I don't think it'll come to that," I say. "Despite appearances, I'm not as stubborn as I look. I can be flexible. Can you?"

"Fine," she huffs, then looks at the time. "How much more? I have a business to get back to."

"As much or as little as you want," Candace says. "There's parenting plans, childcare, communication, religion, parental dating and relationships."

"That," I say. "Let's go over that one."

"Parental dating and relationships?" Candace asks.

I nod.

"Alright, let's see. What if one of you enters into a committed relationship with another person?"

"Then that person will be left at the altar as usual," Regan says with a snicker.

Not amused, I say, "Low blow. But think about it, do you want any girlfriend, fiancée, or wife of mine trying to raise your kid?"

"I'm having a hard enough time at the thought of *you* helping raise my kid, Lucas."

"Okay, so what if we say no overnight guests when the baby is with us?"

"I'm okay with that, but what if you do get engaged? What then?"

"I won't."

"With your track record, what assurances do I have?"

"We'll write it in the contract. I won't live with anyone or enter into a marriage or engagement until the kid is, what... over thirteen?"

"Why thirteen?" Candace asks.

I shrug. "I guess because teenagers seem to know everything already. And they're probably old enough to handle new people in their lives."

Candace raises a brow in Regan's direction.

Regan says, "I guess that's okay. It doesn't forbid any kind of long-term relationship though, does it? Short of living with the other person?"

Candace looks to me. I try to picture Regan with another guy. Another guy who's holding my kid, going to baseball games or recitals. The thought sickens me. But I have a feeling asking her to refrain from *any* relationship because I'd be jealous is going too far.

"I don't think a legal contract can preclude either of you from entering into a romantic relationship," Candace says. "Provided it doesn't affect the child in any way and doesn't violate the aforementioned rules. Agreed? Okay, and to the other points?"

"I'm okay leaving anything else under the 'we'll figure it out' section," I say. "I don't intend on forcing my political, cultural, or religious views upon anyone." I look at Regan. "As long as you don't."

"Lucas, I don't *have* any political, cultural, or religious views."

I laugh. And she does too. Our eyes connect and it's like we're both thinking the same thing… holy shit, we're really doing this.

Candace finishes typing and closes the lid to her laptop. "Looks like we're finished here. If either of you think of anything we haven't covered, or want to make changes, let me know. I should have a contract drawn up for you by next week."

I stand and shake her hand. "Thank you."

She opens the door and escorts us out, all the way past reception, where I don't miss how she shoots Stacey another warning glance. It makes me wonder if she's had issues with her assistant blabbing in the past or if she's just putting an exclamation point on her earlier warning. Either way, Candace McMillan is not a woman I'd like to cross. My dad is always saying what a pitbull she is. Someone who'd eat you for breakfast and use your bones to pick her teeth. Someone I'm glad is on my side for sure. But in this instance, I get the idea she's not just working for me, she's on Regan's side, too.

"That was… surreal," Regan says on the elevator ride down.

"It's definitely up there with the meetings I never thought I'd have."

"Are we really doing this?"

We exit the elevator. "I guess we are."

In the parking lot, I open the back door of her ride, just now realizing I still don't know what she expects from the actual baby-making process. "I'll send the contract over when I get it. After that, I guess call me when…"

You want to fuck? You want me to jerk off into a little plastic cup?

"I'm ready to make a withdrawal from your bank?" She winks and smiles that quirky dimpled smile.

I laugh. Because if the way she's looking at me right now is any indication, we'll definitely be fucking. She's back to her calm, carefree self. Hopefully because she's been put at ease by what we just agreed to.

The car drives away and I'm left with only my thoughts. After the last few days, the idea of having a child has become more and more appealing. But one thing occurs to me. No matter how much I've decided I want a kid, I'm not sure I want it happening on the first try. Because the thought of all the *trying*, has me just as excited as whatever else lies in my future.

Chapter Nineteen

Regan

It's Friday afternoon. The contract was signed last week. I still haven't told a single soul.

And I'm staring at a positive test. I'm ovulating. Or I will be within twenty-four to forty-eight hours.

I know because I went back to the city and bought several dozen ovulation tests. I take a deep breath. Now is the time. We have to start tonight.

I'm excited, but at the same time, terrified. What if it doesn't happen? What if I'm one of those women who can't get pregnant? Or what if I simply waited too long? What if I finally figured out what I want out of life and it's unachievable?

I can't think about any of that yet. I pick up my phone.

Me: It's time. Are you around?

Lucas and I haven't texted much. The time I told him I agreed to his first proposition. Then when I agreed to the second. And when he told me the contract was ready. The last time we texted was last week, after a courier brought me the contract and he asked when he might expect to hear from me because his job entails out of town commitments and he'd have to plan accordingly.

Plan accordingly. Like I'm something on his schedule to be checked off.

I stare blankly out my front window thinking about how crazy this is. I may have a baby with the one man in this town who is the polar opposite of me. Signing his contract, taking these ovulation tests this week, that's about the most planning I've done since before I dropped out of college thirteen years ago.

If I were to bet on it, I'd say he has my name written on some calendar or list somewhere, along with all his other projects.

Project. I think about his 'mission' to make me come. The things he whispered in my ear. The way I'd actually looked forward to being with a guy—something that hasn't happened in eons. I haven't thought about it in weeks. Not since I completely changed directions and went on a mission of my own. Am I disappointed that is no longer the objective here?

No. I don't think I am. Having an orgasm is overrated. I think society puts too much pressure on women as it is. And to then expect them to just 'let Calgon take them away' and forget about everything else in life just for five to ten seconds of pleasure. It's a ridiculous thought, one I'm embarrassed I ever agreed to.

I stare at my phone. He hasn't texted back. He's normally much quicker than this. What if he's not available? Or worse, out of town. I close my eyes. I should have kept him more in the loop. I gave him an approximate time frame, but never having done this, I couldn't be sure. Since my period decided to be almost a week late last month, who knew when this might happen? It's why I've been peeing on ovulation tests for the last six days.

I should have warned him that once a test strip indicates impending ovulation, it's imperative for success that we do it as soon as possible. The articles I read said all the studies show sex *before* ovulation is best. Having sperm right there, waiting for the egg to be released so they can jump all over it as soon as it's in the fallopian tube, is ideal.

Okay, so maybe I've gone a bit overboard these past few weeks with my internet research.

I check my phone again. Still nothing.

Texting him a second time would seem desperate. So I busy myself. I clean the dressing room. Put some dresses back on the rack. Count today's profits. I stare at the calendar. June 20. Could today be the day I—*oh shit*—it's June 20th. I haven't done my quarterly sales tax filing.

I spend the next two hours going over receipts and ledgers from the past three months, and then make the bank transfer, coming in just under the wire.

The front doorbells chime. I don't look up. I'm staring at my laptop waiting for the acknowledgement of filing.

Deep, male laughter fills the air, pulling my attention from my computer.

Lucas is standing on the other side of the counter, bags in hand, staring at the complete disaster I've made. Papers are strewn everywhere. It looks like a tornado came through here and upended my entire bookkeeping system.

"You look how my brother Dallas looks at the start of each April."

I nod. "Yeah. I almost forgot to file my quarterly sales taxes."

His eyes narrow. "How could that even happen? Don't you have reminders on your phone? A digital calendar? Alarms so you don't forget? A wall calendar with important dates circled and noted? Hell, even a Post-it note affixed to your ledger would do."

I stare at him with crazy eyes. "No."

"Why not?"

"Because I'm not a freak, that's why. Do you seriously do all that crap you just said?"

"Any diligent businessperson would."

I study him. "Lucas, have you ever been diagnosed with OCD? And if so, is it hereditary?"

His head bobs with laughter. "You're not the first person to ever ask that. But no, it's just good business practice."

He steps forward, clears a spot on the counter and puts down a large take-out bag from Lloyd's Steakhouse. Then he gets the bottle of wine he'd tucked under his arm and sets it down as well.

Involuntarily, my stomach grumbles as the incredible smells of the food hit me.

"So you *did* get my text?" I purse my lips. "What kind of good business practice has you not responding to texts?"

"This isn't business."

I scoff. "It is according to the contract I just signed."

He leans over the counter, inching closer. "The contract has nothing to do with this part."

"Even so." I tear my eyes away from his, refusing to succumb to his alluring gaze. "You should have texted me back." I touch the takeout bag. "What's this?"

"Dinner."

"This isn't a date, Lucas. This is a business transaction."

"Can you not talk about my cock like it's a commodity?"

"It's not your cock I'm interested in. It's your sperm."

As soon as the words leave my mouth, I wonder how much truth there is to that. His cock *is* fascinating. The thought has me wondering if I'm not just a little disappointed that the friends-with-benefits thing didn't actually happen. Then again, I am about to be bedded by the man.

He walks around to my side of the counter and whispers in my ear. "Then why didn't you have me jizz into a cup?"

I step away. "Better odds this way."

"Actually, the best odds are intrauterine insemination."

My eyes widen.

"Don't look so surprised, Regan. I've done my homework."

I motion to his offerings. "You didn't have to do this."

"So you've eaten? It's only five thirty."

"No, but—"

"We're going to spend the next eighteen years around each other and you're complaining about one dinner?"

I sigh. "We might not, you know. There's no guarantee this will happen."

"It's going to happen." He pats the front of his pants. "I'm shooting only the best swimmers."

"How could you possibly know that?"

"Got tested last week. Wanted to make sure I'm not shooting blanks."

My jaw slackens. "You did?"

"You'll be happy to know my sperm count is very high. Motility is good. Along with morphology and vitality and density. Basically, if sperm testing was an exam, I just aced it with flying colors." He turns in a circle, arms held out. "You're welcome."

I roll my eyes. But secretly, I'm delighted to know he's highly fertile. At the same time, I know that means if we can't conceive, *I'm* the culprit.

"Also." He winks. "You'll be happy to know I tested negative for any and all STIs."

Inwardly, I scold myself for not thinking of this. But I don't say anything. He already thinks I'm a kook of epic proportions. I can imagine what his desk calendar must look like.

Tuesday: Get tested for diseases.

Thursday: Go to sperm doctor.

Friday: Impregnate Regan.

I shake off the thought. "Well, that's a relief. And so you know, no STIs here either."

"I figured." He picks up the wine and Lloyd's bag. "Come on. Let's eat before it gets cold."

Before I even get a chance to call him out on his blatantly obvious stab at my long dry spell, he's flipping around my sign and locking the front door. He really does hate me leaving it unlocked. He turns. "I should have had Candace write into the contract that you'll keep your doors locked when my kid is with you."

"Must you always call it *your* kid?"

"Fine. *Our* kid."

He traipses upstairs like he owns the place, and then—*like he owns the place*—he goes right to the kitchen and plates our food.

I don't resist much, however, because the mouth-watering beef tenderloin on my plate is just about the nicest meal I've had in… well, since I can remember. It makes me wonder, is this how it's going to be? When he's depositing thousands of dollars into my account every month? When he's expecting our child to be raised with the same socioeconomic standards he has?

"Where did you have the testing done?" I ask.

"I'm not an idiot, Regan. I went to the city."

"Good. That's good."

He tops off my wine. "What did Maddie and Ava say about this whole situation?"

"Didn't tell them," I say around a bite of baked potato. I swallow it and add, "What did Blake and Dallas say?"

"I haven't told anyone either."

"Why is that?"

"You tell me."

I gaze across the living room. "I suppose because I didn't want to be talked out of it."

"Yup. Same." He takes a bite of steak.

"So if you're afraid of being talked out of it, and I'm afraid of being talked out of it, does that mean we're making a huge mistake, Lucas?"

He puts his fork down. "It means it's nobody's goddamn business except ours."

I nod, knowing exactly what my friends would say. They'd probably show up with slide shows, graphs, and statistics about how epically bad this plan is.

"When are we going to tell them?" I ask. "Assuming it happens."

"I was going to leave that up to you."

"Can we just play it by ear? Even if I do get pregnant, there are still things that can go wrong."

His head cocks to the side. "But you aren't planning on waiting too long are you? I mean, it'll be obvious after a while."

"I'll have more time than most," I say, glancing down at my fluffy midsection. "I've seen women my size go into their third trimester without it being obvious."

"You want to wait *that* long?"

"I don't know."

He tops off my wine. Again.

"I'm a sure thing, Lucas. You don't have to get me drunk."

He chuckles. "Yeah, but who knows, this may be one of the last drinks you get to have for a long long time." His finger taps on his lips as he watches me take a sip. "You aren't going to drink when you're pregnant, are you? Jeez, there's something else I should have told Candace to add."

"I'm not going to do anything to put the baby at risk. Sushi will be the one that kills me. I love sushi. Especially the raw stuff. But from what I've read, that's a hard no." A thought occurs to me, making me smile like a Cheshire cat. "So listen, since I'm going to have to give up drinking, raw sushi, and a whole slew of other stuff with nitrates and all, I think it's only fair that you have to give up something too."

He touches the wine bottle. "I work in the business, Regan. Sorry, but I'm not giving up drinking. That's a hard no."

I'm somewhat amused he thinks that's what I was talking about. I reach across the table and pull a half-full pack of smokes from his breast pocket, tossing them on the table.

"You want me to quit smoking?"

"God, yes. First of all, you can't smoke around the baby." My head falls back, and I sigh. "Guess I should have had Candace add *that* to the contract. Second, you'll no longer smell and taste like a chimney. And third, and most importantly, you'll live longer. Won't you want to be around for his or her graduation? Wedding? Grandkids?"

"Jesus." He swipes a hand across his jaw. "This really could be happening."

"If you're having second thoughts, now is the time to pull out."

"I'm not." He puts a hand over mine. "Pulling out is not going to help us, Ray. I'm pushing in. I'm pushing in all nine inches. But before I do, I'm going to make sure you're ready for me." His eyes fall to my cleavage. "I'll suck your nipples until you squirm." He waves his fingers in the air. "I'll use these on your clit. And inside you. I'm going to find that little pebble of a spot deep within and massage it until you're so wet you're dripping. I'll use my tongue on you. *Everywhere*. And maybe my teeth. Your pussy is going to beg for my cock, Ray. It's going to drag everything out of me." He leans close. "Every last fucking drop."

I clear my throat, unable to speak or eat another morsel.

He stands, goes to the very drawer that holds my wine stopper, corks the wine, then pulls me to my feet. "Let's go make a baby."

Chapter Twenty

Lucas

On the way to her bedroom, her cat watches me from the doorway across the hall. His eyes say it all: he doesn't like me.

"What's your cat's name again?" I ask.

"Joey."

"Like from the Pussycats?"

She laughs. "That was Josie. He's Joey, as in Tribbiani."

"You gave your cat a last name? That's weird."

The light flicks on and Regan stares at me. I don't like this look.

"What's wrong?"

"There's something else we didn't have Candace put in the contract." She sits on the bed, not looking interested in the least in the very thing we came in here for. "The baby's last name."

"Oh, right." I sit down next to her. "I didn't even think of that."

"You just assumed he or she would have yours."

"I didn't say that. I said I didn't think of it. But if you're asking, yeah, I'd like our kid to have my last name."

"Of course you would. But I started this thing. Don't you think it's only fair it's *my* name?"

"Kids traditionally have their father's last name, even when the parents aren't married."

"Traditionally?" Her eyes blaze into me, and not in a good way. "If I did everything traditionally, we wouldn't be in this situation."

I turn, hitch a leg up on the bed, and face her. "Is this one of those things we're going to have to get an uninterested third party to decide?"

"Why is it so important to you?"

"For one, I have a family business that bears my name. What if he or she wants to be a part of it one day? It would just make sense."

"If it's a girl, though, she'll most likely change her name when she marries, so what does it matter?"

I stare at the abstract painting on her wall. "What if we compromise and say if it's a girl, she gets your name and if it's a boy, he gets mine?"

"That's not a terrible idea," she says, relaxing her tense shoulders.

"See?" I crack my knuckles. "I knew we'd be able to do this. Our first conflict, and already resolved. We won't have a problem as long as you don't decide to call her Rainbow or him Zephyr or some other hippie name."

"Rainbow Lucas," she says, nodding with a funny grin that means she's clearly joking. "I kind of like it."

I stiffen. "Wait. I'm changing my mind."

"I'm not going to name her Rainbow. I think we should each have a little veto power when it comes to the name, don't you think?"

"Yeah, sure, but, Regan"—I get on the floor on my knees, put a hand on her leg, and look her straight in the eye—"I changed my mind about the last name. I want it to be Montana regardless of gender. When you just said it out loud, it dawned on me that my daughter's last name would be my first. Can you imagine me introducing us? 'I'm Lucas Montana and this is my daughter, Sarah Lucas.' It's weird."

She brushes my hand off her leg. "One, we're not naming her after your mother. In fact we're not naming him or her after anyone. I hate that. And, two, you're demanding she have your last name because it's *weird?*"

"Think about it. What if my last name was Regan and we had a boy and called him, for argument sake, Mitch. He'd be Mitch Regan. And when you'd enroll him in school, people would think it's strange that you'd have a kid whose last name is your first. Admit it… it's weird."

She blows out a breath. "I guess it would be." She picks a piece of lint off her comforter. "Fine."

"Seriously?"

She nods.

I was ready to put up a fight to the death on this issue. Yeah, it was her idea. And yeah, she's the one carrying the baby. But having a kid who doesn't have my last name? Call me old fashioned, but I'd have a really hard time with it.

Now that that's out of the way, I'm once again amazed by Regan. By her ability to adapt. To listen to reason. To compromise. I guess it shouldn't surprise me, though. She's definitely a go-with-the-flow type of person. And for sure not as stubborn as a lot of women I've dated.

You're not dating.

It's a fact I've had to remind myself of for weeks. In all honesty, however, whatever this is—it's not *not* dating. It's *something*. I just can't put my finger on what it truly is.

"What made you choose the name Mitch?" she asks.

I shrug. "Just pulled it out of thin air."

"Mitchell Montana."

She says it like she's trying it on for size. And I really like the way it sounds. "Has a nice ring to it, doesn't it? And how about Mitchell Lucas Montana? That way he has your name too."

She cracks a grin then flops back on the bed, her eyes fixated on the ceiling. "Did we really just name our kid? I still can't believe we're doing this." But then, she cocks her head. "Wait. If the baby's name is Mitchell Lucas Montana, he's getting *both* of your names. I know that's not why you chose it, but it's how people will see it."

"So now you don't want his middle name to be your last name because it's my first name?"

"I don't know."

"What if it's a girl?"

Her head shakes. "I don't think it will be. I've never thought of myself as someone who would be a good girl mom."

I chuckle. "Says the woman who owns a boutique with a lot of froufrou clothes. Come on, let's think of some."

She looks away. "I don't want to. I think we should just wait and make sure this even happens. I don't want to jinx it."

"You believe coming up with names will jinx it?"

She shrugs.

"Okay then." I take the opportunity as I see it, and crawl on top of her. "We'll come up with a girl name later. Right now, it's time for me to make a deposit."

She pushes my chest. "Can you get the light?"

I don't want to, but I don't refuse. I've won one battle today, I don't need to enter into another. But one of these days, I'm going to leave the light on. One of these days she's going to let me see her totally naked. My pants tighten at the thought.

When I turn back, she's already undone the first two buttons of her top.

"Hey," I say, striding over. "You're taking half the fun out of it. Who wants to get an unwrapped birthday present?"

Light from the hallway illuminates her expression. "This isn't supposed to be fun, Lucas. It's a business transaction."

I chuckle. "Regan, if you don't go into a business meeting prepared, you'll never get what you want."

"What's that supposed to mean?"

I unbuckle my belt. "It means if I'm not prepared—and by that I mean if I'm not properly stimulated enough to get a full-on stiffy, and if *you're* not prepared—and by that I mean if you're not turned on enough to be lubricated so you can take said stiffy—we might as well fold our cards right now."

When I unbutton my shirt, her eyes are glued to my lower abs. I take it off and drape it over a chair, slip out of my Ferragamo loafers, then remove my pants. With the way she's staring at my package, I know it won't be long before I'm hard.

I strip out of my boxer briefs and stand so I'm all full frontal in the dim light. I sway my hips back and forth to get some momentum going then helicopter my cock around a couple times.

She giggles at the sight. "Dinner *and* a show. You really know how to treat a girl."

I laugh. Then I take *the show* a step further, palming my dick and giving it a few tugs.

Her breath hitches.

I get on the bed, perched on my knees, dick in hand. "Does that make you hot?"

"I… uh…"

I smile and pump myself slowly. "It works both ways, you know. It would get me totally hot if you did it."

She reaches out for me, but I bat her hand away. "That's not what I mean."

If it were lighter in here, I'm sure I'd see her face turning crimson.

"I'm not... no."

"Okay, we'll save that for another day."

"Lucas—"

I lean close and put a finger to her lips. "Shhh. Just watch. A minute of this and you'll be so wet I'm sure I'll be able to slip easily inside you. Why don't you finish undressing? That'll get me hot, too."

She swallows hard. It's like she wants to protest. She doesn't want me watching her undress. She's in quite the predicament.

Her eyes don't stray from my cock as she finishes unbuttoning her Bohemian style blouse. Then she removes those same ripped jeans she had on a few weeks ago—they must be her favorite. She hesitates at her bra, like she's considering keeping it on.

"That too. Your tits are amazing."

It comes off and her large breasts spill to the side.

She goes for her panties when I stop pumping. "Wait. I want to do that."

I hook my thumbs onto the black cotton fabric on either side of her hips and lower them down. She raises her butt to assist, and I get a whiff of what my erotic display did to her. It makes my cock throb.

With her panties off, I graze her inner thigh with the palm of my hand, slowly moving it upwards. A satisfied smile crosses my lips as I detect a shiver running through her when I reach the area between her legs. As suspected, she's wet and ready, making it easy for me to slide in one finger, then another.

When my tongue toys with her left nipple, she moans and presses her head back into the mattress. Jesus, those noises. Is today going to be the day I make her come?

I double my efforts and lower my head until I'm between her legs. When I lick her clit, a hand pushes me away. "Lucas, I'm ready."

"You don't want me to…"

"We're not here for that."

"Right. Because this is just a business transaction."

"That's right, it is." She rises on her elbows. "Was it the contract we signed that clued you in?" she says sarcastically.

"Doesn't mean we can't kill two birds with one stone."

"That's not the objective anymore." Her head shakes. "Besides, there's not a chance in hell of that happening with all these thoughts racing through my head. Will I get pregnant? If I don't, how long will it take? What if it never happens?"

"Can't you just forget all that and be in the moment?"

She laughs. "Let me educate you on the female brain."

"Okay, okay. I get it. You're just using me for my body."

"No, Lucas. I'm using you for your sperm. Your body is just a bonus."

That makes me smile. And even more determined to make her come. I push a finger inside. "Come on, Ray. Let me try. Give me ten minutes. It'll be good, I promise."

Her demeanor shifts. *She* shifts. Almost like she's going to get out of bed.

I sigh in defeat. "Fine. You want my cock, you got it." I climb on top of her and push inside her. It's a little more difficult today. All the talking must have dried her up a bit. I look down. "You okay?"

"I'm good. Just do it."

Not exactly the tantalizing encounter I was hoping for. But it's Regan. And my dick is inside her. I can't help but enjoy it, no matter what circumstances brought me here.

It doesn't take me long to get there. I'd refrained from any manual activity this week knowing this was in the forecast. When she begins to make some sexy little noises, I wonder if they're even real. My dick doesn't seem to care, however. He likes them. He likes them a lot. The moans and sighs and mewls. She definitely knows what it takes to urge a man along.

I grunt and tense and spill myself inside her.

When I roll to her side, I ask, "Did you get *anything* out of that?"

"I'm hoping a baby."

I elbow her gently. "You know what I mean, Regan. Those sounds you made, were they real or just for show?"

She shrugs without answering.

"Why do you do that?"

"I find it gets guys there more quickly."

"But it's deceptive. And it doesn't give us a chance to get *you* there."

She gets under the blanket and switches on the bedside lamp. "Are you mad about that?"

"Not mad. Just disappointed I guess. It's always better if both people get off."

She narrows her eyes at me. "You sure you aren't mad?"

"Why would I be mad, Regan?"

"He always got mad."

"He?" I cock my head and then it occurs to me. "You mean that David guy?"

"Would you mind getting me a glass of water on your way out? I don't want to get out of bed for a while. It'll increase our chances."

She's shutting me out. Not to mention *kicking* me out, for the third time.

I've never been kicked out. I'm usually the one who does the kicking. But it's clear to me that Regan is the one wearing the pants in this… whatever this is.

I get out of bed and put my clothes on. The whole way to the kitchen I wonder about this David character and what he could have done to make her the way she is. Before she left for college, she was different. She wasn't a slut, but I swear she must have dated half the football team. I know because I'd dream of killing every guy she ever went out with.

And although our paths didn't cross much after she came back, I never heard a goddamn thing about Regan Lucas dating anyone. Maybe she did it secretly. Or maybe she didn't do it at all. But one thing is for sure—this David asshole, he's the reason.

I hand her a glass of water and sit on the bed. "Tell me about David."

She takes a drink and sets the glass on the nightstand, flipping off the light. "I'm tired."

I perch myself against her headboard. "I'm not leaving until you do."

"Why, Lucas? What does it even matter?"

"We're friends now, aren't we? And you may very well be the mother of my child soon. It's only natural that I'd be curious about your exes. And it's only fair. After all, you and this whole town seem to know everything about mine."

She turns on her side and fluffs her pillow, settling in then looking at me. "He was my boyfriend in college."

"And he would get mad if you didn't come?"

She nods silently, as if embarrassed.

"Tell me why."

"It's kind of a long story. You sure you want to hear it?"

I take my shoes off again and settle in, leaning back against a pillow. "I don't have anywhere to be at the moment."

"Well, as you know, I played volleyball in high school."

"You were an amazing player."

She smiles, but it's a sad one. "I loved it. I even made the JV team my freshman year at Houghton—you knew I went there, didn't you? My parents wanted me to attend a Christian university. They made it clear it was the only way they'd pay my tuition. It's a small school, so making the JV team as a freshman wasn't that big a deal. Still, I was happy to be playing my favorite sport.

"Anyway, one day early on, I was working out in the gym and there was this gorgeous guy who always seemed to be there the same time I was. Turns out he was on the baseball team. And he was a year older. We became friends even though I was totally smitten. By spring semester, he made it clear that he'd be open to a relationship if I were 'more his type'."

My stomach turns. "You mean if you were thin."

"Exactly."

I shake my head in disgust. "Regan, you didn't."

"I was a love-sick nineteen-year-old who was being propositioned by the hot first baseman on the varsity team. Of course I did."

I have a feeling I know where this is going, but I let her tell me.

"I wanted him so badly, I began starving myself. I let him become my personal trainer. He'd push me so hard, even my fingernails would hurt. And he'd always dangle the carrot of a potential relationship. He even had me weighing myself. Promising if I got down to a certain weight, he'd take me to his parents' second home, a beach cottage in Maine."

"Jesus."

"I dropped weight so quickly I started passing out at practice. I blamed it on a virus and the coach believed me. By the end of the spring semester, David and I became a couple. While most students went home, we both stayed on campus for the summer, taking an easy class or two while continuing to hone our athletic skills. And he made good on his promise. He took me to Maine."

I tense. "What did that motherfucker do?"

"He didn't hurt me, if that's what you're thinking. It was the first time we got naked together. He was so appreciative of my newly sculpted body that I didn't even care how controlling he was becoming. It didn't even occur to me until later that he dictated everything in our relationship. Where we partied. When we worked out. What I ate."

"What you ate," I repeat angrily.

"If he saw a hamburger on my plate, he'd ask if I wanted to go back to being the fat girl. He insisted he was only looking out for my health, and my future on the team, but I knew what he really meant—that he'd break up with me.

"By the time fall semester rolled around, my diet consisted strictly of salads, chicken breasts, and broccoli. When my coach saw me, he freaked and asked if I was sick. Needless to say, I didn't make the team sophomore year, not even JV. But by then, I was too far gone. Too much under his spell. He took care of me like I was an injured bird. He protected me—or so I thought."

"And the orgasm thing?"

"It didn't bother him at first. I think all men get that women don't come every time, and especially not until they're comfortable with their partners. But after we'd been doing it for months, he started to get mad. Like, he'd yell at me, asking what's wrong with me, telling me I didn't love him if I couldn't come.

"So I started faking it. It was so much easier that way. He'd get his rocks off, and he'd be happy that I did too. It went on that way for almost two years, until he graduated."

"What happened then?"

"Believe it or not, I'd never met his parents until his graduation. It was the most eye-opening moment of my life. When I saw his dad, it was like looking at an older version of David. And his mom, she was this pathetic little puppy who followed his dad around and obeyed his every command. She was a Stepford wife. My future flashed in front of me, and I knew if I didn't get out then and there, I'd never be the same. So I broke it off."

I smile and nod. "That-a-girl."

"If it were only so easy."

"Ah, shit. What did he do?"

"He stalked me at my school apartment. He said he still wanted me even though I'd immediately started gaining back the weight I'd lost. A few months later, he broke in and"—she turns and looks away—"killed my cat."

My entire body stiffens. "Holy shit. What happened?"

"The school security cameras showed him breaking into my apartment. They arrested him for that and the cat, but he was only found guilty of the break-in because he took a plea. It still makes my skin crawl that he got away with murdering Chandler."

Finally understanding her feline naming nomenclature, part of me wants to laugh. I hold it in, however, because what she's telling me is so utterly disgusting.

"Did he go to jail?"

"Only for ninety days. Then he was on probation for three years with strict orders to never contact me."

"Has he ever contacted you?"

"No."

"Good." I breathe a little easier. "He's the reason you learned self-defense, isn't he? And that dickwad is the reason you can't have an orgasm with a guy."

"Yup."

"Is he also the reason you've never married?"

"I don't think so. I'm pretty sure I decided long ago that book boyfriends are so much better."

"Book boyfriends?"

"You know, guys in books. Fictional characters. I do own a bookstore, you know. Unlimited fantasies at my fingertips."

"And an arsenal of toys in your bedside table?"

She laughs. "Yeah. And that." Her eyelids flutter. She wasn't kidding. She really is tired.

"Regan?"

"Mmm?" she says sleepily.

"I'll quit smoking. Once you get pregnant, I'll quit. Okay?"

"Mmm…. kay… good," she says drifting off to sleep.

I watch her face relax, selfishly hoping she didn't get pregnant this time.

And it has absolutely nothing to do with me not wanting to quit smoking yet.

Chapter Twenty-one

Regan

Sunlight coming through the window wakes me. I must have forgotten to draw the curtains. Rolling away from the light, hoping to get a few more minutes of sleep, I bump into something. I put my arms out to pet Joey, only, it's not him. My eyes fly open to find I'm caressing Lucas's arm.

"What the…?" I quickly take stock. He's fully clothed, but I'm totally naked. Under the covers, but naked. "Why are you still here?"

Lucas wakes, looks around to get his bearings, then rolls to his side. "Sorry. Guess I fell asleep right after you did."

"Well, get up and go." I pull the blanket tightly around me. "And use the back door so nobody sees you." I shake my head. "We have to be more careful."

"Relax," he says. "It's okay."

"It's not okay. We've been doing this all of one day and we already violated our own agreement. No overnight guests." I reach over and try to push him off the bed. It doesn't do any good. He doesn't budge. Of course he doesn't—he's two hundred pounds of pure muscle.

"Technically the agreement isn't in effect until the baby comes." He works his chin with a few fingers. "And I didn't think that rule applied to *us*."

"Of course it applies to us. It especially applies to us. You wouldn't want the baby getting the wrong idea, would you?"

"You think it happened?" he asks, looking at the covers over my stomach.

I shrug. "Statistically, it probably didn't."

He gets a cocky look on his face and rises on an elbow. "Maybe we should double down and go for it again."

"Double down?" I sit up, covers still around me, take my robe from the bedpost, and put it on without revealing much more than my bare shoulders before I stand with my back to him. "We shouldn't do it more than once a day. Like I said, use the back door."

Leaving my room before he can say anything else, I walk down the hallway, passing my not-so-happy cat, and enter the bathroom.

Slowly opening my robe, I stare at my belly in the mirror. I know the odds of it happening on the first try are slim. But it *could* happen. Could there be a baby in there? Could last night have been the night that changed my life forever? Is there one tiny bundle of cells, smaller than the head of a pin, that could end up being my son or daughter?

During my shower, I promise myself I won't become one of those women obsessed with getting pregnant. One who takes a pregnancy test twice a day even a week before a missed period. But no matter how hard I try to deny it, I know I will be. The ten pregnancy tests I bought alongside the ovulation kits tell the tale. I rationalized it was just good sense to go ahead and get them as long as I was in the city. It's not like I can pop over to Truman's and buy one off the shelf.

Combing through my wet hair, I hear a noise. More curious than suspicious, I hang up my towel and pull my robe back on.

"What was that?" I ask Joey, when I almost trip over him because he's stretched outside the bathroom door like a draft stopper. "And what's with you this morning?"

I hear the noise again and roll my eyes as I stomp out to the kitchen. Hands on my hips, I ask, "Why are you still—"

Then the smells hit me. Bacon. Pancakes. Coffee. I quickly glance at the platters on the table covered with enough food for an army. I look up at Lucas.

"Did I forget to mention I'm a killer cook?" he says, grinning from ear to ear.

"Lucas…"

"I get it. I'm not supposed to be here. We're violating the agreement. Yada yada yada. But, hey, I figured if you did get knocked up last night, might as well start off by giving our kid some good nutrition." He takes a carton of orange juice out of the refrigerator and brings it to the table. "Sorry, you're out of syrup. But you have whipped cream and strawberries."

He studies the can of whipped cream like he has other ideas on what to do with it.

I swipe it from him and he laughs.

"Fine. You can stay for breakfast. But then—"

"I know, I know. Go out the back door."

He scoops a healthy portion of eggs onto my plate, then his. I take two slices of bacon off the pile and a couple of pancakes as Lucas pours us each a glass of juice.

"What's Ryder up to these days?" he asks. "Last I heard he and Amy were living in Colorado Springs."

I tilt my head. "You don't keep in touch? But you were such good friends."

"It's been a few years since we talked. And I'm not on Facebook, so I never get updates."

I put my fork down. "You're not on Facebook? *Everyone* is on Facebook."

"Obviously not everyone, Regan." He looks at the ceiling in thought. "I don't think my brothers are either."

"You guys are clearly freaks of nature." I try not to laugh as I point my fork in the direction of his lap. "And I don't mean because of that thing in your pants."

"Hey now, that *thing* is going to give you a kid. Don't knock it."

Out of curiosity, I ask, "Do your brothers, you know…" My gaze drops to his crotch.

"Have big cocks?"

I feel my cheeks heat up, and I shrug. "There were never any rumors or nicknames about them like there were you."

"You think Blake, Dallas, and I sit around and talk about our dicks?"

"I think you've probably compared notes." I squirt whipped cream onto my pancakes. "Tell me I'm wrong. Women aren't the only ones who talk about that stuff."

"You're not wrong. And no, they weren't blessed with the extra inches I have."

"Blessed or cursed?" I ask with a raised brow.

"Ouch." He grabs his chest. "Regan, you're killing me here."

I take a bite of pancakes and giggle. "Sorry. I'm not one to talk. I know what it's like to carry extra inches. *Everywhere.*"

"I happen to like all of your inches."

"Do you really?" I study his face. "Some guys say that, but honestly, it's hard for me to wrap my mind around the fact that guys actually like this." I squeeze a handful of side belly.

"Don't sell yourself short, Regan. For one, you rock that body. And some of us care more about what's up here." He points to my head. "And what's in there." He points to my heart.

I'm trying to figure out why he cares about any of that—this is just a mission after all—when Joey meows loudly. In my surprise at finding Lucas cooking breakfast, I plain forgot to put his food out.

I reach down and pull him onto my lap. "Sorry, buddy." I kiss his head. "I'll feed you in a minute."

"I already fed him," Lucas says.

My head snaps up in surprise. "You did?"

"I'm trying to make friends. It clearly didn't work." He nods to Joey's food bowl full of untouched food. "He wouldn't eat it."

I cock my head and study Joey before putting him on the floor, getting up from the table, and going to his bowl. I pick it up off the floor then put it back down. I can't help laughing when he immediately digs in. "He really does hate you. I just don't get it."

"Me neither. Pets always love me. My niece's cat doesn't hiss at me like Joey does. He scurries over and purrs against me. And Dallas's dog thinks I'm pretty fucking cool too." He eyes Joey, now devouring his food. "There must be something wrong with him."

"There's nothing wrong with Joey. The problem is with you."

"He's jealous."

"Jealous? Of a human?"

"Tell me, Ray, how many men have you had up here in your apartment?"

I narrow my eyes. "Are you asking about my sexual history? Don't you already know enough about that?"

"I just think Joey believes *he's* your guy."

I regard Joey as he eats. *Does he?*

"In order to see if my theory holds weight," he says, "it's important to know if other men come up here. And how he reacts to them."

I guess I've never really thought about it before. But with Joey only being a few years old, there haven't been many. Oh my god, have there been *any?* "I, uh, respectfully decline to answer that question on account of how pathetic it would make me look."

He laughs out loud, and I swear he looks more than a little happy. I guess he likes to be right. This time… he is.

"You never answered my question about Ryder."

"They're still living in Colorado," I say, scooping the leftovers into containers. "We've never been super close. I saw him and Amy in Sarasota at Christmas. Amy and I have even less in common than Ryder and I do. We've never really acted like sisters-in-law or even gotten along that well. I don't like the way she tries to control him. And it's always been a herculean task to get her to Sarasota every other year for the holidays. It was almost painful, the five of us sitting around with nothing to talk about. I guess because of our age difference, Ryder and I never really connected. And my parents, we just have different values. They'll probably disown me after this."

"When are you going to tell them?"

"I'm not."

His eyes widen. "You aren't going to tell your parents you're having a kid? Won't they be a bit surprised when you show up with one on your next visit?"

"Yes, they will. I've thought about it, and that's the plan—to just show up. At that point, there's nothing they can do or say. They either accept it or they don't. And if they don't, they'll never see me again."

"And Ryder? Will you tell him?" His brows shoot up. "You think he's going to want to kick my ass?"

"I'm thirty-five, Lucas. There will be no ass kicking of any kind."

He laughs. "Every time you mention your age, I have a hard time wrapping my head around it. I still see you as that eighteen-year-old fantasy girl."

I cover my eyes. "I'm sleeping with my little brother's best friend."

"Former best friend." He nudges me. "And there's nothing little about me."

"Stop," I say. I put the leftovers in the refrigerator then lean against the counter. "I'll probably tell him, but not before we tell everyone else." I look at the time. "I've got to finish getting ready and open the shop. Thanks for breakfast."

"My pleasure." He goes for the door, then turns. "What time tonight?"

"Mmm?"

"We should do it again tonight, right? And for the next three or four days probably. To give you the best chance."

"I suppose we should."

"You don't have to look so sad about it." Pouting, he strides back over, tugs me toward him and says, "If you'd just let me go for objective number one, it would be a whole lot better." His eyes capture mine. "Just tell me how you want me to do it. Fingers? Cock? Tongue? Hell, we can even incorporate a toy if you think it'll make it happen. I'm up for anything." He leans in. "I've heard a finger up the butt can really help."

My jaw drops. He did not just say that. But secretly, my insides are swimming in warm gooey juices.

"I'm just sayin'. Whatever it takes, Ray."

With that, he spins on his heel and leaves. I race to the bedroom window to make sure he goes out the back as promised. He does. He starts walking down the alley, lights a cigarette, then turns to look at my back door, staring at it intently. Then his head tilts and he catches me in the window. With a smirk and a wink, he salutes me.

I shrink away from the window, not wanting him to get the wrong idea. Then I go get ready. Taking a few minutes for one minor detour.

Chapter Twenty-two

Lucas

Did I really just ask if she wanted me to finger her ass?

What the hell is it about Regan Lucas that has me wanting to do things like that? Things I've never done before. Things like dirty talk. Whipped cream. Anal play.

And when did I become so forward and demanding? Sure, I'm that way when it comes to business. But not in the bedroom. Never in there. I've always let the woman take the lead, afraid to push the boundaries of regular, vanilla sex.

I look back down the alley. Maybe *that's* what's been missing.

Ever since we signed the contract last week, I've wondered if she would have done it if she knew I still had a major boner for her. Even after all this time, through all the women I've been with—it's still there. I just didn't realize it.

Does that make what I'm doing unethical?

I think it must be the whole orgasm thing. I've always been competitive. I hate to lose. And I've been confident in my abilities as a lover, as mainstream as it's been for me.

Ah, shit. What if all the other women were faking it?

Not possible. I'm getting all up in my head. And I vow tonight, I'm going to bring my A-game and prove to Regan and myself that it's achievable.

I need another cup of coffee. I round the corner at the end of the alley and head into The Criss Coffee Corner. It's bustling on this Saturday morning.

Ava is behind the counter, busy with the cappuccino machine, and I notice Gray Calloway taking orders. I step up when it's my turn. "Didn't know you were working here."

"My dad made me get a job. He said I can't work for his security company until I'm twenty-one because of all the regulations. Gotta be that old to get a gun carry permit."

"My brother Blake worked at Gigi's Flower Shop when he was your age. I worked at the hardware store. I can't remember what Dallas and Allie did. We all had to have other jobs before the winery. It's good to get different experiences. How's your dad's business doing?"

"Great. Storm started working with him last year. Colt will as soon as he graduates. He says as each of us join him, the business will expand. He's thinking of getting into personal security, too."

"As in bodyguards?"

He nods. "Wouldn't that be badass?"

Ava comes up behind Gray and clears her throat. "We've got quite a line of customers. I'll take him. You take the next."

Gray looks guilty for making others wait. "Sure thing, Ms. Criss."

Something tells me she's taking me for reasons other than moving the line along.

"Good morning, Lucas," Ava says with a shit-eating grin.

And there it is. My head bobs to the side. I thought Regan wasn't going to tell anyone.

"How's your quest *coming*?" She giggles. "No pun intended."

Right. Regan told them about our original mission. Maybe she didn't bother telling them that deal was off. That way she could explain any awkward moments of us being caught together.

"I never kiss and tell."

"Good thing *she* does." She refills a large canister of sugar, completely unaware that Regan has no intention of telling a soul about what we're doing. She looks up. "I'm sure I'll hear all about it."

I ignore her comment and peruse the menu over her head. "I'll take a caramel macchiato."

She grins. "*Coming* right up."

Outside, my drink in hand, I park myself on one of the benches lining The Circle. It's a pretty good place to people-watch. Several families are in the park across the way, beyond the statue of Lloyd McQuaid that stands tall in the middle of the roundabout at the end of McQuaid Circle. I cock my head as I observe them, wondering if that will be me soon, holding hands with my daughter or pushing my son in a stroller.

I lift my chin when I see Jaxon Calloway and one of his daughters Ashley or Aurora—I can never remember which is which—walking their golden retriever in the large grassy area. I wave when Ginny Ashford emerges from the jewelry store across the street. I laugh when two kids come racing down the sidewalk on skateboards, remembering all the shit I did with my brothers when we were kids.

"This town sure is a wonderful place to raise children."

My head swings up to see Rose Gianogi standing next to my bench.

She motions to the empty space next to me. "Do you mind? It's a long walk here and I need to rest."

"Please. Sit."

"I like to get my steps in," she says. "I walk here almost every morning. I usually go to the park and feed the birds, but when I saw you here, I thought I'd stop and make conversation."

Finding it unusual that Rose Gianogi wants to talk to *me*, I ask, "Is there anything in particular on your mind?"

"I know things." She looks directly at me with her old, weathered eyes. "I *see* things. And I'm very protective of the ones I love."

"I'm sure you are," I say, not liking where this is going.

"You're a nice boy, Lucas. I like you. I think you have a good heart. But Regan is like a granddaughter to me. I don't fancy seeing her get hurt."

Amused that she called me *boy*, I say, "I'm not sure what you're talking about, Mrs. Gianogi."

She scoffs. "I'm old, but I'm not senile. Saturday mornings aren't the only times I'm around. I've been filling in at the flower shop a few hours a day so Maddie can spend more time with that precious baby. I know The Circle. Which means I know you don't spend much time here."

"Don't have much reason to." I hold up my cup. "But I do enjoy a good cup of coffee."

"You also seem to have a penchant for pastries, no?"

My eyes snap to hers.

"I told you. I see things. When you're old like me, with nothing better to do than watch people, you notice differences. Patterns."

I set my coffee down and lean my elbows on my knees, settling in for what I'm sure is going to be a lecture.

"I'm the last one to argue that people aren't allowed second chances. My husband is a prime example. He wasn't exactly the Norman Rockwell poster boy. But I saw the good in him. Saw his potential. And look at us now. But, second chances are one thing. With your... track record... a second chance is miles behind you. And with that track record, I'm not sure you're capable of making promises. So best you not be makin' any." She stands. "You've heard the story of the boy who cried wolf?"

I nod.

"It may not be exactly the same. But one of these days, you're going to find the person who completes you unlike any other. The person you're sure you can't live without." Her pointed stare bores into me. "What'll you do when you decide she's the one, but this time you're the person being left behind?"

"You've got it all wrong, Mrs. Gianogi. I know my own faults. I never plan to marry."

She flashes me a disapproving glare. "You young people think you can get the milk without buying the cow."

I want to tell her she has no idea what she's talking about. That if anyone is the cow in this situation, it's me. That Regan is merely using me as a sperm donor and nothing else. That Regan hasn't so much as looked at me as anything more than a means to an end.

That this.... whatever we're in... is completely one-sided.

I pick up my cup and stand. "I'm not looking to get the milk, Mrs. Gianogi. And rest assured, nobody will be getting hurt. I've decided I need a change, and I like it here on The Circle, that's it. So I guess I'll be seeing you around."

"Mmm," she mumbles as I walk in the other direction, crossing the street until I get to my car in the parking lot behind Donovan's Pub.

I wonder why the change of heart. When she saw me in Regan's shop a few weeks ago, I could have sworn her intention was to marry us off. I must have read that situation all wrong.

When I reach the Jag, Cooper Calloway is carrying a bag of trash toward the alley twenty feet to my right. I lift my coffee and tip it at him. His face scrunches in thought. "Interesting how your car was parked in that exact same spot last night when I closed."

"Nice to see you too," I say and get in.

The people in this town have far too much time on their hands.

~ ~ ~

Me: I'm at the back door. Can you let me in?

I stand out back, my head on a swivel until she lets me in. *This* door she locks.

She looks beyond me. "You didn't park back here, did you? That's just for business owners." Then her gaze focuses on my face. "You're all sweaty."

"I jogged here."

"Why?"

"Because there are a lot of nosey people in this town."

Upstairs, I tell her about Rose and Cooper. "And Ava wanted to give me the third degree this morning when I stopped for coffee."

"We need to be more careful. And don't go to Ava's shop anymore."

"But she has good coffee."

"I know she does. Too bad, though. Go somewhere else."

"You could always come to my place."

"I don't have a car. And unlike you, I'm not a runner. Five miles each way—not going to happen."

"I'll pay for an Uber."

"I guess that'll work." Her nose crinkles. "Wait, no. What if the Uber driver is someone we know? Is Dax Cruz still doing it?"

I shake my head. "He's working at the auto shop with the rest of his family."

"I thought he was moonlighting."

"Hmm. I don't know, and I don't keep tabs on them. So, no Uber. I could just keep running here."

"No. It'll raise too many suspicions."

I uncork the half-full bottle of wine from last night, and pour us each a glass, thinking of our options. "I could meet you somewhere and drive you the rest of the way."

"Somewhere prying eyes won't see?" She snorts. "Me getting into your car may be far worse than people just seeing you hanging around McQuaid Circle."

"That's true, especially because you're hard to miss." I take a sip, eyeing Joey who's staring at me from behind a chair. When I look back at Regan, she's glaring at me. "What?"

"Low blow, Montana."

I replay my words and feel guilty as hell. "Shit, not because… no, I meant your clothes. Those striped tights you wear. The extremely loud shirts. They practically scream 'look at me.' Maybe if you tamed it down and wore normal clothes…"

She glares in dissonance. "You want me to wear sweatpants and a Nike T-shirt?"

"It wouldn't be the worst thing." I tap a foot on the floor. "You have a clothing shop, Regan. I'm sure you can find something that won't make you stick out and be so obvious. Then we can meet in the very back of the parking lot behind the train station."

Her mouth moves from side to side as she contemplates it. "I could say the same thing about you. Nobody else in this town drives a dark green Jaguar."

"Wyatt Ashford drives a Jag. But he owns the four-door sedan. And it's silver. I'm the only one with an F-Type coupe."

"Yeah, that's not conspicuous at all."

"Got any better ideas?" I ask.

"We could meet in the city."

I shoot her a cockeyed stare. "You want to take a train all the way into the city and get a hotel room, for what, an hour? And then come back on the train? Seems like an awful lot of trouble."

"It would be more like three or four hours," she says.

My mouth forms a grin.

"Easy, Casanova. It's so I can lie down for a while. Not so you can work your magic, or whatever you had in mind. And definitely not so you can stick any fingers up my bumhole."

"Hey, maybe you shouldn't knock it until you've tried it."

"Have *you* tried it?" she asks with an inquisitive leer.

"Nope." I smile. "But I might be willing to if you—"

She covers her eyes with her hands. "Oh my god, we're not having this conversation. We'll try it your way tomorrow. I'll dress down and meet you in the back parking lot. Just text me when you get there. If there's anyone around, we'll move locations."

I smile.

"What?" she asks, clearly irritated.

"I'm kind of liking this covert operation."

She rolls her eyes, takes a very large gulp of wine and heads to the back. "You coming or what?" she shouts over her shoulder.

I laugh, thinking about how I should be asking her the very same question. Then I stride to her bedroom, full of determination, only one thing on my mind. Making. Her. Come.

Chapter Twenty-three

Regan

I stare at myself in the mirror. Plain blue shirt. Yoga pants. Long, lightweight cardigan. Tennis shoes. I look like I should be going to the gym, not going to get laid. I turn sideways, then fully around, looking at myself from all angles.

I look stupid. I feel stupid.

But I suppose it's better than having to let Lucas stay until after midnight and then sneak out in the dark and jog home.

I can't help but feel a little sorry for the guy. Once again, he failed at his quest last night.

It's not so much he failed as I didn't succeed. Didn't even try is more like it. Wham bam, thank you sir was the order of the day— and *all* days. I know myself. It's just been far too long. Add in the fact that all I can think about is getting pregnant, and it's just not going to happen.

"Be a good boy," I tell Joey, feeding him and then grabbing my purse and heading out the door.

I go out the back. Halfway down the alley, the back door to Maddie's flower shop opens and her grandmother steps through holding a bag of trash. She does a double take. "Regan? Why, I almost didn't recognize you." She eyes me up and down. "Is it laundry day, my girl?"

I laugh awkwardly as my head spins, conjuring up a believable story. "I was, you know, just on my way to Truman's for some sugar. Don't you hate it when you run out?"

"Truman's doesn't have a back entrance, dear."

"Yeah, I know. But I didn't want people seeing me like this. As you said… laundry day."

"As it happens, Maddie keeps a large container of sugar in the shop. She does love her coffee. How much do you need? I'll get it for you."

"Um… that's very kind of you, but, um… it's brown sugar I'm in need of."

"Oh, well, I can't help you then. What are you making?"

Think. Think. Cookies? Oatmeal? "Coatmeal."

"Coatmeal?" She cocks her head.

"I mean… I meant oatmeal."

"Mmm. An interesting choice for dinner."

I shrug. "I was craving it. I mean, not craving it. I just was watching TV and there was a commercial for it and so I thought I'd make some."

Oh my god, stop talking.

I am such a bad liar. I'm not sure how I think I'll be able to go several months without telling anyone about this.

"Let me take this to the dumpster for you," I say, reaching for the trash.

She lets me take it. "Thank you. I'll just go back inside and close up then. Enjoy your oatmeal."

"I will."

After getting rid of the trash, I glance back to see Rose is still in the doorway. She waves, but doesn't move. I look back once again when I've made it to the end of the alley. She's still standing there. I have no choice but to turn left instead of right. Right is the train station. She'd know I was full of shit and up to something. Rose Gianogi always has her ear to the ground. And she's the last person I need a lecture from, especially since she already laid into Lucas this morning.

I stand along the end of the building, wondering how long I need to wait. If I peek around the corner and she catches me, she'll know something's up. So I lean against the brick building as I wait and weigh my options.

"Regan?"

Oh, for fucks sake.

It's Nikki Calloway. She must have gotten off the train and is walking home.

I put on a big smile. I haven't seen her since I ran into her outside the hospital last month. "Hi, Nikki," I say, trying to think up yet another lie because I just know the question is coming.

Like Rose, she takes in my unusual choice of attire. "I've never seen you look so, well... *not* flamboyant."

"I was just out for a walk. Getting a little exercise." I stretch my arms over my head. "Got winded and stopped for a bit."

She points up. "Best not be out here long. It's going to rain soon."

Nikki should know, she's a meteorologist as well as being the co-host of a super popular news show on XTN. She's for sure living her best life. Great career. Great kids. Great husband.

"I'm heading home now," I say. "Say hello to everyone for me."

"Will do."

It occurs to me that she can't say the same. She can't say it because I don't have an *everyone*. It's quite the opposite. I have *no* one. Before jealousy can take hold, I remind myself that it's possible in nine months, I *will* have someone. And then Nikki would be saying, "Give Mitchell a kiss for me."

My heart thunders and I just know, despite those pesky doubts that lie in the back of my mind, I'm doing the right thing.

Just as she walks away, a raindrop hits my face.

"Wow," I yell after her. "You're good!"

She laughs and gets an umbrella out of her pack.

Not a minute later, it starts really coming down. I'll get drenched for sure. I contemplate scrapping this whole idea and going back to my place. Then I remember why we're doing this and decide I don't want to give up a chance to conceive.

When I realize everyone coming from the train station is running for their cars or homes, not concerned about me in the least, I make my break for the back parking lot, turning to look down the alley to see Rose is no longer lurking.

By the time I reach Lucas's car, the top half of me is soaked. He leans across the console and pushes open the passenger door. I look inside his sleek car. "You sure you want me getting in like this?"

"Get in, woman!"

I slide into the seat, feeling guilty about getting his car all wet.

"That came out of nowhere," he says, looking up and out the windshield.

"Good thing."

"Why?"

I shake my head, irritated. "People."

He laughs, puts his car in gear, and takes off. He keeps stealing glances at me. I must be a sight. Wet hair. Clothes clinging to my body. And I wonder if my makeup is running.

A few minutes later, when we pull into a parking lot, I remember where he lives and my heart sinks.

"I forgot you lived in an apartment." I look left and right as he pulls into a dedicated spot, right in front of the building. "Yeah, not conspicuous at all."

"Right," he says, and backs out. He pulls around back. "Go through that entrance. The code for the freight elevator is 9638. Take it to the top floor. The code for my penthouse is 4413. It's the one on the right."

I close my eyes and burn it into my memory. "9638. 4413. Got it."

I hop out and race to the door through the rain.

Luckily, I don't run into anyone, and by the time I'm closing the door to his penthouse, I'm letting out a relieved breath. Then, it hitches again when I look around. Holy crap. This place is immaculate.

It's not often I have the occasion to be in places like this. Sure, Maddie's grandmother lives in a mansion with her husband Tucker McQuaid. And Amber and Quinn's house is pretty stellar. But this— I turn in all directions—why would a bachelor need all this space?

The living room and kitchen have ceilings so vaulted it's like they're two stories, making the space seem even larger. I walk to the huge wall of windows that overlooks a picturesque grassy park-like area below.

The door opens behind me. "Nice place," I say. "Sorry I'm dripping on your floor."

"Not a problem. Hold on a sec." He disappears down a hallway and returns a minute later with a sweatshirt. He hands it to me. "There's a bathroom down there. You can change into this."

"Thanks."

I almost ask what the point is. Aren't we about to get *rid* of our clothes? But the part of me that's curious about his penthouse keeps me from saying it.

On the way to the bathroom, I peek into two rooms. One is a home gym, the other looks like a wine cellar. I've never seen so much wine. Rows and rows of it. There must be hundreds of bottles in here.

"See something you like?"

"Why do you keep all this here? Don't you have room at the winery?"

He chuckles and passes me in the doorway. "This is nothing, just my private collection. The winery has room for much more. We produce over three hundred thousand cases of wine per year."

My jaw drops. I knew they made a lot of wine, but I had no idea it was that much. "How many in a case?"

"Twelve."

"That's… I can't even count that high."

"Well over three million bottles."

"Holy shit, Lucas. How do the six of you manage?"

"It takes a lot more than just the six of us. We have a full staff. You should come by sometime. I'll give you a tour."

I snort. "As if that wouldn't have rumors spreading."

"Okay, after everyone knows. Come by then."

I laugh. "When I have absolutely no use for wine?"

"I'll have you know we make some of the best non-alcoholic wine in the country."

"You mean grape juice."

His head shakes. "A common misconception. Grape juice is simply the unfermented juice of grapes. Non-alcoholic wine goes through the full winemaking process, including fermentation, but then has the alcohol removed. It gives you a more developed taste profile and it's much less sugary than grape juice."

"I'll keep that in mind."

"Want to pick a bottle?"

I shoot him a hard stare. "Not a date, Lucas."

"Neither were the others, but we still drank wine. Come on. Any bottle."

"Okay, fine." I close my eyes, spin around twice, then walk forward, carefully extending my arm until my fingers touch one of the racks. I wrap my hand around the first bottle I come to. "This one."

He takes it from me. "I'll open this. You change."

The bathroom is across from his wine room, so I don't get a chance to see what's behind the other two doors at the far end of the hall. I know there's another hallway at the other side of the penthouse, too. That one must lead to the master bedroom. Are there really two more bedrooms over here? And if so, what on earth does he need them for? A home office perhaps. I can just imagine it—a desk packed with lists, calendars, and Post-it notes—all organized and not looking the least bit messy. There would be some sort of ultra-tech high res monitor for video conferencing. Tasteful artwork on the walls. A custom-built desk and ergonomic chair that he drapes his suit jackets over after a long day.

Oh my god, why am I standing here imagining his home office?

I glance at the fourth door, wondering if maybe that room holds even more wine. To impress the ladies? I doubt it. With what he's got below the belt—and I mean both in his wallet and in his boxer briefs—he hardly needs anything else.

Then I remember it's not wine, riches, or a big cock that he lacks. It's respect. The one thing he's lost in this town, and probably the hardest thing to regain.

In the bathroom that I presume is one of many, but that's still three times larger than my only one, I change into the sweatshirt. I'm glad it fits. It would have been embarrassing had it not. But Lucas is a big guy. Not fat big. Muscular big. And tall.

I look at myself in the mirror, running fingers through my wet hair to tame it, and try to figure out if I'd be interested in him if circumstances were different and he weren't the man that he is. Then again, if he weren't the man that he is, he wouldn't be thirty and still single. He'd have been married long ago, probably with at least a few kids.

He's very handsome. Hot even. That's for sure. And he's genuinely nice. I'm sure, having abandoned all the women he has, a lot of people think he's some cocky rich guy. But it's quite the opposite. The man is truly the whole package. With one exception—he's never going to commit. That's what makes this what it is—a business transaction. Nothing more. Even before we were going to try for a kid, it was still basically a transaction. I was giving him sex when nobody else would, and he was going to give me an orgasm.

Has sex *always* been transactional? I scrunch my face. Now that I think of it, I swear it has. Especially with David. He got his rocks off and I got what I needed: love, affection, adoration. The longer we went without sleeping together, the less I'd get those things. So, yes… it was transactional.

What about before David? And the few times after? I think back and rack my brain. Was *any* of it unconditional?

A tap on the door interrupts my mental spiral. "Regan? Everything okay?"

"Be right out." I hang my wet cardigan, shirt, and bra on hooks by the shower and open the door.

"Hmmm," he says, standing back.

I quickly look myself over. "What?"

"You just look so normal."

"Is that bad?"

He shrugs, offers, "It's just not… you," and turns to walk back to the kitchen.

I follow, nearly asking what he means by that, but don't. Could it be that he actually likes the way I dress? Surely not. Not the guy who's never seen out of business attire unless he's out jogging. I narrow my eyes at him as he walks away. Could it be that he likes… *me?*

I shake the ridiculous thought from my mind, not even wanting to think of the ramifications of trying to have a baby with a guy who's been carrying a torch for me all these years.

Lucas pours us each a glass. "To successful baby making," he says, his glass held high.

"I'll drink to that." The incredible flavor of the wine explodes in my mouth. "This is really good."

"I'm glad you think so. It's one of our best."

I almost spit out my next mouthful. "One of your best? Lucas, you shouldn't have let me pick this one. I'm sure it's expensive."

"It retails for about four hundred a bottle."

Now I do choke.

"Lucas, I—"

"Do you think I care, Regan? I have five other similar bottles. And an unlimited supply at the winery."

I put my glass down and glare at him. "I'm telling you right now that I'm going to teach any child of mine the value of money. He or she isn't going to grow up with a silver spoon in their mouth. I get that you have an unlimited supply of cash, but I don't want my kid growing up with a stick up their ass."

"Do I have a stick up my ass? What about Blake—does he? And Dallas and Allie?"

He's got me there. They are all normal people, far different from how the uber-rich McQuaids were when they were younger. In fact, if you were out with a Montana and didn't know they were wealthy, it'd be hard to tell. His parents too. They are incredibly nice. And, wonderful role models for parenting.

This kid hasn't been born yet—heck, he or she probably hasn't even been conceived—but I feel a sense of peace knowing the kind of people he'll be surrounded by.

"Sorry. I was out of line. I, of all people, shouldn't be making assumptions based off stereotypes." I pick up my glass and take another sip. "This may be the best glass of wine I've ever had. Thank you."

He smiles. I like his smile. And I realize I won't be disappointed if we have a son who gets it.

I thumb to the opposite hallway. "Is your bedroom in there?"

He corks the bottle, tucks it under his arm, and leads me to a massive master bedroom suite that could swallow my entire apartment.

"Would you mind if I... I mean it's silly, but I'd love to see your closet."

He laughs heartily. "Go ahead."

I walk through the archway to the bathroom. To the right, a set of open double doors lead into the most impressive closet I've ever seen. Floor to ceiling shoe racks line the far wall. On the right are hanging racks of various heights. On the left are drawers, dozens of them, with cubicle-like shelf space above. There's a tie rack in the corner, electric I presume, with what must be a hundred ties. In the middle of the large closet, a settee covered in brown velvet backs to an island with more drawers and pull-out shelves. On top of the island are fancy trays that hold cufflinks, empty money clips, and cologne.

This closet is every fashionista's dream.

"I could live in here," I say, plopping on the settee and running my hands over the soft seat.

It takes a minute for me to realize the closet is half empty. Right, Lissa used to live here. I look over at him as he leans against the doorframe and wonder if he still regrets what he did to her.

Reluctantly leaving the room, because, come on, I'll never have a closet like this one, I glance in the bathroom on our way out. It's as impressive as the rest of the place. Walking to the bed, I see a picture of Lucas and Lissa on the nightstand. Yeah—definitely not carrying a torch for me.

He follows my gaze then strides over and puts the picture in a drawer. "Sorry. Probably not what you want to see when we're about to do what we're about to do. Guess I should have gotten rid of this a long time ago."

I shrug. "It's not like I'm here for your heart, Lucas."

For a second, I think he looks sad. He must really miss her.

"Get the light?" I ask. "It's time to get down to business."

Chapter Twenty-four

Lucas

I flip the light in the bedroom off, but leave on the one in the closet so I can see what I'm doing. She sits on the bed and tests the firmness. Her hair is still damp from the rain. The sweatshirt she's wearing looks so out of place on her. As did the Nike shirt and cardigan she wore earlier. I tilt my head and study her.

"What?" She looks down at herself. "Did I spill wine?"

"I just can't get over how different you look when you're not wearing your own clothes."

"Tell me about it. I feel like I should be at the gym."

I smile. "Who says you aren't about to get a workout?"

Her lips twitch with a smile, but contrary to her reaction, she says, "Lucas, I'm—"

"I know, I know. You're just here for the sperm." I approach the bed, removing my clothes along the way.

I stand naked next to her, not hard in the least.

My lack of an erection doesn't keep her eyes from looking, though.

"My cock isn't too excited about this being a business transaction. He might need a little encouragement." I sway my hips and it thwaps from side to side.

When her tongue swipes her lower lip, my brain conjures an image of her taking me into her mouth.

She raises a brow. "Wow. All I have to do is look at it and it magically comes to life."

I laugh as I inch closer.

She extends her arm, grips my cock, and gently pulls me toward her until the gap closes between us. The long, slow strokes she starts with rapidly turn into faster-paced tugs with increasing pressure.

She glances up. It's hard to make my eyes stray from the show, but I force it just long enough to say, "Hell, yeah."

With a twitchy grin, she gets back to work, my arousal building by the second.

I've deduced that as we get older, hand jobs become all too underrated. They tend to fall by the wayside as we graduate onto other things. But... Jesus... with the way she's working me, it's becoming clear that this may not even turn out to be the appetizer. It could very well be the main course.

Which is why I grab her hand, stilling it.

"You don't like the way I—"

"Ray, I fucking love it. That's the problem."

"Oh." She scoots back onto the bed. "I guess it's your turn then."

Not wasting a second, I pull the sweatshirt up and over her head. Much to my delight, she's braless. Instantly my mouth falls to a breast, and I toy with her nipple. I take a chance, lightly grazing my teeth across it. When she inhales sharply, I lift my head. "Admit it. You like that."

A slow smile spreads across her face.

"If you like that, just wait until I do the same thing to your clit."

Her head falling back against the pillow is all the invitation I need. I peel her pants down, then her underwear, and I'm bombarded with the unmistakable scent of her arousal. It turns me feral, and I feast on her like Thanksgiving dinner.

True to my word, I gingerly scrape my teeth against her clit. As I'd hoped, her back arches and her hips press into me. I intermittently use my tongue and teeth in an attempt to drive her wild.

It's working. Or I think it is. Because one, she's making all those sexy as fuck noises. And two, she's not pulling away, telling me to just get on with it.

I double my efforts, adding a few fingers to search for that elusive spot inside her that may be the winning ticket.

"Oh… ahh… Luke…"

I almost smile but don't. I can't stop doing exactly what I'm doing. Because I swear she's about to get there. And I'm about to be king of the world.

Then, out of the blue, she stills and grabs my shoulders. "Lucas, please."

It's what every man nestled between a woman's legs wants to hear: her begging for release. But that's not what Regan is asking. She's saying she wants this over with. My dick inside her. For me to do my stud duties.

"One more minute?" I ask, then swipe my tongue across her.

Her eyes close in discouragement. "It's not going to happen."

"But I could—"

"Lucas, please." She rises on her elbows. "I'm asking nicely here."

I sigh and crawl up her body. "One of these days, Ray." I push inside her. "One of these days."

~ ~ ~

"Where did I go wrong?" I ask when it's over.

She shakes her head. "It wasn't you at all. I thought I might even get there. But then when I had that thought, a bunch of other thoughts started creeping in. Am I really going to? What will it be like after all this time? Will Lucas think I'm faking? And it just went away."

"But you were close."

She nods. "Closer than I've been in a long long time."

"Which means all we need to do is get you over the edge."

"Not the objective anymore." She points behind me. "Can you hand me that pillow? I'm going to lie here with it under my hips."

I hand it to her, then uncork the bottle I brought in and pour her a glass. "Stay as long as you like. I'm going to have a shower."

When I return twenty minutes later, her wine glass is empty, and Regan is asleep. Standing in my towel, I lean against the doorway between the bedroom and bathroom, and I watch. She's still on her back, pillow under her butt, her chest rising and falling slowly.

She's the first woman to sleep in here since Lissa. Damn. I hadn't even thought of Lissa for weeks. Not until Regan noticed the picture. And not even then did thinking of her bother me.

It probably should have. I'd brought another woman into the apartment and the bed I'd shared with her for years. But… it didn't.

I know now that I won't be taking the picture frame out of my drawer, not unless it's to pack it away or throw it out. I'm over her. She can go on and marry the senator's son. She can have a dozen kids with him if that's what she wants. She can even come back here and try to parade her happiness in front of me. It won't matter. None of it will. Because my heart no longer belongs to her. And as I look at the sleeping woman on my bed, I wonder if it ever really did.

Fuck.

I turn, go to my closet and pull on a pair of sweatpants, then go out to my kitchen, getting something far stronger than wine. I pour several fingers of whiskey into a rocks glass and sit on a barstool. I should tell her. I should tell her I like the wacky way she dresses and the unconventional way she runs her business. I should tell her I like her nonsensical, carefree attitude. I should tell her I like her in my life. In my bed.

The problem is, I like it *too* much.

Which is why there's one more thing I should tell her. Run away. Run fast and run hard.

I close my eyes and bring the glass to my lips. It may already be too late. What if we made a baby? Telling her now would cause her stress she doesn't need. If we haven't conceived, if she gets her period, I'll tell her then. Because not telling her would be as good as lying.

I'm not going to lie to her. And I sure as hell am not going to hurt her.

I thought it was just a crush. The same old feelings I had when I was a kid.

I quietly make my way back to the bedroom and look at her, sleeping peacefully, maybe even dreaming about the child we might have made. Her face is practically glowing in the dim light. I have the urge to go to her and kiss her. And that's exactly why I know everything has changed. This isn't a crush. I've fallen for her.

And I have to tell her.

I will. Odds are, it'll take months for her to get pregnant. She'll just go to a sperm bank as planned after this doesn't work. And I'll go back to being the idiot who can't commit to a woman.

I spin, pad back to the kitchen, and pour myself a small second glass, downing it in one gulp. When did this happen? When did she go from being my childhood crush to the woman I want? By my side. In my life. Permanently.

Sadness washes through me as indecision niggles away at me. What if she *is* pregnant? What then? Do I live a lie, never revealing my true feelings for the mother of my child? Potentially watch her date other men, have other relationships, even marry?

There's no other choice. I've done all the hurting I'm going to do. I've destroyed countless women over the past decade. I refuse to destroy *her*. And I know if we got together, I'd do exactly that. Only this time would be worse—a child would be at stake. In the middle. An innocent pawn in my deceptive game.

Then I come to my senses and laugh out loud. Because who am I kidding? Regan hasn't ever given me any indication she wants me. I've never seen her look at me with love or adoration. With want or reverence. The only looks I've ever gotten from her are the looks of a woman who knows what she wants... a one-night stand... an orgasm... a kid.

In all those scenarios, I'm the one being used. And I'm the first person to admit I deserve it.

I hear a faint noise and go to investigate.

Regan isn't in my bed anymore. I must have heard the sound of her cleaning up in my bathroom. But the bathroom door is open, and she's not there either. When I pass by my closet, that's when I see her. She's facing away from me, sitting on the settee, staring up at the half-empty shoe racks along the back wall.

I step inside, take some loose bills from on top of the center island, and hand them over her shoulder. "Four hundred and sixty dollars for your thoughts?"

She giggles and pushes my hand away.

"I was thinking how I'll have to get rid of my closet in the second bedroom." She waves her arm around. "It's nothing like this.

Mine is full of freestanding clothes racks and a few antique dressers. Maddie strong-armed Tag into building me a shoe rack a few years ago that holds thirty pairs. My actual bedroom closet is miniscule. I'll have to move most of my clothes to the shop storeroom." She turns. "Don't get me wrong, it's all going to be worth it. I guess seeing this closet just had me mourning mine a little." She stands, wearing only my sweatshirt that falls just past her hips. "I'll get over it."

"You could always move. Get something larger."

"Ha! Like I can afford that."

"Regan, you'll be getting a lot in child support."

"That'll be for the baby."

"No, that's so the baby gets to grow up in an environment he or she would have if we were married. That means a larger apartment for both of you. There are even a few empty units right here in this building."

What are you doing? Stop talking. She may not even have your child. What then? You rope her into moving and then she goes bankrupt having to pay for an apartment she can't afford?

Her mouth opens and closes several times. "You want me to move into your building?"

I shrug, devil be damned. "It makes sense. Think of how easy it would be for me to see the baby. How convenient it would be for you if you had to run out for something. I'd be right here."

"It wouldn't be convenient at all," she says. "My shop is five miles away."

I decide not to press the point. It may be moot anyway. "No decisions have to be made now. Stay at your place if you want. I just wanted to put the idea out there."

She says nothing, but I don't miss how she gives my closet another thorough look. A longing look.

I try not to laugh thinking the woman's love of clothes might be the one thing that works in my favor.

She goes back into the bedroom and finishes dressing. "Mind if I return your sweatshirt later? I'll clean it for you. I'm sure my clothes are still wet."

"Keep it. I have an unlimited supply."

Her eyes scrunch together. "What would I do with a Montana Winery sweatshirt?"

"I don't know. Use it on laundry day."

Her dimples make an appearance, and her laughter hits me in all the right places—or wrong ones.

"What's so funny?"

"Just something Rose Gianogi said earlier." She stands, shoes on. "Ready to take me home? It's dark enough now that you might even be able to drop me off in the alley."

"Sure." I throw on a shirt and shoes and grab my wallet and keys. "I'll bring the car around back."

"Thanks." She smiles. "Same time tomorrow night? I think five nights in a row would be ideal."

The devil on my shoulder almost has me nodding. But the other one, the angel that controls my sense of compassion, has me spouting a lie. "Actually, I'll be out of town. Last minute trip. Just for two days."

Two days should get me off the hook, right?

I'm doing the right thing. If she's not pregnant, I'll come clean and the whole deal will be off.

She looks sad for a second. But the pathetic part, the part my heart hates right now, is that I know she's not sad she won't get to be with *me*—Lucas the man. She's sad she won't get my goddamn sperm.

I spin and leave the room, knowing just how much of a bitch karma can be.

Chapter Twenty-five

Regan

Washed and dried, I fold the Montana Winery sweatshirt and tuck it away in one of my dressers. I stand in the center of my second bedroom-slash-closet and turn slowly. I am going to miss this. I momentarily allow myself to wonder what it would be like to live in Lucas's building, have a larger apartment, and a closet similar to his.

The thoughts have me immediately feeling guilty. Like I'd be benefiting from the child support. I don't have an issue with him paying for things baby-related, but his money being used to pay *my* rent—that seems a step too far even if he did give his blessing.

Besides, would I really want to leave this place? Sure, it's old. It needs to be painted. The kitchen appliances could use updating. And the bathroom is small. But it's mine. Or it will be as soon as I pay off the mortgage.

When my parents handed down the business to me, they owned it completely, along with the apartment. Since Ryder didn't want to run the business, they liquidated half the equity, gave it to him in cash, then signed the shop and its mortgage over to me. They called it our inheritance and told us to expect nothing further when they eventually died, as they planned to spend their retirement savings living out the rest of their days in Florida.

Even though the shops along McQuaid Circle are all connected in one long building, like mine, they are individually owned, not leased from large corporations. A few years back, McQuaid Enterprises, owners of many businesses and properties in Calloway Creek, tried to buy out the businesses on The Circle and then lease them back to the owners. We all banded together to prevent the buyout. Rather successfully, too. As of today, the only part of McQuaid Circle owned by the actual McQuaids is Lloyd's Steakhouse around the corner.

I run my hand across the decades-old wallpaper in the room, wondering if I should go ahead and strip it now in preparation for painting. I picture the room in shades of pink or blue and try to figure out which one I'd like best.

In trying to imagine a color for the walls, I know what I'm really asking. Would I want a boy or a girl?

I thought I really wanted a boy. The name Mitchell Montana swirls through my head. But if I'm being honest, and I know it's cliché, at this point, with me being the age I am, I'd be happy with either.

I turn and leave the room, deciding that stripping the wallpaper would be tempting fate. I'm already having to go with one less try than I'd hoped because of Lucas's last-minute business trip.

We did it four nights in a row. Four nights of him wanting to get me off despite my assurances it wouldn't happen. Which it didn't. To his credit, he never got mad. I think he was just frustrated that I didn't even let him try. But damn, I came so close last night.

He's so different from David. Like in another stratosphere. Hell, he brings me pastries, something David wouldn't have done in a million years. *He* used to bring me laxatives and diet pills and photos of bodies he thought were attractive.

How did I ever get sucked into a relationship with him? If I could only go back and tell my nineteen-year-old self that if a man didn't like me for who I was, he wasn't worth a second thought.

And then there's Lucas. He doesn't seem to have any issues with my weight, my extra inches, or my all-around plumpness. I was sturdy and thick even in my teens, yet he masturbated in high school at the thought of me.

Why is life never easy? Back then, I was willing to do anything, including sacrificing my volleyball career, to get the attention of the star athlete who only wanted to mold me into his version of the perfect girl. And now, the guy I'm sleeping with is a hot, kind, wealthy bachelor who accepts me for who I am and could set any potential kid up for life, yet he's one hundred percent unavailable, unreliable, and unattainable.

Not that I'd want to attain him.

I cock my head at Joey as he watches me from across the living room. *Would I?*

It's a ridiculous thought and I almost laugh at the unconscionable notion of Lucas and me together on any other level than what we are right now.

I think knowing it could never and would never happen is what's making all this possible.

"Are you hungry?" I ask Joey, reaching for a can of cat food. "How about tuna tonight?"

He meows when he hears the familiar 'pffft' sound of me pulling the tab of the can. I dump it on his food plate and allow him to eat it right up here on the kitchen counter. I chuckle knowing Lucas would probably hate it and would sanitize the entire kitchen. But he'd do it without getting mad. Sure, he'd call me careless, breezy, maybe even irresponsible, but then he'd roll his eyes, smile, and meticulously scrub the counter.

I pat Joey's head. "I'm off to meet the girls. Be a good boy."

Down the stairs and out the front door, I stop and turn before crossing the street. I go back and lock the shop. I'm not sure why I do it. Maybe it's Lucas's voice in my head. Maybe I'm already being protective of what may or may not be growing in my womb.

Across the street and around the back of the ice cream shop, I find our usual bench. It's empty. I'm the first one here. I sit and stare at the playground. There are a few kids on the jungle gym and more on the slides. Izzy McQuaid pushes her five-year-old brother Myles on the swing. Their mom, Willow, waves from across the way. As I wave back, I notice something I hadn't before. The distinct curve of a pregnant belly. Willow is expecting.

I wonder if we'd become closer if I had a baby too. Would we go to the same Mommy and Me classes? Would our kids go to preschool together?

"Hey!" I hear behind me.

Ava is walking up, her hands full of coffee in two drink carriers. "We're the first ones here?" She looks around. "I heard we might have a full house tonight. Amber said she wanted everyone here."

"I know. I saw the text. You think she's pregnant?"

She shrugs sadly and I feel bad for her knowing how much she wants it for her and Trev.

I can see it now, all of us cheering and hugging and smiling when Amber delivers the news. It's a far cry from what would happen should I make the same announcement. Looks of disapproval, concern, and maybe even judgment would be more like it. Would my friends even be supportive?

Maddie pushes a stroller up next to the table. Little Teddy is awake, wide-eyed, and utterly adorable. I reach in and touch his hand. When he grabs onto my finger, my heart explodes. I almost tear up with how badly I want this. But with all this pregnancy and baby stuff surrounding me, I get a sinking feeling it won't happen for me. Like maybe I waited too long and missed my chance.

Maddie elbows me, looking across the playground. "I didn't know Willow was expecting."

"Me neither. You think Amber is?"

She shrugs.

"Oh, come on. Tag is her best friend. You must know something."

Ignoring my statement, which means she absolutely knows something, she says, "I'm glad nobody else is here yet. I wanted to ask you how things are going with Lucas."

I stiffen for a second before I realize she thinks we're sleeping together for orgasm purposes. I shake my head. "That's not happening."

"Really? Why not?"

"Because it was weird."

She puts a hand on my shoulder. "It was kinda."

Ava looks up from Teddy and cocks her head. "But he came in for coffee Saturday morning. There are two other coffee shops closer to his apartment."

"Maybe he just likes yours." I hold up my cup. "It is the best."

She eyes me curiously. "But he said he doesn't kiss and tell."

"Maybe he was kissing someone else?" I say, trying to sound uninterested. "I hear Olivia Weston is back in town."

Now both of my friends are eyeing me suspiciously.

"What aren't you telling us?" Maddie asks. "You have a strange look on your face. And you seemed so set on that whole friends-with-benefits thing with him. What's up, Regan?"

"Nothing. It's nothing. I just changed my mind."

It's not a lie. I *did* change my mind. I'm just choosing to leave out the part where Lucas Montana may or may not be about to be my baby daddy. My heart skips a beat wondering if he already is. If not, it won't be for a lack of trying.

Four times in four days. And if the size of his cock is any indication, he may pack more of a punch in the sperm department. I almost smile remembering what he told me about being tested and having 'scored' well.

This really could be happening.

"That right there." Maddie points to my face. "What is going on with you that you won't—"

"Hey ladies!" Serenity sings, walking up arm-in-arm with Amber.

My eyes automatically go to Amber's flat belly that reveals nothing.

Nikki and Dakota cross the parking lot heading our way.

"Willow!" Amber calls, waving her over.

"Amber's definitely knocked up," Ava whispers into my ear.

I grab her hand and give it a supportive squeeze. I know that every pregnancy in this town, every baby, is like another shard being driven into her heart. I feel guilty about what it will do to her if and when I have my own news to announce. I think Ava believes she's safe with me. That because I'm not married and don't have a boyfriend, I'll likely never get pregnant. And I've pretty much told them I'm not the mother type. She probably thinks that if it doesn't happen for her and Trevor that at least she'll have me.

Guilt over what I'm doing crawls up my spine. Maybe I should tell her. Prepare her for what might happen.

Or what might not, I remind myself.

And that's reason enough not to say something about it.

When all of us are settled around the picnic table, and we're expectantly looking at Amber, she beams with a smile. "I have exciting news."

"I knew it!" Dakota exclaims.

Amber shakes her head. "I'm not pregnant, if that's what you were thinking."

"Oh," Dakota says, her brows knitting together, as are all of ours. All but Maddie's.

"But we are having a baby," Amber says. "I was waiting to say anything until we were sure. We're adopting." She bounces up and down. "Eeek! I can't believe it. And it's a boy. He's due next month."

All jaws hang open with the exception of Maddie's, who obviously knew. It's not the news the rest of us were expecting. Then again, this is Amber Thompson. As an adoptee herself, and already mother to one adopted child, this shouldn't come as a surprise.

"Well?" Amber says. "What do you think?"

Simultaneously, everyone stands and moves to take turns hugging her.

Questions and comments get rapid-fired.

"We're so happy for you!"

"Congratulations!"

"When did this happen?"

"Is Josie excited?"

Amber laughs. "Okay, so Quinn and I have been sitting on this for a while. And what nobody knows is that we've been trying to adopt for a few years now. Not because we can't have a child of our own, but because we felt it was our mission. We came close a few times, but those fell through. But this time—" Her hand comes to her heart. "You guys, we met the birth mom last weekend. She's amazing. She's eighteen. She's been through a lot, but she's so strong." Tears come to her eyes. "She reminds me so much of my mom. We just knew this was going to be the one. It was fate that we found each other."

Maddie's husband, Tag, has been best friends with Amber since they were kids. Maddie has shared with us the horrific story of what happened to Amber's birth mom, Piper.

"Was she…?" I can't bring myself to say the word.

Amber nods. "She was sexually assaulted."

Gasps abound, all of us disgusted.

"Like my mom, she has no idea who the father is. It was a random attack, and he wore a mask. We have no clue about the baby's race or ethnicity." She chuckles with a half-grin. "And we don't care. We just knew this one was meant to be."

"You guys will be great parents," Ren says. "Again. But that poor girl."

"Like I said, she's strong. But she basically has no one. She entered the foster system at fourteen and bounced from home to home. She suspects her rapist might have been one of the many boys she'd been in foster care with. It happened when she was seventeen, but she didn't find out she was pregnant until after her eighteenth birthday."

"That's horrible," Ava says.

"Her name is Julia. She's super intelligent and very talented. You should see her paintings. We're going to pay for her to get a college education. Room, board, and tuition. The girl deserves a break, you know?"

"It just goes to show that sometimes good can come from evil." Nikki smiles. "Julia could go on to be the next"—she rubs her chin then laughs—"some news anchor I am if I can't even come up with the name of one famous female painter."

"We're all so happy for you," I tell Amber. "So when is Tag planning the baby shower?"

Laughter comes from everyone. Best friend or not, Tag Calloway won't be throwing *anyone* a baby shower. That's okay, though. Amber is surrounded by friends who will be all too happy to step up.

Willow rubs her belly, shares a look with pregnant Nikki, and leans down to tickle Teddy's chin. "Maybe something's in the water."

I don't tell her I hope something *is* in the water. *My* water.

Samantha Christy

Chapter Twenty-six

Regan

Twelve days and nine pregnancy tests later…

I stare at the test in disbelief. Has it really happened? Am I—thirty-five-year-old Regan Lucas—really pregnant on the first try?

I take a tenth test just to be sure.

All the tests are spread out on my kitchen table. Many are from different manufacturers, so the results show up differently. Some have a plus sign. A few have two pink lines. The rest clearly announce it with one unmistakable word: **PREGNANT**. But all ten are positive.

I'm one hundred percent knocked up.

And suddenly, I'm more excited than I've ever been in my entire life.

Samantha Christy

Chapter Twenty-seven

Lucas

Regan: Can we talk?

I push my work aside and stare at the text. In my experience, never have those words come to mean anything positive. I've said them more than once myself, when I had the balls to have an in-person conversation rather than just not showing up at the wedding.

Could it be Regan has come to her senses and doesn't want to keep carrying on with the likes of me?

That would be a smart move, even if it means giving up the lifestyle my wealth would afford her and the baby.

Or it could simply mean she's not pregnant. This is about the time she'd find out, right?

We haven't talked, texted, or even crossed paths since the night she came to my apartment. And as much as I've tried to deny it, I've missed her. I've missed her way more than I should, given the transactional nature of our relationship. And it's why I'm going to have to hurt her. Not in the way I've hurt the other women in my past, but I know she'll be disappointed that I'm backing out. She's probably gotten used to the idea of me being her baby daddy by now. Maybe she's even gotten a little excited about what the extra money would mean.

But it's the right thing to do. Continuing this has disaster written all over it. For me. And surely for any kid I'd bring into this fucked up situation.

Because I'm pretty sure that over the past six weeks, I've fallen in love with Regan Lucas.

I lower my head to the desk, banging my forehead over and over on the unforgiving mahogany. Of course I've fallen in love with her. I'm Lucas Montana. It's what I do—fall in love with women and then leave them high and dry.

It's why I refuse to do it to Regan. Not her.

She'll get over it quickly. Much more easily than I will. She'll move on and go back to her original plan, never having known my true feelings. She'll just think I did a typical *me* thing, bailing out of something at the last minute. Maybe she'll even hate me. And maybe it's what I deserve.

I grab my keys off the corner of my desk and head down the hall.

I pass Allie in reception. It looks like she's just getting done with a tour. "Leaving early on a Monday?" she says. "Kind of unlike you."

"Just running an errand. I'll be back later."

My younger sister waves and dances happily back to her office.

On my drive, I think about Allie. She's been in a long-distance, friends-with-benefits relationship dating back to last Christmas when she met Dallas's girlfriend's older brother. Her *much* older brother. Although Asher lives thousands of miles away in Florida, he travels a lot for business and they get together every time he's in the city. No planning. No strings. Just a fun, no expectations liaison.

I'm jealous of what they have. Why can't I, for once in my miserable life, not fall hard and fast for the girl?

I could have just texted Regan back, but this conversation calls for more than a 'see you around' blow-off text. Even if I can't tell her my real reason for backing out, she deserves an explanation.

On McQuaid Circle, I park in front of Truman's Grocery. It's early afternoon on a Monday. I thought most people would be at work, but the street is bustling with people. Kids seem to be everywhere. Then I see the red-white-and-blue banners that still adorn all the light posts and remember what week it is. July 4th was just a few days ago. It's summer vacation for kids, and many people have the week off.

Familiar faces are everywhere. This is a bad idea. I put my car in gear and pull down the street, through the roundabout, and park once again, this time behind Lloyd's Steakhouse. Then I walk down the alley, hoping none of the other business owners pick this moment to take out their trash.

Me: I'm at your back door.

It takes far longer than I expect for her to let me in. And once she does, I realize why. Her shop is dark, as if she never opened up for the day. Damn, she must be really torn up. And I'm about to drop even more bad news on her.

"Hey," she says and turns. "Come on up."

Once upstairs, I see her cat and try to lighten the mood. "How *you* doin'?" I say to the furball.

My joke falls completely flat as I follow Regan into the kitchen. She takes a seat and motions to the table. Upon inspection, there must be a dozen pregnancy tests laid out in front of her. I step closer, my eyes darting from one to the next, until my brain catches up with what my eyes are seeing.

I look up and Regan is smiling from ear-to-ear, her dimples as clear as I've ever seen them. "We're pregnant!" She covers her mouth and tears come to her eyes. "Oh my gosh, that's the first time I've said it out loud. This is real. It's actually happening. Can you believe we did it the first month? I'm still wrapping my head around it."

I pull out a chair and fall heavily onto it. She rambles on and on, but only one thing is registering. The woman I'm in love with is pregnant. And I absolutely *cannot* tell her. My plan—my entire plan to walk away and try to forget about her, to move on with my life and let her move on with hers—it's all just gone up in flames. Because I'm tied to her for the next eighteen years. Longer even.

Fuck my life.

I have a feeling I'm going to be living in my own personal hell for... *ever.*

"Lucas?... Lucas, are you okay?"

"What? Oh, yeah. Wow. This is incredible. I told you my swimmers were good."

She laughs. "I guess so."

I pick absently at the table. "So what happens now? Have you been to the doctor yet? When is it due? Can we find out the sex?"

She laughs again. She's downright giddy. Me, I'm miserable. I want to take her in my arms and tell her I'm in love with her. I want to celebrate us becoming a family. I want to actually *make* us a family.

But we're not one. We're the furthest thing from a family as you can get. Technically, we're now bound by the legal contract we both signed. The business transaction we agreed to. The one that has me being the occasional weekend dad and her the primary parent.

I want to find the contract and rip it to shreds. I don't want to be a weekend dad. I don't want every other holiday. I want every holiday. I want every *day*. With her. With them.

"I just found out today," she says. "I haven't even called the doctor. I doubt they'd want to see me for at least a few weeks. It's still so early. But I did look up the due date."

"How?"

"The baby's due date is based off your last period. Mine was June seventh. That puts the baby due on March fourteenth."

"Holy shit."

I feel the blood drain from my face. This is real. I did this. I agreed to this. Hell, it was my fucking idea. And now I have to live with what I've done.

Her hand touches my arm. "Are you okay?"

"Yeah." I shake my head, trying to get my blood flowing again. "It's just... I mean I knew what we were doing, but it's all so unreal."

Her smile falls. "Are you disappointed it happened on the first try?"

"No. Of course not."

"Liar." She narrows her eyes. "Do you really want a kid, or was it a ruse to have regular sex with someone who doesn't think you're a pariah?"

"I want a kid, Regan. I wasn't lying about that." I shrug. "Still, can you blame me if I'm a red-blooded man who wanted to spend a little more time in the sack with a beautiful woman?"

"Sorry," she says, her grin reappearing. "Guess you'll have to go back to spending more time with your right hand."

I snicker disingenuously. "Guess so."

She stands. "I should open the shop. I was just too shocked to do it earlier. I'll let you know how the doctor's appointment goes."

"You'll let me know? Regan, I want to be there."

She cocks her head. "You do?"

"Yes. I do. It's my kid too. Like I said, I want this."

This and more, a voice screams in my head.

"There will be rumors if anyone sees you there."

"I'll have them bring me in the back door or whatever. Ah man, don't tell me Hudson McQuaid is your doctor. Please, anyone but him."

"You think I want my friend's husband all up in my business? No way. It's Dr. Russo. I'll text you the day and time. If you can't make it, I'll give you the CliffsNotes."

"I'll make it."

"What if you're out of town?"

"Regan, I said I'll make it. But listen, here's what you should do. When you get to the office and they take you back to an exam room, that's when you ask the doctor to bring me in through the back door. I'll park a ways down the street and wait there."

"It's going to be hard to keep this a secret if anyone suspects."

"We'll do what we can, but sooner or later, everyone will know."

She nods. "Okay." She motions to the door. "I really should open up."

As I descend the stairs, still in a state of shock, she calls my name. I glance back.

"Don't forget." She smiles brightly. "You have to quit smoking now."

I hold up a dismissive hand. "Yup. Sure thing."

In minutes, I'm back in my car lighting up. I take a long drag off one of the last cigarettes I'm ever going to have and think of how I was just kicked out. *Again.*

Oh, how ironically poetic it is to have the tables turned.

~ ~ ~

I smoke two cigarettes on the way back. It's only a twenty-minute drive from Regan's to the winery, but I sit in my car and smoke two more, emptying my pack, wondering what kind of father I'll be—hoping I'll be a good one. Knowing I can't fuck this up. Not this.

Am I happy? Yes, I think I am. I think I'm fucking ecstatic. I'm going to be a dad. It's something I thought would never happen. I thought the door to that had been closed, sealed, and nailed shut after leaving Lissa.

It's just, when I agreed to this... no, when I *suggested* it, I didn't imagine things would get so complicated.

Back in my office, I sit and blindly stare at the crumpled pack of Marlboros in my trash can.

"What's eating you, brother?" Blake asks from the doorway, a box tucked under his arm.

"You have no fucking idea."

He steps inside, closes the door, and deposits the box on the corner of my desk. "Your industrial sized box of Post-it notes." He sniffs the air around me and scowls. "Why do you smell like a goddamn chimney? I thought you were going to kick that nasty habit."

I nod to the trash. "I just did."

He laughs heartily. "Right." He takes the seat across from my desk. "So what's up?"

I shouldn't tell him. I shouldn't tell anyone. We agreed to keep it a secret as long as possible. But it's eating away at me like a fast-growing cancer. I have to talk about it. I have to tell someone.

"I'm..." I lean back in my chair, look up at the ceiling, and let out a long, deep sigh. "I'm going to be a dad."

Just saying the words knocks the breath right out of me. I knew what I was doing. I knew it would probably happen sooner or later. I just didn't know I would feel like this. I didn't realize there would be this intense need inside me to protect the little being that's no more than a bundle of cells at this point. And more… to protect its mom.

"Holy crap." He scrubs a hand across his jaw. "You got someone pregnant?" His eyes go wide. "Oh, shit, it's Regan, isn't it? Bad move, brother. Thought you were smarter than to let that happen."

"I didn't let it happen. We planned it."

He almost falls out of his chair. "You *what?*"

"Not only that. It was *my* idea." I shake my head, wanting to regret it, but knowing I don't.

I tell Blake everything.

"Dude, are you crazy? So you're just going to share custody, both of you being part-time single parents?"

"We have a contract. Candace drew it up for us. Regan will be the primary parent."

He scratches his head over and over. "Why are you doing this?"

"Same reason she wanted to. Something was missing in my life."

He belts out a maniacal laugh. "You mean other than the four fiancées you ditched?"

"I get enough shit from everyone else, Blake. I don't need it from you."

He holds up his hands. "Fine. Fine. But, damn, you really thought this out."

I rub my eyes. "Wait. It gets worse."

He stares at me, trying to read me. He pinches the bridge of his nose. "Oh, hell. You went and fell for her, didn't you?"

My door swings open. It's Dallas. "I wanted to—" He stops talking when he sees our serious expressions "Okay," he says, stepping inside. "What'd I miss?"

Blake pats the empty chair next to him. "Have a seat, brother. And shut the door."

Chapter Twenty-eight

Regan

I press my cheek against the porcelain throne, exhausted once again from my morning vomit sessions.

Two weeks ago, when I hit the five-week mark, is when it started. As I sit hunched over the toilet, it's hard to believe it's actually gotten better. A few days ago, after a call with Dr. Russo, I discovered if I eat crackers in the middle of the night, my morning sickness isn't as bad.

I chuckle inwardly, thinking how vomiting for a half hour straight is still an improvement over the two hours I was tied to the toilet previously. I wanted this. I brought it on myself. This too shall pass.

The funny thing is, at least having morning sickness is confirmation that I'm actually pregnant. And there *is* a tiny baby growing inside me. It's the thought I cling to when I feel like nothing else can possibly come out of me and then I practically vomit up a lung.

It is strange that, with all the sickness, I still have an appetite. Just not until mid-morning.

I'm sitting slumped against the wall, hoping I'm done for today, when the doorbell rings. I bolt upright, willing myself not to throw up. Because few people know of the hidden doorbell on the back door of the shop.

When I was a kid, there was a group of teenage thugs who would skateboard down the alley and ring the doorbells of every business. My dad got sick of it after a few weeks and disconnected it, only to install a new, hidden one only his wholesale book suppliers knew about.

Oh, no. *No, no, no, no.* It can't be my parents. My head slumps into my hands. That would be the absolute worst thing ever. Please let it just be some kid playing around.

When the doorbell rings again, I look at Joey, curled up outside the bathroom door where he sits every morning, patiently awaiting my return to the living. "It's not them," I say. "Fate couldn't be so cruel."

It rings a third time. I get up off the floor, feeling semi-sure I'm not going to hurl anymore, and slip on my robe. When it registers that it's only eight-thirty in the morning, my heart sinks. It's not a bratty teen playing a prank. Teens aren't up at this hour in the summer.

I quickly swish my mouth out with water and take a long drink. Then I head for the stairs, just as it rings three more times in quick succession.

Is it Lucas? He knows how sick I've been. Is he coming to check on me?

No. He doesn't know about the doorbell. Plus, he'd text. Or just walk in as he likes to do. Then again, I have started locking up for the most part. Unless my pregnancy brain has me forgetting to, of course.

I hesitate as I walk through the shop and approach the back door. I slowly put my eye against the peephole as if the inconsiderate person on the other side might be able to see me. But then, relief envelops me like a warm blanket when I see who it is. I unlock and swing the door open and throw my hands around my brother's neck. "Ryder!"

He laughs as I hug him tightly. "I wasn't aware I'd get such a welcoming greeting."

"Are you kidding? I'm just glad it's not Mom and Dad."

"Why don't you want Mom and Dad here?"

I shake my head, coming up with a plausible excuse. "You know how they can be, wanting to micromanage everything. Trying to tell me how to run the business and all. I just like it better when I see them on their turf, not mine."

"Fair enough. Are you going to invite me up?"

"Yes, of course. Come in." I look behind him for his wife. "Where's Amy?"

"Long story."

I spot his car parked in one of the two spots reserved for me in the alley. "You *drove* here? All the way from Colorado?"

"I did. So I'd really appreciate a cup of coffee while I explain." He follows me to the stairs, taking a moment to look around the shop. "I like what you've done with the place."

"If you'd bother showing up once in a while, you'd have seen all the renovations I made over the years."

He shrugs. "Amy never did like it here."

"So I'm guessing if you're here, that means…"

"Coffee first, big sister."

"Okay. Don't judge. My place is a mess." I stiffen when I think of a few things I don't want him to see. Namely the pregnancy books sitting on the coffee table. "Wait here," I say at the top of the stairs. "I just want to tidy up first."

"It's not like I didn't grow up seeing all your girl shit lying around, Regan."

I shoot him a hard stare. "Just wait here for two seconds."

I race across the room, gather up the books, and do a quick visual sweep for anything else that might give me away. I tuck the evidence in my nightstand drawer and head back out.

Ryder is in the kitchen petting Joey.

I roll my eyes. "Gee, thanks for waiting."

"You got a new cat," he says. "Wasn't sure you would after what happened with that fucker, David."

My stomach rolls at the mental picture of what he did to Chandler, and I will myself not to throw up.

"His name is Joey."

Joey rubs against his leg, purring at the attention he's getting. I narrow my eyes. How come he likes Ryder and not Lucas?

"So… coffee? And can I use your bathroom?"

I motion to the hall, praying he doesn't go through my bathroom drawers. "You know where it is." I start brewing a cup for him. For him, not for me. I haven't been able to stand the taste of it for weeks, which has made Tuesday nights difficult with me secretly dumping Ava's liquid gold under the picnic table.

When Ryder returns a few minutes later, he looks bummed. Oh, god, he saw something.

I hand him a mug and sit at the table, waiting for him to lay into me.

"You made the second bedroom into a closet?" he asks, looking absolutely disheartened as he sits next to me.

"Yeah, so?"

He turns the coffee cup around several times by the handle. "I was hoping I'd be able to crash here for a while."

My hand finds its way on top of his. "Oh, Ryder. Did she kick you out?"

I try to sound sympathetic when saying it. They have been married for years. But I never liked her, or the way she kept him from coming home. The way she dictated where they lived, what jobs she wanted him to have, and how they spent their time. It always reminded me too much of David.

He shakes his head. "I left."

"Finally came to your senses, huh?"

"I know the two of you never got on like sisters, but—"

"But she's your wife and you love her."

He closes his eyes, sighs, then takes a long drink. "Why is that?" He narrows his eyes. "Why do you think I stayed all these years? Wasted all that time on a woman who was clearly so self-involved that she was incapable of really loving anyone?"

I point to myself. "You're asking me? The one who stayed with David, sacrificing my passion and my health?"

He snorts. "Guess we're two peas in a pod then."

"What finally did it? Why now?"

He pinches the bridge of his nose like he's getting a migraine. "She's been cheating on me with one of my co-workers."

My mouth opens wide. "Seriously?"

He nods. "I'm pretty sure it's been going on for a while. She became less interested in sex—another thing she always controlled about our relationship. I should have known what was happening. The guy was just too fucking nice to me at work."

"How'd you find out?"

"Caught them in bed. *Our* bed."

My hand flies to my mouth. "I'm so sorry."

"No, it's good. I needed the wake-up call. I threw all my shit in my car and just drove. I wasn't even sure where I was going at first. All my friends are her friends. It was either Sarasota or here. And well… recreational pot isn't legal in Florida, and we both know how Mom and Dad can be." He motions to the couch. "So, what do you say? Can I crash on your couch until I can figure something else out?"

"You smoke pot? Since when?"

"For years, Regan. Mostly because of anxiety, which I now realize was directly related to my soon-to-be ex-wife."

My head spins. He smokes weed. He's getting divorced. He wants to live here. I can't deny my little brother in his time of need, but… my morning sickness. How am I going to hide it from him?

"I'm not sure how comfortable you'll be on the couch. It's old and lumpy. And no smoking up here. Do it in the alley."

"Fine." He shrugs. "I can pick up an air mattress or something and put it in your… closet."

"Okay."

"Thank you. I just don't know what's going to happen, you know, with the money and all. Amy was the one who paid all the bills and handled our accounts and investments. We have savings, but I'm not exactly sure just how much."

"But *you're* the one with the business degree."

"I know, Regan. You don't have to remind me what a fucking doormat I've been." He scrubs a hand across his stubbled jaw. "Guess I need to hire a lawyer."

I check the time. "Ryder, I'd like to stay and talk, but I'm supposed to meet someone downstairs in a half hour. I have to go get ready. I'll clear a drawer for you in the bathroom. And later, we can clear a space for an air mattress."

He nods sadly.

"You can always come down to the shop. We can talk more there."

"I think I'll probably sleep all day. It was a long drive."

"You drove straight through?"

"Thirty hours straight, including stopping for food and gas."

I get up and hug him from behind. "Thank goodness you're even alive. How did you not fall asleep at the wheel?"

He grabs my hands and squeezes. "Pure rage I suppose."

"I'll get you a pillow. Or… I guess you could use my bed, but the sheets haven't been changed in a while."

"The couch will be fine for today. I'm so tired I could sleep on concrete."

"Okay." I back away and head for my room. "Ryder?" I say, turning.

"Hmm?"

"I'm glad you're here. Despite the circumstances, it's nice to see you again. And I hope you stay in town. I've really missed you. I know we were never that close because of our age difference, but maybe things can change now."

He smiles. "I'd like that a lot."

As I get ready, I realize how much I meant what I said. I would like to be closer. Even if now is not exactly the ideal time. I mean, how am I going to tell my little brother I'm having a baby with his childhood friend and college roommate? And that said friend was nothing more than a fuckbuddy turned baby daddy. Will he be mad? Will he hate Lucas?

Even through all these unknowns, I'm still glad he's here. Maybe being pregnant has made me realize how important family is. How important siblings are.

I drop my shirt and sit on my bed, stunned at the thought. Because even though I'm just barely pregnant, and regardless of the fact that I'm thirty-five, I think I've just decided that I want my kid to have a brother or sister.

I cock my head and wonder if Lucas would be up for the task. Then I laugh. Because we sooooo need to see how this one goes first.

Speaking of Lucas, I pull out my phone.

Me: You'll never guess who just showed up on my doorstep.

Chapter Twenty-nine

Lucas

I still can't believe Ryder is back in town. When Regan told me yesterday, I wanted to go over and see him, but we both thought it would be better if I waited for him to reach out. Or for word to get around that he's here. Which shouldn't take long if he steps foot outside her shop.

But we agreed on one thing—not to tell him he's going to be an uncle.

She still doesn't know I told Blake and Dallas. I swore them to secrecy.

In the same conversation, Dallas swore us to secrecy about his upcoming proposal as well. He's going to ask Marti to marry him. We've all known it was coming. They've been living together for months, along with her son, Charlie. But we assumed it might take longer for him to get there after all he's been through. Losing his first wife and son several years ago really did a number on him.

He, of all people, deserves a happy ending. I stare off in the distance at the rear entrance of the doctor's office. *Do I?*

Finally, after sitting in my car for twenty-five minutes, I get a text.

Regan: Dr. Russo will meet you at the back door in two minutes.

Me: I'll be there.

I hop out of my car, race stealthily across the lot, and stand near the door, shifting my weight from foot to foot in nervous anticipation.

What feels like hours later, but is most likely only seconds, the door opens and an older lady wearing a white coat appears. "Mr. Montana, come in. I've got Regan in the room right over here."

She motions to a door very near where she's standing and ushers me through to where Regan is sitting on an exam table.

"I appreciate you going through all the trouble," I say, removing my ball cap.

"This isn't the first time I've been asked to bring a father in discreetly," the doctor says. "You can sit there. We're going to do Regan's ultrasound. I like to make sure the pregnancy is viable before we go into all the specifics. Assuming we find a heartbeat, we'll discuss the next steps."

"We're going to see the baby?" I ask.

"That's the hope. At seven weeks, the fetus should be about the size of a coffee bean, or M&M if you prefer. About one centimeter in length."

I smile and look at Regan. "M&M? As in Mitchell Montana? That's got to be a sign."

Regan rolls her eyes and lies back.

Dr. Russo holds up a long wand sheathed in what looks like an oversized condom and lubes it up. "This might feel strange."

Regan giggles. "That? Oh, that's nothing." She catches my eyes and grins widely.

Now *I'm* the one rolling my eyes.

The doctor studies the ultrasound screen for a minute and types on the keyboard with her left hand as she holds the wand inside Regan with her right. Then she points. "This here, that black space, is the amniotic fluid. And this right here is the baby. I can visibly see cardiac activity."

She pushes a button on the keyboard, and we hear a fast-paced *thump thump thump* echo throughout the exam room. "Fetal heart rate is one hundred sixty beats per minute. Perfect."

Regan lets out a huge sigh.

Dr. Russo points out some anatomy that I have trouble deciphering. "This bulge is the heart. Right now, your baby is in the fetal pole stage, which means it's curved and has a tail similar to a tadpole. When we do the anatomy scan between eighteen and twenty-two weeks, you'll see quite a difference."

Regan rises up on her elbows. "So everything looks normal?"

"It does. You're measuring right at seven weeks. And based on your last menstrual period, that puts the due date at—"

"March 14th," I say.

The doctor looks up. "I see you've been doing your homework." She removes the wand, throws out the condom thing, and places it back in the holder. "I'll step out for a moment to let you put your pants on, Regan. Normally, I'd have you come to my office for a talk, but why don't we just do it here to reduce the risk of prying eyes. I'll be back in a few minutes." She hands a strip of black-and-white photos to Regan. "These are for you."

As she leaves the room, Regan stares at the printouts. "It's really happening."

I pull the chair closer, but I'm not looking at the photos. I'm looking at *her*. She's so happy she's practically glowing. And she's so goddamn beautiful.

She looks up from the photos and chuckles. "Why, Lucas Montana, don't tell me you're getting all teary-eyed over this."

I sniff and straighten my spine, trying to man the fuck up. "Me? No, uh—"

She touches my arm and a bolt of electricity shoots through me. "I'm kidding. But isn't this exciting!"

"That it is."

She sits up and makes a face. "Lucas? Can you hand me some tissues? I'm all lubed up down there."

I swallow and try to think of anything else but how slippery she might be *down there*.

Well, shit.

I curse my burgeoning erection as I hand Regan the tissues.

She doesn't fail to notice my rising problem, and her eyes home in on my crotch. "Are you seriously turned on right now? Here. In the doctor's office?"

"Like I can help it." I sit back down, hoping for some camouflage. "It's a perfectly natural physiological reaction to a beautiful half-naked woman talking about how slippery her pussy is."

She laughs out loud. "Did you just say pussy?"

"I did. Why? Did it turn you on?"

She laughs again. But I swear, for one brief moment, she's trying to decide if it did.

"Lucas, I threw up five times this morning, and my boobs hurt so much they're practically throbbing. If you think there's any way in hell I could be turned on right now, you're crazy." She wipes her crotch. "Anyway, your job is done." She holds out the tissues. "Here."

I look at the soiled tissues like they carry the plague.

Her eyes roll. "Lucas, if you can't touch a few tissues with KY Jelly on them, how will you ever change a diaper?"

I take them from her carefully, holding them only with the tips of my fingers, and cross the room to deposit them in the trash. Yup, that did the trick, my boner is definitely gone.

Regan gets off the table and puts on her pants. Well, not pants. Tights. Bright blue ones. And damn it if I don't feel another tingle below the belt.

"How are things going with Ryder?" I ask.

"Fine. He's manning the shop."

"Ryder? Selling women's clothing? I find that hard to believe."

"If he wants to keep crashing at my place rent free, he's going to help when I need it."

"You think he's going to stay in Calloway Creek?"

"I do."

"It'll be nice to reconnect with him. If you think he'd still want to be friends after finding out I knocked you up."

"I think Ryder will need all the friends he can get."

"Good." I nod. "That's good."

In spite of the fact that I had ulterior motives for becoming his friend way back when, I was always glad I did. We had a lot in common. We both liked sports and video games. We were interested in going to the same college. And we both got our degrees in business.

When he took up with Amy, I saw him less and less. When they moved in together our senior year, he became almost a stranger. They took off to her hometown after graduation, and other than his wedding soon thereafter, and the occasional phone call, I have no idea what he's been doing.

There's a knock on the door and Dr. Russo comes back into the room. She pulls over the rolling stool and looks from me to Regan. "Well then, let's go over the usual things. Regan, as with any geriatric pregnancy, there are—"

"Excuse me," I say, brows knit. "Geriatric?"

"Regan is over thirty-five. That places her at an advanced maternal age. It comes with elevated risks."

I turn to Regan. "Did you know about this?"

"Relax, Lucas. I *just* turned thirty-five. It's going to be fine."

"Most likely, it will," Dr. Russo says. "But I'll still go over the risks. You have a higher chance of miscarriage, preeclampsia, gestational diabetes, premature birth, and chromosomal and other genetic disorders. And with your BMI being what it is, there are compounding risks. We'll keep a close eye on your blood pressure as you're at risk for gestational hypertension."

"I'll buy her one of those home machines," I say.

The doctor nods. "Being proactive will definitely help."

"What else can we do?"

Regan looks at me and smiles. Does she like how I said 'we?' Because I sure as hell do. But then her words from earlier echo through my head. *'Your job is done.'*

"Make sure all of your preventative care is up to date," the doc says. "Take a prenatal vitamin that includes folic acid. Exercise regularly, even if it's just a brisk walk through the park. Don't smoke or use alcohol. Reduce stress levels and get plenty of sleep. Eat a healthy diet with plenty of fruits, vegetables and whole grains. And with your BMI, I'd like you to keep your weight gain to less than twenty pounds."

"Not a problem with as much as I've been vomiting," Regan says.

"That may be true now, but your morning sickness will probably go away as you near the second trimester."

They talk about her weight for a minute, but I'm still stuck on a few horrible words the doctor said. "Miscarriage... premature birth... genetic disorders. That's a lot of scary shit, Doctor. Pardon my French."

"I don't mean to scare you. We'll do blood testing around ten weeks to rule out chromosomal abnormalities. I'll have you come in for early glucose screening. If you start experiencing frequent headaches, contact me." She pats Regan's hand. "Odds are you and the baby will be fine. Your chances of having a healthy baby are still much higher than miscarriage." She stands. "I'll see you back here once a month until the third trimester. Should any problems arise with blood pressure or whatnot, we will increase that frequency. You can meet with Janice out front to work out the billing."

"I'm not going out front," I say, locking eyes with Regan. "But I'll be paying for all of it." I pull a business card out of my pocket. "Can this Janice be discreet?"

"We're all bound by HIPAA," Dr. Russo says, taking my card. "I'll have her bill you."

I laugh. "HIPAA or not, we all know rumors spread like wildfire in this town."

Dr. Russo nods. "I'll do everything in my power to prevent that. But sooner or later..."

"We're just hoping for later," Regan says, sliding down from where she sat on the exam table. She takes my business card back from the doctor. "I'll pay it myself." She looks at me. "You can transfer me the funds after."

"That might be wise," the doctor says, confirming my fears. She motions to the door. "Shall I escort you out the back, Mr. Montana?"

Right. Regan is going out the front. *Alone.* I'll quietly leave while she pays the bill and goes back to work. There will be no gushing over the ultrasound pictures. No talking about the excitement of hearing the heartbeat. No walking out of the doctor's office hand-in-hand discussing what will happen when we find out the sex of the baby. Just the two of us going about our separate lives.

A deep sense of sadness washes over me when I realize this is the life I've subjected myself to.

Chapter Thirty

Regan

"Another three miles in the books," Lucas says as we approach the trailhead.

Since the day we left Dr. Russo's office, Lucas has insisted I meet him for the 'brisk walk' the doctor prescribed. Three times a week, we secretly and separately meet just before dusk at one of the trailheads at the rear of Calloway Creek Park. If we see anyone approaching, which rarely happens, he jogs ahead as if he's just passed me on his nightly run.

This time, though, our luck runs out and we're caught red-handed as Lucas's brother Blake comes blazing around the last turn and almost plows into me.

"Whoa!" Lucas says, making sure there isn't a collision. "Watch where you're going."

"Oh, hey," Blake says apologetically. "Sorry, Regan." His eyes dart between us, amusement dancing in them even in the ensuing darkness. "How are you?"

"I'm great. Just out for a walk. Lucas here almost plowed into me just before you did," I say, trying to explain our close proximity.

"Of course he did."

I don't miss how Lucas shoots Blake a disapproving glare.

"How's Ellie?" I ask.

"She's good," he says as well as signs like it's a habit. "She mentioned you the other day. She has a big load of clothes she'd like to drop off."

"Tell her I'd appreciate anything she has."

"Will do. See you around." He lifts his chin at Lucas and continues his run.

I turn, hands on hips. "Why didn't your brother seem surprised to see us together?"

Guilt is written all over Lucas's face.

"Oh my god, you told him." I shake my head when he doesn't deny it. "Lucas, we said we'd wait. Do you know how hard it's been for me to keep this a secret from Ryder? For three weeks, I ran down to the shop to throw up in the boutique bathroom just so he wouldn't hear me retching up my insides. Do you realize how difficult it's been not to say anything to Maddie and Ava? To my other friends? Especially Amber, who has a new baby now? And Nikki, who's pregnant herself?"

"I'm sorry."

"Does anyone else know?"

"Just Dallas."

"How long have they known?"

He paces in a circle. "I told them the day we found out."

My jaw slackens. "They've known for months?"

"I'm sorry. I couldn't keep it in. I didn't realize how much finding out I was going to be a dad would affect me. I just had to talk about it with someone."

"How do you think *I* feel?" I touch my stomach. "I'm the one growing the tiny human."

"So tell Maddie and Ava."

"Maybe I will."

"Good. Because it is nice having someone to talk about it with." He nudges my elbow. "You know, other than you."

Sometimes… okay, lots of times… I could swear he's flirting with me. He's quick to grab onto my arm if he thinks I'm about to stumble. And if I'm not mistaken, he holds on a bit too long. He's always complimenting the way I look, even when I'm sweaty after a walk. And he's been sending me deliveries of fruit baskets, my favorite pastries, and even the occasional meal from Goodwin's or Lloyd's.

Oh, and he sends me daily reminders to check my blood pressure. Which I'm happy to say has been near perfect.

He's doing so much for me. Then again, I could be entirely misreading the situation. After all, I am carrying his baby, and all of those things could be related to that.

Or… I'm imagining his sultry looks. His stolen glances. His prolonged touches. Maybe it's just my hormones gone amok. Because for the past few weeks, ever since the morning sickness abated, my hormones have definitely gone into overdrive. Which is to say, I'm horny.

All. The. Time.

And no matter how many times I masturbate—which isn't as often as I'd like, because Ryder is still crashing on an air mattress in the next room—I still can't scratch the itch.

When he leans in to touch my stomach, I almost kiss him. That's how sexually charged I am. I'm willing to complicate things by having another one-nighter with my baby daddy just to satisfy my carnal appetite.

"How's M&M doing today? He kick you yet?"

I'm amused by the nickname he's given our son. Yes—our *son*. Sometimes I still can't believe there is a little Lucas Montana inside me. The blood test we had a few weeks ago confirmed it, along with alleviating any stress we had over congenital defects. Everything was normal. So far, I'm having a textbook pregnancy.

"I told you that's probably not going to happen for months. Maybe longer since I have a little extra padding."

"Yeah, but he's a Montana," he says, in that flirty tone of his. "We've always been over-achievers."

I laugh, but in all honesty, I can't wait to feel those first kicks and flutters.

Then I realize we've been standing around far longer than necessary. And that maybe I'm enjoying his company a little too much. Damn hormones. "I'd better go before anyone else sees us."

He touches my shoulder. "See you Wednesday for another three miles?"

"That's the plan," I respond, as heat sears through me at his touch. I shake the feeling away and walk off toward home.

~ ~ ~

One hour, and two self-imposed orgasms in the shower later, I'm sitting on the edge of my bed feeling anything but satiated. My clit is practically tingling against the seam of my tights. And I can't get Lucas off my mind. His light touches. The way he smelled, both before *and* after our walk. His uber-sexy smile. How it's been months since his large hands wandered my body. His huge cock slid inside me.

Oh. My. God. I almost come just thinking about it.

"What is wrong with me?" I shout.

Ryder knocks at the door. "Everything okay?"

Making a split-second decision, I hop off the bed and stride to the door. I rip it open, catching him a bit off guard. "I'm fine. I'm going out."

"You hungry? You going for dinner?"

"Yes. I'm hungry. I'm very, very hungry." I hold out my palm. "Can I borrow your car?"

He shoves a hand in his pocket and comes out with his keys.

I'm through the door and heading down the stairs when he calls after me. "At least you could ask me if I want anything."

I throw up a dismissive hand, not bothering to turn around. I'm a woman on a mission, after all. "Not today. Sorry. See you later."

Ten minutes later, Lucas opens his door. His eyes widen in surprise. "Is everything okay?" He looks at my stomach. "The baby?"

I don't answer. I just push him back inside, shut the door behind me, and crash my lips to his.

Chapter Thirty-one

Lucas

I'm surprised as hell, and for a moment I think I must have fallen asleep and I'm dreaming. But I don't let my shock of reality keep me from kissing her back the way I have been in my dreams. I don't let it stop me from devouring her lips. Exploring her mouth with my tongue. Wandering her body with my hands.

Our mouths part momentarily. "Is this okay?" she asks, breathing heavily.

No. It's not. That's exactly what I should say. That it's most definitely not okay. Because it's hard enough to see her, go on walks with her, sit at her doctor's appointments, without saying something that will change the whole dynamic in this thing. Something that may even have her running back to Candace for legal advice. So I should one hundred percent tell her it's not okay and she should march back out my door.

But I don't say it. Even when I know it's wrong not to. That I'm deceiving her. That I have way more invested in this relationship than just my sperm.

"Hell yes it is."

"Good." With a huge smile, she grabs my hand and pulls me toward my bedroom, tossing me a sexy look over her shoulder. "Because I have needs."

I'm hard as a rock by the time we get there, thinking about her needs. I have my own needs. The need to bury myself deep inside her. The need to be with the mother of my unborn child. The need to tell her things I know I shouldn't be telling her.

Nearing the bed, she drops my hand and starts removing her shirt. I stop the motion. "Regan." I look her in the eye with dead-set determination. "I have needs, too. And one of them is to unwrap you like my favorite candy bar."

Her neck extends as she giggles. She holds her arms out, putting herself on display. "Unwrap away."

I take the hem of her long, bohemian-style shirt dress thing and pull it up and over her head, leaving her in only a bra and—surprise—brightly colored tights.

Kneeling, I undo the straps on her clunky black shoes, then I peel her like an onion, stripping the tights right down her legs.

Her belly is at the same height as my eyes. It's soft and squishy and round, but not any larger than I remember. *My kid is in there*. It's a concept that still boggles my mind every time I think about it. I stare at her middle and imagine a time when her belly will become prominent and hard. I touch her there as if waiting for the kicks I know I won't be able to feel for some time.

Regan clears her throat and looks down at me expectantly.

It's now that I realize she never asked me to turn off the lights. And I don't dare bring it up. Because I may be about to live another one of my fantasies.

"Sorry," I say at my hesitation. "I was just wondering if M&M is going to be bothered if he gets poked by the beast."

More laughter flows out of her.

Jesus, I love her laugh.

"He'll be fine. He's happily floating in a protective sack. Now can we get on with this? I'm hella horny."

Now *I'm* the one laughing. But it doesn't last long. Because now I understand what this is. I have the books. I've read about this. Regan is in her second trimester now. The morning sickness is gone. She's got extra blood flowing to her girl parts or something.

This is one hundred percent a bootie call. Nothing more.

And while a pang of disappointment jolts through me, who am I to waste time sulking over it when I have something so magnificent standing before me?

I push her panties down around her ankles and she steps out of them. Finally, I stand, reaching around her to unhook her bra. When it falls down her arms and I get my first look in three months, my eyes bug out.

My hands are immediately on her breasts. And, holy god. I thought her tits were great before, but these... these are fucking spectacular.

She exhales a mewl when I run my fingers across her nipples. When I take her left breast into my mouth, her body practically convulses. She fists my hair, tugging it hard as I twirl her nipple with my tongue.

Gently, my mouth still working her breast, I guide her a few steps back and urge her onto my bed. The seal gets broken when she sits. I push her back. Her plentiful breasts spill to the side and bounce when she crawls backwards on her elbows until all of her is on the mattress.

My pants are bursting at the seams with how hard I am. I'm rock fucking solid, and she hasn't even touched anything but my hair.

She eyes my captive bulge. "Are you going to stand there and stare at me, or are you going to get naked?"

I watch her watch me as I shed my clothing and climb on the bed next to her. The way her eyes rake over my body has heat building inside me. She looks at my tight abs like she wants to lick them. My thighs like she wants to squeeze them. My cock like she wants to—

"Fuuuuck," I drawl when her hand circles around my dick.

As she pumps me, I reach over and bury a hand between her legs. She's soaking wet, her pussy already drenched with her arousal when I slide a finger inside. Her back arches and her hand momentarily falls away. She touches me again, but when my thumb finds her clit, she moans loudly and loses her grip.

When her hand searches for me a third time, I brush it away, wanting her to lie back and enjoy this.

She doesn't fight me, and exhales another moan when I insert two fingers and crook them inside her. Her breathing is heavy and labored. Gentle high-pitched squeaks come out with every breath, driving my desire to achieve what has proved to be a near-impossible goal.

I can't help but scratch my own itch at the same time, rubbing my cock against her leg as I enjoy the soft noises escaping her.

And as her body writhes, her noises amplify, and her breathing quickens, I realize it might not be so impossible after all. When I think she could be on the precipice, I don't change a single goddamn thing I'm doing. All my motions remain the same. The way my thumb rhythmically circles her clit. How my fingers concentrate on one spot within her. I'm afraid if I change one miniscule thing, move one single iota, I'll break the pattern and pull her out of where she is. Because if I'm not mistaken, she's exactly where she needs to be.

Confirmation comes when her body seems to tighten, and her eyes fly open, capturing mine. My heart sinks, expecting her to tell me not to bother. That despite my efforts, there's no way she's getting there.

Miraculously though, that doesn't happen. I keep up those efforts, because I can see the surprise in her eyes even before I hear the keening in her voice.

"Oh… ahhh… oh, my god… ahhh!"

I can't tear my eyes from her face as she comes apart right before me. Sensationally. Magnificently. Phenomenally.

Holy shit, I've never seen such a sight.

I swear her orgasm lasts ten seconds. Maybe twenty. I don't change a goddamn thing I'm doing the entire time. Not even when my balls tighten up and I swear I'm about to explode.

"Lucas… ahhh!"

That's it. I'm fucking toast. Hearing her shout my name has me jizzing all over her hip as I join her in the last few moments of her orgasm.

I remove my cramped fingers and drop onto my back next to her, amazed at what just happened.

She's breathing heavily. I listen as it calms, then turn and wait for her eyes to open again.

When they do, her cheeks flush. "Oh my god, I just—"

"Yeah you did. Spectacularly, I might add." I laugh out loud. "So spectacularly, in fact, that I did too."

Her eyes widen and a hand flies to her mouth. "Seriously?" She belts out a sigh. "Thank god, because I thought I might have wet myself."

Now I'm laughing even harder. Her amazing giggles join in.

When we settle, she stares at the ceiling. "That was… wow. I mean, I've been super horny lately, but I still didn't actually expect it to happen. But once it started, unlike all the other times, it was like a freight train I had no chance of stopping." She looks around. "Did we really keep the lights on?"

I chuckle. "You were a woman on a mission." I hop off the bed. "Be right back."

I go into the bathroom and get some tissues. Back at the bed, I'm wiping my jizz off her thigh when she squirms. I raise a brow at her.

"Sorry. You touching me there is getting me all tingly again."

I perk up, having thought that was it, that's all there was. "Seriously?"

She nods, face reddening. "I just can't seem to get, I don't know, satisfied."

I toss the tissues off the bed and spread her legs. "Challenge accepted."

"You don't think I could…" Her head shakes. "No way."

I position myself between her legs and lower my head. "I think we're about to find out."

Not more than two minutes later, she's coming again under the ministrations of my tongue. I reach up and play with a nipple, hoping it'll prolong it. It does. And, holy shit, those noises. I'm already hard again.

Before she's done quivering, I crawl up and hover over her. "Regan, can I…?"

"Yes. God, yes."

I slip inside her, groaning as her last few pulses squeeze me. She's slick and tight and warm. It's the trifecta of perfection. Every man's dream. And I'm able to enjoy it longer this time, having come not five minutes ago.

As I slide in and out of her, I try to remember if this has ever happened before. I honestly can't remember one single time. In and out. One and done. I've never in my life given a woman multiple orgasms, and I sure as shit have never had two in the same night. Not unless one of them was at the mercy of my own hand.

This woman, though, she's different. She turns me on in ways I didn't think possible. The sweet, smooth, comforting timbre of her voice. It's like being wrapped in honey every time she speaks. The energy of her hips and the sensual silhouette of her body whenever she walks into a room. And her laugh. Jesus, her laugh. It hits me square in the balls every goddamn time. *Not only in the balls*, I think. *In my goddamn heart.*

I thrust into her gently again and again, feeling the sensation build with each deep penetrating plunge. My elbows lock and my jaw tightens as I grunt and spill my load inside her.

My head comes to rest on her shoulder as I catch my breath. "Jesus, Regan."

"I know." She giggles. "If I weren't already pregnant, I imagine that would have done the trick."

Pregnant. Right.

I roll off her. That's the only reason she's here. She's pregnant and horny and I'm the only viable candidate to satisfy her craving.

"Can I use your bathroom?" she asks.

I relax into my pillow. "Mi casa es su casa."

She shoots me a strange look. "Okay. Thanks."

I watch her curvy backside as she gathers her clothes and disappears into my bathroom. I follow, detouring at the closet to pull on a T-shirt and joggers.

Before I even have my work clothes off the floor and in the hamper, she's fully dressed. She smiles almost guiltily. "Well... thanks, I guess."

"You got it."

Her head tilts and she studies me. "You okay, Lucas?"

"Hey, I'm great," I lie. "I'm just happy it finally happened for you. Glad I could help."

"I didn't mean to barge in on you unannounced. I just—"

"Had needs. I get it."

Her eyes narrow, but she doesn't say anything else. She smiles one last time, walks out of the bedroom, and moments later I hear the front door close.

I sit on the bed that smells like sex warmed over, slumped down, forearms on my knees, feeling every emotion I imagine all my exes ever felt. And knowing I deserve every goddamn one.

Chapter Thirty-two

Regan

Lucas rolls off me, our bodies slick with sweat. "You're really making up for lost time, aren't you?"

Suddenly embarrassed that I've shown up unannounced for the fifth time in two weeks, I pull the covers over me. "I'm sorry. I know I'm probably being a big inconvenience."

He laughs and perches on an elbow. "Do you see me complaining? Every time just gets more incredible." He touches one of my ultra-sensitive nipples through the sheet. "I've never seen a woman come by nipple stimulation alone. That was seriously crazy."

"You're telling me. Three months ago I couldn't orgasm to save my life. Now you practically look at me and I do."

He eyes me strangely. "I'm just curious. And this is purely for research. But do you almost come when *other* guys look at you?"

"Other guys aren't exactly looking at me, Lucas."

"Oh, they are. You just don't realize it."

I roll my eyes. "Oh, you mean the way women look at you?"

"In case you missed the memo, women in this town are staying far, far away from me."

"Not that reporter lady, the one who keeps trying to get an interview with you. She definitely looks at you with fuck-me eyes."

He chuckles and leans over to take a sip of water from the bottle on his nightstand.

While staring at his back, I feel a strange twinge deep inside me. For a moment—just one brief second—I wonder if that feeling is jealousy. I shake it away as quickly as it came. Because that's ridiculous. Anything I'm feeling right now would simply be a product of my hormones.

I start to get up but realize I'm sore in places I didn't even know had muscles.

"I don't think I can move," I say, resting my head against a pillow.

"Then stay." He clears his throat, and I could swear he mumbles, "Bad idea, Montana," right before taking another drink.

"Stay?" I bring a hand to cover my heart in mockery. "And violate our contract with a forbidden overnight visit?"

I'm joking. But internally, something shifts. *Would I* want *to stay?*

Maybe morning sex with Lucas wouldn't be the worst thing. But it's an epically bad idea on so many levels.

"I wouldn't want to have to explain myself to Ryder. Speaking of which, did you know he's trying to clean up my ledgers? I think you and he are cut from the same cloth. He's much more organized than I am. How we share the same DNA surprises me."

"He's always had a good head for business. I knew that about him even back in college."

I turn on my side and face him. "You should stop sending me stuff. It's getting harder to explain it to him. He knows I don't make a ton of profit at the shop."

"I'm just trying to make sure my kid is eating healthy."

I rub my belly. "I'm getting all my fruits and veggies. I'm eating so well I've actually lost weight instead of gaining."

Shocked, he rises back up on an elbow. "Regan, that's not healthy."

"It's perfectly fine. I've talked about it with Dr. Russo. I'm not losing weight on purpose. I'm just eating better. And then with all the morning sickness I had, and growing a baby burns extra calories." I pat his hand. "Don't worry, I'm sure the weight will come back soon enough."

He traps my hand. "Promise me you're taking care of him. M&M is counting on you. *I'm* counting on you."

There's deep concern in his eyes. And there's something else. *Love.* He's already acting like a father. He's protecting his child.

"I promise I'm doing everything I can to keep us both healthy."

He nods in relief. "Good."

His hand falls away from mine and I swallow at the brief moment of emptiness I feel. Then I curse my hormones.

"Do you know I offered Ryder a job at the winery?"

I shift in bed. "Really? He didn't say anything."

"Probably because he turned me down."

"Why would he do that? I know he's been trying to figure his shit out while he waits for the divorce to go through, but why not make some money in the meantime?"

Lucas shrugs. "He says he has a plan and he's trying to come up with a way to make it happen."

"Plan? For what?"

"He wouldn't say."

"And I can't ask." I lean into the pillow and stare at the ceiling. "Otherwise he'd know you and I are talking."

"We should tell him. Isn't it safe to tell people now?"

"Now? Are you crazy? Now is most definitely not the time."

"Why not?"

"*Why not?*" I motion to the bed. "Because of this."

"This?"

"You and me. Sleeping together. I was going to tell Maddie and Ava weeks ago, but then this happened." I sit up, pulling a blanket around me. "Explaining having a kid and co-parenting with a friend is one thing." I wave my hand around. "If they found out about this, I'd be the laughingstock. The desperate hormonal single pregnant lady."

"No you wouldn't."

I shoot him a hard, challenging stare.

"Okay, so maybe there would be some gossip about how fucked up this situation is."

"Some? Lucas, the whole town will salivate over this. No, we need to wait."

"Until?"

"Until this passes. Until I'm not so flippin' horny all the time and sneaking over here for bootie calls." I glance at the soiled mattress between us. "Until *this* ends."

He sighs. He sighs big time. I can practically see disappointment ooze from him.

I'm just trying to figure out if he's upset that I'll eventually cut off the gravy train, or if he's frustrated about my hesitancy to tell people.

"Besides, it wouldn't hurt to be further along. Just in case."

He sits up, a sheet around his lower half, and scoots next to me. "You're still worried about miscarriage?"

"No." I shrug. "Yes." I sigh. "I don't know."

But what I don't tell him is that's not my only worry. I don't tell him that over the last few minutes I've now added to the list of things I have to worry about.

And when I look up and into his chocolate brown eyes, the twinge in my gut becomes a knot. Because I now know that what sits at the top of the list—my number one concern—is this unfamiliar feeling in my heart.

Chapter Thirty-three

Lucas

I swipe my phone back from Dallas when the waitress at the pub comes to take our order.

Both my brothers snicker loudly after she's gone.

"You really expect to keep this under wraps for *how* long?" Blake asks.

My eyes are glued to my phone as I stare at one of the pictures from the anatomy scan done earlier today. My kid. My son. All the parts of him are there. Everything measured exactly how it should have. We even saw him moving, which was all kinds of relief for Regan considering she hasn't felt him kick yet.

"I told you," I whisper. "She doesn't want it coming out while we're sleeping together."

"And that's going to end when?" Dallas asks, amused.

I look away. "Whenever she says it does."

"Damn." Blake whistles softly. "You've really got it bad, brother. And she doesn't even suspect?"

I shake my head. "I'm not going to ruin what we have because of my one-sided feelings."

Dallas's brow lifts. "You mean you don't want her taking away the milk."

"It is *so* not that," I say with a biting stare. "If I tell her, she'll pull away completely, and who knows, I may not even be invited to the birth. When we're together, she acts like we're best friends or something. Best friends who scratch each other's itches. If I go and ruin what she thinks we have—this amazing co-parenting relationship that comes with zero strings—it could change everything."

"So you're just going to spend the rest of your life pining for the mother of your kid?" Blake asks.

"I don't know." I throw my hands in the air. "I don't fucking know, okay?" I stare back down at the photo.

"What don't you know?"

My heart races as I look up at my sister. I hadn't even realized Allie was here. She scoots in next to me, pushing me over, and grabs my phone. Before I can take it away from her, her eyes bulge. "Lucas! Oh, my god, who's ultrasound is this?"

I stiffen and crane my neck around to see if anyone heard. "Would you shut up," I hiss.

"Wait." She covers her mouth in surprise. "Is this... *your* baby?"

My mind spins trying to come up with some reason—*any* reason—why I'd have an ultrasound photo on my phone. But there isn't one.

Blake and Dallas both cock their heads in amusement. They know I'm backed into a corner.

"You cannot tell *anyone*," I whisper between gritted teeth. "Not even Mia. Swear it."

"Oh, come on. Mia can keep a secret."

I cringe. "She was the first one to blab about Denise leaving Carter and Christian."

"She was a teenager. All teenagers gossip."

"That wasn't gossip. That was spilling the beans on a family secret."

Allie looks down at the table. "Lucas, believe me, she *can* keep a secret."

Something about the way she says it has me believing her. Like maybe Mia *has* kept a secret. For *her*. "Does this have anything to do with your fuck-buddy boyfriend?"

"His name is Asher. And he's not my boyfriend. But no. Nothing to do with that."

Oh, it's something. I can tell. But I don't push her, because I'm about to tell her *my* secret. "Don't tell her, Al. It's just for a little while, okay?"

"Fine," she huffs. Then she looks across the table. "Why don't the two of you look surprised?" Her hands go to her hips, elbows out in consternation, and she glares at me. "They already know?"

I shrug.

"Since when did the three of you become a boys' club with no girls allowed?"

"Since I know they can most definitely keep a secret."

"Says who?"

"Allie, they've known about this for four months. If they'd told anyone, *everyone* would have heard about it by now."

Her mouth opens so wide she could catch flies. "Four months?" She takes my phone again, and when the lock screen appears, she shoves it close to my face to unlock it. Then she studies the picture, tracing the baby's head with a finger.

"Next week will be halfway. Twenty weeks."

She uses her thumb and forefinger to zoom in on the photo. I know what she's doing, but she won't find it. When I took pictures of the photos, I made sure to exclude the name across the top. Then again, maybe she's looking for a penis. Or the lack of one.

"Who is she? When is she due? Is she from around here? Is the baby a boy or a girl?"

I answer the easiest question first. "It's a boy. See?" I take the phone and page through the photos until I find the penis-between-the-legs one. "He's due in March."

Her brow furrows. "A boy?"

She looks sad. Why would she be sad that it's a boy?

"Is he okay?" she asks. "I mean, did you have all the genetic testing and stuff?"

I'm surprised she's choosing to grill me over the baby and not the baby's mom.

"We've had all the testing. He's fine. This is the anatomy scan. We had it today. Everything is right on track."

She sighs, looking relieved. I find it strange that she'd be so worried.

"So, whose is it?" She claps, bouncing in her seat. "Oh please tell me it's someone I know. I love a good messy situation."

"It is." I shake my head. "Both messy and someone you know."

More clapping. "And you said 'we' had the testing done. Are you secretly a couple? What's the story?"

"Allie." I glance around again. "Would you keep your voice down?"

"Sorry. I'm just so excited I'm going to be an auntie again."

The waitress brings our food and we fall silent. Four pairs of eyes wait for her to leave. She looks at us strangely and says, "Hey, Allie. Do you want anything?"

Allie grabs one of my fries. "No thanks, Marci. My brothers like to share." She rolls her eyes. "Except when it comes to secrets that is."

I kick her foot under the table. "Thanks, Marci. I think we're good." Marci leaves and I glare at Allie. "*That's* why I didn't want to tell you."

"Relax. It's not like I'm going to *tell* her the secret. Jeez." She crosses her heart. "I promise I won't tell a living soul, including Mia. Okay? Now come on, are you going to make me guess?"

I sit back. "Well, that might be fun. Who would you guess?"

She chuckles. Then she thinks on it. "Ava Criss?"

"What? No. She's married."

"And she and Trevor have been trying to have a baby like forever. I figured maybe they talked you into knocking her up or something."

I huff out several incredulous breaths, because damn… she did hit it a little close.

"Nancy Leonard?"

"Nancy? I didn't even know she was in town."

She nods. "Her husband had an affair. She came back early this year. She's been lying low."

"It's not her."

"Can we be done with this game?" she asks, stealing more fries.

I lower my voice even more. "It's Regan."

Allie blinks repeatedly, then shouts, "Lucas?"

Thank god nobody would think anything of her shouting *my* name. "Jesus, Al."

"Sorry." She smashes her lips together, then whispers, "Lucas?"

"Do you know any other Regans?"

She looks from Dallas to Blake and then back to me. "But she's... I mean the way she dresses. And her attitude. Her whole way of life is just... just..."

"Different. I know."

"How did this happen? Are you dating? I mean, of all the people in this town, she's *the last* person I'd have guessed."

I snort. "Yeah, me too."

"So it was an accident. A one-night thing? Have you told Mom and Dad?"

"No. No. And no. It was intentional."

She swallows. "You *tried* to get her pregnant? So, you're together? Then why all the cloak and dagger?"

"We're not together. She wanted a kid. I wanted a kid. It just made sense."

"You want a kid? Since when?"

"It's a long story. But yeah, I want a kid. I'm serious about you not saying anything, Allie. She hasn't told anyone, not even Maddie and Ava."

"Why not?"

"At first, she didn't tell them because she knew they'd try to talk her out of it. Now, well, she just doesn't want to be the newest Calloway Creek gossip fodder."

"But she can't hide it forever."

"We know that. We just want a little more time."

She narrows her eyes. "What's she getting out of this? Did she talk you into this for your money?"

"She's not like that. She didn't even want to accept the child support recommended by our lawyer."

"You have a *lawyer?* What, did you sign some pre-baby contract that says what days you'll each get with him and shit like that?"

"Actually, yes."

Dallas and Blake watch our back and forth like a tennis match, stuffing their faces with cheeseburgers while enjoying the entertainment. Me—I push away my food. I'm not hungry.

I tell Allie everything. Well, not *everything*. I leave out the part that makes me look like a douchebag when I wanted hookups just to make Regan come. I also leave out the minor detail that, oh yeah, I'm in love with her.

"She should be able to hide it better than most," Allie says, taking a bite of my untouched burger. "Remember when Lily Knutson got knocked up? She's about Regan's size and she was able to hide it the entire time. Nobody knew she was pregnant until she left the hospital with a newborn. Sheesh! If that whole thing wasn't a scandal."

I remember that. It was about seven years ago when Lily Knutson and Doug Peters—both married at the time, and *not* to each other—became parents.

"We're not going to take it that far," I say. "I think once she tells Maddie and Ava, and maybe Ryder, she'll be ready to tell everyone." I point a finger at her. "If I hear even one rumor before then, I'll know it was you."

She holds up her hands innocently. "I'm *not* going to blab." She motions to my meal. "Are you going to eat the rest of that? Because I'm starving."

I push it toward her. "Go ahead."

"Um, brother?" Blake says, looking behind me. "Not to make a bad situation worse, but your ex is on TV again."

I rotate for a better position and see a new photo of Lissa and the senator's son. Their *wedding* photo. I stare at it for a second when it hits me—I have no regrets. She got her happily ever after. The one she deserves. I turn back around, unaffected. "Good for her. I hope she's happy."

Allie stares at me through slitted eyes, chewing her food. Then her eyes fly wide open. "Oh. My. God. You love her!" she whisper-shouts. "You love Regan."

I close my eyes, lean back, and try to sink into the booth. I'm not ready to have this conversation again. Because every time I do, I lose another piece of my heart.

Chapter Thirty-four

Regan

I page through the ultrasound photos, my eyes getting misty. It's happening. These photos prove it. Despite the fact that most days it doesn't feel like it. I cup my belly, that isn't much bigger than it usually is, and long to feel the hardness of my growing uterus underneath. The movement of my baby. *Any* signs of the life growing inside me.

Dr. Russo said those things will happen soon enough. Still—I crave them.

Is that why I haven't told anyone? Because it's just not real enough for me yet?

I trace my finger along the photo on my phone remembering Lucas's reaction to the ultrasound. His eyes were glued to the screen. When little M&M started moving around and we saw it, he took my hand and squeezed. I'm not even sure he knew he did it. It felt good. Normal even. It was comforting and exciting at the same time. And when he moved it away to point to something and ask Dr. Russo a question, I immediately wanted it back.

I've lost count of how many times I've visited Lucas over the past six weeks. A shameful amount, I'm sure. It's as if I'm addicted to his touch. Or the orgasms he provides. I've tried to convince myself the feelings aren't real. That those twinges inside me every time I see him, hear his voice, or even receive a text, aren't genuine. I tell myself it's the hormones. That I'd be sleeping with anyone who offered at this point. But I know I'm only fooling myself. Because I've gone and done the worst thing.

I've fallen for him.

I set down my phone, cover my face with my hands, and sigh. Because I know what this means. I can't go over to his place now.

Or ever.

It would be torture pining away for someone who is not, nor will ever be, able to commit to anything but the family business. And I'd be crazy to think I'm any different than all the other women.

He's committed to the baby.

But I guess we'll see about that. Only time will tell.

My heart hurts. I feel like I'm going through a breakup even though we were never technically together. Not really. And I only have myself to blame. I mean, I practically threw myself at the man. We've spent so much time together. On our walks. In bed. Of course I fell for him. He's handsome and kind and funny. And a stallion in the sack. What's not to love?

I stiffen. *Love?* No. No, no, no. That's not what this is. It's a crush. A crush fueled by my out-of-control hormones.

The bells over the front door chime and Maddie's grandmother comes into the shop. I paste on a smile. "Hey, Rose. I didn't know you were bringing anything today."

"I'm not. I was walking by and saw you sitting there looking sad. Is everything okay, sweetie?"

I nod rather unconvincingly.

She walks up to the counter. "Sometimes it helps to talk."

I swallow the tears that threaten, cursing my hormones once again. "Really, I'm okay, Rose."

She puts her old, weathered, freckled hand over mine. "It looks to me like you're anything but." She gives my hand a squeeze. "Does this have anything to do with that boy, Lucas Montana?"

I straighten and my eyes connect with hers. "No," I lie. "I mean, of course not. Why would you say that?"

"I see things, dear. And I get feelings. You're usually such a happy person, but to look at you now, nobody would think it. You have such a sad energy about you." She gazes right into my eyes and seems to leap directly into my soul. "The life in you normally shines so bright—" She stops talking mid-sentence and looks at my stomach, which I instinctively try to suck in. She nods over and over and pats my hand.

Could she possibly know?

"There are times in a woman's life where she just needs her friends," she says. "I think now is one of those times, no?" She's staring back into my eyes, waiting for me to disagree with her. "Fine, then. I'll send Maddie and Ava right over."

"I... I..." I can't think of a single reason why not. Rose is right. Whether or not she knows what's really going on with me, she's right. And it's time. I've put it off long enough. I blow out a deep sigh. "Okay. I was about to close up anyway."

"Everything will work out in the end, Regan."

"Thanks, Rose."

Thirty minutes later, my two best friends knock on my door. "Hey, guys. Thanks for coming."

Both of them look at me suspiciously. "Why did my grandmother arrange this meeting?" Maddie asks.

"Are you okay?" Ava says, eyeing me up and down. "You're not sick are you?"

I lead them into the living room. "Wait here, I'll get drinks." I look at Maddie. "Are you still nursing?"

"I am, but I can pump and dump." She narrows her eyes. "But, why are we drinking on a Monday night?"

"Just sit."

The apartment door opens, and Ryder walks through. *Oh, Jeez. Ryder.* I wasn't even thinking. Almost immediately I surmise this must be some sort of divine intervention, because honestly, do I want to have to do this twice?

Ryder sees Maddie and Ava on the couch. "Hey, guys." They wave as my brother slips by me and reaches for a beer. "I'll just take this to my room and give you some girl time."

"No, don't. Join us."

"Okay." He pops the top on his drink and plops down in the chair across from them.

I pour two glasses of wine and tuck a bottle of water under my arm and cross the room. Three pairs of eyes stare at me. It's Ava's I'm focused on. Because I know what I'm about to say might be a nail in her coffin. Trevor was on leave the entire month of September. They were practically like newlyweds. And it was just ten days ago when she discovered all their efforts once again were for naught.

Will she hate me? My eyes flicker to Ryder. *Will he hate Lucas? Will all of them call me a fool?*

I hand Maddie and Ava the wine. Maddie tilts her head as she takes it from me. "You're not drinking?"

I shake my head and sit.

Ava's hand flies to her mouth. "Oh my god! You're pregnant."

~ ~ ~

Joey curls up next to me on the couch.

"It wasn't that bad," I tell him. "Ava still loves me. And Ryder didn't even seem pissed at Lucas. Although he did leave right after, so who knows, he could be over at the penthouse giving Lucas a piece of his mind."

Joey stares up into my eyes.

"Okay, okay. So they all called me—us—crazy. And so I may have left out one minor detail about my ridiculous feelings for Lucas. But I just wasn't up for an 'I told you so' from Maddie." I tug him close. "You're excited, right? I mean, you and me and Lucas may be the only ones who are." I pat his head. "They'll all come around sooner or later. Even if they think we're going about this the wrong way, they're still being supportive. And Rose was right. I did need to talk to friends. I do feel better."

My phone buzzes with a text from Lucas.

Cue the tingles.

Lucas: A little heads-up would have been nice.

Me: I'm sorry. Was it bad?

Lucas: We're all good. He may have threatened me within an inch of my life if I ever hurt you or his nephew though.

Me: He's harmless.

Lucas: After I nearly shit myself, we ended up having a drink. He's still a good guy and I

realized how much I missed having him around.

Me: Yeah, me too. We've become a lot closer. I think he'll be a good uncle.

Lucas: Were you planning on coming over?

The momentary butterflies dancing in my stomach have me thinking I just felt M&M move, but sadly, no, it's just my irrational, unreasonable, ludicrous crush.

Me: Not tonight.

Or ever.

Lucas: That's too bad. Because I was just thinking about that time in the woods.

I pull a throw pillow onto my lap and let my mind wander back to the moment he's referring to. We were on one of our walks. I saw Lucas adjusting himself in his shorts, and I got horny. So horny in fact that I pulled him behind a grouping of trees off the path and told him to put his hand down my pants. Fifteen seconds later, I was done and returned the favor in what he said was one of the best hand jobs he'd ever had.

Probably because of the excitement over the fear of being caught.

Aaaaaaaand, now I'm hot and bothered again.

Crap.

Lucas: Come on, Ray. You know you want to. Just thinking about that day has me hard. And if you don't come over, I'm going to have to take things—and by *things*, I mean my cock— into my own hands.

Oh my god. Now I'm imagining him touching himself.

I squirm right here on the couch. *Just ignore him.* Ignore him and go to bed and get out a Lucas replacement toy.

My chest heaves. Because there's a little voice in the back of my head that assures me there *is* no replacement for him.

Lucas: Regan? Are you there? I'm dangerously close to getting myself off. Do you really want to miss the party?

Warmth spreads throughout my body. My clit is already engorged. I'm almost thrumming with arousal. Maybe I could go over. Just this once. One last time.

Lucas told me that when he quit smoking, he finished off his pack, smoked them all, got one last nicotine high, and went cold turkey. That's all this would be. One last high before I quit. Quit him.

I spring up off the couch. And as I text him back, I wonder how one can be so sad and so turned on at the very same time.

Me: I'll come to your back entrance.

Lucas: See you soon. And, Ray, maybe I'll come at YOUR back entrance.

The thought of it. Of him. Of everything we've done together. All the wild and crazy things neither of us had ever done before. All of it makes me crave more. More of him. More of us.

I'm down the stairs and in Ava's car before I can talk myself out of it.

Every bump in the road along the way—every picture in my head of what he's going to do to me—increases my excitement. By the time I'm pulling up to the back parking lot, I question whether or not I'm even going to make it to his apartment. Maybe he'll get down on his knees and make me come in the elevator like he did last week.

Not helping.

I let out a guttural groan of frustration. Then I laugh, wondering if this is what it's like for hormonal teenage boys who are perpetually horny.

I park and am out the door in a rush, quickly striding to the rear entrance. In perfect synchronization, as some of our orgasms have been, he flings the door open and smiles. Almost immediately, though, it falls, replaced by a grimace.

Has he changed his mind?

Then I realize he's not looking at me. He's looking *behind* me.

I spin and see a beautiful, vaguely familiar woman approaching. "Mr. Montana," she practically sings. Then she looks at me. "And Ms. Lucas. What a pleasure."

This lady knows who I am? And what's up with the sinister grin on her face?

"What the fuck are you doing here?" Lucas barks.

"Lucas?" I say. "What's going on?"

"That's Sylvia Franco. From the news. She's one of the reporters who was hanging out for weeks trying to get my story after Lissa got engaged." He moves to stand in front of me, almost protectively. "I thought you'd given up months ago. Why are you stalking me again? I saw the pictures. I know she got married. And I couldn't care less. There, that's my statement—I couldn't care less if Lissa rides off into the sunset with the senator's son and lives happily ever after."

Sylvia smiles. "Why is that, Mr. Montana? Is it because you've moved on with Ms. Lucas?"

Lucas fumes. "It's none of your fucking business what I've moved on to. Please leave."

"Or perhaps it's because Ms. Lucas is pregnant with your child."

The world falls silent. There's no rustling of fall leaves. No humming of streetlights. No sound whatsoever. With the exception of my pounding heart.

One look at Lucas has me knowing he feels exactly the same way. He composes himself much more quickly than I do, however, and takes a step toward her. "Get the fuck out of—"

"Mr. Montana, we can stand out here shouting about your illegitimate child, or you can invite me up to your apartment where we can have a conversation."

"You're crazy, lady," he says, turning and taking my elbow and leading me to the door.

"I've had you followed," Sylvia says. "I know about the appointments, the back-door entrances to the OB's office, the secret meetings here at your apartment. I also know that nobody in this town has a clue." She holds up her phone, showing us a photo of us walking in the woods. She swipes to a photo of him pulling me through the back door of this very building. Another shows him being greeted by Dr. Russo at the rear entrance.

"Shall I go on? The story is going to run, Mr. Montana. But if you give me thirty minutes, I might just let you convince me to tell your side, even though from here, the story I could make up seems so much juicier." She looks between the two of us. "What's it going to be?"

Lucas shuts his eyes and shakes his head. Then he looks at me, guilt written all over him. He walks to the door and holds it open. "Thirty minutes," he says.

Sylvia and I follow him inside.

Chapter Thirty-five

Lucas

I have to park down the street due to the number of cars lining the cul-de-sac. Regan and I barely said two words to each other on the way here. What is there to say really? We agreed last night to tell them only what we told the reporter. Nothing more. Nothing less.

I race around the car, open her door, and help her out. I scan the cars as we walk up the sidewalk toward Blake's house. Familiar cars owned by family and friends.

At the door, I reach over and squeeze her hand. "It's going to be okay."

"That's easy for you to say. You're used to being gossiped about."

Before I can ring the bell, Blake's wife, Ellie, opens the door. She looks a bit confused that Regan and I are standing together—proof my brother really has been keeping our secret.

"Come in," she signs.

"Thank you," I say and sign back. "Nice to see you."

"Hi, Ellie," Regan signs. "How are you?"

The two women have a short conversation in ASL. Sometimes I forget Regan knows it. And as I watch them sign, I realize it's one more reason I'm drawn to her. She fits. With me. With my family.

"You ready for this?" Dallas says, coming over to greet me.

"I'm not sure. But we don't have a choice. Thanks for helping put this together on such short notice."

Blake's house is abuzz with conversation. Nobody seems particularly interested when I walk into the room. Nobody knows why they're here. Everyone close to me is standing in this room. My family. Close friends. Most of the Calloways. There must be at least three dozen people.

Dallas and Blake arranged this emergency gathering after Sylvia gave us forty-eight hours to tell everyone before the story comes out.

Mom walks over. "Do you have any idea what this is all about? Nobody seems to know anything, and your brothers are being all secretive."

Regan stares at me from ten feet away.

I nod. "Yeah. I do. And you'll know in about two minutes."

"Oh, Lucas… you aren't quitting the business, are you?"

"It's nothing like that. I promise." I kiss her cheek. "Just please be happy for me," I say, then walk over and stand in front of Blake and Ellie's massive fireplace—as good a spot as any to announce our news.

"Thank you all for coming," I say loudly.

Instantly, the room falls silent, everyone eager to hear why they've been summoned here so urgently.

Regan is standing off to the side, nestled next to Maddie Calloway as if she's worried she'll faint at any second. I'm not sure she'd be wrong. She *is* looking a bit pale. A few of my friends and relatives have noticed her and are giving second glances. Makes sense considering Regan is the one person who seems out of place. She's the only person in this room who doesn't have ties to anyone else here.

"We all know how the rumor mill goes in this town. I wanted to bring you all here and make sure you know the truth before you start hearing reporters spin the story."

"How come Regan Lucas is here?" Storm Calloway calls out from the far corner.

Suddenly, three dozen pairs of eyes are trained on Regan. Despite her always saying she couldn't care less what people think of her, I think she might actually collapse. I go over to her, take her elbow, and lead her back to stand beside me. "It's going to be fine. It'll be over in a second," I whisper.

"Oh my god," my cousin Sydney shrieks. "Are you a couple? Are you getting married?"

Gasps, incredulous huffs, and even laughter echo throughout Blake's living room.

I'm about to open my mouth, when Regan speaks instead.

"No! No, no, no. Absolutely not," she says, her steadfast denial driving a spike deep into my heart.

"Then what's this all about?" Addison Calloway asks.

"We're not getting married," I say. "You all should know better than to think I'd put anyone through *that* again." I chuckle awkwardly. "And, um… we're not… together." I glance at Regan. "But we are having a baby."

More gasps. People look to each other to make sure they heard correctly.

"You're *what?*" someone shouts from the back.

"We're having a baby." I reach over and touch Regan's stomach. "Regan and I are having a child together. It's a boy. He's due in March. And we're going to co-parent."

"But..." Amber Thompson steps forward, studying her friend. "You're not together?" She turns to me, raising a glaring brow, and I just know what she's thinking—that I knocked her up and am refusing responsibility.

"By choice," Regan says. "I turned thirty-five. Then Teddy was born. And you and Quinn adopted. I knew something was missing."

"Same for me," I assert. "I can't seem to stick to any relationships with women, but I've always wanted kids. It seemed the perfect solution for both of us."

"Wait," Dani Calloway says, "so this wasn't an accident?"

"No, Dani, this wasn't an accident," I confirm. "This was planned. And it wasn't impulsive either. We have a contract outlining the legalities of how we'll be raising our son."

My mother steps forward, tears drowning her eyes, and takes Regan's hand. "Contract or no, you're having my grandchild, and that makes you family."

She pulls Regan into a hug. Regan hugs her back. Her eyes even close. I know she's thinking about her own mother and how she wishes she might react when hearing this news. But from what she's told me, it'll be nothing like this.

People swarm around us, firing off questions.

"Calm down, calm down!" I yell. "We'll answer all your questions. That's why we're here. For damage control. There will be a story coming out tomorrow about this. A reporter who tried to get an interview from me after the whole Lissa engagement story hired someone to follow me. She has pictures of me going into the OB's office. Photos of Regan and me together. She gave us two days to tell family. I have no idea what her story will be. She promised if we told our side, she'd be merciful. I guess we'll see. But we wanted to make sure you knew the truth."

The truth.

The words swirl in my head. *The truth* is we're secretly sleeping together—even Sylvia Franco knows that, though she promised not to report it. *The truth* is I want more than a co-parenting situation with our son. *The truth* is I love the woman standing to my left.

But no one outside my siblings will ever know *that* truth. Not Sylvia Franco. Not the dozens of people in this room. And especially not Regan.

After answering what seems like a hundred questions, the room is quiet again.

"So that's it?" Sydney says, her eyes bouncing between us. "You're *just* going to co-parent? There's *nothing* between you?"

I swallow and look at Regan. For a fraction of a second, I think I see something in her eyes. Something that's obviously not there.

I shake my head, doing my best not to look disappointed, and say, "There's nothing there. Nothing but friendship and a desire to have a child."

And scorching hot sex.

I leave that part out. Not just because they don't need to know about it, but because, sadly, after Sylvia showed up, Regan assured me that was ending.

Demographically, the people in Blake's living room part like the Red Sea. The women gravitate toward Regan, wanting to see ultrasound photos and feel her belly. The men pull me aside, asking if I realize what I'm in for as a single dad.

For the better part of the evening, Regan and I are apart. We're in the same place, but we're not together. And I realize it's just a taste of what's to come.

Mom pulls me aside and hugs me. "If you're happy, I'm happy."

"Yes, Mom. I'm happy."

"Are you sure?" She eyes me like only a mother who has decades of experience reading her children can. "Because if you don't stop looking at Regan the way you have been all night, I doubt anyone in this room is going to buy your friends-only story."

"What? That's crazy."

"A mother knows," she says with a hard, all-knowing stare.

I blow out a long, painful sigh. "It's completely one-sided." I lean against the wall and lower my voice. "Karma is a real bitch. After all my trials and mishaps, I finally find the person I think is the one, and she wants nothing to do with me other than honoring the contract we signed."

"Are you sure about that?"

I nod.

"You've told her how you feel?"

I shake my head. "I can't risk it. It would ruin everything. Even if by some miracle she felt the same—which she doesn't—I won't hurt her. I won't hurt her like the others. Because I know I would."

"This is different than all the others, sweetheart. She's having your child. That bonds you in a way you never had before."

"I can't. I'd rather have what we have. She's become like a best friend, Mom. I can't risk it. I won't."

"Having a best friend is important." She pats my arm. "But having a best friend who is also your lover, the parent of your child, and your soul mate, is the ultimate bliss." She rises up on her toes and kisses my cheek. "I'm just saying… the greater the risk, the greater the reward."

And with that, she floats across the room right into Dad's arms. He pulls her close, kissing her temple, and whispers something in her ear that makes her blush. Thirty-three years they've been married, and they still seem like newlyweds.

I told myself I was getting that with Kaitlyn. I swore I was getting it with Simone. With Veronica. With Lissa. I stare across the room. Regan smiles brightly when she catches my gaze. She's relieved we've finally told everyone. She can breathe easier. It's not a secret anymore.

No. She has no more secrets to bear. Now *I'm* the only one who has to live with that kind of torture. The kind that has you wanting something so badly… something right there in front of you, yet still so out of reach.

Chapter Thirty-six

Regan

I'm awake, but for a moment, I can't see clearly. A headache splits my temples.

I lie here and take deep, cleansing breaths, feeling for movements from my little M&M. Granted he's not so little now. And he's been doing somersaults in my belly for months. It's a feeling I crave even if half the time he's bouncing off my bladder.

The headache isn't subsiding, despite my controlled breathing exercises.

I get out my phone and text Lucas, who made me swear to contact him with every craving, every nuance of the pregnancy, and lately, especially since it's been creeping up ever since I hit the third trimester, my daily blood pressure.

Me: Something's not right.

As usual, I get an immediate response. It's as if his phone never leaves his hands. I say jump and he asks how high. It's endearing if not mildly annoying. He has no idea how him acting like a doting partner is messing with my head. Because all those feelings and emotions I had sworn were tied to my orgasms, they haven't subsided. Even when I haven't been in his bed for thirteen weeks. Not since the day Sylvia Franco showed up at his back door.

We've been together a lot. On our walks. When he brings me meals several times a week. During his late-night treks to fetch things like ice cream, pickle sandwiches, and my oddest craving: Cheetos dipped in strawberry yogurt. Not to mention the holidays he insisted Ryder and I spend with his family. Sure, my brother and I had to tell a few lies to get out of Christmas with our parents, each of us still closely guarding a secret—a divorce for him, and M&M for me. We'll tell them in good time. But not yet.

Luckily, Sylvia's story wasn't as popular as she had hoped it would be. Apparently, the heir to a winery having a baby with his gal-pal isn't as newsworthy as say… a waitress marrying a senator's son. I doubt the story even made it as far as Florida, making us basically local gossip fodder.

Lucas: I'm on the way.

Quickly, I change into the pajamas Mom sent me for Christmas and discard the Montana Winery sweatshirt I've been sleeping in. He doesn't need to know I've gone to bed wearing it every night for the past few months. That the soft, fleece-lined fabric makes me feel closer to him.

I take my blood pressure for the third time, hoping I'd simply misaligned the cuff and it isn't actually continuing to go up. I've always prided myself on having textbook blood pressure. Even for the first twenty-seven weeks of my pregnancy, it was excellent. But lately, I swear it's gone up just a little every day. Today is the first time it hit 140. 140 over 90 to be exact. And I sigh, knowing this isn't good. It's the exact number Dr. Russo warned me about.

At least I don't have to worry about the shop. Ryder has been pulling his weight around here, letting me sleep in every day as he takes the morning shift.

He's still crashing in my 'closet.' His divorce isn't final yet and he doesn't have access to the funds he needs to get his own place. But Ryder swears he'll be out before the baby comes.

My brother and I haven't discussed Lucas's idea of me getting a place in his building. I haven't even discussed it with Lucas yet. And the sad thing is, he hasn't mentioned it again since that first time. Maybe he's changed his mind, having decided my being that close wouldn't be good for his dating life.

Despite the fact that I haven't seen him out with another woman, my guess is he'd have to venture quite a ways from Calloway Creek. Everyone here knows not only about his past as a runaway groom, but about the impending birth of his kid with me. I swear, every single woman in this town has a sign they hold up around Lucas that reads, *'I wouldn't touch you with a ten-foot pole.'*

While part of me feels sorry for him, the other part, the deep-down part of me that wants him to my very core, is glad he's not the highly-sought-after bachelor he should be.

I hear the front door to the apartment open and then Lucas is standing in my bedroom doorway.

"What's going on? Is it your blood pressure?"

I nod.

He strides over, sits on the side of the bed, and picks up the cuff. "Let me do it."

I don't object. I never object when he does anything that has him touching me. Though my incessant horniness has abated, the jolts of electricity I feel when his fingers brush against my arm are just as intense as always. The man has no idea that every time he accidentally touches my hand, when his arm swings against mine on our walks, when he wipes a spot of pizza sauce off my chin—that my heart races and butterflies not brought on by our little M&M dance in my stomach.

He has no idea that every time I look at him, I have conflicting emotions about Lucas the man and Lucas the father of my child. He has no idea that I dream of the three of us becoming a family. A family like his brothers have. Like Maddie has with Tag. Like Amber with Quinn.

Most of all, he has no idea that over the course of the past several months, I've fallen head over heels in love with him. *Him*— Lucas Montana. Runaway groom. The most unattainable, unfettered, unbridled man in the history of men.

"One forty over ninety," he says with a frown. He stands and offers me his hand. "Get dressed. I'm taking you to see Dr. Russo."

~ ~ ~

As we have for every appointment since the anatomy scan, we walk in the *front* door of the doctor's office. Yes, we often get stared at. Whispered about. Even laughed at. But after months of this, it just rolls right off us.

While Sylvia's story was surprisingly tactful, it made waves locally and there have still been rumors. Some of them crazier than the actual truth itself. They range from us being secretly married (my favorite), to Lucas hiring me as a surrogate, and me getting pregnant by IVF, because come on, why would a guy like him ever actually want to have sex with a girl like me?

"The doctor will see you," Carrie says.

We're escorted back, all the usual vitals are taken, and then we're led to an exam room.

Dr. Russo enters, asks all the normal questions, palpates my tummy, takes my blood pressure for the second time since we got here, and settles onto her stool. "Regan, it's good that you came in. Your blood pressure is elevated. It's at the point where we need to monitor you more frequently. I'd like you to be on modified bed rest. I'm ordering a twenty-four-hour urine test to screen for preeclampsia. We'll do twice weekly ultrasound biophysical profiles to monitor the baby's health. And of course, I'd like you to continue taking your blood pressure and report any fluctuations. If it reaches one-sixty, we'll admit you to the hospital and start hypertensive protocols."

I place my hands protectively over my stomach. "I'm only thirty-two weeks. Will he be okay?"

"There's no need for alarm. Most likely the modified bed rest will help. You don't have to be in bed all day. I'd just like you sitting or lying down for the most part. Binge your favorite shows. You can even continue working a few hours a day if you wish. Just have this big strong man here move a recliner behind the counter and let your customers do most of the work. No more walks in the park. Short walks only. To Ava's coffee shop. Over to Goodwin's Diner. Nothing more than a few minutes. Light housework is okay, but you let that strapping brother of yours do the heavy lifting."

I look up at Lucas. "I don't even have the nursery done. Not to mention I'm not even sure where I want it to be."

He cocks his head oddly.

"You let others take care of that," Dr. Russo says. "Your job—your most important job—is to protect this baby and yourself by taking it easy." She stands and pulls over the ultrasound machine. "Now, let's take a look at your little slugger, shall we?"

~ ~ ~

"Don't freak out," Lucas says when we leave. "We knew this was a possibility. If you do what Dr. Russo says, it'll be fine."

"I'm not freaking out, Lucas."

He opens the car door for me. "You really aren't, are you?"

"Since when have you known me to be the freaking out type?"

"Oh, I don't know… that time when we stood in front of half the town and told them about our news?"

I roll my eyes. "Lucas, God himself would have freaked over that."

We both laugh.

He gets in the car and sighs. "I'm really going to miss our walks."

I look at him strangely. "You are? I always got the impression you'd rather be out running."

"Are you kidding? I love our walks. Especially that *one*." He whistles low and slow. "I don't think I'll ever go on a walk better than that."

My cheeks flush.

He chuckles. "Why, Regan Lucas, did I just see you blush?"

I swat his hand. "Just drive."

When he passes my shop, I turn and raise my eyebrows. "Um, where are we going?"

"You heard the doctor. I need to get you a recliner. We're going to the furniture store."

"I do have a couch there."

"That old antique thing? It's stiff as a board. We're getting you a plush, comfy recliner. One you can pop your legs up on and sink down into."

I laugh. "You mean one I won't be able to get out of? Do you know how hard it's getting to stand up?"

He works his upper lip with his thumb and fingers. "How about one of those electric recliners for old people that rises up?"

"I'm not getting an old-person recliner. I'll make do."

"Whatever you want." He smiles. Then it fades. "What did you mean back at the doctor's office when you said you didn't know where you wanted the nursery?"

"I was just thinking how it's going to be all kinds of crowded at my place when the baby arrives. And I'm not sure Ryder can afford his own place yet, not until the divorce is final. So I was thinking maybe I'd get someplace new. A little bigger."

"You want to move into my building?"

The amount of surprise in his words is alarming. It has guilt careening through me. Living in his building means using the child support for me, not just M&M. And despite what he says about it being okay, I'm still not sure I'm okay with it.

"I don't know. Maybe not."

His expression falls, as if he was truly excited and then I squashed his hopes. I get it. He wants to be close to his son.

Emotions bombard me as well, but for a much different reason. Because for a second, I got excited about seeing Lucas more often. In the parking lot. In the elevator. Maybe even in each other's apartments. Mixed with that, however, is hesitation over him being so close yet at the same time, so far.

On some level, though, wouldn't it be what's best for the baby? Having both parents there, ready and available?

What's best would be having both parents *together*, a voice whispers in the back of my mind. I silence it, because I really don't like what it's been telling me. That I may be subjected to a lifetime of wanting a man I can never have. Needing something he can never give me. Craving things he's incapable of.

"You don't have to decide now," he says. "But I'll look into it just in case. I believe there might be two units available. I think you should get the larger one. I'm fairly sure the closet alone will give you an orgasm. It's not quite as big as mine, but we all know none are."

Heat crosses my face as I'm fairly sure he's no longer referring to closets. "Um… okay. But no promises. I'm not sure about anything at this point."

"Right now, our mission is to get you the biggest, baddest recliner there is," he says as he turns into the parking lot of the furniture store. "Then we'll work out a meal schedule. You shouldn't be cooking."

"Nonsense. Dr. Russo said I can do light housework."

"She also said staying off your feet is better for you and the baby." He turns off the engine, gets out and races around to help me up and out. "You're the mother of my child. It's my job to spoil you." He touches my stomach. "Both of you." His face lights up when he feels a sharp jab. "See? M&M approves."

I laugh. "I'm not sure that was approval. More like a stay-in-your-lane jab."

"You think I'm going out of my lane?" His hand falls away, as if bereft. "Are you telling me to back off, Regan?"

As much as I want to say yes, I can't. Because as much as I know seeing him, smelling him, being around him will kill me, it's what I crave.

"No, Lucas," I say with a grin. "I wouldn't dare."

He smiles like the proud father he's about to become.

Chapter Thirty-seven

Regan

Lucas's face beams as he holds our little boy. Mitchell is adorable in his footed pajamas with pictures of the Grinch and Max the dog all over them. At almost two years old, he's incredibly excited to see all the presents underneath the massive Christmas tree.

"Mommy!" he exclaims when he sees me. "Pwesents!" He squirms in Lucas's arms. "Daddy put down."

Mitchell skitters across the room and goes right for the largest package. Lucas laughs heartily as he turns to me. "I have something for you, too." He pulls a small square jewelry box from his pocket. It's unwrapped but has a thin red bow tied around it. "And it comes with a question."

Tears well in my eyes. Today is the day I've been waiting for. Dreaming of. Fantasizing about. He drops to a knee and tears the ribbon off the box.

"Regan, will you—"

"Regan… Regan!"

My eyes fly open. Ryder is standing over me. I shift in the recliner and get my bearings. I'm at work. I must have fallen asleep. Again.

I sigh heavily and silently curse my brother for interrupting my dream.

Oh my gosh. The dream. It comes back to me as powerfully as if I'd lived it. My face is still wet with tears. My heart is still thrumming with excitement, so full of... love.

Instinctively, my hand goes to my belly. I saw him. I saw Mitchell. It's the first time I've ever dreamed of him. He was Lucas through and through. Dark hair. Chocolate eyes. Strong jawline. But with my dimples.

"You okay?" Ryder asks.

I wipe my eyes. "Yeah. I guess I was dreaming. What's up?"

"Mrs. Mulrooney just dropped off all these boxes of clothes, and two teachers from the deaf school have questions about a collection of books you have for sale. Sorry to wake you, but I know nothing about the books or ASL."

"It's fine." I start to get up but feel lightheaded. "Whoa."

"What's wrong?"

"Nothing. I just got up too quickly."

"You want to take your blood pressure?"

I motion to the customers. "After I take care of them."

Ryder helps me to my feet. Lately, it's been a lot more difficult to get up from sitting or lying down—two things I do a lot of since Dr. Russo put me on modified bed rest two weeks ago.

I help the deaf customers, happy to tuck a large wad of cash beneath the register.

Ryder counts it out. "That's the largest sale you've had this week. Those books must be good."

"It was a series of eight books. All signed by the author. And yes, they're good."

He cocks his head. "Regan, don't you think it's sad that a two-hundred-sixty-dollar sale is the largest you've had this week?" He motions an arm around the shop. "I've been working here for months. I see the trend. I've been going over your ledgers. Profits have been steadily declining for years. We need to make serious changes or you won't be able to pay the mortgage."

I shoot him a hard stare. "We?"

"You have the baby coming. I figured we could do something together. Make this place into something super lucrative. Keep up with the times."

I settle back down into the recliner and put my feet up. It's amazing how much they ache after only being on them for a few minutes. "Ryder, you hate this place. Selling books and women's clothing is not something I see you doing long term. And now you want to help me make it successful?"

"Well..." He leans against the counter. "I wasn't exactly thinking of keeping the shop the way it is. I was thinking of changing the inventory to something else."

I roll my eyes. "We're not turning *Booktique* into a sporting goods store just because you hate selling books and women's clothing."

His arms cross in front of his body, and he looks at me with more determination than I've ever seen. "Not a sporting goods store."

"What then?"

"Don't freak out."

"I don't freak out, Ryder. Just tell me."

"I've been doing tons of research on this, Regan. I have a business plan and everything. I was looking into other locations, but lately, I've been wondering if maybe this is the perfect spot. And remember, I do have a degree in business. We could make this work. Just hear me out."

"Oh my god, spit it out."

He chews his lip for a moment. "I want to turn this place into a cannabis dispensary."

It takes my brain a few seconds to process his words. "You… want to open a pot store?" I glance around. "Here?"

"Yes, here." He gets on his knees and looks me right in the eyes. "Regan, I've done my homework. The nearest dispensaries are in White Plains or the city. We'd be the only one around. It would be a gold mine."

I blink repeatedly. "You want to open a pot store."

"It's fully legal in New York for anyone over twenty-one. Just listen before you shoot down my idea. I've been thinking about this for a few years. I first came up with the idea in Colorado, but out there, dispensaries seem to be on every corner. Amy hated when I talked about it. I think it's one of the reasons she did what she did. She never liked the fact that I used it to control my anxiety."

"It's… crazy."

"It's not crazy, Regan." He pulls a large binder out from a cabinet beneath the counter. "It's all in here. Licensing, operational costs, hardware, software, security and other tech stuff, staffing, inventory, taxes. You name it, it's in here."

I take the thick, heavy binder from him and flip through it, my eyes widening the farther into it I get. He's right, it's all here. Everything he said and more. "I can't believe you've done all this."

"Even the location is perfect. We're not within five hundred feet of a school or community center or two hundred feet from a church. The square footage is spot on for a dispensary."

My eyes bug out when I see the bottom line of start-up costs, then snap up to his. "Let's pretend for a second that I agreed to go along with your insane plan, this is over five hundred thousand dollars. You don't have that kind of money."

"A large part of that is real estate costs." He waves a hand. "We already have that covered. Once the divorce is finalized, I can withdraw my half of the money. I still have a lot saved from when Mom and Dad gave me my portion of our inheritance. Amy gets half," he scoffs angrily, "but there's still a good amount. I can get a small business loan for the rest. I've done the math. I *can* make this work. And done right, it could be ten or twenty times more profitable than *Booktique* has been."

He nods at my flamboyant maternity top. "Look at you, already looking the part. You and your eccentric clothes and your incense and carefree lifestyle—no one would even bat an eye."

M&M jabs my bladder. "I can't think about this right now, Ryder. Maybe not ever. It's seriously impractical."

He laughs. "Since when has Regan Lucas ever been practical?"

The baby kicks again. "I have to pee."

Ryder pulls out the BP cuff. "Hold on a minute. You said we could take your blood pressure first."

I hold out my arm and push up my sleeve. "Let's make it quick. This kid is dancing on my bladder."

He's an expert at it by now and does it quickly. A look of concern etches his brow. "Regan, it's one-fifty-two over ninety-six."

I remove the cuff. "Of course it is. You just dropped a bomb on me." I shake my head. "Pot store. It's ludicrous. Now help me up so I can use the bathroom unless you want me to pee all over this chair."

After relieving my bladder and washing up, I stare in the mirror. Is he right? Do I look the part of a pot shop owner? Maybe I need to start dressing more conservatively. I am about to be a mom after all.

M&M kicks me and rolls around. I put my hands on my belly and push back at a protruding foot or elbow. "Listen, I know you're running out of room in there, but cut me a break."

Ryder is hanging up the phone, looking guilty when I emerge from the back.

He holds up his cell. "I called Lucas. He's on his way."

"Well, call him back. He doesn't need to rush over every time the baby kicks."

"It's more than that and you know it."

"Whatever." I sit back down. "While you were at it, did you tell him your insane idea?"

"I haven't told anyone other than you and Amy. And she hardly counts anymore."

"Mom and Dad would freak," I say in amusement. Then I smile. "Maybe you should do it. It'll take some of the heat off me for this." I point at my fast-growing bump.

"Me? This is your place, Regan. It would be *us*." He nods to the ceiling. "I'm going up to make us a few sandwiches. You think it over."

He disappears up the stairs as I mumble to myself, "It's still a stupid ide—"

I stop talking mid-word when a man walks into the shop. But it's not just any man.

It's David.

My head starts swirling. I must be hallucinating.

Painstakingly, I get back on my feet.

As he approaches the counter, his sinister smile widens. My heart pounds and I instinctively look around for Joey, wanting to protect him even though I know he's not down here.

"Well, looky here," he says, his rough voice like gravel on my ears. "I had to come see for myself."

"Wh-what are you doing here?"

"I've been out of the country. Japan. I play baseball there. Have for years. I came back to New York to see family before spring training starts up again. Imagine my surprise when I open an old magazine to see a story about you and Lucas Montana having a kid in some kind of fucked up relationship."

I can't form words. My mouth doesn't work. My brain is malfunctioning. I'm twenty years old again. Back under his thumb where he can manipulate me to his will.

"What's wrong, Regan? Cat got your tongue?" He laughs boisterously. "Oh, right. You don't have a cat. At least not *that* cat."

I feel sick to my stomach. I only hope this isn't real. It's a nightmare. I've fallen asleep again and this monster is invading my dreams.

"You know, now that I'm here, I question why I came." He eyes me from head to toe as if appraising the most hideous thing he's ever seen. "Especially when I see how you let yourself go. How could you get so fucking fat?" He shakes his head in disgust. "I get that pregnancy adds twenty or thirty pounds. But this... Jesus, Regan, this kid has added what, a hundred?"

"Get out," I manage to say even as my entire body shakes.

He snatches a book from a nearby shelf. "Is that how you treat paying customers? Not very good for business if you ask me."

"Why are you here?"

"Curiosity," he says. "You know how they say it killed the cat. Then again, so did antifreeze and rat poison." His evil laugh makes my skin crawl. "Had to see how a mousy, weak person like yourself was able to get a billionaire like Montana to even give you a second glance."

"I'm not mousy or weak," I say defensively, feeling nothing but. "Only *you* made me that way."

He pretends to read the back cover of the book. "Whatever helps you sleep at night." He looks back at me. "But seriously, how could someone like you get a man like him into bed?" He puts down the book and takes a step closer. "Did you drug him?"

My pulse pounds in my ears, and his voice echoes through my mind as if I'm in a tunnel. My head twinges with pain as I become vaguely aware of the chimes over the door.

"Regan?" a familiar voice asks. "Are you okay?"

"Lucas!" I steady myself on the counter, feeling myself starting to spin.

"Lucas?" David says. "Well, if it isn't the baby daddy."

Lucas steps around the counter, putting himself protectively between David and me. "And who the fuck are you?"

"David," I say, my vision narrowing. "It's David."

Then everything goes black.

Chapter Thirty-eight

Lucas

I catch Regan and ease her to the floor. She's out cold.

"Call a fucking ambulance!" I yell as fear paralyzes me.

David holds up his arms and backs away. "I'm outta here."

"Regan!" I put my fingers to her neck and feel a pulse. It seems slow. I dip my cheek to her face to confirm she's breathing as I pull out my phone and call 911.

Ryder appears at my side. "What the hell happened?"

"I don't know. She just collapsed. That David asshole was here. Go make sure he's gone."

"David? Her college boyfriend?"

"Yes, *that* David." I motion to the door. "Make sure he's nowhere near this place when the ambulance comes."

He darts to the door and when it opens, I can already hear the sirens.

Regan starts to move. "Easy there," I say, brushing a hand down the side of her face.

Relief floods through me. She's not dying. She just fainted. I could kill that asshole for coming in here and scaring her like that.

The paramedics come in and rush to Regan's side.

"I'm… I'm okay," she says, clearly out of breath.

"Why don't we let the professionals determine that?"

I step aside and let the paramedics do their thing. I don't recognize one of them, but I went to school with the other.

"Regan, your blood pressure is dangerously high," Jessica says. "We're going to take you to the hospital."

"I'm coming," I say and turn to Ryder. "Man the store?"

He scoffs. "I hardly think the store needs to stay open."

"I don't need you both hovering," Regan says to him. "Please stay here."

"If anything happens, I'll call you. I promise." I glance around. "And if that asshole comes anywhere near here, let me know. Better yet, call Sheriff Niles and tell him what happened."

"Will do."

Regan is loaded into the back of the ambulance and I crawl in after her and take her hand. "We're lucky you fainted," I say.

"Lucky? How's that?"

"Well, I'd probably be in police custody if you hadn't because I'd have killed that motherfucker."

A half-grin brings out one of her dimples. Then she rubs her belly. "I just hope he's okay. Why do you think I fainted?"

I shrug. "Stress, I suppose. Ryder said your BP was already getting up there."

Her eyes close tightly and the fingers of her right hand pinch her brow. "My head hurts."

I look at Jessica. "She's developed preeclampsia, hasn't she?"

"Highly probable," she says. "We've called ahead. Dr. Russo is already on her way to the hospital. You'll know more then."

My worst fear is happening. I thought we had it under control. But now... all the horrible things I've read about the condition sweep through my mind. Organ damage. Stroke. Stillborn baby. Maternal death.

I've never been so scared in my fucking life.

I'll rip that David asshole apart limb by limb if anything happens to either of them.

Dr. Russo is already in the ambulance bay when we arrive. Regan is taken to a room in the emergency department where they hook her up to all kinds of monitors.

I tell the doctor about David.

"The stress from the situation may have caused a temporary spike in blood pressure. If it doesn't come down soon, though, we may be looking at an early delivery."

"She's only thirty-four weeks."

The doctor nods. "The baby will be small. At thirty-four weeks, he'll be late preterm. Late preterm babies may look and act like full term babies, but they aren't fully developed. They are at higher risk, but they usually do well in the long run." Dr. Russo continues to diagnose Regan out loud. I know she's doing it so I have all the info as well, but it's not doing anything for my blood pressure either. "Regan is currently presenting preeclampsia with severe features, which is to say not only is her blood pressure high, but she's also experiencing headaches, visual impairments, and has swelling."

She turns away from me. "Regan, just to be safe, we're going to administer steroids to encourage fetal lung maturity. We'll also put you on an IV with antihypertensives." She takes Regan's hand. "If we can't get things under control by this evening, we'll use Cervidil to ripen your cervix overnight and then Pitocin in the morning to induce labor."

Regan's eyes go wide. "You want me to have the baby *tomorrow?*"

"It's the safest option for both of you if we can't get the preeclampsia under control."

There is a whirlwind of activity. Regan is hooked up to more things. An ultrasound is done which brings a modicum of relief knowing he's okay… for now. And we get moved up to labor and delivery.

When things calm down and it's just the two of us, I ask, "Would you mind if I step out and make a few calls. I need to update Ryder and my family. You want me to call Maddie and Ava?"

She nods, her lip quivering. It's the first time I've ever really seen her show fear. Well, if you don't count two hours ago when she was being confronted by that cat killer.

I squeeze her hand. "It's going to be okay."

I swallow hard and stare at her for a long moment. I swear for a second in the shop, when she was lifeless on the floor, I thought I'd lost her. I thought I'd lost them both. And my future flashed before me. My empty, pathetic, lonely future. One without the child I've come to long for much more than I dreamed possible. Without the woman I love so much that it hurts every time we're together and I can't tell her.

Tell her.

"Regan, I…" I close my eyes, determined not to make this moment about me and what I want. Because there's just so much more at stake here. "I know this is scary. But it's going to work out. I don't know how I know, but it is. I promise."

A tear slips from her eye. "I think so too. I had a dream earlier." She touches her stomach. "About him. Mitchell. It was Christmas and he was two. You were holding him. He had on these ridiculous Grinch jammies."

I laugh, tears caught in my throat. "Of course he did. You're his mom."

She wipes her tears, and I follow the motion of her hand, thinking I should be doing it. *I'm* the one who should be wiping her tears. I should be kissing her forehead. Hell, I should be sitting on the bed beside her and wrapping her in my arms.

"You can make your calls," she says, appearing to be a bit calmer.

"I'll be quick."

Before I'm out the door, she calls out. "Lucas?"

I turn.

There's something in her eyes. The way she looks at me. I know it's just gratitude mixed with exhaustion and anxiety. For a moment, however, I could swear it's more. But I know it's just my mind playing tricks.

"Thanks for always being there. I'm not sure I could have done this without you."

"It doesn't stop when we leave this hospital with him. I'm going to be there. Wherever and whenever you need me. Always."

She smiles sadly, as if it's something she both wants and doesn't want.

I thumb out the door. "I'll go make those calls. Be back soon."

~ ~ ~

Visitors have come and gone all afternoon. Maddie and Ava played cards with Regan. Ryder brought food after closing early for the day. Allie and my parents came and told tales about my childhood. They've all taken turns trying to distract us from what seems inevitable. Because we can see her blood pressure. It's taken automatically every so often. And every time it is, Regan and I lock eyes. We know what this means. We're going to have a baby tomorrow.

A premature one.

Chapter Thirty-nine

Regan

As another contraction hits, which thankfully isn't as bad as before thanks to the epidural, the nurse injects something into my IV line.

"This is magnesium sulfate," she says. "It helps prevent seizures during labor."

Lucas and I share another concerned stare.

Nurses are constantly checking on me, watching my blood pressure, asking about my vision, headaches, nausea, pain, and swelling.

And they're obsessed with the fetal monitor. Probably because if the baby's heart rate shows any sudden changes, I'll be whisked away for an emergency C-section.

This is not at all how I planned for this to go. Months ago, when I'd think about M&M's arrival, it was much more serene. Me laboring to my favorite playlist. Lucas offering his luminous smile and encouraging words with every one of my contractions. Mitchell coming into the world and being placed into my arms, everything and everyone else falling away as we share our first moments together.

But now... there's barely a moment when we're alone. A few minutes here and there.

Earlier today, more friends and family stopped by. I got tired of everyone telling me it was going to be okay. Like they thought maybe it wasn't. I didn't need that negative energy. So we kicked them out and it's just been the two of us all afternoon. Well, the two of us and the slew of nurses scurrying about.

Once Seizure Nurse leaves the room, Lucas sits down again in the chair by the bed.

"Tell me something to keep my mind off all this," I say.

"Okay, let's see... well, you know Dallas and Marti got engaged recently. So guess what? They picked a date. The wedding will be this spring and it'll be a destination wedding."

"They don't want to get married here?"

"Dallas's first wedding was at the winery. He's not about to have a second one there. I think he just wanted something completely different so there would be no bad memories of his late wife."

"Right. That makes sense. Where is it going to be?"

"Antigua."

"That sounds fun. You'll have a great time I'm sure."

"You know you're invited, don't you?"

I raise a brow. "Me? Why?"

"Regan, my family considers you family. M&M is their grandson, their nephew, a cousin. And they aren't about to leave you out of anything just because we aren't... you know."

Lucas looks away, out the window, like he's upset. I think this whole labor and delivery thing is freaking him out way more than he's letting on.

"You think the baby will be ready for an international trip in the spring? Lucas, I don't know. I'll bet the flight will be long and uncomfortable for an infant."

"Don't worry about that. We'll be flying down on a private jet."

I'm not sure why I'm surprised by that, other than I keep forgetting how flipping rich the Montanas are.

"I've never been out of the country. I've barely been out of New York. The extent of my world travels consists of Connecticut, Maine, and Florida."

"We'll get you a passport." He touches my stomach, careful not to dislodge the fetal monitor. "Him too."

The door opens and Dr. Russo walks in. She puts on a pair of gloves. "Time to check your cervix."

I assume the proper position, having done this more times than I'd like to think about today. At least it's not uncomfortable. I send some silent gratitude to the anesthesiologist and the epidural as Dr. Russo finishes her exam.

She removes her hand with a smile. "You're at nine centimeters. It won't be long now." She repositions the fetal monitor and checks the displays again. "I'm pleased with the progression of your labor. The next time I see you, it'll be to welcome this little guy into the world."

I smile, happy to be so near the finish line. I know delivery is the 'cure' for preeclampsia. My blood pressure should start dropping almost immediately and could even be back to normal in days. I'll no longer be at risk for seizures, and M&M will be out of the woods. Well, barring any complications due to him coming early.

I can't even think about that. I try to remain positive. I think of one of my favorite childhood movies when Tom Hanks declared, *'Looks like we just had our glitch for this mission.'*

My blood pressure. The preeclampsia. This is our glitch. Everything else is going to be fine. M&M will be tiny, and he may have to stay in the hospital for a bit, but he'll be perfect. I can feel it.

Another nurse comes in. This one I know. Mackenzie gives me a comforting smile reminiscent of our high school days. She asks the same old questions. Analyzes the machines. And glares at Lucas like he's a leper.

I get it. There's still gossip being tossed around. People don't believe we did this on purpose with zero intentions of being together. They think it was an accident and that he should man up and marry me. They're all crazy if they think it'll happen.

My heart seems to get squeezed along with my uterus. Because that picture of how Mitchell's birth would be—over the past weeks and months it's morphed from me bonding with the baby to the three of us becoming a family. Not the traditional family, because no way would that ever happen, but something else, something that's just as special. Maybe something that's even *more* than special.

I close my eyes, hoping once this is over my hormones will go back to normal and I'll get over these deep, unforgiving, unrelenting feelings I've developed for Lucas.

"You okay?" Lucas asks. "Another contraction?"

"Yes, but it doesn't hurt. It's just pressure."

He holds up his phone. "Another text from Ryder. He's really concerned."

I shake my head. "Tell him to chill. Jeez, he's worrying so much that I don't even need to."

"You guys have gotten close."

I nod, happy to affirm. "We have. Oh my gosh, I totally forgot. I finally found out what his big 'business' plan is." I air-quote the word *business* because it's just so ridiculous.

"He's kept it close to his chest," Lucas says. "He wouldn't even spill when we got pretty drunk watching the basketball game last week. So, what is it?"

I shake my head, still finding it unbelievable. "He wants to open a pot shop."

His mouth falls open. "A cannabis dispensary?"

"Yup. Crazy, right? And here's the nuttiest part, he wants to turn *my* shop into his marijuana business."

He seems to go inside himself, deep in thought. "Actually, no. It's not crazy. I know you love your shop and all, but realistically it's not sustainable in the long term. Not in this consumer climate. I think transforming it into a dispensary is a brilliant idea."

My head snaps to the side. "What?"

"I've often thought it would be a good investment to get in on a dispensary. Even talked to my brothers about it a few years ago when recreational cannabis became legal here. But then Dallas lost Phoebe and DJ and I guess we just never picked up the conversation."

My eyes are bulging in surprise. "But... but you own a winery. Isn't that like a conflict of interest or something? Wouldn't owning a pot store take away from your wine profits?"

He laughs. "On the contrary. A lot of people who get high love to enjoy a glass of wine as well. And they're much less likely to care about the cost." He cocks his head. "Is he looking for investors?"

I point at him. "You're as crazy as he is. Both of you have lost your minds."

"Says the Boho Gypsy girl who has twenty-five kinds of incense."

My planned retort to him is cut off by a strange feeling down in my nether regions. "Lucas, I'm feeling a lot of pressure down there. It's almost like I have to push."

He presses the button to call the nurse. Within minutes, Dr. Russo has confirmed I'm nearly crowning.

"Here we go," she says. "Take the cues from your body, Regan. When you feel the pressure, go ahead and give a big push."

I look at Lucas. He nods. "You've got this."

He grabs my hand, and for a second, my mind swirls with the dream of the perfect family and the perfect birth. The perfect exit from the hospital, car seat in Lucas's large hands as we go back to his perfect penthouse.

I steel myself and settle for one out of four. The one that is the most important. My perfect son. Right now, nothing else matters.

The pressure is building.

Dr. Russo puts a hand on my lower belly. "The baby is positioned very well. And because he's small, it might not take very many pushes to get him out."

I nod, trying not to take notice of the team of specialists who just arrived in my room and are standing in the corner. Dr. Russo told me they'd be here. A neonatologist. A special care nurse. A respiratory therapist. All standing at the ready to assess and possibly resuscitate the baby if needed.

I push a few times with every contraction. It doesn't hurt, but I can feel him coming out, like my body is a large tube of toothpaste and I'm squeezing it.

Suddenly, the pressure is gone.

"He's here," Dr. Russo says.

I stiffen and rise on my elbows, my heart pounding so hard I fear it will come right out of my chest. "He's not crying."

Lucas's hand crushes mine as we both stare over at the doctor. "Give him a second."

Then I hear it. It's not anything like I expected. It's not like what you hear on TV, the high shrill of a baby getting his first lungful of air then expelling it with a forceful wail. This is more like the soft cry of a baby bird.

"There he goes," Dr. Russo says.

"Because he's early, his breathing and muscle development are still maturing, so his cry will be quieter than a full-term baby," the NICU nurse explains.

"But he's okay?" I ask.

Nobody answers me for what seems like a decade but is probably only a few seconds. I grab onto Lucas's hand for dear life.

"He appears healthy," one of the doctors says. "We'll do a full workup back in the NICU."

Dr. Russo is still holding him. She looks up at Lucas. "Would you like to cut the cord, Dad?"

Lucas beams. We were told it might not be possible. This is a good sign. He's going to be okay.

Lucas cuts it, then we watch as he's immediately handed off to the NICU team and put into a clear plastic incubator as three people hover over him doing all kinds of things.

Mackenzie puts an ID band on my wrist, then Lucas's. "This matches the baby's and lets everyone know he's yours."

Mine. Ours. I swallow hard. We have a son who belongs to us.

They wheel him over to me.

I try to sit up, but Dr. Russo is still down there waiting for the afterbirth. "Can I hold him?"

"Soon," a doctor says. He opens the side of the incubator. "You can touch his hand right now, but we need to get him to the NICU for assessment."

I reach in and touch his tiny hand, almost the only part of him that isn't currently under a hat or blankets. I can't quite believe he's real. "He's not crying anymore," I say in distress.

"He's tired," one of them says. "Being born so tiny is exhausting. You'll be brought to the NICU to see him as soon as you're able."

They start to move away. "Wait!" I call out and touch his hand again. "I love you." The words come out along with a hundred tears.

"I love you, too," I hear Lucas say behind me, emotion etched in his words. When I turn to look at him through my tear-blurred vision, I could swear he's not only looking at Mitchell, but at me.

"Lucas," I say, finally letting myself succumb to every fear I never let myself have, and I bury my head into his chest as our son gets whisked away.

Chapter Forty

Lucas

After Dr. Russo finishes up with Regan, the nurse helps get her changed into a pair of pajamas.

"When can we see him?" Regan asks.

"As soon as you want," Mackenzie says.

Regan looks like she's going to get up.

Mackenzie stops her. "Whoa, there. You may be unsteady on your legs for an hour or so because of the epidural. I'll send in a wheelchair."

When the nurse leaves, we're alone. Alone and without our kid. I sit in the chair feeling overwhelmed by everything that's happened in the last twenty-four hours.

"He's going to be okay," Regan says. "I just know he is. Did you hear his little cry?" Her hand covers her heart.

My phone vibrates on the side table. I've been ignoring it for the past few hours.

"Are you going to answer that?" she asks, eyeing it.

"I want to see Mitchell first." My heart thumps. It's the first time I've ever called him by his real name. He *is* real. I have a son. I'm a father. *Holy shit.*

"Lucas, you alright?"

I nod. "I think it just hit me. Regan, we have a kid. We're parents."

There's a knock on the door and then it opens. But it's not Mackenzie with the wheelchair. It's one of the team of doctors who whisked Mitchell away.

I stand. "What is it? Is everything okay?"

He smiles. "Everything is fine. I'm Dr. Ford. I'll be your son's neonatologist during his stay."

"I went to high school with your daughter, Leanne," Regan says.

Dr. Ford smiles again. I get the idea he has to do that a lot to reassure the freaked-out parents of his patients. "Yes, that's right. I believe you were on the volleyball team together. Anyway, I wanted to update you on your son and tell you what to expect."

"Mitchell," Lucas says. "His name is Mitchell Lucas Montana."

"A strong name," Dr. Ford says. "Mitchell looks good. He's just a hair under five pounds. He's breathing on his own with a little oxygen support to help keep his lungs open. He's likely going to stay in the NICU for a week, perhaps a little longer. We'll be closely monitoring his vital signs and providing necessary medical interventions like oxygen therapy and feeding support. Before he goes home, he'll have to be stable in terms of breathing, heart rate, and temperature regulation. He'll also need to be feeding orally, breast or bottle. And of course he'll have to be free of any medical complications that require ongoing monitoring or treatment."

The door opens again. This time it's Mackenzie with the wheelchair.

Dr. Ford motions to the wheelchair. "You can contact me with any questions after you've seen him. The NICU nurses will also be very helpful in getting you the information you need."

"Thank you, doctor," I say as Mackenzie and I help Regan into the wheelchair. Mackenzie gets behind it, but I urge her out of the way. "I've got it."

Regan cranes her neck and smiles at me.

"Right this way," Mackenzie says.

We're led through a set of double doors that Mackenzie has to use her badge to open. We approach another door with a sign to the right that reads Neonatal Intensive Care Unit.

Intensive Care. My son needs intensive care. My stomach turns at the thought of him struggling in any way.

A woman wearing scrubs with teddy bears on them comes through the door. She's vaguely familiar. Then again, in a town this size almost everyone is. "I'm Christa," the woman says. "I'll be your son's day-shift nurse for the next few days. Kayla will be here in a few hours. She's the night-shift nurse tonight. "Do you mind if I see your ID bands?"

We both hold out our arms and Christa scans the code.

"You'll have to show these every time you come in here, even when all the nurses know you. It's a security measure."

"Understood," I say.

Mackenzie leaves us and Christa leads us to a wall with two sinks, one regular height, and one lower so a person in a wheelchair like Regan can use it. "You'll wash up every time you come in. It's important to keep germs out of the NICU, not just for your son, but for all the babies." She points to a carton of alcohol wipes. "If you plan to use your phone for photos, please go ahead and sanitize it here. Also, put it in airplane mode so it doesn't interfere with any electronics. And turn it to silent."

Christa sanitizes the handles of the wheelchair as we wash our hands. I'm not sure I've ever washed them so thoroughly.

"Do you mind?" Christa says, touching one of the handles of the wheelchair. "There's lots of medical equipment."

I step aside and let her take over. She presses a button on the wall and the automatic doors open.

Sounds immediately bombard me. I'm not sure what I was expecting. I mean, there are fragile preterm babies in here. I assumed it would be quiet and serene. This is anything but.

Regan looks up at me. She's obviously thinking the exact same thing.

It's all so surreal as we walk through the large, bright, loud room filled with incubators. Two of them are empty. The other four have babies of various sizes. A couple I recognize as Sam and Kendall Willis are standing over one and talking with a nurse or doctor. Dang, I knew they were expecting, but not for a while. Their baby must be even earlier than Mitchell. Sam sees us pass and lifts his chin at me. I do the same, noticing his red-rimmed eyes and puffy cheeks.

Christa was right, there's tons of medical equipment attached to every incubator. The sounds all around us are a combination of beeps, voices, and humming of ventilators. Several staff are conversing over another incubator. A young girl, maybe even a teenager, is sitting in a rocking chair holding a tiny baby with tubes coming out every which way. A nurse hovers closely.

An alarm sounds, and the hairs on the back of my neck rise.

"That's not him," Christa says quickly as a different nurse rushes by and goes to an incubator we already passed. "That's Little Hulk."

"Um... did you say Hulk?"

She smiles. "We give all our babies nicknames here. Little Hulk is small but mighty." She thumbs to the left. "That there is Cuddle

Bug because she loves being held and won't let go of your finger. The little princess at the front is Tiny Tornado. She keeps us on our toes."

"What have you named Mitchell?" Regan asks.

"We haven't yet. He's only been here thirty minutes. He'll earn his nickname in a day or so when we get to know him better."

Christa pushes Regan up next to the last incubator in the row. My gaze falls immediately inside it. And my fucking heart plummets into my stomach.

"Oh my god," Regan gasps. "I thought Dr. Ford said he was okay."

"He's doing well," Christa says. "Don't let all the tubes and wires upset you. These here are his EKG leads. This is his oxygen saturation monitor. The nasal cannula is providing him supplemental oxygen. And the other tube is a nasogastric tube for feeding."

Regan looks up, clearly as distressed as I am. "I can't nurse him?"

Christa shakes her head. "Not quite yet. You can pump and we'll feed him through the tube. Once he's more stable, we can feed him through a high-flow bottle. Breastfeeding takes a lot of energy, and the little ones wear out quickly."

"Can I… touch him?" Regan asks hesitantly.

"I'll do you one better," Christa says. "You can hold him."

Shock, surprise, and elation cross her face all at once. "I can?"

"Yes. Of course. Human touch and cuddling are very therapeutic for preemies. You'll even see nurses holding the babies if they haven't been out for a while."

"How often can we come here?" I ask. "What are visiting hours and limits?"

"There are none. You can come anytime you want, day or night, and stay as long as you wish."

Christa unhooks a few things, gets Mitchell out of the incubator, and settles him into Regan's arms where she re-hooks everything.

Regan's whole face changes. I can't look away. It's like she's having every single emotion all at once. Fear. Uncertainty. Nervousness. Excitement. But mostly what I see is love. It oozes from her every pore as she gazes at our son through teary eyes.

"Hey, buddy," she says, hiccupping her way through the words. "I'm your mom. I'm the one you've been kicking all this time."

As if he understands, Mitchell's eyes open and his head turns slightly, looking up at her. My heart splits open and love pours out like a fucking tsunami. I had no idea. No goddamn idea how instantaneously it could happen. I knew I loved him. I loved him even before I saw him. But this… this is the most intense feeling I've ever had in my entire thirty years. It's all-consuming. It's so powerful it actually hurts.

And I know right here and now that for the rest of my life I will do anything for him. My eyes flit back to Regan's face. And for his mom.

Regan cries in happiness. "Can he hear me?"

"He can," Christa says. "He can see you, too. Babies love to stare at faces, especially when close like yours is now."

The floor is hard and unforgiving, but I lower to my knees anyway and lean near her shoulder. I reach out and touch my son for the first time, more emotions catching in my throat as I feel his soft hand. It's so damn little. His skin is thin, delicate, a bit wrinkly, and slightly translucent, with visible blood vessels underneath.

His tiny hand wraps partially around my finger and I lose all my breath. "He's holding onto me."

"He's got a good grasp reflex," Christa says. "He's probably been practicing on his umbilical cord for a while."

"He's…" Regan has a hard time finding words. "He's perfect."

I wholeheartedly agree. Despite all the tubes and wires obstructing our view of his small face, he *is* perfect. "Of course he is," I say. "He looks like me, after all."

Regan laughs. "On that we'll have to agree to disagree. He most definitely has a Lucas nose."

"That's what I said. He's all me."

"That's not what I meant." She glances at me with a smile and an eye roll. "Oh, forget it."

Regan talks to Mitchell. Her voice is calm and gentle, her tone soft and endearing. She was made for this. Made to be a mom.

"You're a natural," I whisper in her ear.

When she turns her head and smiles, our lips are inches apart. I long to kiss her. We've just welcomed our son into the world. I should kiss her. Her eyes fall to my lips for just a second, but then she looks back at Mitchell, and the moment is gone.

I kiss her anyway. On the cheek. "Thank you," I say.

"For what?" she asks, touching his little cheek.

"For him."

"Thank you too," she says, looking back at me.

Now's your chance. I lean in. I can feel her breath on me. Is she going to let me kiss her?

An alarm behind us sounds and Regan pulls away, looking back. "Is everything okay?" she asks Christa.

"You'll hear alarms sounding often in here. Most of the time it's not a real emergency, just a change in vitals that is easily fixed by altering a ventilator or other piece of equipment. And sometimes leads and wires come loose. You'll get used to all the sounds soon enough."

I stay on the ground so long, my knees bruise and my legs go numb. But I need to be close. I want him to see me.

"You want a turn?" Regan asks after holding him for a long time.

I want to. More than anything. But seeing the two of them together as mother and son is the most amazing thing I've ever witnessed. She's earned the right to these moments. And no matter how much I want to take him in my arms, she needs it more than me.

"I'll have my turn later. I'm good just holding his hand."

A few minutes later, it dawns on me that I haven't taken a single photo. I get my phone from my pocket and take two dozen pictures. Of him. Them. Every part of him. His little hand. His face. I open the blanket and take one of his foot. I push back the beanie and take one of his fine, dark hair.

Christa changes her gloves and holds out her hands. "Here. I'll take one of all of you."

I shift around on my sore knees, put a hand on Mitchell, and lean close to Regan while Christa snaps another dozen photos.

"You'll send all those to me?" Regan asks.

"You and the whole damn town," I say proudly.

She smiles then yawns. Christa doesn't miss it.

"You need to sleep, Mom. You've had a long day."

Regan frowns. "I don't want to leave."

"You'll be better for him if you're rested," Christa says. "And you can come back any time, even in the middle of the night."

"But he'll be alone."

"I promise he won't be. We're all here for him."

"I'll come back and sit with him," I assure her. "When you're sleeping, I'll be in here. I'll stay with him. Okay?"

Regan nods reluctantly. "Promise?"

"We have family here," I say to Christa. "Can they come in?"

"Grandparents only. We have to limit the number of people. More people mean more germs."

I feel bad for Regan. My parents will get to see Mitchell, but she hasn't even told hers about him. Will she? Now that he's here, will she tell them?

"Now kiss your little one goodbye for now," Christa says. "I'll get him tucked back into his temporary home."

Regan lowers her head and kisses him. Then I do. I lean over and place my very first kiss on his little head. I'm not going to be one of those dads who thinks it's unmanly to kiss and hug and show affection. I'm going to hold him every chance I get. Show him that, like my dad did for me, hugging a child might just be one of the manliest things you *can* do for him. "I'll be back," I whisper.

Christa takes him, and I wheel a sleepy Regan back to her room knowing our lives are forever changed. Because of the little man in the incubator. The tiny human that has ripped a giant-sized hole in my heart and filled it with more than I could have ever anticipated.

Regan reaches a hand up by her shoulder, rooting it around, searching for one of mine as I push her. I grab it and squeeze, wanting so much to say the three words caught in my throat. I do say them, but only to myself. Because I'm not about to ruin the monumental moments we just experienced with our son.

Our son.

I'm a fucking dad.

I still can't believe it.

Chapter Forty-one

Lucas

Regan is asleep before her head hits the pillow. I'm not surprised. I've heard labor and childbirth is more taxing than running a marathon.

I watch her sleep for a minute. Her face is clean of all makeup. Her hair isn't washed. But somehow, she's even more beautiful than she was yesterday. Or last month. Or when she was eighteen and I was the horny adolescent lusting after her.

My feelings are more intense than before. But she's the mother of my child. I'm sure that has everything to do with it.

You loved her before.

I scrub a hand across my two-day stubble as I glance around the room at all the flowers and teddy bears that got delivered when we were in the NICU. Which reminds me, my phone is blowing up with calls and texts.

I promised Regan I'd sit with Mitchell. But first, I have to let everyone know what's going on.

I make my way to the waiting room, surprised to see it filled to capacity with friends and family. A dozen people spring off couches and chairs when I appear in the doorway. All I have to do is smile and the whole room seems to sigh in collective relief.

"Lucas!" Allie screams, bounding forward to punch me in the arm. "For Christ's sake, couldn't you at least have texted?"

"Is he okay?" Mom asks.

The room falls silent as I tell them everything. Then my phone gets passed around so everyone can see pictures.

Allie cries uncontrollably when she sees him. Big, snotty sobs.

Mom sidles up next to her, almost having to hold her upright. I had no idea my little sister would be so affected by me becoming a dad.

"He's small, but perfect," I say. "I bet he'll be out of here even before they anticipate. My kid is strong."

Dad pats my shoulder. "Of course he is. Congratulations, son."

I pull Mom and Dad aside. "I'm going to sit with him now. Regan doesn't want him to be alone. Grandparents are the only other people allowed, so do you think—"

"Whenever you need us," Mom says. "We can take shifts."

I nod. "Thanks."

I look back at everyone in the room. Regan's friends. Mine. Ryder and my entire family. And I know with this many people pulling for him, Mitchell is going to be just fine.

Before leaving, I pull Ryder aside. "What did Sheriff Niles say about that asshole?"

"No trace of him. Gone. Vanished like a puff of smoke. He made his deputies aware, and they'll be on the lookout, but he honestly believes she's seen the last of him."

I breathe a deep sigh of relief knowing a weight has been lifted and Regan will have one less thing to worry about.

I clasp his shoulder. "Thanks, brother."

He looks at me oddly. When it dawns on me that I called him brother, I backtrack quickly and say, "Or should I say *uncle?*"

He smiles, clearly liking the title.

I wait outside the NICU for someone to let me in, then wash up and sanitize my phone in case I want to take more pictures. Because of course I will. Then a nurse scans my ID band and I enter.

"He's been doing very well," Christa says from across the room. "I'll be right there." She finishes doing whatever she's doing and then comes over. "You ready to hold him, Dad?"

"Like you wouldn't believe."

"It was really nice of you to let Regan have all that time with him. I know it must have been hard."

I shake my head, thinking of how happy she looked with Mitchell in her arms. "It wasn't."

Christa cocks her head and studies me. She knows about me. The whole town does. Even people I don't know, recognize, or remember—they all know about the infamous runaway groom. Finally, she looks away and pulls over a rocking chair. "Sit here and take off your shirt."

I raise a brow.

She chuckles. "Relax, sailor. I'm not hitting on you. We call it kangaroo care. It's a technique for holding preemies that involves placing the baby directly on your chest for skin-to-skin contact. It not only promotes bonding, but can help your baby sleep better, keep them warm, and improve their heart, breathing, blood pressure, even their glucose levels. It's amazing what it can do."

Before she's even done explaining, my shirt is off.

When she unwraps him from the blanket, he's just in a diaper. I'm amazed they even make diapers that small. His body is so tiny.

He looks much smaller than he did just an hour ago. His little arms and legs look so frail I'm almost scared to hold him.

"It's okay," Christa assures me, sensing my anxiety. "He won't break."

When she places him on my chest, my entire world stops. Everything else falls away. It's just me and him. My son. My new purpose in life.

"Ho-lee shit," I murmur.

"Pretty incredible, huh?" Christa says.

"I had no idea."

"Nobody does. You can try and tell people how it will feel to have a child. But until you experience it, there just aren't enough words to truly express it."

"Why haven't I ever done this before?" I whisper. "I swear to god I'm going to give you a dozen siblings."

I think I hear Christa chuckle before she walks away and leaves me to bond with my son.

Sometime later—I don't even know how long it's been. *Ten minutes? An hour?*—Christa comes back and leans over the top of his empty incubator. "You're going to be a good dad. I can tell."

"I plan on it."

"I read the article," she says. "Saw the news stories too."

"You and everyone else," I say, not looking up from my incredible sleeping son.

"They didn't tell the whole story."

I glance up. "What do you mean?"

"They left something out."

I narrow my eyes at her.

"You're in love with her."

"What?" My heart pounds. "You're crazy."

"You're the one who's crazy if you don't tell the woman who just had your kid that you love her."

I look back at Mitchell, not having the energy to deny it. "It's way more complicated than that."

"Complicated. Right. You just had a baby together. There's no clear answer here."

"Whatever, Christa."

My stomach grumbles. I'm not even sure how long it's been since I've eaten. It's been even longer for Regan since they didn't want her eating during labor. She'll be starving when she wakes up.

"Hey, Christa." I nod to my phone sitting on the little table. "Mind doing me a favor?"

"More pictures?"

"No. I need you to place an order for me. Regan will want to eat when she wakes up. Can you call Sushi King?"

"Sure. What kind of sushi do you want to order?"

"All of it," I say. "One of everything. She's gone all these months without eating it. I want to make sure one of them is her absolute favorite."

She laughs, makes the call, then sets down my phone. She leans close. "No one has ever done that for me. Not even my husband." She walks away, tossing me a look over her shoulder. "But, yeah... it's soooo complicated."

~ ~ ~

Regan wakes up and looks around. "What time is it? How long did I sleep?"

"A few hours. It's eight o'clock."

She sits up slowly with a slight grimace on her beautiful face. Her arms reach for the pillow next to her, so I move it to support her back. She must be uncomfortable. With all thoughts on Mitchell, it's easy to forget she just pushed a five-pound human out of her.

Her shoulders slump. "I thought you said you'd stay with him."

"I did. And then I came to sit with you. You need people, too, Regan. My mom has been with him for an hour or so. Dad says he'll come too. Between the four of us, he'll have a lot of company."

"Good. I'm glad he won't have to be alone."

"There are plenty of nurses around to keep an eye on him."

Her head shakes. "It's not the same."

"I know."

Her eyes widen then dart around the room. "What's that smell? Is that sushi?"

I roll the tray table over. The spread I got barely even fits on it. There are salmon rolls, spicy tuna, crispy shrimp, and a dozen others. Her eyes bug out.

"I wasn't sure what kind you like."

"Oh my gosh... all of it!" She rips into a pair of chopsticks as I start opening little plastic containers.

Her eyes roll back as the first piece goes in her mouth. She chews it like it's the best thing she's ever tasted. She picks out another, and moans when she bites into it. I stand completely still and watch as this happens over and over.

It's really hard to keep myself from getting turned on. Because... *shit*.

"You can't be serious," she says, eyeing my rising problem.

"It's your fault," I say. "You're making all those noises. And you cut me off months ago."

Her chopsticks come to rest on the table. "You haven't...?"

I shake my head.

"Not since...?"

I reach out, grab a piece of a spicy tuna roll with my bare fingers and pop it into my mouth. "Nope," I say around it. I wiggle my fingers. "My hand is the only thing I'm dating these days."

I could swear the hint of a smile crosses her lips. Because she thinks I should abstain since she did? Or because she's happy I'm still being boycotted? As I study her for an answer, her cheeks flush. She turns away and picks out her next piece of sushi.

"Maddie and Ava were here," I say. "They sat with you when I was with Mitchell earlier. They said they'd come back tomorrow."

The door opens and a different nurse comes in with a strange-looking machine attached to tubes and funnels. She eyes the sushi table and shakes her head in amusement.

"You want some?" Regan asks. "I think he got everything on the menu."

"I'd love a piece or two. Thanks. My name's Lola. I'll be your night nurse. I came in to help you pump. Baby needs all that great colostrum."

"Well then," I say, moving toward the door. "I think I'll go check on my mom. How about I come back in fifteen minutes or so and take you to the NICU?"

Regan looks at Lola who nods.

"Perfect." Regan peruses the table for another bite. "And thanks for this, it was really sweet of you."

"It's nothing. See you in a few."

"Lucas... it's not nothing. Really. Thank you."

"You got it."

Our eyes connect for a long moment before she goes in for another bite. But damn, in that moment, it's like something was connecting us. Something more than Mitchell. More than what we've gone through or are going through. More than what any contract binds us to.

I leave the room, press my back against the wall just outside it, and grip my shirt right over my heart. Because I've got it bad for the woman on the other side of that door. And it's killing me that when we leave this place, we won't be leaving together.

Chapter Forty-two

Regan

Pumping is strange. And not at all the intimate experience I was hoping for. The plastic bottle doesn't grip my finger while taking nourishment from my body. The motorized buzzing is not the soft suckling sound I find myself craving.

I can't wait to hold Mitchell in my arms and nurse him.

When I gaze at the empty chair next to the bed, remembering how Lucas was looking at me, I start crying for no reason at all.

Lola gobbles down a piece of sushi and pats my arm. "Everything okay?"

"I don't know." I sniff. "I mean, I guess so." My chest heaves as my eyes are glued to the chair. "How am I going to do this alone? What was I thinking? I don't know how to raise a kid and run a business at the same time."

"I'm confused," Lola says, glancing between me and the door. "Aren't you two...?"

"No." I cry harder. "We're doing this together, but we're not *together*."

"Oh." She checks the pump and removes it from my right breast. "I guess I just thought with the way you guys looked at each other…"

I swallow. "Wh-what do you mean?"

She shrugs. "Well, it just seemed obvious that you guys were a couple."

I laugh snottily. "We're not. We never have been. We're friends. Good friends. But… Oh my god, why am I crying? This is ridiculous. I never cry like this."

"It's the hormones."

My eyes snap to hers. "I thought all that crap was done as soon as I delivered."

She looks mildly amused. "Quite the opposite. After childbirth there is a dramatic drop in the estrogen and progesterone in your body. There also may be a sharp drop in hormones produced by your thyroid gland. All of that can lead to emotional mood swings, sluggishness, even depression." She puts her hands on her hips. "Haven't you read anything about the postpartum period?"

"No." I cover my face with my hands. My shoulders shake with more uncontrolled sobbing. "I… I just thought everything would go back to the way it was." I glance at the chair again. "Or… something."

Her hand lands on my shoulder. "It's okay to feel whatever you're feeling. Some of it may be real. Some of it not. But for most people, the 'baby blues,' as they call it, will go away within a few weeks. So by the time you and Mitchell head home, you could be ready to conquer the world."

Ready to conquer the world.

With a baby.

By myself.

The door swings open. I wipe my eyes and blow my nose.

Lucas rushes to the side of the bed. "Regan, what's wrong?"

I shake my head. "Something about hormones and mood swings. Lola said it's all perfectly normal. I'll be fine."

He stares at me and pushes a piece of errant hair behind my ear. The way his fingers sweep against my cheek almost has me breaking down in sobs again.

"Can I go see him now?" I ask Lola.

"If you can make it to the bathroom and back without help, I'll let you go without the wheelchair."

"Deal."

My legs feel a little funny when I get up, like I haven't walked on them for a while, and when I pee—*geesh!*—it stings like a mother.

Afterward, I look at myself in the mirror. Bad idea. I need a shower. And makeup. And maybe ice packs for these huge bags under my eyes.

"I'm a total wreck," I say, emerging from the bathroom.

Lucas hands me the plush new robe his mother, Sarah, gave me. He grins. "You look like a mom." I look up to meet his gaze and our eyes connect like they did right after Mitchell was born. "Beautiful," he whispers.

How can he even think that? I'm fat and ugly, I have blood and mucus coming out of me, and I basically look like the living dead.

Lola is standing directly behind him, her eyebrow cocked whimsically, grin on her face.

"I… you're crazy."

"I'm not crazy," he says. "You're glowing."

I roll my eyes and ask Lola, "Did I pass the test?"

She motions toward the door. "You know the way." Then she picks up the tiny vials of milk or whatever. "I'll get these to the NICU. Thanks for the sushi."

Lucas holds the door open. On our way to see Mitchell, he takes my elbow as if to steady me. "Mom just left. She'll be back tomorrow. Everyone else is wondering when they can see you. Maddie, Ava, Ryder. Your other friends. They know they can't see Mitchell, but they were hoping to visit. Can I tell them to stop by tomorrow?"

"I'll be with Mitchell."

"You can't sit with him all day every day."

"Says who?"

"You're going to need breaks, Regan. He sleeps most of the time. Even if he were at home with us…" He shifts his hold on my arm. "I mean at home with you or at home with me." He sighs. "Even then, he'd sleep a lot and we wouldn't be hovering over him twenty-four seven."

I nod. "You're right. I guess they can come tomorrow."

"Are you excited to see him?"

"So excited. Have I missed anything? Did he roll over yet?"

He laughs heartily. "Well, you know, the Nighthawks are already recruiting him for shortstop."

I feel a smile splitting my face. How is it that I always feel better when Lucas is around? The smile falls, because in a day or two, he won't be around. He won't be around when I wake up. When I break down. When I need anything. When I need… *him.*

"Here we are."

My heart pounds excitedly as I wash my hands. I'm going to see Mitchell. My baby. My son. Before I can stop it, tears start streaming down my cheek.

"What is it?" Lucas asks.

"I just can't believe I'm a mom."

He cups my face and wipes my tears with his thumbs. "I know. I'm the same way. Earlier, I nodded off in the chair by your bed and when I came to, it was like I'd forgotten for a second. But then, wham! It hit me and kind of took the wind out of me. I'm a dad. You're a mom. We're parents." He shakes his head. "Unbelievable."

His hands fall away. I miss them. I miss them more than I want to admit.

A nurse comes out to scan our ID bracelets, then we go through the doors. The last time I was in here, I was in a wheelchair. My mind was all over the place. All I could think about was seeing Mitchell. But now that I'm up and walking, I notice things I didn't. Like what I can only assume is a micro-preemie who is barely even there, tubes and wires overtaking the entire body. A tiny mask over the eyes. I cover my mouth. "Oh my god."

"That's Sam and Kendall Willis's daughter. She was born last week at twenty-seven weeks."

I continue to stare at the miniscule human, wondering how it's possible a baby that small can even survive. When I arrive at Mitchell's incubator, he suddenly seems so much larger, even though he himself is so small.

A nurse I've never seen before comes over and introduces herself. "I'm Kayla. You must be Regan. Your husband told me all about you."

"Um... what?" Lucas hems and haws. "We're not... she's not..."

"We're just friends," I say.

Lucas sighs heavily beside me, probably relieved the pretty nurse knows the truth now.

"I'm sorry," Kayla says. "I'm fairly new here. And to Calloway Creek. I just assumed by the way he spoke about you. Anyway, are you ready to hold him? He's a cutie."

Before I can register what she said about Lucas, an alarm sounds. Unlike when I was here before, it's not behind us, or on the other side of the room. It's right here. It's Mitchell's alarm. My heart goes into overdrive. Something is wrong.

Kayla immediately goes into action. She reaches into Mitchell's incubator, puts a hand on him, and shakes slightly. My feet almost go out from under me. I stop breathing. Arms come around me, holding me up.

The alarm stops, but my heart doesn't start. And I feel like I might vomit.

"What's happening?" Lucas asks, horror lacing his words.

"It's okay," Kayla says. She touches my arm. "He's okay. Look, he's even awake now."

My hand comes to my chest as I stare at his open eyes. "But… what happened?"

"He stopped breathing for a sec—"

Lucas's grip tightens on me. "He stopped *breathing?*" he exclaims, pulling the words straight from my brain.

"Oh my god!" I cry.

"Breathe, Mom," Kayla says. "It's not uncommon for this to happen with preemies. It's called an A & B episode. That stands for apnea and bradycardia. It's where they temporarily stop breathing and experience a slowed heart rate. We call them 'spells' here."

I reach out and touch the plastic side of the incubator. "Has he had one before?"

"No."

"Will it happen again?" Lucas asks.

"Hard to say. Maybe, maybe not. His nervous system isn't mature yet. That can lead to irregular breathing patterns. But you can see all it took was a light shake, just a little gentle stimulation, to get him back on track. The doctor will discuss it in more detail, but that's the gist of it."

"What if it happens when he's at home?" My chest seizes. "Could he just die in his crib?"

"First, it's unlikely that will happen. Second, he won't be allowed to leave the NICU until he's gone five days without a spell." She sees the tears pooled in my eyes. "Regan, it's okay. That's why he's here and hooked up to the monitors."

Lucas's arm is wrapped tightly around me. He squeezes my shoulder. "Hey, it's okay. He's okay. Look at him. He's perfect."

My heartbeat slowly returns to normal as I watch Mitchell's little hand twitch. As I see the steady rise and fall of his chest. "Can I even hold him now?"

Kayla reaches in to prep him. "It's preferable that you do. Babies respond very well to touch."

He's placed in my arms for only the second time in his short life. I want to squeeze him against me and never let him go.

Kayla pulls over a rolling stool for Lucas and he sits at my side, reaching over to touch various parts of our son.

"I'll leave you to it," Kayla says. "I'll be close if you need me."

I'm not sure how long we sit and stare at Mitchell. We watch as his little eyes flutter open and closed. As he squirms just a bit, like even those small movements are a lot for him. As he sleeps. As he breathes.

Hours later, I can't keep my eyes open despite my earlier nap.

"Come on," Lucas says. "You need sleep. I'll get you settled and come back and sit with him."

He calls Kayla over and she puts Mitchell back. I gaze into his incubator saying a silent goodbye.

It's almost midnight when we get back to my room. I pee again and get into bed. I can't help it when the waterworks start again. "What if... what if it happens again and that was the last time I ever see him?"

Lucas takes my hand. "That is not going to happen."

"But you can't be sure. Lucas, our baby almost just died."

He tenses and his shoulders shake. He's trying to hold it together for me, but like me, he's about to fall apart.

"How can I fall asleep knowing he could stop breathing?" I ask through my tears. "I don't think I'll ever be able to sleep."

"You have to. For him. You'll be no good to him if you aren't rested."

I shake my head. "I don't think I can."

"Can I try something?"

I shrug.

He drops my hand, crosses the room, turns out all the lights, then gets up on the bed. "Scoot over a bit," he says.

"But Mitchell needs you."

"You need me too, Regan. Please."

I scoot over and he settles in next to me. He wraps an arm around me, and instinctively, like it's the most natural thing in the world, I nestle my head into his shoulder.

"I'm here for you, Regan. You and Mitchell." I can feel the wind of his voice through my hair. His face is tucked against my head. He kisses me. "I'm here for you."

I cry in his arms. I cry for Mitchell. I cry for myself. I cry for the man whose very arms surround me like those of a husband. A lover. A life partner. And I cry knowing he'll never be any of those.

And as his steadfast arms envelop me, I realize this big, strong, virile man is crying too.

Chapter Forty-three

Regan

Light is pouring through the window. I throw an arm over my eyes, groaning. But then I bolt up, fully awake once reality sets it.

Mitchell.

Lucas is sleeping on the couch under the windows.

"Lucas," I call, getting out of bed and into my slippers.

He wakes, taking a moment to orient to where he is, and sits up quickly. "Everything okay?"

"Yes. I mean, I think. Why did you let me sleep that long?"

"You obviously needed it," he says, wiping his eyes. "You slept all night, Regan. That's a good thing."

"But—"

"I sat with him twice. Held him for hours. He's good."

I sit next to him in relief, then notice a new bag on the floor next to him. "What's that?"

"I had Ryder drop off another pair of pajamas and all your bathroom stuff. Figured you'd want a shower."

"A shower sounds heavenly. But—"

He holds up a hand. "I'll go sit with him." He stands, straightens the wrinkled shirt he's been wearing since yesterday, and goes for the door. "Take all the time you need and try not to worry about him, okay?"

I nod. After he leaves, my hand wanders the fabric of the couch cushion he vacated. I look at the bed and wonder how long he lay beside me last night, holding me, crying with me, before he moved. Part of me wishes he'd still been there when I woke up. But that would mean he wouldn't have been with Mitchell. And no matter how my heart feels about Lucas, that's not what's important here. The little warrior down the hall—he's the only thing that matters. Not my ridiculous pregnancy emotions or postpartum feelings about the warrior's father.

Thirty minutes later, clean, but feeling guilty about taking even that long, I arrive at the NICU.

I know something's wrong the second I see the way Lucas is looking at me. He's holding Mitchell, but there's so much pain in his eyes. My heart thunders as I approach. My legs almost fail me. Is he holding our dead son? Sitting here grieving for him as he waited for me?

But then I see Mitchell move, and my lungs fill with air.

"What is it?" I ask.

"He had another episode, or spell, or whatever they call it."

My hand flies to my mouth as I choke back sobs.

"He's okay. I talked to the doctor. He assured me it's not uncommon. Listen, everything else is good. His fluid intake and output is stellar." He smiles. "Did you know they monitor *everything* that goes into or comes out of his body? And apparently our kid pees and poops like a champ. Then again, I'd expect no less from any son of mine."

How Lucas can make me laugh when I want to scream and crumble apart is beyond me.

I step next to him and hold out my arms. "Can I. Please? I need to."

He stands confidently and, without any help from a nurse, shifts Mitchell into my arms. I kiss my sweet boy and then look up. "You're getting pretty good at this."

He takes a bow, making me smile.

"Were you here when it happened?"

His head shakes as guilt crosses his face. "It was early this morning. I should have been here."

"Lucas, remember what you told me. We can't be here twenty-four seven. We're here enough. And he has a great team of doctors and nurses."

"Wow." He tilts his head and studies me.

"What?"

"A good night's sleep and a shower really did you good. You aren't freaking out nearly as much as I thought you would."

I look at our sleeping son, relieved with each and every rise and fall of his chest. "I'm sorry I sort of fell apart on you last night."

"Regan, you just had a baby. Even if he was full-term and totally healthy, you'd still be allowed to do that."

"Well, thanks. I wasn't sure I'd get any sleep at all before you climbed into my bed."

Unwittingly, my cheeks flush. Lucas smiles. "You okay, Ray? Your whole face just turned three shades of red."

Ray. It's been a while since he's used that nickname.

"I'm just... so happy to be here holding him."

Lucas seems content just sitting by my side for hours.

Christa, Mitchell's first nurse from yesterday, comes over. "Mom and Dad, why don't you take a break. I need to weigh him and do some other nurse things. Go get breakfast. It's not the best food in the world, but the pancakes in the cafeteria are edible."

"No need," Lucas says.

I glance at him as Christa takes Mitchell. "But I'm starving."

"Got it covered."

I narrow my eyes. "Lucas Montana, what did you do now?"

"You'll see."

I kiss the baby, and we go back to my room where Maddie and Ava are waiting with several steaming Criss Coffee Corner cups along with bags of pastries from my favorite bakery and a gigantic basket of fresh fruit.

I turn to look at Lucas, positive he's responsible for all of it.

He just shrugs. "I'm going to go home for a shower and a change of clothes. I'll be back in an hour."

He kisses the side of my head, spins, and leaves.

"Oh. My. God."

My eyes snap to Ava. "What?"

"You're totally in love with him."

I pull the door shut. "Lucas? What… no."

"It's written all over you. You love your baby daddy. Admit it."

Maddie's eyes widen like dinner plates. "You are, aren't you?" She sighs. "Regan Lucas, you went and did it, didn't you?"

I close my eyes and crumple onto the bed. "I didn't mean for it to happen. It just sort of did."

Two pairs of arms come around me. I sit up and hug them back.

"It's the hormones," Maddie says.

"That's what I've been telling myself for months."

"Wait." Maddie pulls back. "Months? You've been feeling this way for months? I thought it was just because of the birth and you bonding over the scary stuff."

"Go ahead and say it." I sit back and wait for her 'I told you so.'

She perches on the bed next to me. "I'm not going to say it, Regan. I'm not sure I need to. Because it looks like… Well, it kind of looks like he might feel the same way."

My gaze darts to hers. She looks to Ava for confirmation. "I saw it too. And the way he sounded on the phone, wanting me to bring just the right things. That man wants to make you happy."

"I just gave him a son. Of course he's taking care of me."

"It's more than that," Ava says.

"It's not," I assure them. "The man isn't capable of more. We all know it."

"I don't know," Maddie says. "There's something about kids that can change a man's whole perspective on life."

"I'm not sure what you think you saw, but it wasn't that. He's really just pampering me. End of story." I gaze out the window, sadness becoming a dominant emotion once again. "It's just sometimes I worry about my ability to do this alone."

Maddie's arm comes around me. "No matter what happens, you're most definitely not doing this alone. We're here for you. All of us."

Are they all? Will they all be? Will he be?

Sure, Lucas has been kind, generous, and super attentive. But now that the baby's here and I'm no longer this fragile vessel carrying his child, things will change. No more walks through the park. No catered meals once I'm out of the hospital. No daily checks to make sure I'm okay.

I sigh, pushing the thoughts out of my head, then motion to the bag of sweets. "Now if you don't mind, I recently pushed a human out of my vagina and I'm starving."

Samantha Christy

Chapter Forty-four

Lucas

My back is killing me from sleeping on the couch in Regan's hospital room for two nights in a row. Not to mention how sleep deprived I am from waking every few hours to go be with Mitchell so Regan can get a full night's sleep.

This morning, knowing Dad is with him, I let myself linger in bed—or on couch, as it may be—and watch a sleeping Regan. She looks peaceful despite our situation. She has this quiet little snore/snort that occasionally wakes me. Has she always done it, I wonder? Only once have I slept in bed with her all night. A fact that is becoming more painful the longer I have these feelings.

Her eyes open and she stares at me sleepily. I'm ten feet away, but I might as well be right next to her with how she's looking at me. I see the appreciation in her eyes for all that I've done. But what she doesn't realize is that *she's* the one who did everything. She did all the hard stuff. Going through morning sickness, monitoring her weight and blood pressure, making sure she was eating all the right things. Giving birth.

"You're my goddamn hero," I say. "I hope you know that."

She smiles lazily. "I like waking up to your smile. It lets me know everything is okay."

I sit up. "Everything *is* okay. My dad came around four this morning."

Her arms stretch above her head as she yawns. "Your parents have been amazing."

"I told you, the Montanas do anything for family."

Her gaze falls to the floor. She's suddenly sad. I bet she's wishing she had a better relationship with her parents.

"Do you know if Mitchell had another spell last night?"

"Not as far as I know."

"Good." She sits up, puts on her slippers and robe, and heads to the bathroom.

I take the opportunity to run down the hall and get her some crappy hospital coffee since the breakfast I ordered won't be here for a few hours.

"Thanks," she says, taking the cup from me when I return. She sits morosely on the couch, moving aside the blanket I was sleeping under. "I was just thinking, they're going to kick me out today. I'll be ten minutes away." A tear rolls down her cheek. "I know he's okay without us here twenty-four seven. And I know we'll be here a lot. But when I envisioned going home from the hospital, it was a whole lot different."

I sit next to her and let her cry on my shoulder. I hate that she's crying. But I love that she's leaning on me in her time of need.

"What if something happens and I'm not here?" She sniffs and snivels. "What if he—" She full-on sobs into my chest.

I take the coffee from her and set it on the floor. "Hey. He's not going to. You heard the nurses yesterday. He's doing very well despite his spells. He may never even have another one. His nervous system is maturing more and more every day."

My shirt is soaked from her tears. Damn, I wish there was more I could do.

I brush a hair off her forehead. "You know what? If you want to stay, I'm sure we can arrange something. The hospital must have an empty room somewhere. I'll pay whatever it takes if that'll make you feel better."

"I can't let you do that." She pulls away and wipes her face. "I'm just being hormonal. I'll only be a few minutes away. I just hate the idea of leaving this place without him."

I nod. "I know. Do you… want me to come sleep on your couch or something?"

Her head shakes. "Ryder is still there. He can take care of me."

Her words are like a vise around my heart. *I* want to be the one there. *I* want to be the one taking care of her.

"As long as they have both of us on speed dial," she says.

"I'll make sure of it."

"Are you ready to go see him? Or do you want a shower first."

"I want to see him. If your dad has been there since four, he needs to go home."

Within a few minutes, we're entering the NICU. Faces of the other parents, all familiar by now, look up in greeting. Not happy greetings. None of us are delighted to be here. It's more of an acknowledgement of presence. We're all part of a club nobody wants to join.

Yesterday, Sam and I had a long talk about becoming dads. He has a long, long road ahead of him, though. His daughter, Gemma, affectionately known as Tiny Tornado, has all kinds of health issues. I feel for him. And it's hard not to feel fortunate that my kid is *only* experiencing spells. Sometimes I catch him looking at us with envy.

Just as I look at them with a broken fucking heart. Because I can't imagine how it would feel if Mitchell had even a fraction of the things his daughter does. Low blood pressure, infection, intraventricular hemorrhage, and a slew of other conditions I can't recall.

It's kind of wild to even think for a second that I feel lucky with my four-pound-fifteen-ounce son who occasionally stops breathing. But in here, it's hard not to.

"You've got yourself one hell of a kid," Dad says, letting Christa take Mitchell and pass him off to Regan.

"You're just in time," Christa says. "We're going to try feeding him with a bottle this morning."

"A bottle?" Regan looks up. "Why not my breast?"

"Nursing is very taxing on the little ones. The high-flow bottles will let us know how ready he is. If he does well over the next day or two, we'll transition him to your breast. Don't worry, he'll still be getting your breast milk. Just don't forget to pump every three or four hours. And supplementing with the bottle while he's here and you're at home will be necessary as these little ones need to eat every two hours."

Regan sighs. I know she's still thinking about how much she wants to be here. But, man, every two hours? I'm kind of glad she won't be. She needs her sleep.

Christa hands Regan a very small bottle with a tiny nipple. There's hardly any milk in it.

"That's all he's going to get?" I ask.

"At this age, he'll take about twelve to fifteen ounces per day. Because he'll be fed every two hours, he doesn't need very much at each feeding. But what he does get is full of nutrients since it's Regan's colostrum."

"What if he chokes on it?" Regan asks.

"I'm right here," Christa says. "I think he's going to do just fine."

Dad quietly slips out, wanting us to have this moment together. I nod my thanks.

When Regan carefully touches the nipple to Mitchell's tiny lips, he immediately turns away.

"It's okay," Christa says. "Try again. Preemies have all kinds of unpleasant things going in their mouths. It won't take him long to figure out this is the good stuff. Try putting it on his cheek first. Babies have a rooting instinct."

She gently rubs the nipple on his cheek. He does turn and take it in his mouth, but I don't see him suck.

"I don't think it's going to work," Regan says, sadly.

Christa touches her shoulder. "Give him a minute."

Mitchell looks like he's going to fall right back to sleep with the nipple still in his mouth. But then… then his mouth moves, and I can see him sucking. My eyes instantly go to Regan's face. She's beaming. Happy tears pool in her eyes as she watches our son take his very first bottle.

"He's doing it!" She looks up and catches my eye.

"He's a natural," I say. "So are you."

"Do you want to do half?"

I shake my head. "I'll do the next one. This is all you."

I stand and lean against the wall next to his incubator, watching the interaction between my son and his mother. Every once in a while, his eyes open and he looks directly at her. As soon as they close, she looks up at me. And there's so much love there. She loves him as fiercely as I do. Perhaps even more, if that's possible.

Christa steps next to me and whispers, "Looks like the news story left out *two* vital pieces of information."

I tilt my head, waiting for more.

"She loves you. She loves you, too."

My eyes blaze with amusement. "You're insane."

"Oh, come on, Lucas. With the way she looks at you? That woman is head over heels in love with you."

Regan looks up to catch us talking. "Am I doing it wrong?" she asks Christa.

"No, ma'am. You're doing everything exactly right."

Christa shoots me a playful look and walks away.

~ ~ ~

Damn. I didn't think it would hurt this much. Like physically hurt like a punch to the gut. But here I am, dropping Regan off at her place. Helping Ryder carry up all the cards, flowers, teddy bears, and other shit from the hospital.

But the one thing I'm not helping carry up her stairs is the only thing that matters. Our son.

He's only a few minutes away, but he might as well be halfway across the country. It still hurts like hell. I should have insisted we stay. But we have no idea how long he'll be there. Hopefully it's just a week. Maybe two. But realistically, it could be longer.

"I have a little surprise for you," Ryder says as we approach the top of the stairs.

"You didn't put the nursery together, did you?" Regan asks. "Because I don't want to. Not until we're sure he's coming home."

I nudge her arm and look right into her eyes. "He's coming home, okay? He will. He just needs more time."

She nods.

"It's not the nursery. Besides, with Mitchell coming early, I'm still living here, so there's nowhere to set it up. I promise to be out of your hair by the time he comes home."

"Where will you go?" Regan asks. "It's not like you have a ton of money lying around."

"We'll figure it out." He kisses her head. It's something I've never seen him do. I'm pleased they finally have the relationship I've always had with my siblings. "The only thing you need to worry about is that amazing kid of yours." He stops at the door handle. "You do not need to worry about what's on the other side of this door, okay? I mean it."

"Ryder," she scolds. "What did you do?"

He opens the door and Regan walks through first. "Mom? Dad?"

Ryder raises a brow at me as I try not to shrink back into the fourteen-year-old kid who got caught with my pants down.

I shake my head, glaring at Ryder. "A little fucking warning would have been nice."

"Baby, why didn't you tell us?" her mom cries, crossing the room.

The three of them hug and cry together for minutes. It's family time. I should leave.

I turn to slip out quietly, when her dad, Darrin, corners me with his booming voice. "Lucas Montana."

Suddenly, I *am* that kid again.

"Sir, I can—"

His arm extends as he approaches me, his hand out in a kind gesture. I shake it, confused.

"Ryder told me everything. Especially how much you've taken care of our baby girl. It may not be exactly what we envisioned for her, but any man who's gone through what you have for her can't be all bad."

"Thank you, sir. I just want the best for her and Mitchell."

"I know you do."

"I'm going to leave and let you all catch up."

"Don't be a stranger. And, son, let's go grab a drink soon. Just the two of us."

Regan is standing behind him, her dumbfounded reaction mirroring mine.

"I'd like that, sir."

"It's Darrin."

"Okay, Darrin. Thank you."

I look behind him. "I'll be going back to the hospital in a few hours. Want me to pick you up?"

Joyce, her mom, puts an arm around her. "We'll get her there. We can't wait to meet our grandchild."

Sadness overcomes me. Immense, indomitable sadness. Because now, not only is Ryder here for her, her parents are as well. And as happy as I am for her that she has more support, I'm devastated that I'm not the one getting to provide it.

I nod. "I guess I'll see you all there."

Regan's mouth tugs into a faint smile, but the melancholy on her pale face tells me she's feeling exactly the same way I am—that we'd rather be somewhere else. *With* someone else.

I give a wave of my hand. Then I leave.

~ ~ ~

Home doesn't feel the same anymore. I've only been here once since Mitchell arrived, and I won't be here long now, but it's so much different than it ever was.

It's larger somehow. And a whole lot emptier. Despite the changes I've made over the past few months, it still doesn't feel right. Without her. Without him.

I sit on the couch feeling miserable. Regan and Mitchell should be here. Is this how it's going to be for the rest of my pathetic life?

Then Christa's words echo through my head. *"She loves you. She loves you, too."*

It couldn't be true, could it? I mean, it's crazy to think someone like her would fall for a fool like me. One with my history. Someone who should never be trusted with the long-term wellbeing of another's heart.

Is it possible that over the past seven months we've fallen for each other? That perhaps we're both feeling the same way but have each concluded it's a bad path to travel?

But damn… it's a journey I want to take. And it's not about Mitchell. Baby or no baby, in some way, it's always been Regan.

Is that why I never followed through with any of my other relationships?

Holy shit. Did I just *shrink* myself?

But if she is *the one*, how could I ever get anyone, her included, to believe it? There's not a person in this town who thinks I'll ever cross that finish line. No one but me. I've never been so goddamn confident that I could. That I will.

Then again, Christa could be wrong. All these *ways* she claims Regan has been looking at me could just be hormones. Or the situation we're in. Or the result of me taking care of her. Hell, it could just be gratitude for all I know.

I stand up and cross the room, open a bottle of tequila, and down a shot, hoping it will drown out all this tangled confusion inside my head.

A noise behind me has me turning. Dallas is standing in my entryway.

He shakes his head. "You didn't hear me knock?"

"Sorry if I'm a bit preoccupied at the moment."

He eyes the empty glass in my hand. "Brother, I'm about to school you the same way you did me. If you don't tell her you love her, you're a fucking idiot."

I laugh sadly. "I think we have a little too much going on at the moment. Not to mention I don't want to fuck things up."

"If you think this little situation of yours isn't already fucked up, you're not as smart as I thought you were. Lucas, man the hell up and tell her. What if something happens to Mitchell? She's going to need you more than ever. On the flip side, what if something doesn't happen and he gets released tomorrow? What if the two of them go back to living in her little apartment over her little shop, and you become the part-time dad who has to watch from the sidelines?

"Or... what if you tell her how you really feel and you get everything you've ever wanted since you were fourteen fucking years old?"

My eyebrows shoot up. "You knew? All that time you knew, and you never said anything?"

"Brother, everyone knew you had a boner for Regan. Then *and* now."

"*She* didn't. Neither did Ryder. Not back then." I snort and jerk my wrist. "Her dad definitely did."

A sour look crosses his face. "I'm sure I don't want to know what you mean by that."

"No." I laugh. "You don't." I thumb to the back. "Listen, I have to shower and grab a bite to eat and then get back to the hospital."

"Hey, before you get back to dad life, do you have any idea why Allie is acting so goddamn strange?"

"She is, isn't she? And no. Maybe that Asher guy dumped her."

"Not according to Marti. They're seeing each other at least every other month. Texting a lot too."

"Is there something there?"

He shrugs. "Nothing she'll admit. But you know Allie, she's never been one for relationships. Not since that guy Jason way back when. Anyway, is there anything I can do for you? Here or at work? You know you don't have to worry about work, right? We've got you covered as long as you need."

"I know. All I need is to get back to my son and—"

"And Regan." He snorts, clearly amused by his masterful observation skills, and heads for the door. "See ya soon, brother."

I stare at the tequila bottle, contemplating another shot. But if I take one, I won't be clear. And believe me, the first time I feed my son, I want to remember every goddamn second. Every suckle of his lips. Every tiny movement of his body. Every look from his mother, who will most definitely be watching.

I set down the bottle and stride to the bathroom. Fuck eating. I just need to get back there. Because I can't wait. I can't wait for the rest of my life to start. And I vow right here and now that some way, somehow, I'm going to make it be with *them*.

Chapter Forty-five

Lucas

"Two days without a spell," Christa declares as soon as I walk through the door. "Progress."

I breathe.

There's this moment I have every time I enter the NICU. A moment where I stop breathing because what if he had another episode? Or worse. Time ceases to exist and doesn't start again until I see that he's okay.

The rocking chair next to his incubator is vacant. I look around. "Am I the first one here?"

She holds a small bottle out. "Early bird gets the worm."

Yup. That's me. The early bird. I'm here at five o'clock in the morning because I haven't slept more than a few hours each night. Hell, I slept better the two nights I was here at the hospital even though I kept getting up to go to the NICU.

I smile, sit, and wait for Mitchell to be placed in my arms. This is when my heart starts beating again. When the world is right.

Because when I'm outside those doors—when I'm at home without him—the world is definitely not as it should be.

I glance at the empty stool next to me knowing it's still not right. There's one more thing missing.

"He's been eating so well," Christa says as he takes to the bottle. "In fact, at this morning's weigh in, he's back to his birth weight. It takes some preemies much longer to achieve that."

I beam. "That's my boy."

I hold him for two hours, until my eyes can't stay open anymore. I need coffee.

Christa puts him back for me, and I watch as he settles in, relaxes, and immediately dozes off.

When I look up, I see Regan crossing the room. And, holy crap, I can't stop staring at her chest.

"Yeah, yeah, my milk came in." She tugs at her top. "Nothing fits anymore. It's annoying."

"It's… wow." I lean close. "Is it wrong that I'm turned on around all these babies?"

She giggles and it reaches all the way into my body and wraps around my heart. I love her laugh. It's not something I've heard a lot over the past five days.

"My dad is with me. He's just outside. It looked like you were getting ready to leave."

I see Darrin behind the glass and wave him in. The rule is no more than two family members in the NICU at a time. "I was going for breakfast. Can I bring you anything?"

"Dad made it for me. He came over early. Mom was still at the hotel sleeping after being here until about two in the morning."

I love how accepting her parents have been. Even if Darrin sometimes still looks at me like I'm the pervy teen jerking off while watching his daughter. I get it though, now that I'm a dad. If Mitchell were a girl and I ever caught a boy pleasuring himself at her image, I'd pummel him to the ground.

Just as Darrin walks up and I'm set to leave, the alarm near Mitchell's incubator sounds.

My heart splinters. Regan cries out. Christa rushes over.

Unlike before when we witnessed this happen, a gentle shake doesn't have the alarm stopping. Christa pulls something out from a drawer under the incubator. It's a mask. She puts it over his face.

"What's going on?" Regan asks, holding onto me so fiercely I'm sure I'll have bruises on my arm.

"He just needs a little positive pressure ventilation," Christa says.

I watch the nurse's face for any telltale signs of panic. Because me—I'm fucking panicking. I'm panicking so hard it's turning my insides to mush, and I very well might vomit. But her face gives nothing away. Either this isn't the dire emergency the three of us standing here think it is, or she's really good at hiding it.

The alarms continue to go off. How long has it been? How long can they continue to sound? How long can my son go without breathing before… before…

The alarms cease.

Regan cries out. This time in relief. And she falls against me.

My arms encase her. "Shhh. I'm here. I'll always be here. He's going to be okay." I turn to Christa. "Right?"

She doesn't respond. Instead, she removes the mask then holds a stethoscope to Mitchell's chest.

"Christa?"

She listens intently on one side, then the other. Finally I think I see a hint of relief cross her face.

"It's okay. He's fine. I was just checking for pneumothorax—collapsed lung—which can sometimes happen when we bag and mask them."

Regan buries her head in my shoulder, sobbing.

"But he doesn't have that?" I ask.

"No. He's good. I'll listen to his lungs again in a minute to be sure."

"Does this mean he's getting worse?" Regan asks from her perch against me.

"Not at all," Christa says. "It just means his nervous system isn't quite there yet." She touches Regan's back. "It'll happen. He might never have another spell. And if he does, it might be like the others and not this one."

"But it might not be," Regan says to put a point on it.

Christa's shrug is not all that reassuring. But I get it. She can't predict the future. And she's not going to stand here and lie to us.

Regan peels herself out of my arms and hovers over the incubator. I go around and do the same at the other side. Our hands connect over the top as Darrin watches on.

A tear rolls down Regan's face. "I don't ever want to leave him. I want to be with him every second of every day."

I squeeze her hand. "I know how you feel. But I'm not sure you know how *I* feel."

She looks up. "What do you mean? I'm his mom. Of course I know."

"You don't." I shake my head and draw in a deep breath. Because, *fuck*, here it goes. "In five days, or a week, or two weeks, or however long it may be—*you* get to take him home. *You* get to be with him all the time. I'm the one who goes home alone. I get him for a few weekends." I stare down at him. "I know what the contract says, but, Regan, a few weekends and holidays isn't enough. I want more. More than summer vacations at the beach and trips to Disney World. I want him every minute of every day. I want to be there when he wakes up. I want to feed him his midnight bottle. I want to be there when he rolls over, smiles his first smile, takes his first steps. I want to be there for every birthday, every fall off the skateboard, every broken heart. My apartment is so goddamn empty. I've been wandering around it for days. It's what I do when I'm not here. I wander around my huge apartment and think about how empty it is. I think about how empty *I* am. Without him." I clear my throat. "Without you."

She tilts her head, staring at me like I'm an alien.

"When we leave here, I want you to come home with me. Wait, that's not true. I want *you* to come home with me today. Tonight. I don't want to spend another sleepless night without you. I want you to come home with me today and him to come home with us when he's ready. I want... I want us to be a family."

"I... Lucas, I—"

"Sorry," Christa says. "I need to check him again."

Our hands come apart as we both back away. We want to look at each other, but right now, looking at Mitchell is more important.

Christa listens to his lungs then turns to us. "So, who wants to hold this little Comeback Kid?"

I raise a questioning brow.

Christa smiles. "He just earned his name."

"Comeback Kid," I muse. "I like it. Not as good as M&M, but it'll do."

Regan seems to be in a daze as she sits in the rocking chair.

Mitchell gets placed into her arms. She looks at him, then at me, then back at him.

I step near her side. "What do you say, can we give it a go?"

"I..."

Darrin's arm clasps my shoulder. "Why don't you go for a cup of coffee, Lucas? She seems a little overwhelmed at the moment."

Lucas. Not *son.*

Regan's entire focus is on Mitchell. She doesn't even glance up at me. I nod and leave, thinking about how colossally I just fucked everything up.

~ ~ ~

Sitting on a hard chair outside the NICU, I stare into my cold, untouched coffee. I replay the words in my head. I know I didn't say it right. I want a do-over. She probably thinks I'm crazy rambling on like that about being empty and shit.

Someone sits next to me. "What's your endgame, Lucas?"

It's Darrin.

I lean back and let my head thud against the unforgiving concrete wall. "This isn't a game, Darrin. I love her. I'm *in* love with her."

A deep sigh comes out of him. "You loved all the others too, no?"

"She's different."

"Because she had your child?"

I shake my head. "I know you won't believe me. Nobody will. But I think she might be the reason I could never be with the others. I've asked myself for years why I could never follow through. Was it them? Me? Was I just that scared of commitment? But it was none of that." I close my eyes. "It was her. It was Regan. It's always been her. She's the one. I think I've loved her since I was fourteen. I *know* I've loved her since before she got pregnant. And now… seeing her with him. I'm not sure I can ever live without her."

Sniffles have me opening my eyes. I turn to see Regan standing near Darrin.

She looks stunned. "They, um… kicked me out for shift change and rounds."

I spring out of my chair, certain by the look on her face that she heard most or all of what I said.

"Regan, I know I'm putting it all on the line here. But he's worth fighting for. *You're* worth fighting for. I know I can never be a husband. I've proven that. But I can be a good partner. A good boyfriend. And I *will* be a good dad. I plan on being the best goddamn father any kid ever had. What I said is true. Every word of it. I love you. We're great together, you and me. We laugh. We cry. We're the most unlikely pair, but maybe what they say is true about how opposites attract. You're more than my child's mom, you're my best friend. And maybe in time, you could come to feel about me the way I feel about you."

She takes two steps closer. "I already do, you dummy."

"Regan, baby," Darrin says. "Don't give into this. It's your hormones. Now is not the time to make any rash decisions."

She turns to him. "I love him, Daddy."

My heart explodes and expands all at once, the same way it did the moment Mitchell was born. "You do?"

She laughs and cries. "I do." She takes another step toward me. "I thought you'd bail," she says. "When things got serious with the baby. When he was born early and then had his episodes, I thought you'd bail. But you didn't. You're here. You're always here. And I love the way you love him."

"It's not just him I love."

I'm vaguely aware of Darrin's hasty departure as I draw her into my arms and kiss her. I kiss her sweet, salty mouth knowing it's the only mouth I ever want to kiss for the rest of my life.

"It's about damn time," someone says.

I look over Regan's shoulder to see Christa putting on her coat and slinging a purse over her arm.

Regan and I embrace long and hard. But it's much more than a hug. It's a promise of love. Of commitment. Of always being there for him and each other.

When my brain has fully wrapped around the fact that this is actually happening, I ask, "So you'll come home with me? Today? You'll move in? Both of you?"

"I don't know." Her dimples make an appearance. "We'd be violating the contract."

"Fuck the contract." I cup her face in my hands. "Fuck all of it. Let's tear it to shreds."

She wipes her tears and shrugs nonchalantly. "Well, I mean, you do have that closet."

I laugh out loud and pull her against me once more.

Then she gets serious and looks into my eyes. "Just promise me one thing."

I caress the side of her cheek with my thumb. "Anything."

"Never ever ask me to marry you."

I laugh again, knowing for sure she's the one. The one who will always make me laugh. The one who I can feel comfortable crying with. The one who will never need a piece of paper to know that I'll love her forever.

"Deal."

Chapter Forty-six

Regan

It's eight pm and I'm exhausted. Being at the hospital is more than a full-time job. But I'm not complaining. I'll never complain about getting to spend time with our son.

"Are you sure your parents don't mind doing the night shift?" I ask in the elevator.

"They're happy to do it. Between our four parents, M&M gets a lot of overnight company."

The elevator dings and the doors open to the penthouse level. I step off, but before we go inside, Lucas holds a key out to me.

"Why do I need that thing?" I ask. "I still know the code." I punch in the numbers and the door clicks open.

He laughs but shoves the key into my hand anyway. "Take it. And tomorrow I'll call the security company and put you on the list. By the way, my security password is *Fruit Bomb*. Just in case the alarm ever trips accidentally, and they call you."

I giggle. "Only you would have a password like that." I step across the threshold and stop. "Lucas, are you one hundred percent sure this is what you want?"

He pins me to the wall. "One hundred and ten."

I smile as he kisses me, and I can't mistake the feel of his erection against my thigh. "Hold on there, Wine Boy. You know Dr. Russo said at least four weeks."

"It's a perfectly natural reaction, Regan. Besides, I'm not with you for your body." His eyes roll. "Okay, not *just* for your body."

I'm not sure how this man can make me feel sexy when I'm only five days postpartum. But it's one of the reasons I know this is right. I don't care what my parents think. What the rumors will be. What anyone says. This thing between us is real. I think my heart knew it even before my head did.

"We probably should have stopped at my place to pack up a few things."

"No need," he says, motioning to the living room.

Tucked into a bright, cozy corner is my favorite reading chair. The one I kept by the window in my apartment. The one you can sink into and get lost in a book.

"My chair." I stare at it in wonder. "How did it get here?"

"Along with everything else," he says, gesturing toward the dining room where Joey is cowering behind the leg of his table.

"Joey!" I go over to pick him up and smile back at Lucas. "You did all this?"

"My brothers, Ryder, and your dad moved everything."

"*All* of it?" I feel my cheeks flush.

"Don't worry. I told them not to go in any bedroom drawers if they didn't want to be traumatized for life. I had Maddie and Ava pack all that shit. Along with your clothes."

I put Joey down and press myself against Lucas's back, wrapping my arms around him. "Thank you."

He turns in my arms and kisses my forehead. "Anything for you."

"They left most of your furniture in the apartment for Ryder. But anything else you really want, I'll get moved."

"I don't need anything else. Just the chair." I lean into him. "How did you know?"

"Because I know *you*, Ray."

I gaze up at him. "I think you really do. And you're one of the only ones who does."

"Come on." He takes my hand. "Let me give you a tour."

"I *have* been here before," I say. "I know it's been a while. Not since Sylvia Franco interviewed us. But I'm sure nothing's changed other than my clothes." I do a little jig, excited about getting to share his massive closet.

"Oh, there may be one or two things that are different."

He drags me down the hallway and stops at one of the rooms I never looked in. When he opens the door, my eyes completely bug out of my head. It's a nursery. Complete with professionally painted light-blue walls with white paneling, the most beautiful baby furniture, baby contraptions I didn't even know existed, and toys upon toys upon more toys.

"Oh my god. You did all this? *Today?*"

He shakes his head. "This was done weeks ago."

My jaw hangs open. "Weeks ago?"

He shrugs. "Even with him only being here every other weekend, I still wanted it to feel like home."

I slip a hand into his. "It *is* home. And it's incredible."

"You haven't seen the best part."

He grins and motions to the closet.

I smile in anticipation and then race over to open the sliding door. I'm bowled over in surprise for the umpteenth time today when I take in a walk-in closet full of baby clothes. This closet is a fraction of the master bedroom one, but there are still rows and rows of rods, a large bank of drawers, and a wall of cubbies. Every nook and cranny of drawer and cubby space is filled, as is every inch of the hanging rods.

I open each and every drawer. They are filled with onesies, rompers, matching sets of shirts and pants—clothes for all seasons and in sizes up to toddler. Never in a million years would I have expected him to be so completely immersed in our child that he would do this.

I turn. "You couldn't have possibly done all this yourself."

"My mom was in heaven when I asked her to help me. Allie helped too. She wasn't quite so enthusiastic, though." His brows knit together. "In fact, it was strange. She seemed almost sad every time she was here setting up the room. She's always been so great with Maisy and Charlie. I thought she'd be thrilled to be getting another nephew."

I shrug. "They were both older when they came into her life. Maybe babies scare her. She'll get used to him and love him just as much as his cousins."

"Yeah. I'm sure she will."

I walk back out into the nursery. "I love it. All of it. Except maybe this." I pick up a hideous-looking stuffed... something. "What is this?"

"It's a groundhog. You do know our kid was born on February second, right?"

A hand covers my laugh. "I hadn't even thought of that."

He chuckles. "I fear our son may be cursed by many more of these to come in his lifetime. I figured we better get him used to it now."

"You thought of everything." Tears pool in my eyes. "What could I ever give him that you haven't thought of?"

He wraps his arms around me. "The one thing nobody else can give him. *You*. You can give him *you*. You're already the best mom to him."

"I miss him so much. Even though we only left thirty minutes ago, I miss him like it's been days. Weeks. I want to be with him all the time."

"I know." He kisses my head. "Me too."

"Lucas?"

"Yeah?"

I extricate myself from his arms, sit in the glider-rocker in the corner, and pull a nearby stuffed animal into my lap. "What if... what if I told you I never want to be apart from him? Would you call me crazy?"

"Of course not. I just told you I get it."

I shake my head. "That's not what I mean." I blow out a stress-filled breath.

He gets on his knees next to me. "What is it, Ray?"

"I know you just asked me to live here, and this is all so new and who knows what the future will bring. But Ryder wants to open a pot shop and even my mom and dad think it would be a good idea and he's going to live there and I'll be here and I don't want to work at a pot shop and then again I don't really want to work at *Booktique* and be away from Mitchell so—"

Lucas puts a finger to my lips. "Regan, you're all over the place. Just spit it out."

"I want—" I hide my eyes behind my hands. "I know it will be a huge imposition and maybe it's totally stupid and I'll end up hating it but—"

"Ray?" He chuckles. "Are you saying you want to be a stay-at-home mom?"

I dare to look at him. "Is it a terrible idea?"

"Are you kidding?" His face lights up. "It's an incredible idea."

"But the financial burden would fall completely on you."

He looks at me like I'm crazy.

I hold up a hand. "I know, I know, you're rich. But I'd feel really guilty about not being able to contribute."

He traps my hand against his chest. "Regan, I was going to pay an arm and a leg to get Mitchell the best goddamn nanny in the country. Believe me, this is actually a win-win situation."

"It is?"

He sighs heavily. "Is *this* what's been eating at you all afternoon? Jesus, Ray, I thought you were having second thoughts."

"I'm not. I've wanted this… *us*… for a while now."

"Tell me." He looks into my eyes. "Tell me how long you've wanted it."

"Come here." I scoot to the edge of the chair. "And I'll show you."

He gifts me with one of his huge luminous smiles—the one I hope Mitchell inherits—and he crashes his lips onto mine.

~ ~ ~

I wake up and look at the clock. It's four am. I watch Lucas, wondering how long I can stand to let him sleep before I poke him and demand he take me to Mitchell.

But I don't have to poke him. It's like there's this tether between us. One that pulls at him, letting him know what I'm thinking.

"Good morning," he says, kissing me.

"Mmm." I pull back slightly. "My lips are sore from all the kissing."

"Believe me," he says. "My balls are sorer."

I laugh.

"You want to go see him, don't you?"

I nod. "I can survive on far less than six hours' sleep."

"Me, too. But first, I need you to clear something up for me. Last night, during your rambling, you said your parents are in favor of the pot shop, er… cannabis dispensary?"

I tuck an arm under my pillow and face him. "Turns out my dad has been using medical marijuana for years down in Florida." I shrug. "For his glaucoma." I snicker. "And apparently my mom partakes upon occasion."

Lucas sits up, stunned. "Wow. Strait-laced Joyce and Darrin smoking weed. Who'd have thought? *And* they're being supportive of Ryder's divorce?"

"Wait. I didn't tell you that."

"Your dad and I talked yesterday after you went back to the NICU. We had a great conversation. Came to an understanding."

"What understanding?"

"Well… he understands I won't hurt you. And I understand he'll cut off my balls and serve them to me for dinner if I ever do."

I laugh so hard my stomach hurts.

"Are you and my dad becoming friends?"

"I think we are." He gets out of bed and offers me a hand. "Now let's go see our son, shall we?"

At the mention of Mitchell, my boobs leak, soaking my sleeping shirt. I cup them to try and stop the waterworks.

"Wait here," Lucas says. "I'll go get the pump. We need to catch every last drop for the amazing Comeback Kid."

I smile as I watch my... *boyfriend?*... race out of the room. And for the first time, I honestly feel like all this might turn out exactly as he has planned.

Chapter Forty-seven

Regan

"Are you really sure he's ready?"

Christa is helping me bundle Mitchell up in his go-home outfit. There are no more tubes. No wires. And I've been nursing him for the past five days. Over the past two weeks, he's gained more weight than even the doctors anticipated. He only had one more A&B episode, and slowly, he was weaned off the oxygen and other therapeutics. He finally looks like a healthy baby. Still only five and a half pounds, but healthy.

He's healthy, I think again as I pull a tiny arm through his long-sleeved bodysuit.

I look back at Sam and Kendall—the couple we've become close with over the past three weeks—and feel a pang of guilt that we're leaving with Mitchell and they have such a long journey ahead. Other parents and babies have come and gone, most only staying a day or two. The teenage mom, Tarryn, went home with her baby just a few days ago. I remember how envious of her I was.

Now, it's our turn. And although part of me is nervous that we're going to have to do this ourselves, without the twenty-four-hour care and help from the NICU, I'm relieved that Mitchell gets to come home with both of his parents.

We pull on his tiny socks and cute little preemie pants with teddy bears on them. It's much different from the going-home outfit I bought for him months ago. It seems like another life when I went into the city and got him a newborn jumpsuit with giraffes on it. Eventually, the newborn clothes will fit him, but he'll be swimming in them for a while. I want his going-home pictures to show how I see him: a perfectly sized amazing little version of Lucas.

We have plenty of photographic evidence of how tiny he is. Lucas has captured everything on his phone, snapping pictures and taking videos of Mitchell at every turn. From day one, something I didn't know about until yesterday, he's been snapping photos of our son next to common household items so we won't forget how small he was. There are pictures of Mitchell next to a water bottle. A cell phone. Even a banana.

It's incredible how Lucas has literally thought of everything.

When Mitchell is dressed and I pick him up, still amazed at the feel of holding him in my arms without any tubes and wires, I turn around to see a small crowd gathered in the washroom just outside the inner doors of the NICU. Dr. Russo is there. Dr. Ford is there, too. As are several other nurses, doctors, and techs who were either at the delivery or have had a hand in caring for Mitchell.

I smile as my eyes fill with tears. I knew it would happen. Any time a baby stays more than just a day or two for observation, they get a 'graduation' sendoff.

"First things first," Lucas says, bringing over the car seat.

He sets it on the floor and holds out his arms.

Some dads would have no idea how to put a newborn in a car seat. Not Lucas. He seems to be an expert at it. *Has he been practicing?* I'm not even sure I'd know how to do it. Any knowledge I have comes from watching Maddie and Amber with their babies, not from firsthand experience.

As I watch him get our son settled and snug, I once again thank my lucky stars that we're doing this together. I don't even have Mitchell home yet, but I still have a newfound admiration for single parents who have to do all of this alone. I make a promise to myself to reach out to Tarryn who, as far as I know, only has her aunt helping her. She never spoke about friends, her parents, or even her baby's father. She's got a long and bumpy road ahead of her, I'm sure.

Lucas proudly picks up the car seat. He exhales and closes his eyes at the weight of it. I know what he's thinking. He's happy this day is here. He's grateful we get to take home a healthy child. He's beyond words at the thought of our son being carried out through the doors of the NICU and into the beginning of the rest of his life.

He opens his eyes and holds out his hand. I take it, and we walk toward the exit.

Those who aren't leaving with us—other nurses, a few parents—clap as we pass.

I stop and give hugs to the Willises. "Your day will come," I whisper to Kendall. "I know it will."

When it does, I plan to be one of the people waiting on the other side of that door.

As we step through the inner doors, I look back, giving one last glance to Mitchell's first home. And I hope with all my heart that this is the last time he'll ever be in a hospital.

In the washroom area, there is a chalkboard with Mitchell's name on it, how many days he stayed here, his birth date and weight, today's date and weight, and, of course, his nickname: The Comeback Kid.

I smile, just knowing it's how Christa, Kayla, and all the other nurses in the NICU will forever know him.

There's a pink and blue balloon arch—the same one they use for all the 'graduations'—and a large banner for us to stand next to and have our pictures taken with all the people who have helped get us to this moment.

There are many tears, mostly mine. Lots of hugs. And a few laughs. Then Rondell, an orderly we've gotten to know over the past few weeks, comes out with a cart loaded with the things we've accumulated here over the past weeks. A throw blanket. Some reading material. A pair of slippers. And the typical hospital sendoff gift including various baby items, postpartum things, nursing aids, and informational packets.

Flowers, gifts, balloons, and teddy bears were all taken home long ago as those aren't allowed in the NICU.

After we say our goodbyes, Dr. Russo escorts us to the elevator. "Well, you did it," she says, putting a motherly arm around my shoulder. "And just look at you now. You're quite the family."

Family. We're a family.

I look at Lucas. He looks at me. We both look at Mitchell. And we smile.

Down in the lobby, another crowd waits for us. My parents and his. Siblings. Friends. They all gather around, but not too close, to get their first look at Mitchell.

Maddie and Ava hug me from behind.

"You know," Maddie says. "We never had a chance to throw you a baby shower."

"That's okay," I tell her. "Have you seen who I'm going home with? I promise, I have everything we need."

"Still," Ava says. "Every mom deserves one."

It's not lost on me how she's looking at Mitchell, with a deep longing that I hope one day will be fulfilled.

"You just let us know when you're ready. Next week. Next month. Whenever. Because it's happening, Mama."

I envelop them in one of our threesome hugs. "You guys are the best."

"We're happy for you, Regan," Maddie says. "Genuinely."

"I know you still have reservations. But you don't have to. I don't."

"Did you really tell him never to ask you to marry him?" Ava asks in a whisper.

"Wow, news travels fast. But yes."

Lucas butts in. "While you ladies finish talking about me, I'll go get the car."

I roll my eyes and crouch next to Mitchell's car seat, happy he's not getting touched, poked, and prodded by the two-dozen people here. It makes me wonder if Lucas asked them all to steer clear. It's still winter, after all, and who knows what germs are going around.

As if Ava reads my mind, she gazes at Mitchell. "I cannot wait to get my hands on him."

Yup—Lucas definitely issued some sort of warning. I'm sure of it.

Allie gets down on her knees, a foot or so away, tears streaming down her cheeks. Of all our friends and family, she has been the most emotional.

"He looks amazing." A hand flies to her mouth, covering a sob. "I'm so happy for you."

"Thanks. Once we get settled, I hope you'll come over and hold him. He has a lot of blood uncles, but you're his only blood aunt."

She reaches out and touches his foot that's tucked under a thick winter baby blanket. "I can't flippin' wait. I'll be the best auntie ever. I promise."

"I know you will."

After a few more minutes of well-wishes, my dad comes over and lifts the car seat. "Your ride is here."

I make sure the blanket is securely tucked around Mitchell, turn and thank everyone for coming, then Rondell follows us to the front doors.

Exiting into the brisk winter air, I look for Lucas's Jag, but don't see it. It takes my tired brain a few seconds to remember his car doesn't have a back seat, so he wouldn't be driving it.

As I wonder what he has planned to get us all home, a massive SUV, a Lincoln something or other, pulls up and Lucas gets out of the driver's seat. He walks over with a smile. "It's for you." He winks. "All part of the contract."

My mouth hangs agape, staring at the gigantic silver SUV. "I thought we were tearing it to shreds."

"Incinerated." He chuckles and leans close. "If you decide you don't like this one, we'll trade it in for whatever you want."

"Are you kidding? It's as big as a tank. He'll be safe there. I love it."

He opens the back door and snaps Mitchell's car seat into the base in the center seat. Then he motions for me to get in.

I raise a brow. "You're going to be our chauffeur?"

He tips his invisible hat. "I'll take you anywhere you wanna go." Then he leans in and kisses me on the lips. "Come on, Ray. Let's go home."

Chapter Forty-eight

Regan

"I thought this was a baby shower," I say, opening the fourth gift that is most definitely not for the baby.

I narrow my eyes at Lucas.

"We already have everything we could need for M&M." He motions across the room to Maddie and Ava. "This was their idea."

The gifts I've opened so far include certificates for massages, spa days, mani/pedis, and one super cute and comfy outfit that will fit right into my eclectic wardrobe.

I scan the room filled with family and friends, knowing how lucky I am.

Allie is in my reading chair over by the fireplace. I don't even think she's paid attention to any of this. She's snuggling five-week-old Mitchell the same way she always does when she's here—like she's afraid every moment she has with him could be the last one.

I get it. I was the same way when he was in the NICU. But he's good now. He's nursing like a champ and growing like a weed. And, as the nurses promised, he's most definitely found his lungs. The kid can cry. And boy does he like to be the center of attention—just like his daddy.

Lucas and I share a look. He's noticed the way Allie is around the baby, too. He shrugs and hands me another gift. This one is from Mom and Dad, who decided to hang around for another month to help out.

It's a leather-bound book titled *Letters to My Son.*

"It's a journal," Mom says. "So you can write down everything about his childhood. It'll be something he'll always cherish when he's older and can appreciate it."

"What a thoughtful gift." I frown. "I wish someone would have thought of that when you had me."

Mom holds out another gift. "Someone did."

I tear up as I unwrap it. I stare at the thick journal, the words *For My Daughter* embossed on the front cover. Tucked into a clear plastic flap is a picture of my mom holding me as an infant.

I look up, stunned that she did this. We were never all that close. I was always jealous of friends who had that special bond with their mothers. But Joyce Lucas has been making up for lost time over the past several weeks. And now this... what an amazing surprise.

I pull it to my chest. "I can't wait to read it. Maybe I'll read it to Mitchell."

She chortles. "Might want to leave out some of the colorful language."

I cock my head, stunned.

"Oh, don't look so surprised. You weren't the easiest of kids, you know. I may have vented a time or two in there."

"Thank you," I say. "I'll cherish this forever."

When I'm finished with all the gifts, there are a few silly shower games. Like seeing who can chug beer from a baby bottle the fastest and other equally outrageous challenges.

Ava is holding the baby when her husband, Trevor—on leave for two weeks—comes up by her side. He admires the way she's holding Mitchell. And I could swear, he swallows tears.

"I want one," he says.

Ava smiles sadly, not looking up from my son. "So much it hurts."

"Let's do it." Trevor touches Mitchell's head. "Let's do whatever it takes to make it happen."

Ava finally tears her gaze from Mitchell. "Whatever it takes?"

Lucas squeezes my shoulder and winks. "Regan might have some old sperm bank brochures."

Ava snorts incredulously, but Trevor doesn't even flinch.

"Wait, really?" Ava asks, turning wide-eyed toward her husband. "But I know how set you are on having a child of your own."

"I've been doing a lot of thinking lately." He nods to Amber and Quinn. "They have two kids who aren't biologically theirs. You think that makes one bit of difference?"

She shakes her head, not believing what he's saying. "No, it doesn't. So we can think about it?"

"Sure. Why not? But under one condition." He waves a hand around. "I don't want to miss any of this. Not one minute. I don't want to be seven thousand miles away hearing about the first time you feel the baby kick. I don't want to have to watch my kid being born via FaceTime. I don't want to miss the first smile or laugh. I want to be here for all of it. So, yes, get those brochures from Regan. Pick a donor. Find a doctor. But Ava, I want to be a part of it. All of it."

She hands Mitchell to me, tears rolling down her cheeks, and flings herself into his arms. "Now that's a deal."

Lucas chuckles behind them and clasps Trevor's shoulder. "Lucky bastard."

"How do you mean?" Trev asks.

"Unlike me, you won't have to watch the woman you're secretly in love with have your baby."

We all share a laugh.

"Speaking of that." Lucas suddenly looks all nervous as he takes the baby from me and hands him off to his mother.

He pulls something from his pocket and my heart stands still. It's a... *ring*.

He gets down on a knee and I try to urge him up. "Lucas, no. You promised."

He bats my hand away. "It's not what you think."

"You have an engagement ring and you're down on a knee," I whisper-shout through gritted teeth.

He holds up the ring. "It's not a diamond. It's an amethyst." He nods to Mitchell. "His birthstone. Clearly it's not an engagement ring."

"But—"

"Ray, will you shut up and listen for a second? Please?"

His eyes plead with me, so I do what he asks, despite the fact that he's about to ruin a perfectly good party, and perhaps a perfectly good relationship.

Why here? In front of all our family and friends? And why is he breaking his promise?

"Regan Lucas," he says, his voice cracking—though I'm not sure why. He has, after all, done this four times before. "These past few weeks have been the best of my life. I've had some harebrained ideas in my life, but none of them has ever been as brilliant as the one I had nine months ago. I had no idea at the time that it would end up like this. But then again, I know deep down I wanted it to. Because this, right here, is everything I've ever wanted since I was twelve years old watching you play volleyball in the sandpit at the county fair."

Even as sighs are heard throughout the eerily silent room, my heart sinks. Because he's making a monumental mistake. And the thought of hurting him here in front of everyone is turning my stomach. "Lucas—"

"I'm not quite done," he insists. "Your turn comes in a second."

"Regan Tallulah Lucas,"—he holds up the ring—"will you make me that happiest guy in the world and *not* marry me?"

"Wait... what?"

Laughter echoes behind me, confirming that I did in fact hear him correctly.

He takes my left hand. "You heard me. Will you do me the honor of *not* marrying me? Even though it sentences us to a lifetime of being teased about our names. And in spite of the fact that we'll have to explain ourselves to everyone who sees this happy couple, this amazing family, these two parents who love their kid and each other so much it confuses the hell out of everyone as to why we don't make it official. But, Ray, I don't need a piece of paper to prove how much I love you. I don't need an official document to make us family. We're already a family." He nods to the ring. "But I sure as hell need this ring on your finger so that every red-blooded man in the universe knows you're mine."

I fall to my knees, sniffling and crying and laughing all at the same time. I cup his head in my hands. "Yes, Lucas Christopher Montana, I would be honored to not marry you."

Applause roars around us as he slips the beautiful purple stone onto my finger.

Chapter Forty-nine

Lucas

Today is the day my son was supposed to be born. Instead, he's six weeks old.

Today is also the day I swear myself to Regan for the rest of my life, for better or worse.

The winery venue is all decked out. It looks like a wedding, only it's not. After a lot of convincing on my part, I talked Regan into having a ceremony. I wanted her to know that even if we're not getting married, I'm in this. I'm in this forever.

So today, on the day our son was due, we commit ourselves to each other.

Everyone we know, and a few I could swear I don't, is here.

I'm wearing a suit. She's wearing a dress. Not a regular dress. In full flower-child fashion, Regan looks like she could have stepped out of a magazine from the seventies. Her paisley-print three-quarter length dress, complete with frills lining the bottom hem, looks amazing. She's paired it with flat sandals that have long straps winding up her legs, and amethyst earrings I gave her this morning as a 'commitment day' gift.

There will be no walking down the aisle. In fact, there *is* no aisle. There will be no wedding party. No officiant. Just the two of us standing up declaring our dedication to each other while Regan's mom holds Mitchell in the front row.

We walk to the front of the hall, holding hands. I can tell she's nervous. Me—I'm just excited. I still can't believe she agreed to this.

As planned, before we say our 'vows,' Ryder comes up and gives a short speech. It's entertaining, mainly making fun of me and the obsession over Regan nobody knew I had, but that, in his words *'explains so much about how I behaved back then.'*

Dallas says a few words about love and shit that make women in the audience cry.

Blake comes up last, saying and signing his speech. "I don't think I've ever been so happy to stand up for Lucas and have him *not* getting married." The guests laugh. "But seriously, I'm lucky enough to have a brother—brothers really—I'm so close with that we can talk about our fears and hopes and dreams." He looks around me to Regan. "And believe me, Regan, it's been a tough number of months watching this man fall head over heels in love with you thinking he'd sentenced himself to a life of torturous, unrequited longing."

Regan's dimples come out when she smiles.

"Brother," Blake continues, "the two of you may be opposites in almost every way, but anyone who looks at you can see the way you love each other. And Regan, there's nobody I'd rather have as my not-sister-in-law. I wish both of you and my nephew a wonderful life together."

When the applause dies down, it's just the two of us in front of the crowd.

"Ladies first," I say, putting her on the spot.

"Really?" she asks nervously. "This is your gig. I figured you'd want to take the lead."

I shake my head. "You know how much I like to have the last word."

Chuckles are heard among the hundred or so people watching.

"Okay." She shifts uncomfortably.

I squeeze her hands in encouragement.

We never talked about our 'vows,' so we have zero idea what the other is going to say.

"If someone had told me nine months ago that I'd be standing up here making a commitment to the infamous runaway groom, I'd have called them crazy. But now I realize, it wasn't so crazy after all." She tilts her head. "Or maybe it was. I mean, our life together so far is the very definition of crazy. It's unexpected and thrilling, and so perfectly imperfect." Her eyes become glassy. "Sorry," she says. "I didn't think I'd make myself cry. But that's what you do to me, Lucas. You make me feel more than I've ever felt. You make me look at things differently than I ever have. You make... *being me*... easier and more fun than I ever dreamed. So I'm happy to stand here today and tell the world that I love you. Despite the crazy. Despite the imperfections. Or maybe... *because* of all that." She wipes a tear. "Okay, your turn."

"My turn." I blow out a long breath. "Finally."

Everyone laughs.

"Regan, ever since I *didn't* propose to you last week, I've been waiting. Waiting for the apprehension. The nerves. The second thoughts. I thought I'd at least have a small freak out when I got here and saw the venue all decorated like a wedding. But the truth is..."

Truth.

I stop talking as the word floats around in my head. I look at her and her spectacular flamboyant dress. I scan our surroundings, making eye contact with my loved ones. I look at the empty spaces next to us and realize the truth is… this isn't what I want at all.

"The truth is"—I sigh big time—"this is all wrong."

Regan's smile fades. Gasps are heard from the crowd. Chatter echoes throughout the room. I think I even see money changing hands in the third row.

Regan leans forward and whispers, "It's okay if you don't want to do this. I still love you."

I stare into her forgiving eyes knowing that right there is why I'm about to do what I'm about to do. And that it's unequivocally the right thing.

I swallow and breathe and shore myself up. I turn to the audience and raise a hand. "Can you all quiet down please? You've got it all wrong." I take both of Regan's hands. "I thought this was what I wanted. Me standing here telling you I'll always be here and that a piece of paper doesn't mean shit. But the truth is, I'm a goddamn liar. I want so much more. I want Maddie and Ava standing next to you. Blake and Dallas standing next to me. I want a pastor. I want rings and vows—*wedding* vows. I want it all, the whole nine yards. I want to marry you, Regan. Right here and now. Today. We already ripped one contract to shreds. Why not just go all the damn way?" I lean in. "How's *that* for crazy?"

When I look into her eyes, I realize she's not crying at all. She's laughing.

But the rest of the room is so quiet you could hear a pin drop. Then Mitchell lets out a howl.

"See?" I say. "He agrees."

She giggles jubilantly. "Yes." She throws her arms around me. "I say yes."

My eyes go wide. "Yes? Are you serious?"

"I said I wanted to keep the crazy going, so yes."

I turn to the crowd. "Is there anyone here who can marry us?"

"I can," a low voice booms.

Judge Elfman, friend of my father, is standing near the back.

"But not until tomorrow," he says as he approaches. "You need a marriage license." He checks his watch. "The courthouse is open for another few hours. You can apply today, and we can meet back here twenty-four hours after."

Shit. I forgot about the marriage license.

Regan waves the judge over. "Let's do it anyway," she says. "I don't want everyone to have to come back tomorrow. As long as we're here, we might as well."

I raise my brows at Judge Elfman.

"I don't see why not." He comes up and stands in front of us. "We'll have the ceremony now, then you get the license, and we can meet at my office tomorrow to make it official."

"But tomorrow's a Saturday," I say.

"I don't mind," he says. "I owe your dad a favor or two."

I turn to Regan. "Are we really doing this?"

She nods. "We really are."

Maddie and Ava race to Regan's side. My brothers come to mine. Mom and Dad offer us their wedding rings to use.

Someone holds up their phone and plays *Here Comes the Bride.*

I take Regan's hands once again. The hands of my fiancée—even if it's only a title she'll hold for the next two minutes. Then I pour my entire goddamn heart out to her and say all the things I never got to say—never *wanted* to say—every other time I stood in this exact spot.

Chapter Fifty

Regan

It's my wedding night.

Technically that will be tomorrow. But I'll always think of today as the day we got married.

Lucas's parents took Mitchell for the night, along with some breast milk from the freezer. It'll be strange to be without him, but if I've learned anything over the past six weeks, it's that I have this new extended family I can rely on who loves that kid as much as we do. I have every confidence that Mitchell is in good hands.

The elevator opens and we approach the penthouse door. He looks at the door, then at me. He holds out his arms as if I could possibly jump into them and be carried across the threshold. "Shall we?"

Warmth flows through me knowing I have a man who accepts me exactly the way I am.

I give him a sultry wink. "How about you just show me how strong you are in bed?"

"Your wish is my command," he says, pulling me impatiently through the door.

Tingles bombard my insides. Tonight is the night we'll be together for the first time in five months. We've done stuff. Other stuff. Mostly to him because I wasn't sure if my 'parts' were ready. But with the way I'm feeling right now, I know they are. And I can't wait to make love to my… *husband.*

I say the word in my head, still not believing it. Because in my heart, that's what he is and what he'll always be.

"So… wife," he says as if we're telepathically connected. "What about the honeymoon? Where should we go? Anywhere. Just name it. Nothing is off the table."

We walk into the living room, greeted by Joey. Or *I'm* greeted by him anyway. He still hasn't fully warmed up to Lucas.

"At the reception, I was talking with Marti about their upcoming wedding in Antigua. I think it's the perfect time. M&M will be three months old. You said we'd take a private jet. Your entire family will be there for at least a week to help babysit so we can have some alone time."

As I talk about it, his smile grows larger. "I think you read my mind, Mrs. Montana."

Mrs. Montana. Everyone started calling me that right after. The first time it happened, I watched Lucas's reaction to see if it bothered him. It didn't. In fact, he was beaming, his smile splitting his face from ear to ear.

Regan Montana. Lucas Montana's wife. My stomach flutters and my heart floods with warmth. Who'd have flippin' thought?

"Yeah." I lean down and pick up a pair of baby booties and set them on the table. "One night without him will be hard enough. I can't imagine going a whole week or two not being around Mitchell."

He pins me against the wall, my hands trapped over my head. "Just one more reason we belong together."

When he goes for my neck, I extend it to the side, giving him plenty of room to tease and taunt me the way he has been these last weeks. It's been weeks of torture. Of sentiment. Of pure bliss.

"Tonight, I make you mine."

I giggle as he sucks on my throat. "I thought the ceremony earlier today did that."

"Are you thirsty?" he asks, peppering my jawline with kisses. "Hungry?"

"Mmm." I lose myself in the feeling. "I'm only hungry for one thing."

His lips disappear from my skin and he takes my hand, dragging me through the living room, past the kitchen, and down the hall into our bedroom.

Ours. It's never felt more like it than it does right now.

I stand next to the bed, his eyes feasting on me before even one scrap of clothing has been discarded. "I love this dress." He unties the bodice bow, leans down, gathers the hem, and pulls it up and over my head, tossing it to the floor. "I love it even more now."

I laugh, but then stop when his stare devours me.

"Holy crap, Ray."

I run my hands seductively down the front of my new strapless lacy shapewear, then slowly twirl around so he can see me from all angles. Knowing I'd never be walking down any actual aisle at any real wedding, I thought this was my one chance to wear something like this. Who knew it would end up being my actual wedding night attire? "You approve?"

"Do you even know what you do to me? You look incredible."

My cheeks heat. "Well, I *have* lost the seventeen pounds I gained with Mitchell and then some. Breastfeeding is amazing."

His hands come up to cup them. "One of the wonders of the world, I'd say."

"Careful, or they'll leak all over you."

"I wouldn't mind." He kneads my super-full breasts that are much more than a handful. "I wouldn't mind one goddamn bit."

He guides me down onto the bed. Then super-seductively, and in slow motion as if just to torture me, he unwraps my lengths of strappy sandals from my calves.

Tossing them aside, he invites me to undress him with a sexy nod toward his belt.

Wasting no time, I remove it. Then his tie, his shirt, his pants, and finally his socks. I have no idea when he took his shoes off. I'm definitely otherwise occupied by his throbbing cock. I've certainly learned my way around it lately. What drives him wild. What my mouth can do for him. What makes him come quickly. Even how I can get him to last longer.

A few strokes of him elicits groans. He encircles my wrist with his hand and pulls me away. "This night is all about you, wife."

"No." I shake my head. "It's about us. Just as the rest of our lives will be."

He gently eases me down until I'm lying flat on my back then crawls up on the bed and hovers over me. "You bet your perfectly round ass it is." He roots around at the crotch of my silk panties. "Please tell me you aren't attached to these, because I'm about to rip them clean off."

Before I can even answer, I hear the material rip, chuckling at the sound. "Guess I wasn't."

"I'll buy you a thousand pairs." He kisses my lower stomach where the teddy is rising up. "I'll buy you anything you fucking want, Mrs. Montana."

His head springs up in surprise. I was waiting for this.

"You got waxed?"

I shrug. "It was my wedding day."

He runs a finger over the smooth, sensitive flesh that's never been completely bare. Only now. Only for him. My insides quiver even before his finger touches my clit.

"Shit, Ray. I'm going to come just touching you."

"That's okay." I lie back and wait for his sensual assault. "We've got all night and zero interruptions."

I moan loudly when a finger glides inside me. He's gentle. Much more so than he's ever been. He's testing the waters. Making sure I'm not sore. I'm not. Not one little bit. I'm ready for this. Ready for him.

"You don't have to play nice," I say, running my fingers through his hair. "I won't break."

He glances up. "Are you telling me you want me to ravage you, Regan Montana?"

I bite my lip then smile. I don't need to answer. My eyes and my body do that for me.

"You think I can get you there when your body isn't all hyped up with hormones?"

"There's only one way to find out."

He inserts another finger, crooking them and causing my hips to rise off the bed. When his tongue finds my clit, his name comes off my lips in a sensuous cry as a tickle creeps up from every corner of my body.

"Jesus, Ray," he murmurs around me, the words vibrating against my swollen nub.

My body reacts in a feral way. I rise to his lips. I press him into me with demanding hands. I want everything he has to give. Everything and more.

All my senses are heightened. I'm not sure if it's because of the waxing. The ceremony. The way he looked at me all day. Or maybe it's because I know I'm making love to the father of my child. The man who just promised himself to me forever. Whatever the reason, I feel it building. It's not an unfamiliar sensation. It's one I've had before. I'm climbing the mountain. One step at a time, I'm climbing. Hoping to reach that elusive peak. Get to that undefined pinnacle.

Building even further, I know I'm there. I'm at the precipice. The cliff. The point where I either fall forward or retreat back.

Suddenly his face appears within my mind like a dream. Only it's not a dream. Everything I see actually happened. Him saying his vows. Caressing me with his words. Declaring his love.

I feel myself teetering on the edge of the ridge. One small breeze could sway me one way or the other.

The breeze comes in the form of my name. "Regan," he whispers loudly as his mouth surrounds my soft, slick center.

So I do it. I leap. And I fall. And everything everywhere ceases to exist as I tumble spectacularly beneath his hands. His fingers. His tongue. His promised love. Nothing is clouding my head. Nothing is holding me back. Sensations, feelings, emotions… they all bombard me as I detonate beneath him, allowing the explosion to go on and on as the euphoria draws out every last spark. Each remaining ounce of energy. I let it drain me until I'm nothing but a languid pile of rubber limbs.

I can't talk. I can't move. I can't think.

"Oh. My. God," Lucas's words tickle my ear as he settles in beside me. "That was ten times better than when you were pregnant because I know it was *me* who did it."

It takes a moment to find my words. To gather my thoughts. To remember my name. "You can say that again." It takes all my energy to open an eye. "I'll deal with you soon. I just need a minute."

He laughs. "Oh, believe me, after that glorious display, I've already been... dealt."

I hear him get tissues from the drawer and wipe up any mess.

Joey meows and jumps on the bed. I'm about to kick him off when he circles around me and rubs against Lucas's arm. I shoot up. "Did he just...?"

"You see that?" Lucas's smile is as big as Texas. "I think he just gave me his seal of approval." He runs a hand down Joey's back. "You think he was just waiting on *that* to happen?"

"Um... no." I roll my eyes. "That's ridiculous. I've seen the way he's been looking at you lately. He likes the way you hold Mitchell. He sees you as a caregiver."

"Nah," he says, picking Joey up and setting him on the floor then snuggling behind me, his front to my back, securing me against him. "He was watching and waiting. He knows better than to trust a man who can't make a woman come."

"You're crazy." I turn my head and side-eye him. "You know that, don't you?"

He kisses my shoulder. "Crazy about you."

"You know..." I turn in his arms and face him. "It's okay if you don't show up tomorrow."

His eyes narrow. "Why wouldn't I show up?"

"It's what you do."

He traces my jawline with a finger. "I showed up *today.*"

"That's different. It wasn't an actual wedding."

He pulls me tight. "It was, Ray. We're married now. Tomorrow is just about making it legal."

"I get that. But I want you to know it's okay. You said your vows. I know you love me for better or worse. And if you don't show up, I'll still be here. I'm not going to leave like the others."

He scoffs. "I'm going to show. I promise."

"I hear you. But just in case, you need to understand that no matter what, I'm in this. I'm here until the end. So if you get to Judge Elfman's office tomorrow and you just can't go through those doors, you don't have to. I know we belong together. Everyone does. Even Joey. So whatever happens, it's okay. You're stuck with me." I take his face in my hands. "It's okay if you don't show up."

Lucas's eyes become misty. He climbs on top of me, hovering, staring, loving. He lowers his head slowly. Then, right before his lips touch mine, he whispers. "And that's exactly why I will."

Epilogue

Regan

He showed up.

Acknowledgments

After writing the previous book, *Loud Unspoken Memories*—a story heavy on angst and emotions—I needed something a little lighter and more fun. I had no idea I would enjoy writing Lucas's and Regan's story as much as I did. The twists and turns surprised me, and I just loved their personalities.

I hope you enjoyed reading it as much as I loved writing it!

Crazy Imperfect Hearts is my thirty-first book!

As I enter my eleventh year as a published author, I continue to hope my stories hit you in all the right places and give you all the amazing feels. It's because of you, my dear readers, that I remain on this amazing, wild, unpredictable journey.

I feel as though I'm always thanking the same people. But they do SO much for me, my continued gratitude is the least I can offer them.

First and foremost is my PA, Julie Collier. Julie always pushes me outside my comfort zone and encourages me beyond belief. She is usually the first person I communicate with every morning, and often the last one (other than Mr. Christy) before I go off to bed.

My editor, Michelle Fewer, always manages to work me into her schedule even when I forget to book her. She's just great like that.

I have the utmost respect for Kimberly Kernek, M.D. FACOG (fellow of the American college of obstetrics and gynecology), who is my go-to gal for all things OB/GYN. She is always quick to answer any medical questions I have, and she never makes me feel stupid for not knowing even the simplest of things.

Last but certainly not least, my steadfast beta readers. The women who keep me honest. Kellie Shanks, Joelle Yates, Shauna Garness, and Laura Conley. Thank you for your keen eyes, quick input, and wonderful suggestions.

While most of my series have ended at three books, this one continues on to a fourth! *Tiny Precious Secrets* follows Allie Montana. I just love it when I'm writing and a character calls out to me for a story. As Allie's did while I was writing *Quiet Beautiful Things*, Ava Criss's story wouldn't get out of my head while writing *Crazy Imperfect Hearts*. So for the first time in forever, I'll be writing a non-series book—though it will still be set in the Calloway Creek world. Hold on for a wild ride as Ava and Trevor find their way back to each other after a tragic accident.

About the author

Samantha Christy's passion for writing started long before her first novel was published.

Graduating from the University of Nebraska with a degree in Criminal Justice, she held the title of Computer Systems Analyst for The Supreme Court of Wisconsin and several major universities around the United States.

Raised mainly in Indianapolis, she holds the Midwest and its homegrown values dear to her heart and upon the birth of her third child devoted herself to raising her family full time.

While it took time to get from there to here, writing has remained her utmost passion and being a stay-at-home mom facilitated her ability to follow that dream.

When she is not writing, she keeps busy cruising to every Caribbean island where ships sail.

Samantha Christy currently resides in St. Augustine, Florida with her husband and the two of her four children who haven't yet flown the coop.

You can reach Samantha Christy at any of these wonderful places:

Website: www.samanthachristy.com

Facebook: https://www.facebook.com/SamanthaChristyAuthor

Instagram: @authorsamanthachristy

E-mail: samanthachristy@comcast.net

Made in the USA
Middletown, DE
02 February 2025